season
of second
chances

AIMEE ALEXANDER

ISBN: 9798633298635

SEASON OF SECOND CHANCES

Copyright © Aimee Alexander 2020

This first paperback edition published 2020

All rights reserved.

No part of this publication may be reproduced, stored in a retrieval system or transmitted in any form or by any means without the prior written permission of the author, nor be otherwise circulated in any form of binding or cover other than that in which it is published and without a similar condition being imposed on the purchaser.

The right of Aimee Alexander to be identified as the Author of the Work has been asserted by her in accordance with the Copyright, Designs and Patents Act 1988. Aimee Alexander is the pen name of Denise Deegan.

*To Jean Grainger, one of the kindest,
most thoughtful people I'm lucky enough to call a friend.
This book would not exist without you.*

one

Rain slams against the windshield. The wipers swipe full pelt. It's dark and the road is narrow and winding. The silence in the car has lasted six hours, all the way from Dublin. Grace Sullivan glances at her daughter Holly, asleep beside her. Mouth open, she looks younger and more vulnerable than her fifteen years. In the rearview mirror, Grace's dark and broody son, Jack, at sixteen, looks on the verge of manhood. Ear pods in, he glares out the window, angry at the world. Grace can't remember him any other way. She wants to tell him she's sorry. For snatching him from his friends, his school, his life. For the lies he had to tell. (Oaths, not lies. Worse.) Most of all, she's sorry for not getting out sooner. But she says nothing. She knows how Jack feels about her sorries. To him, they've always made things worse.

She raises her chin and reminds herself it's over. They got away.

Fresh start. Hope.

The Jeep is packed with everything they own or, at least, everything they've taken. Possessions are not important when it comes to freedom.

Grace tries to imagine the new life that lies ahead. And has to calm her breathing. Confidence is like a precious diamond that has been taken from her. Not just once but over and over. And, though she has left Simon behind, he keeps on taking.

But here they are. Miles away. Free. That didn't happen by chance. It took guts and planning, patience and ruthlessness. She was careful. She did her how-to-leave-an-abusive-man research in the library where he couldn't track her browsing history. With money she squirrelled away (and more borrowed from her unsuspecting father) she bought a second phone and hired a lawyer, Freda Patterson, a Rottweiler of a woman. One thing her husband taught her: to fight a bully you need a bully. While Freda took care of the legals, Grace worked out where to go, how to earn a living free from him, and most importantly, how to get as far away as possible. He knew that there was something different about her, a focus, a determination she tried to hide. He got rougher, crueller, to get her back in line. But she was determined. *Determined*.

They received the court judgement today. And here they are, already miles away. The law is on their side. They did everything by the book. Apart from the lies. But there are bigger crimes than lying.

The headlights of the Jeep fall on the ruins of the old church, then on the moonlit sea as Grace takes the last turn into the village where she grew up. There it is, Killrowan, standing still and colourful with its dainty street lights, like a postcard image. Memories flood her mind. Carefree memories. Of ice cream and sailing boats, of laughter and innocence, of fancying boys who didn't fancy her back. Of life before Simon.

The main street is deserted. But Grace crawls through anyway. So much has changed. (A new craft shop. A crêpe place. An art gallery. A florist.) And still so much has stayed the same. (Shopfronts painted in the vivid pinks and blues and yellows that have always spelled home; the same names claiming ownership above the newsagents, the butchers and post office.)

Holly stirs, wiping her mouth. "Are we here?"

"We are," Grace says quietly.

At the top of the street, the home where Grace grew up comes into view. Only in West Cork would white look imaginative. Despite the pretty climber trailing under the eaves, the house seems tired, old and somehow lonely. Returning home at the age of forty-seven, single again, children in tow, tastes like failure.

"We're not telling Grandad why we left, okay?" she confirms what they've already agreed. "He has enough on his mind. Plus, he'd probably want revenge," she says fondly. Des has always been the problem-solving type of dad. Suddenly, she can't wait to hug him.

Holly nods. "It's over."

Grace reaches across and squeezes her hand.

As they pull up outside the house, the front door opens and Des appears as if he has been looking out for them. Grace's heart pangs at the sight of him. He has aged so much. Fully grey, he seems to have shrunk. If Grace didn't know already that he had Parkinson's she would now from his slow, shuffling gait. He still looks dapper in his tweed jacket and corduroy trousers. That, at least, is encouraging.

Grace and the children climb down from the Jeep.

"Welcome to West Cork!" Des says with an official arm roll. "I have the fire lighting." He gazes up at Jack. "'Tis bigger you're getting. And you can't deny the Sullivan genes," he says proudly, referring to Jack's heart-shaped face, green eyes, dark hair and slim build. "And look at you," he says to Holly, "like a young Snow White."

"Hi Grandad."

"Come on in. I've made sandwiches."

"Wait. Don't I get a hug?" Grace asks.

Smiling, he opens his arms. She slips into them, closing her eyes. For the briefest moment, she pretends she's a child again, carefree, optimistic, her future a blank and hopeful canvas.

Until her mother died, Grace had always associated home with the smell of baking. Now, her nose is greeted by the smell of must and possibly damp. She takes comfort in the dark green carpet that she learned to crawl on, walk on, leave the house in teenage strops on. The orange and brown wallpaper makes her nostalgic for that life. She catches Jack frowning at a Sacred Heart of Jesus night light, glowing red on the wall. And takes a deep breath. Yes, there will be adjustments. Holly, rubbing her arms, darts Grace a look. The fire might, indeed, be lighting in the sitting room but the rest of the place is so cold their breaths are fogging up. Grace nods but says nothing to Des, for now, just follows him into the kitchen.

The sight of the sink and her mother not at it sends an ache of loss through Grace. She is distracted by Holly mouthing, "It's freezing!" Her daughter is new to heat rationing, having grown up in the kind of luxury one might expect from a plastic surgeon with a penchant for display. Everything was plush, perfect. Comfortable.

"Mind if I turn on the heat, Dad?" Grace finally asks.

"Sure I have the fire on," he protests.

She imagines the bedrooms upstairs, damp and unaired. "I'll pay the bills while we're here," she says. Paying the bills with money she borrowed from him makes no actual sense. And the look he gives her says exactly that.

"Turn it on, so," he says picking up the tray of sandwiches, neatly cut into quarters and heading through to the sitting room with them.

Jack and Holly look at Grace for direction. She nods at them to follow their grandfather.

"I'll make tea," she calls, wishing she'd thought to buy hot water bottles.

Carrying in a tray of teas, Grace spots Jack eyeing the old-fashioned TV that extends about a foot and a half at the back. She remembers that they are now in two-channel land. No Sky. No Netflix. The look he gives her says: my PlayStation will never work on that antique.

Grace sets down the tray.

Holly is peering at the sandwiches her grandad made. "Is there ham in *all* of them?" she asks, looking, indeed, like a young Snow White, with her dark hair, pale skin and the blue eyes she inherited from her father.

"You don't like ham?" Des asks incredulously.

"I'm a vegan."

He waves a casual hand. "Yera, you're in the country now."

"So?"

"Well, it's just natural to eat meat. Aren't humans omnivores?"

"What about the *planet*?" Holly sounds very South County Dublin. And equally miffed.

"Ah, let the next generation worry about that," he says, taking what looks like a huge protest bite out of his sandwich.

Holly stares at Grace like she can't believe where the conversation is going. "My kids will *be* the next generation!"

Des squints at her. "You're way too young to be worrying about the next generation, girly."

"My name is Holly."

Grace's heart fills with hope at how her daughter is standing her ground. If only Grace had stood hers, all those years ago. Well, she did. In the beginning.

Des glances at his daughter in surprise.

Grace shrugs. "You don't call people girly anymore, Dad."

Jack looks up from his phone. "What's the Wi-Fi password?"

"The what?" Des asks.

Jack stares at his mother in horror. "There's no actual service here. We need Wi-Fi."

Grace is furious with herself for not thinking of it; Wi-Fi is their oxygen. But there was just so much else to organise. "I'll get it set up first thing in the morning," she promises.

"On a Saturday?" Des looks doubtful.

They carry their things in from the car in exhausted silence. No one complains. They know why they're here.

Upstairs is draughty, the windows single-glazed and in need of filling. The grouting between the bathroom tiles is black. The bedrooms are boxes with sixties décor, featuring pink bedspreads with ropey waves. Holly looks like she's fighting tears.

"It's only temporary," Grace whispers. With her first paycheque, she'll find them a place of their own. Well, her second or third paycheque. She has to return the money she owes her father. And it's not as if she can rely on the court ruling for maintenance. It would be just like Simon to simply not pay. Anything to wreck her head. The last thing she expects from him is fairness. He'll want to punish her for this treachery.

"Don't apologise," Jack snaps at her.

He has earned his rage, Grace thinks, and lets it go. "Sleep with your clothes on tonight, till the place warms up."

She follows Holly into her room. "It'll be okay, sweetie."

Holly collapses into her arms, letting loose a body-wracking bawl. "I hate him!"

"Hey," Grace says gently. "This is going to work out. I promise. It's going to be good here, Hol. I can feel it." She'll make this up to them. A million times over.

two

Jack paces the tiny room, punching his fist into his palm, over and over. He shouldn't be here. He should be out with his mates, right now, having a laugh. His automatic reaction is to blame his mother, to call her all the names his dad used to. That's why he lied in court. He knew that if he stayed around his father any longer, he'd turn into him. So many times, he caught himself thinking like him. It was becoming harder and harder to keep those thoughts in. Sometimes they did escape as words and the hurt in his mum's eyes, the pain, floored him. If he didn't get away, if he didn't lie, he might have killed his father or at least broken his perfect nose.

He wonders what he's doing now with no one to take his anger out on – and some anger it will be – outsmarted, outlawyered, outdone. Will he just take it lying down, this man so used to getting his own way? Or is he planning something?

Jack drops to the ground and starts into a hundred vigorous press ups, counting them out to drown the thoughts in his head. He'd go for a run if the roads outside the village were lit and had paths – and he had a key to get back in.

"Twenty-three, twenty-four, twenty-five…"

Will his dad appeal? Can he? Or will he take the law into his own hands, like he has always done with his wife? Jack needs to know. He glances at his phone beside him on the threadbare carpet. Two bars of service upstairs in that exact spot. Jack gets up onto his knees. From his back pocket, he whips out his wallet. From it, he takes his old SIM card, rescued from the bin his mother flung it into. Best to cut all ties, she said. So did Jack. Still, he couldn't just let that SIM go; he doesn't know why. Now, he replaces the new one with it. Just for a minute. Just to see. He has to be ready. For anything.

There are six missed calls from his father. And three voice messages. His stomach cramps. Is he strong enough for this?

He has to be.

He taps the screen, then closes his eyes.

"Jack. It's me. It's your dad. Why did you lie? You *know* I never did any of those things. Wouldn't. Couldn't. I'd never hurt you, Jack. Call me. We need to talk."

Jack feels like some sort of Judas. It was his idea to lie. Otherwise, his father would have got access to them – and their heads. They'd never have escaped his control. Hearing him now, though, reminds Jack of all he's going to miss: breakfasts out on Sunday mornings, just the two of them; the man-to-man talks; his actual wisdom on lots of issues. His humour. The monster could be funny. And loving. Kind, even. Just not to his wife.

Jack could call back, explain that hurting her was hurting them in a million different ways. But that would be stabbing her in the back. And his father would twist everything anyway and then never stop calling. So, Jack doesn't call back. Instead, he makes himself listen to the next message.

"I love you, Jack. I love Holly. I even love your mum. She just drives me crazy sometimes."

Jack understands that. She drives him crazy too. The placating. The pleading. The sorries.

"Come home. Back to your friends, your school, your hockey, *your life*."

Everything Jack aches for.

"I forgive you, Jack. It'll be different if you come home. I've changed. Why don't you tell your mum you need to come home? Tell her it'll be too hard there, miles from everything you know."

Jack kills the message.

The great manipulator is at it again. He'll never change.

Jack scans the missed calls and messages from friends who don't know his new number. Mostly girls. Right now, he is the mystery boy, the one who disappeared. Everyone wants to talk to him. Everyone wants to know why the hell he took off to West Cork. Well, he's kept the family secret all his life. He's not about to spill the beans now. He removes the SIM and slides back in the new one.

He has missed a call from Ross, his best friend since the age of four, the one person he trusted with his new number. He longs to call him back, tell him everything, somehow make a joke of it all. But Ross will be out with everyone else. Probably getting hammered. And what's the point anyway? Before they left Dublin, Jack fully thought that their friendship would survive, that he'd invite Ross down and they'd just carry on. Now he sees how dumb that was. Where would his (minted) friend stay? On the manky carpet in this tiny, back-in-time room? He knows that Ross wouldn't mind. *Jack* would, though. Dragging his friend all the way down to this hellhole where there's nothing to do, nowhere to go, no way to use the PlayStation, not even a decent TV. And it's not like you can keep a whole friendship going on phone calls. Jack doesn't want to watch what they have peter out like air from a half-empty balloon. Better to let it go. Save Ross the guilt. He gets up from the floor and flops back onto the bed. This is the price for not becoming a monster.

"Suck it up, Willoughby," he tells himself, staring up at a stained and stippled ceiling.

Grace lies in her narrow childhood bed, listening to the ticking of a small square alarm clock from the seventies and watching its luminous hands slowly advance time. It is incredible to her that her life has flipped on its head in just one day. She has finally done the one thing that terrified her most, the thing she never believed she would actually do. Until she did it.

No arm will swing at her tonight. No whispered threats will invade her ear. She won't wake with his hands on her neck because of something he imagined, something she said or didn't say. She can breathe again. Nothing to harm her in this innocent bed. She should be celebrating. But this is no celebration for Jack and Holly. They have left their father, their home, their lives. They have sworn under oath that he beat them. They have lied for her. She begged them not to, reminding them that, despite everything, they love their father, he loves them and they should continue to see each other. With Jack's first lie, there was no going back. Grace supported her children as they were supporting her. Simon was incredulous at the judgement. Livid. Puce. He could not believe that his children had accused him of doing to them what he had done to her. The hurt in his eyes.

This is not over. Grace will be made to suffer somehow. That is how he rolls. Her body tenses, her muscles returning to their default position. Her head feels like it's in the grip of some great force. She reminds herself of the barring order. Of the six hours between them. Of his obsession with his career. None of these will stop him, though, if he wants to hurt her, come for her, come for them. He has lost control. And that is what drives him.

If he comes, he'll choose a weekend. That's when she must be at her most alert. No. She must be alert around the clock. He knows where they are. The law demanded that. He could come at any time. He could be on his way now. She sits up. She should install an alarm. But how would she explain that to her father, in this sleepy village?

She gets up, steals to the window and peers out. The street is deserted as rain pelts down outside. She watches it as though hypnotised. She used to love the sound, tucked up safely in her little bed. How innocent she was then. Before she learned that bad things happen.

Where is he? What is he up to? The silence is terrifying. If only she'd kept her old SIM Card, she'd at least be able to check her messages, see what he's thinking, planning. With him, you have to be so smart. Ten steps ahead. Think like he does. Cut him off at the pass. But no. He'd just wreck her mind. Push her buttons as only he can. She could end up giving in, lose control again. No. She did the right thing. She just has to stop thinking about it, about him. Move forward. Sink her roots into this rural land, make it her home again, her children's home. Find the person she once was, the person who'd be able to stand up to him – knowing him for what he is. Anyway, she had to get rid of the SIM. Otherwise, he'd have continued to track her every move as he had always done. She wishes she'd thought to insert some kind of tracking device on *his* phone.

Will the dread ever go away? Will this ever be really over?

She leaves the window and goes to check on the kids.

Holly is deeply asleep, lips swollen and parted, cheeks flushed. Grace brushes her hair back from her forehead, stoops down and gently kisses her forehead. Holly didn't share her new number with anyone. She had no one to share it with. Grace prays that life will be better for her here, that she will find friends, happiness, peace. Is that too much to ask for her baby?

Jack is frowning in his sleep. Grace worries about the toll that all this is having on him. What is his view of girls? Yes, he's incredibly popular with them. But is he good to them? Does he respect them? Or does he hold them in the same contempt that his father held her in? She should have got out sooner. She should have got out the very first time he hit her. But then she wouldn't have had Holly.

"Back off!" Jack calls out in his sleep, his voice a mix of both fear and aggression.

She wants to tell him it's okay. But if he woke to find her gazing down at him, he'd probably freak. So Grace does as instructed and backs off.

She sneaks downstairs to check the locks.

All is quiet, the kitchen softly illuminated by a street lamp outside. Her eyes dart from corner to corner, finding them reassuringly empty of him. She strides to the back door. Her heart jolts to find it unlocked. Imagining a hand reaching for it on the other side, she rams it shut and slams the bolt across. She hurries to the front door and puts the latch on it. Then snaps every curtain shut, upsetting years of dust.

Only now does she turn on the light. Standing in the middle of the kitchen, she wraps her arms around herself. She will have to talk to Des about security – without alerting him to the reason for it. Her head is pounding. She finds her bag and roots in it for her pack of Nurofen Plus. She should have thought to stock up before she left Dublin. Pharmacists are so careful about codeine now. In Dublin, she had hundreds of pharmacies to choose from. Here, there is one. As a family doctor, she can't develop a reputation as an addict of any kind. Not that she is an addict. She has just come to rely on them a little. She started taking them for the endless headaches but continued for that extra little something they gave her. She puts the blister card back in the box. She's away from him now. She doesn't need a psychological crutch anymore. She can stop. Anytime. It's mind over matter.

The first-aid box is in its usual home, in the cupboard by the oven. Grace takes two paracetamol and downs them in relief. Spotting her father's Parkinson's meds, laid out in a weekly pill organiser, she goes through them. No surprises. Exactly what she'd prescribe. Still, she goes upstairs in search of mobile phone service.

In bed, she googles Parkinson's disease. The latest treatments. Alternative treatments. Not just physio. They say that dancing is good. And cycling. The video evidence is extraordinary. Grace looks up from her phone filled with possibility. But how can she tell Dr. Des Sullivan how to manage his own health? Especially as he has just retired. She knows how useless a doctor feels when they can no longer practise. It was Simon's idea for her to stay at home when Jack was born. If she'd known then that this was his first big step in controlling her, she would have kept her job. If she'd known then what was to come, she'd have got the hell out. It sneaked up on her. He did. Worked on her mind first – when she became pregnant. Broke her confidence. Then, when Jack was born, he moved onto her spirit. Her body. Her soul. He took the holistic approach. He swallowed her whole.

As soon as the children started school, though, she quietly rebelled, landing a part-time position two mornings a week at a practice far enough from home that she wouldn't bump into patients. She would have loved more hours but couldn't risk being found out. This was enough to keep on the Medical Council register, to keep up to speed, and to hold onto her sanity. She used her income to pay for continuing medical education, then saved what she could in a secret bank account, the details of which she hid at the surgery. She never really believed she would get beyond quiet rebellion.

Well, now she has. The phoenix is out from the ashes and rising.

three

Des shuts off his alarm before it wakes Grace or the children. He's not going to become a man who sleeps in on retirement. He's not going to let himself go. He dresses in a flannel shirt, beige chords, a navy pullover and cashmere socks. On a whim, he adds a cravat.

Gripping the bannister, he goes downstairs, avoiding the steps that creak.

In the kitchen, he turns on the heat for them and a light for himself. He opens the curtains though it's still dark outside. He likes the company of the streetlights. He stands looking out at the stillness of the world.

Putting on the kettle, his eyes fall on a small, navy, velvet box. With a sigh, he picks it up and opens it. He stares at the shiny gold watch inside. What fool started the tradition of watches as retirement presents? Any thinking person would know that the last thing a man would want is to count all the time he now has on his hands. He shakes his head and tucks it away into a cupboard so he doesn't have to face it again.

He hears the flap on the front door and the post fall. He waits for Tim, the postman, to appear at the window on his way past. They raise their hands in greeting. This is their routine now. And there's comfort in it.

Heading for the front door, Des reminds himself to take big steps as he does every time he walks. His body needs the nudge.

At the kitchen table, he flicks through the four envelopes – three bills and a bank statement. He turns one over. On the back, he starts a D.I.Y. list; all the jobs that have been piling up over the years, waiting till he's not too busy or tired. Now that he has company, he has an incentive.

Clean out shed.

Sand and repaint facia boards.

Fix windows.

Clean grouting.

Clear out gutters.

Climbing a ladder is as exciting as things have become around here.

Des turns back to the window and stares out. He wishes something were urgent. He remembers the kettle and gets up again. Another trick to break the silence. Miriam has been dead for five years but the loss has never hit harder than this week. While he had work, his mind was occupied, home late every evening, a quiet whiskey, then bed. Up early and straight out to the surgery next day. People needed him. And he needed that need. Who'd have known that the stillness of a house could drive a man around the bend? Two days into retirement, he remembered the radio. Keeping it on in the background has saved his sanity.

Oh, but it was good to see them arrive last night. Not the sadness they carried with them like a low wail on the air. But just to have them here with him, his flesh and blood, his family. Precious beyond belief. He couldn't let them know how glad he is to have them here. Because home is where they'll be happiest. They need to return. And, so, the gruffness.

He looks down at his shaking hand. And instantly picks up the kettle. The tremor is only present at rest. It was a patient, sitting across from him, who first noticed it. Curious as to why she was staring at his hand, he glanced down. Immediately, he froze. Could it be? Could it really be? He moved the hand, picking up his pen and twirling it between his thumb and finger. He was fine. Too much caffeine.

Over the next few months, as his symptoms increased, so did his mortification. It was as if he had failed as a doctor, unable to stop disease in his own body.

The symptoms seem so much worse this week. But that's just because he has had time to notice. Maybe not, though. Maybe they *are* worse.

He hears the floorboards creak upstairs, the lovely reassuring sound of company. But he has to think of them, not himself. He has to send them home.

Des has just seated himself back at the table when he hears gentle footfall on the stairs. Glancing up, he's struck by the contrast between the daughter who appears now and the girl who used to thunder down those stairs with so much energy. How carefully she holds herself. How neat she looks, how conservative. She could – easily – be a different person.

Her smile holds the same affection though. "Hey, Dad."

"Hi, love. How did you sleep?"

"Great."

Everything is always "great" with Grace even when it's very clearly not.

"You look tired," he says.

Another smile. "Tea?"

"I'm grand, love, thanks." He holds up his mug.

Des waits for her to sit down, wondering how best to approach it. Whatever he says, she'll argue that she's due to start in the practice on Monday. Well, he'll just tell her that they can get someone else; it's not the end of the world. A broken marriage however....

Grace joins him at the table and puts a mat under her mug, though there's no need. The fading pine is already stained and ancient.

"Dad, you left the back door unlocked last night."

This throws Des. But just for a second. "Yera, I always do."

"You can't!"

His daughter has been in Dublin too long. Des takes a sip of tea, a hint for her to do the same, to just sit back and relax. Life is easier here. She just needs to remember that.

But her eyes grow more panicked. "You're a doctor! What if junkies come looking for drugs?"

Des gives her a look. "We're in Killrowan, Gracie."

"There are drugs everywhere! And... there are children in the house now!" She looks up at the ceiling as if she can see them through it.

"Grace, love, you were eighteen years growing up with the back door always open. Killrowan hasn't changed."

"But the world has!"

Des, sensing real distress, is instantly sorry. "Of course. You're right. I'm sorry. I'll lock it."

Relief floods her face.

Then he understands. "You were broken into, in Dublin, weren't you?"

"No! We were not broken into! I just want the door kept locked."

"Alright, love. Locked it is." He can't believe how stressed she has become. You can't even break a traffic light in Killrowan; there are none. One thing's clear: being here does not seem to be helping her stress levels. He takes a deep breath and puts down his mug. "Is this madness, love, this bolt from home?"

Her body tenses, shoulders rising. "No, it's not mad! It's the opposite of mad!"

"I know you're upset but what could be so bad for you to walk out on… how many… years of marriage?"

Grace's hands wrap around her mug and she stares into her tea. "Eighteen," is a whisper.

"He's just such a smashing fellow, Gracie. And a great dad. Have ye tried counselling, at all?"

Her eyes stay glued to the tea but her fingers whiten as they tighten their grasp on the mug. "Just trust my decision, Dad," she says through gritted teeth.

"It's just that people give up too easily, nowadays."

She looks up, eyes filled with rage, jaw jutting forward. A flash of teenage Grace. But, unlike teenage Grace, she keeps her words in.

"Some of us don't get a second chance." That's his main point, really. "Some of us have our loved ones snatched from us, overnight," he adds with an ache in his heart.

Grace's face softens. "You and Mam were so happy together. And I know the pain you feel. I miss her too. So much. But I've tried with Simon. I've given him so many chances. Too many chances. I've been a fool. I have to do this, Dad. For myself. But mostly for the kids."

"Did he have an affair? Is that it? Because lots of marriages survive–"

She shoots to her feet. "Right. I'm going to the shop. Need anything?"

He sighs. Then he checks the beloved leather watch on his wrist with its almost human face. "I don't think it'll be open, love."

"Fine. I'll go for a walk first. What do you need?"

"I'm grand, Gracie. Thanks."

She flings open the fridge, snaps open cupboards and when she finds nothing but milk, butter, ham and bread, she gives him a look that says: "You're anything but grand."

four

Grace marches down the narrow footpath, oblivious to village life starting up around her, lights clicking on, doors opening, deliveries arriving. Smashing fellow! Smashing in more ways than one! He has everyone fooled. His patients think he's God. His pro bono work (representing international, humanitarian cases of badly burned and scarred victims) sets him aside as a pillar of the medical community. He is Mr. Charming. Mr. Handsome. Mr. Fake. Even his appearance is fake. Letting his hair grey naturally has people assume that he is embracing the ageing process. Meanwhile, he injects his face with a perfectly balanced mix of Botox, fillers and collagen. Fake, fake, fake, fake, fake, fake, fake. Grace storms past the supermarket, failing to notice that it's about to open.

Startlingly quickly she finds herself at the edge of the village where the path falls away. Up a slope to the left is the surgery and its carpark. Across the road, the police station. Beyond them are fields and the old church ruins. To the right is the sea.

Muttering to herself, she turns around. But she's not ready to face a whole village with the polite face she shows to the world. She's not ready for anything except a long loud scream somewhere private. She needs to lose this *rage*. She needs the sea.

She strides across the road, cuts through the car park and playground, then comes face to face with a natural beauty that stops her. It is blues and greens where sky meets sea, and everything bathed in morning sunlight. Down at the pier, a small, red fishing boat heads out for the day, a flock of optimistic gulls flying behind. The water carries the sound of their racket, the "Ow, ow, ow," that always reminds Grace of home.

Everything slows, her heartbeat, her breath and, when she resumes walking, her pace. Down to the pier she strolls, breathing slowly and deeply like she's starting a meditation. Maybe she is.

At the pier, people are boarding the ferry to the island, everyone armed with provisions. Every two weeks, Grace will have to make the trip, out to the clinic there. She feels her body tense at the thought of her first visit, which is only days away. Is she really ready to return to full-time practice?

She turns from the pier, taking a narrow path that leads through fields bordering the inlet. She fills her lungs with briny air that smells faintly of cow dung. Cattle graze in the fields but Grace isn't concerned. She knows as well as any local that they're used to strollers passing through and never pay them any attention.

She gazes down at the tiny, pebble beaches where she used to skim stones as a child. What a joyful little person she was with her buddies, her dreams and her absolute belief that the world was a good and happy place. There was nothing she couldn't do, no dream she couldn't achieve. She'd be a doctor like her dad. No problemo. She's still the same person inside. He hasn't killed every spark. He couldn't have. As if to prove it, she trots down the next set of steps. One by one, she gathers flat, round stones. She squats down and flicks them out to sea, then laughs at her dismal performance. She needs practice. But that's fine. She *can* practice. She's in the right place. And there's no one to tell her what she can or can't do.

Grace scrambles up one of the rocky outcrops like the kid she used to be and perches on a lichen covered, pockmarked prominence, watching the gentle ebb and flow of the waves, down below. The sun rises higher and the sea takes on the turquoise hues of the Caribbean. Grace understands how ancient peoples worshipped this ball of light. It is magnificent. She turns her face to it and closes her eyes. It's October and it's Ireland but the sun is shining. Like a sign. Everything will be okay. It has to be.

Her pace is slower on the way back. Reaching the village, she catches her reflection in a shop window and comes to a halt. This is not the person who skimmed stones on the beach moments ago. This is a person whose whole look has been designed by someone else. Bobbed, brown hair – ordered by Simon. Conservative designer clothes – ordered by Simon. French manicure – ordered by Simon. Grace takes a deep breath. She looks beyond her reflection. A hairdresser is standing in front of a mirror, blow-drying her hair in an otherwise empty shop. Grace admires her confidence, her sparkly black top, her leather trousers. Grace is a fan of sparkles. Not that you'd know it.

She pushes the door in.

A bell pings but the hairdresser doesn't hear over the noise of the dryer. Grace takes a seat in a waiting area. She loves the way this pretty young woman tackles her hair, like she's in charge and she expects no argument. Grace needs to be more like her.

"Done!" the woman says to herself, clicking the hairdryer off. She points at her reflection. "Looking good!"

Grace smiles. "I agree."

The hairdresser swivels around, touching her heart. "Holy Mother of God! I didn't see you there! I'm so sorry. Have you been waiting long?"

"I literally just came in."

"And there I was gawking at myself in the mirror, going on like a total looper."

"It made my day, to be honest."

"It's early." She smiles then touches a black swivel chair that faces a wall of mirror. "Come, have a seat."

The children won't be up for ages, Grace tells herself. She deserves this. Maybe she even needs it. She is *not* the person he wanted her to be. She is herself. She has broken away from him. She is free. Free to be the person she was before she ever met him. If she could just find that person, the energy of her, the confidence, the strength…. Well, hair is a start.

Grace sits into the chair with a new determination.

"So! What are you having done?"

Grace eyes her reflection like a dare. "Something drastic."

"I knew you were fun the minute I saw you!"

"*Really?*"

"Oh yeah. And I was right. No one asks for drastic." The vivacious blonde swings a black silk cape over Grace's shoulders as though she was born to do so. She ties it with Velcro at the neck then looks at Grace in the mirror. "I'm Jane," she says, a question in her voice.

"Grace."

"You're not from around here?"

Grace hesitates. News in the village is everyone's. It just takes a few minutes. On this occasion, that's fine. Grace should probably get word of her arrival out now, acclimatise people before she appears in the surgery on Monday.

"Actually, I am! I'm Des Sullivan's daughter, back from Dublin!" She says it like it's a great thing. It could be. Eventually. Maybe.

"Oh, *yeah*! I *heard* you were coming. Sure, that's great altogether. Welcome to Killrowan. The real capital! You have kids, don't you?"

Grace smiles and nods. "So, I want it all off," she says, to end that line of inquiry. "Especially the fringe. Maybe feather it or flip it to the side or, I don't know, both?"

"So, you definitely want it short?" Jane confirms, like she's experienced some post-cut changes of heart.

"Yup."

"Short short?"

"Short short."

Jane nods seriously like she's about to perform surgery. She lifts pieces of hair and lets them fall. "Okay, I have a suggestion. It's a little bit mad. But hear me out."

Grace glances at the people going by outside. No one rushing. Lots of chat. A few laughs. It's October and the tourists have gone. Just locals now. Farmers, new age hipsters and people working in the town. Grace had hoped to be here by September for the start of the school year but the legals took longer than expected. She hopes that Jack and Holly will settle in and that the change won't swamp them. Starting over is never easy. And life in Killrowan couldn't be more different to the one they have left.

Jane works fast, snipping away with the same confidence she tackled her own hair. Grace watches strands fall like shackles. Her heart lifts at the thought of no longer being designed by Simon. Even thinking his name makes her skin crawl.

The cut is definitely short short. It frames her face, highlighting its heart shape and her delicate features. But Jane was right.

"It needs something more."

Jane grins, then disappears. She returns with a trolley and gloves on her hands.

The bleach goes in. Grace's scalp tingles and her eyes smart. There's a moment of doubt as she remembers her request for drastic. But there's no going back now. And, however terrible it turns out, it won't be what it was. It won't be his.

"Will I do your nails while we're waiting for that to work?" Jane asks.

Grace looks down at her hands and splays out her fingers.

"Ah, sure you're grand," Jane says when she sees the French manicure.

"Actually, no. I want that off."

"But it's perfect."

The way Simon wanted Grace. And it was easier, in so many ways, to go along with it. The only thing she kicked back on was plastic surgery. No matter how much he criticised her face, it was hers. Her biggest disincentive, though, wasn't her appearance but the niggling fear of going under an anaesthetic while he hovered with a scalpel.

Grace doesn't know which he hated most, red or black nails. Right now, black feels more rebellious. She picks up the varnish and hands it to Jane. Who smiles.

"That'll be so cool with the hair."

While Jane has been working on Grace, the place has been filling up. Another hairdresser has arrived and conversations are humming. Grace overhears "Young Dr. Sullivan." a few times and feels the glances she is getting. She closes her eyes.

"Young Dr. Sullivan, back again like a bad penny?" a voice booms.

Reluctantly, Grace opens her eyes. In the swivel chair beside her, an overweight, middle-aged woman with a ruddy face is smiling at her.

Grace's return smile is gracious. "Hello."

"Hi, I'm Jacinta Creedon, the butcher's wife. Jacinta O'Donovan that was."

"Oh, my goodness! I remember you from school!" Jacinta is only three years older than Grace but looks at least ten. "How *are* you?"

"Ah, sure. I could complain but who'd listen?" She chuckles like she's very contented with her life. "You're going fierce mad with the hair."

Grace looks in the mirror. And barely recognises herself. Her cropped hair has been entirely bleached of colour. "Silver" tones have been added. Grace was expecting that. What she wasn't expecting was to have years taken away with the colour. Her light green eyes seem suddenly huge, making her look like one of those anime characters. Or a pixie. Her features were drowned by the bob; she sees that now. Grace looks like someone entirely new. Someone cool, maybe even fun. Someone not afraid of adventure. Not afraid of anything. Maybe.

"It's gorgeous," Jacinta says.

Grace turns and smiles at her, thinking her lovely. She'd forgotten how friendly people were here. Nosey, yes. But warm too. Genuinely warm.

"And look at those nails," Jacinta says, like a fan.

The other hairdresser arrives behind Jacinta and looks at her through the mirror. "So Jacinta, what'll it be?"

"Oh. The usual."

five

The hair has taken up most of the morning. Grace texts Des to let him know she's on her way, then dashes into the supermarket. She ignores turning heads and flies down the first aisle, snatching things up. She stops, trying to decide between two brands of peanut butter. That is when she realises just how good her hearing is. From someone in the next aisle, she catches:

"Young Dr. Sullivan down from Dublin."

"With her notions," someone else chimes in, sotto voce.

Grace's heart lurches. Notions are the worst thing you could possibly have in Ireland. Notions about yourself and how brilliant you are. What makes anyone think she has notions? Her hair? The nails? What? She feels herself colour. It can't be a good look. Silver head, red cheeks.

"The cut of her!" the clandestine conversation continues.

"And when she opens her mouth, you'd never think she was from here at all."

Grace tells herself she doesn't care. Let them think what they want. Whoever they are, they don't know her. They just want something to talk about. Something to entertain themselves with. She has bigger things to worry about.

"I wonder what has her coming down here… without the husband," the conversation continues.

Right! That's it! Grace swings her trolley around into the next aisle. There they are, huddled together. One, she doesn't know. The other is Jacinta Creedon who Grace had decided was lovely, half an hour ago.

Seeing her, the women clam up.

"Oh Grace, 'tis yourself," Jacinta says, innocently.

"With my notions," Grace replies, eyeballing her.

Jacinta blushes.

Grace pushes the trolley through them.

She'll have to come back to this aisle when she's done.

In the meantime, she is going to live up to their expectations. They think she has notions? She'll show them notions. Into the trolley goes freshly blended coffee that smells like heaven, homemade cheeses from West Cork, the finest of breads and salami. An expensive wine. She collects tofu and chickpeas and quinoa for Holly, delighted with the health food section. She spots tortilla chips and goes a bit mad. In a frenzy of rebellion, she starts snapping up all the foods that Simon used to disallow. Tortilla chips (three packs). Ingredients for chilli con carne. Salsa. Guacamole. Beer. To hell with him. To hell with Jacinta and her pal. To hell with everyone. Grace will answer to no one. Ever again.

In the household section, she finds some bleachy concoction that should work on the black stains in the bathroom. She also picks up a candle. Not the fanciest candle she's ever seen. But it'll cheer the house up a little. She hopes.

The checkout girl – who Grace has never met – addresses her as Young Dr. Sullivan, proving that, not only has news spread of who she is, but her title has been decided upon. Something tells Grace that fighting it would be a spectacular waste of energy. As would pointing out to the checkout girl that "Young" Doctor Sullivan is probably twice her age.

"So, that's it. We'll never see Dr. Sullivan out anymore now," the young and, until now, chirpy blonde says with regret.

Grace frowns. "What do you mean?"

She scans the wine casually. "Oh, just that he hardly leaves the house now, only to come down here for his few messages."

"Why is that, do you think?" Grace asks, trying to hide her worry.

The girl lowers her voice and leans across the conveyer belt conspiratorially. "I'd say he's embarrassed. You know, on account of the Parkinson's."

No filter, Grace thinks. And just as well. This is information she needs to know.

Out on the street, laden with bags, (Why didn't she think to bring the car?) she spies a florist called Petals. And hurries inside. She can't go around changing her father's home but there's nothing to stop her from brightening it up. She chooses lilies. Waiting for them to be wrapped, to avoid conversation, she wanders into another part of the shop. Oh. It has a lovely line of interiors brands. She spies gorgeous towels and tea towels. Which she brings back to the till. Too late, she remembers that she is spending borrowed money. She will have to change her ways. Simon encouraged her to spend, wanting her to look good, the house to look good, the children to look good. He just didn't care how they felt.

"You've great taste, Young Dr. Sullivan," the florist says, taking the towels from her.

Inside, Grace groans. "Thank you…. I don't know your name?" she says, to equal the playing fields.

"Petal," she says, so quietly that Grace isn't sure she's caught it.

"Petal?"

The florist closes her eyes and nods. "I was doomed from the start."

"But you called the shop Petals!" She must like it.

Petal shrugs. "Well, it makes sense to call it Petals, doesn't it? I mean, I'd be stupid not to. Everyone knows I'm Petal."

"I think it's a lovely name."

Petal places the towels carefully into a tasteful, coffee-coloured bag bearing the Petals logo in pink. "You didn't grow up with the teasing I did. I should hate flowers. Instead, I love them."

"It shows," Grace says, glancing around the shop at the beauty, the creativity.

"Aw, thanks."

"You know, you could always change your name." Grace has changed hers back and the sense of freedom has been amazing. But then she notices Petal's professionally branded apron, matching the bags and the shopfront outside. With all the branding, Petal is probably stuck with her name.

But the florist brightens. "I could! Couldn't I? I mean, I could keep the shop the same. It still makes sense even if I'm not Petal."

"What would you go for?" Grace asks, encouragingly.

Petal taps her upper lip. Then brightens like she's having a Eureka moment. "You know, I've always liked Jacinta."

Grace's reaction is from the gut. "I'd stick to Petal if I were you."

Struggling to carry everything, Grace passes two men in their twenties jumping down from a tractor in mud-splattered Wellington boots. They step back to let her pass.

"Here, let us give you a hand," one says.

"It's fine. Thanks, though."

They take the bags from her anyway. All of them.

"Thanks so much," she says awkwardly. "I'm just up here."

"Oh, you must be Young Dr. Sullivan, so," says the more confident of the two…brothers? Non-identical twins?

It's one "Young Dr. Sullivan" too far. "I'm old enough to be your mother."

"Ah, 'tis just to distinguish you from the other Dr. Sullivan," one says, reassuringly.

The other is busy looking into her eyes. "You don't look it."

He's not flirting, Grace tells herself.

"Would you ever give over?" his companion scolds him.

So he was flirting. When is Grace going to start trusting her gut and stop making excuses for people?

"If I see a beautiful woman why wouldn't I share my appreciation?" he asks, continuing to look into her eyes.

Stunned and wholly unused to male attention, Grace feels herself blush. Luckily, they're almost at the house.

She takes back the bags with a quick, "Thanks very much."

She just wants to be home and stay inside forever.

Home.

Grace brightens at the thought that this word no longer means a palatial mansion in South County Dublin where the air is laced with fear but a tiny, draughty, country house where she is loved.

Three spoons drop into Cornflakes when Grace hurries inside.

"Sweet divinity," her father says. "Hardly the look of a country GP."

That's becoming very clear to Grace.

Jack is staring at her with a look of horror. "You're not looking for someone else, are you?"

"What? *No!* That's the last thing I'd want, right now. Or *ever!*" She seems to be making the same look of horror back.

"Okay. Good." He returns to his Cornflakes.

"Well, *I* love it," Holly says, getting up and coming for a closer look. "And the nails!" She lifts her mum's hand and laughs. "Wow."

If only all of Grace's patients were fifteen-year-old girls.

"Still," Jack mumbles into his cereal. "It's like you're looking for attention or something."

Holly pivots around. "You just don't get it, do you? All Mum wants is to start over."

Grace looks at her fifteen-year-old daughter, stunned by her insight. "You're right, Holly. That's exactly what Mum wants." Minutes ago, it had been to escape Simon, shake him off. But escaping Simon is still all about Simon. Grace sees that now. What she must do is start over. Because that is about Grace.

She hugs Holly tightly. "You're wise beyond your years, young lady."

"I know!"

Grace laughs. And when she sees the look of surprise on her children's faces she wonders how long it's been since they've heard her laugh. Years? There and then, she makes a promise to herself.

six

Everyone helps to put the shopping away, Jack sampling as many delicacies he can get his hands on. Grace smiles. This is one thing he has never lost: his love of food. His very first word – while eating – was "More!" Jack's appetite has always reassured Grace.

"Where does this go?" Des asks of the tofu. He looks at Holly as if she must be the intended recipient of this strange food.

"Fridge," she says, taking it from him and putting it in the door.

"Dad, after lunch, I'm bringing the kids to Drim to get uniforms. Will you come with us?"

"Ah, sure I'm grand here, love," he says, looking baffled by guacamole.

"Fridge, too," Holly says, taking it from him.

"I know you're grand," Grace persists, "but a change of scenery might... be nice."

"Mum, you're sounding all Cork," Jack says, screwing up his face like there's a bad smell.

"Maybe because I *am* from Cork," she says taking the Gubeen cheese from him before he polishes it off.

"Yeah, but you're down here, like, two seconds."

She turns back to Des. "So, Dad, why don't you come along? Get a coffee and a scone. Have a read of the paper." Scones, in particular, are Des's great weakness.

"I've things to do, pet."

"Can't they wait?" she asks lightly. "Isn't your pal, Tadhgh, in Drim? Ye could have an old pint of Guinness and a chat."

"Mum, seriously," Jack says of her accent.

At the same time, Des says, "Don't mother me." He lifts a cucumber from the shopping bag and looks relieved.

Grace feels her stomach tighten. This is not just about getting her dad out and moving. It's about making sure that no one's home should Simon show up. Grace can't have her father face him alone. Simon would run rings around him. He'd probably be sitting by the fire when they came home, whiskey in hand. Should she tell Des? No. She can't tell him. Should she cancel the trip? No. They need uniforms. She is stuck.

But then Jack puts down a jar of posh olives he was about to open, goes over to Des and puts an arm around him, surprising everyone, especially Des.

"Grandad, I'd like you to come."

Grace wants to hug her rage-filled son and magic away the past. She also wants to thank him.

Des perks up. "Alright so. I'll come."

"And I'll have a pint with you," Jack says with a wink.

Grace's head turns at superhuman speed. "You will not!"

"Joking, Mum. Joking."

"Ah, sure, the boy will be grand to have a pint at sixteen," Des teases, grinning at Jack.

And the most beautiful thing, a smile from Jack.

"I'll have to watch out for you two," Grace says.

"You will," grandfather and grandson say together.

Though the sky is low and grey, and the sea reflects that bleakness, the drive to Drimaleen lifts Grace's spirits. To be surrounded by nothing but nature makes life seem simple, uncomplicated, hopeful. The yellows, oranges, browns and vivid reds of autumn inject the landscape with warmth. The car in front whips up leaves from the narrow road making them dance. More swirl down from trees like lazy, autumnal confetti. A fir laden with cones seems to wave at the car as they pass by. It's just the wind at work, but, in her mind, Grace waves back. She feels her shoulders lower, her breathing ease.

Then everything changes as Simon's car comes into view. She stops breathing. Her heart pounds in panic. Her hands grip the wheel as her body tenses like a board.

What can he do? They're in the car and moving.

He could follow them! Have a showdown in front of her father, a whole town!

Maybe he won't see them.

On this road? In a Jeep this size?

Grace pulls right up to the car in front, hoping to hide. It's almost as big as theirs.

"Grace, slow down," her father warns.

He's right. This is dangerous. Grace eases on the brake.

His car is almost on them. What should she do? Keep her eyes dead ahead? Lower her visor? Stare him down like she's not afraid? Then all her thoughts go out the window. She can't help herself; she looks into the oncoming car.

Relief floods through her. It's not him! It's not even a man! She feels like laughing. She's still free. They're still okay. It might just take her body the rest of the day to recover.

Getting out of the car in Drimaleen, Des stumbles. His heart jolts but he catches the door to stop a fall. Jack rushes to help but Des holds a hand up and Jack steps back. Des closes the door.

"Will I come with you, Grandad?"

"I'm grand. You go get your uniforms. Then, if you like, you can follow me into McCarthy's and I'll treat you to a scone."

Jack smiles. "Deal."

Des starts to make his way up the street. He could do with a stick. But he's not going to give into this illness. He's going to take big steps, push back his shoulders, lift his chin and fight the pull it has on his body. He remembers how he used to stride everywhere, always in a hurry, never appreciating the ease at which he moved or the respect in people's eyes as he passed them on the street. He is mortified by the image he now presents, the shuffling, slow gait, the posture of a man whose body is calling the shots, despite his best efforts. At least, here, no one knows him. Or mostly no one.

In the coffee shop, Des makes his way to the counter where he selects the biggest scone on display. He picks up a copy of *The Southern Star*, arguably the best source of local news around.

Carrying his tray to a table, it occurs to him that he never fully appreciated how his Parkinson's patients felt; he doesn't know which is worse, the disability or the shame. When he finally sits, he glances around to see if anyone has been watching his struggle. The only person looking his way is a very thin woman – checking out his scone.

He opens the paper and goes straight to Rosie Shelley's health column. His patients were always quoting her. He started to read the column so he'd be ready for their questions. Now, he wouldn't be without her weekly, alternative take on things. He folds the paper to give him room to go at his scone. The smell is making his mouth water. He cuts it open in anticipation and adds generous dollops of cream and jam. The first bite is heaven. So is every one that follows.

He glances around. Everyone is busy with their own lives. No one has any interest in him whatsoever. He lets his eyes wander, over the people, the shop, life outside the window. It's good to be out of the house. He hadn't realised it but cabin fever had started to set in. One simple change of scene and it's like his horizons have broadened.

Holly had a bad feeling the minute they walked into the shop. It's not a uniform shop like you get in Dublin, where there's nothing but uniforms. It's just a shop selling clothes for, like, old people, with a uniform section stuck down the back. Now, they're telling her they don't have her size skirt. Well, they have to find one! They just do!

"I can't go to school on the first day in half a uniform!"

"Sweetheart," her mum says, "I'm sure they'll understand at school that they just didn't have your size."

"No! No one will understand. I'm already the new kid. D'you want me to look like one too? D'you want me to be bullied? I, need, a, skirt. I don't care if it's too small or too big but I'm going in there in full uniform!"

Her mum starts to rub her nose intensely.

"What?" Holly asks on full alert.

"Nothing," comes too quickly.

Holly knows her mum. She knows what it means when she rubs her nose like this. "You're upset."

She shakes her head. "Only that you're upset."

"Don't worry, we'll sort you out," the motherly shop assistant reassures, as if this is nothing compared to some of the meltdowns she has seen.

"What other sizes do you have?" Grace asks.

"We have one size up and one size down," she says – calmly – the way she says everything.

"I suppose we should get the bigger one, then. We can always get it taken in."

"If you don't mind a suggestion?"

Holly looks at the assistant like she's her only hope.

"They're wearing the skirts fierce short altogether these days. You can hardly see the things."

"But isn't it a convent school?"

Sometimes, Holly wishes her mum would just stay quiet.

"Oh, I know the school. Sure, my daughter goes there. I'm telling you. The way they wear those skirts would leave little to the imagination."

Standing nearby, picking out a school tie, Jack's head pops up. Holly rolls her eyes.

The assistant looks at him. "And the boys wear the shirts tight. To show off their guns."

Grace laughs.

"I'll get an extra-large so," Jack says defiantly.

Holly stares at him. "That's social suicide."

"I'm going out to Grandad," he says, already on his way.

Holly hears her mother sigh.

"Don't worry; we have his measurements," the assistant reassures.

"What about a school coat?" Holly asks her like she's an all-knowing guru.

Making sure that her superior at the register is occupied, the guru lowers her voice. "Oh, I wouldn't bother. They all wear whatever coats they want. In fact, from what I'm told, you'd be a right eejit altogether if you wore the school coat. That's what my one says anyway. As long as they're non-regulation, anything goes."

Jack storms from the shop. He doesn't want a new uniform. He doesn't want a new school. He doesn't want a new life in the middle of nowhere. As for tight shirts, if that's what the culchies are wearing, the farmers, he'll go as loose as he can. Why did his father have to ruin it for everyone?

He finds his grandfather tucked into the corner of the coffee shop, completely absorbed by the sports section. Seeing him, something melts in Jack. He goes over.

Straight away, Des gets up.

"Come on up with me. I spotted a great big sugary donut you'd love."

Smiling, Jack goes with him.

The donut will hit the spot alright. A donut and Coke. But his grandad doesn't stop at that. The man who didn't want to leave the house helps himself to another scone and cup of tea.

"Sure, I'm out," he says.

Jack smiles, warming to the man he's only really getting to know now, at the age of sixteen. Why didn't they visit Killrowan more? But then, he knows why.

Back at the table, Des tosses the newspaper aside. Grandfather and grandson sit together – eating – in contented silence.

"It must be very hard for you, coming down here?" Des says at last.

"It's fine," Jack says, reminded that it actually is fine. Because they've got away. And that's the main thing. That's what he needs to remember – every time he forgets. They're free. "I'm glad you came with us, Grandad."

Des smiles. "Me too." He dabs his mouth with his napkin. "D'you know what we might do if we have a few minutes?"

Jack raises his eyebrows.

"I spotted a nice cravat across in Brady's. I think I'll go back and buy it."

"Good plan."

seven

That evening, leaning over the old, beloved AGA stove, Grace closes her eyes and inhales the smell of simmering chilli con carne, the smell of freedom. She finds it incredible not to have to worry about adding too much or too little (or what *Simon* considered too much or too little) salt, pepper or whatever ingredient he chose to zone in on, incredible not to have to watch every step, question herself, try to second-guess him. She can just cook. Breathe. Be.

She opens a bottle of Corona for herself and one for her dad. She could get used to this.

She calls the kids.

Jack, never far away when food is being prepared, thunders down the stairs, followed closely by Holly.

They sit together, this new family, everyone tucking in, worries on hold.

"It's so good to be here, Dad," Grace says, rolling her shoulders, enjoying the sensation of her body loosening up.

"It's good to have ye here," Des smiles, looking from Grace to the kids.

"We'll start looking for a place at the end of the month," Grace says. "Get out from under your feet."

Jack darts her a reluctant look.

Seeing it, Des misinterprets. "Would ye not go back?" he asks his daughter.

The air changes. Three bodies tense. Jack and Holly look to their mum.

"No, Dad," Grace says. "We would *not* go back."

Des puts down his fork. "It's just such a disruption for ye." He looks at Jack.

"We are well able for disruption. Aren't we, guys?" Grace can hear the switch in her voice, back to South County Dublin.

Holly nods like crazy.

"Yup," Jack says.

"I know but, whatever he did, I'm sure he's sorry."

Holly stares into her tofu chilli.

Jack's jaw shifts.

Grace tries to keep her voice steady as she says: "Dad, I've told you already, this is what we want. You have to trust our decision."

"But–"

Jack drops his fork. "Leave it, Grandad."

"Marriage–" Des persists.

Jack shoots to his feet. "You don't know what you're talking about!"

"I was married–"

"Oh my God! He hit her, okay?" Jack blurts out. "Not once. Not twice. But all the time. He put her down, tried to turn us against her, look down on her." Grace bows her head. "And we stood by and did nothing. Nothing! It doesn't matter if he's sorry or not because sorry doesn't stop him. Nothing does."

Des stares at his grandson, then turns to his daughter. He reaches out, then stops as if he doesn't know what to do, what to say, how to fix this. "Oh, pet," is all that comes out. Then, "I'll kill him."

Grace looks up. "No, you won't," she says calmly. "Because we're here now. Away from him. We've done it. This is our new life. Our new start. So, if you want to do anything to help, just love us, that's all we need. A little love."

Dazed, Jack sits back down. Hiding behind a curtain of hair, Holly silently cries into her tofu chilli. Des gets up. Forgetting to take big steps, he shuffles to his daughter. He puts his arms around her shoulders and hugs her. He rests his head on hers.

"How did I not see?"

The children are in bed, Grace having struggled to reassure each of them that it was not up to them to stop their father. It was up to her. And she did it – finally – with their help. There is nothing, *nothing* to feel guilty about. Grace knows that they will need to hear this again. She knows, more than most, that guilt doesn't stop on demand.

She stares into the fire now, her father by her side. She has tried to answer his questions honestly, admitting to when it started, why she stayed, and why she never told them. When he asked if Simon ever hurt the children, she rushed to reassure. But there are things that Simon did to her that she will never tell him. So, there are lies. Lies to protect her dad.

"I'm sorry for being so blind." His eyes beg forgiveness. "I've come across this so many times in the practice. I thought I knew the signs."

"He hid it well. Especially from you. The golf. The whiskeys by the fire." On the rare occasions they saw each other, Simon behaved impeccably, affectionately even.

Des slams his fist down on the arm of the chair.

Grace jumps.

The colour drains from his face. "Oh, love. I'm sorry. I didn't mean to–"

"I know. I know you didn't. It's okay. It's over, Dad. I'll be fine. We'll be fine."

"What if he comes down?" Des asks, glancing around as if his little house is made of straw.

"There's a barring order. He could get twelve months in prison if he breaks it." She's reassuring herself as much as him, here.

He frowns. "Do the kids have to see him?"

Grace shakes her head. "The courts allowed us to relocate without access."

"Things must have been bad." His eyes search hers.

She looks away. Into the flames she says, "We had a great lawyer." It's not a lie. Grace will be forever grateful for the strength of that woman.

"But it's unusual for a parent to be denied access," he insists.

She can't let him imagine the worst, stew on it, blame himself for not spotting it. So she turns to him and looks deep into his eyes. "You can never tell anyone this." She glances at the door, then lowers her voice. "We lied in court," she admits. "We said he hurt them so they wouldn't have to see him. Jack and Holly are going to carry that for the rest of their lives."

His face is a blank canvas. "Did you ask them to lie?"

She shakes her head. "It was Jack's idea. Then neither of them would back down."

He reaches out and squeezes her hand. "Well, fair dues to them, that's what I say. They put a stop to his gallop. They shouldn't feel one ounce of guilt. They should feel proud. Hats off to the pair of them."

The relief is huge. "I wasn't going to tell you. Didn't want it hanging over you, too."

"No more secrets, Gracie. I'm in your corner, now, okay? You're not alone anymore."

Her throat burns and her eyes smart. She looks back into the fire. More than anything, more even than the fear, she has felt alone. Funny she is only realising this now.

"You got away from him. That's the main thing. We'll make a good home for you here in Killrowan. You mark my words."

She looks at him. "I love you, Dad."

"I love you too, pet." His eyes well up. "I just can't believe–"

"It's all right. It really is."

But his hands curl into fists and his jaw hardens.

"Another briquette?" she asks.

He looks at her and softens. "Ah, sure, go mad. Put on two."

After years of doing every little thing carefully, Grace tosses the briquettes in like a mini rebellion. Bright orange sparks rise up, reminding her of the phoenix. That's who she is now.

"What made you leave in the end?" Des asks like he's afraid of the answer but is determined to hear it.

"He killed the dog. He killed Benji. Said it was an accident. Left him in the boot of the car on the only hot day of the year." Her sigh shudders with oncoming tears and she wipes her nose with the back of her hand. "It *could* have been an accident. I don't think he'd have hurt the children like that. Me? Yes. The kids no. But that's when I decided. No more. *No more.*" She wipes away tears, knowing what her father is probably thinking: You let him break you but left for a dog? What she doesn't say is (because she'd choke on the words) Benji was more than a dog. He was family. And her defender. Tiny little ball of fur rushing to the rescue. Or trying. Tiny little ball of fur that brought so much comfort to all three of them, Holly especially. Benji knew when they needed love and he gave it in spades.

"We'll get you a dog," Des says.

"You're grand. There's no room." Des might trip over one. But the biggest reason he's "grand" is that no one could replace Benji. That's when it hits Grace: Benji saved them. Benji made them leave.

eight

Holly lies awake, listening to the gentle murmur of voices downstairs. It's a relief that her grandad knows now. Their lives have been one long secret. And this is a new start. The less secrets the better. She turns over and closes her eyes. The radiator gurgles as air runs through the pipes. Above her head, in the attic, she hears the water tank refill. There's a faint tapping sound too that she can't figure out. There better not be mice up there.

She still can't believe that they are here, that her mother finally did it. Holly had nagged her, googled stuff for her, found out about shelters. She didn't care where they went as long as they got out. She never thought that Benji would have to die, though. Her throat burns and her eyes smart. She knows that Benji would be happy that they escaped. She wishes he were here beside her, snuffling his little wet nose into her face, letting her know that everything's going to be okay. This whole thing would be so much easier with him.

But he got them away. Got her mum moving. Gave them a reason to lie in court. If only Holly had made her dad hit her. Her mum would have left then. Before anything happened to Benji. But every time she thought about it, she worried that he'd just get madder with her mum and take it out on her instead of Holly. And she was never brave enough to take that risk.

They are away, now, though. And that's so good. But scary too. How will she walk into school on Monday? There are bullies in West Cork, too. She knows she should be more like Jack and just not care. But how do you make yourself not care? She has tried. She still cares. About everything. Everyone. And what they think. She's still super careful, afraid to do anything that will bring it down on her. Still, she doesn't want to be a person who is angry at the world, a person who wants a fight, dares the world to bring it on. There has to be an in-between place between herself and her brother. She just wishes she could find it.

She pulls her turquoise velvet throw up to her face like a comfort blanket. If only she'd brought more stuff from home. She has tried to make the room cosy. And the bed does look better with the throw. If only she'd brought her lamp and the rainbow rug beside her bed. They'd have made all the difference.

She hopes the woman in the shop was right about the skirt.

Grace wakes gasping for air. His hands were around her neck. Pressing. Squeezing. Choking. She was slipping into unconsciousness when she jolted awake. She sits up, trying to calm her breathing, her hands holding her neck. It felt so real, as if she were back in time and it was happening all over again. Is it a sign? Is he coming? Is he already here? Rigid with fear, she listens intensely.

But it's just the ticking of her clock and the gentle chime of the grandfather clock at the end of the landing. Far from reassured, she goes to the window.

The street is empty but for a fox padding across it. She watches him in all his grace until he disappears.

It's okay. Everything's okay. It's just her imagination. He's not here. He's not on his way. He's lying asleep on a silk (wrinkle-preventing) pillow.

Checking on the children, Grace finds them reassuringly deep in sleep. She steals downstairs.

In the kitchen, she touches her heart. Not only is the back door locked, her father has jammed a kitchen chair underneath the handle. Her heart swells with love.

She is home. She is safe. There is a barring order. All is well.

And yet she still craves codeine.

She pours herself a large glass of water and gulps it back. She wanders around picking up things, putting them down. She gazes at her graduation photo. Her mother was so proud of her that day. So proud of her always, really. Grace feels like she has let her down. Her mother never said that she didn't like Simon. There were only ever two questions that might have made Grace wonder, both before she married. The first was asked tongue-in-cheek: "Do you do *anything* without Simon?" The second should, at least, have made her pause, question, *look*: "You don't think he's a little controlling?" Grace thought her mother was being ridiculous; he was just passionate, intense, in love. She touches her mother's face in the photograph, so like her own: tiny nose, full mouth, pointed chin and big, round, trusting eyes. If only she'd listened. If only she'd asked herself where those questions were coming from.

With one of the new tea towels, she brushes dust from the picture then puts it back. She wipes the mantlepiece. This starts a frenzy of cleaning, mopping and scrubbing. She snaps on a pair of rubber gloves and, with a toothbrush and the bleachy concoction she bought in the supermarket, goes upstairs to tackle the grouting in the bathroom.

Catching her reflection in the mirror, she is reminded of her new silver-haired, pixie self. This is not the kind of woman to clean grouting to silence. She needs Spotify. Sitting on the side of the bath, with two bars of service, she downloads a new playlist, a pre-Simon collection of her favourite tracks from the eighties, Sinead O'Connor and The Cranberries featuring strongly. She puts in her earphones and closes the door.

As she scrubs in tiny circles and sees the black give in to her vigour, her mood starts to lift. She doesn't realise she's singing until she hears herself pelting out the words, "This is the last day of our acquaintance, oh, oh, oh." She stops, hoping she hasn't woken anyone. In her head, though, she continues to shout the words to a plastic surgeon with a penchant for silk pillows.

"The Emperor's New Clothes" and "Mandinka" take Grace back to sleepovers that involved no sleep, to a snowball fight outside a disco, and the giggly recounting of her first clumsy kiss. She shared everything with her friend, Yvonne. More than a friend, really, a soulmate. They used to finish each other's sentences, read each other's minds, plan futures that involved marrying brothers and staying together forever. How did they ever lose touch? It happened slowly. Grace moved to Galway, the only university to offer her a place in medicine. She was studying hard and playing hard as med students do. But she still came home every few weekends. Then Simon, seven years older, swept her off her feet, gobbled up her every free second. Why, he wanted to know, would she want to go home to Cork when she could stay with him? She sees now what she was too in love to see then. To control a person, you isolate them – from family, from friends. You do it slowly, patiently. Ruthlessly. You occupy their every available minute, showering them with a wonderful – fake – version of you, a shiny, glossy, caring you. When he got his consultancy post in Dublin, that was it, they were gone.

She wonders what Yvonne is doing now. Did she move away from Killrowan? Most young people do. She wonders if she's on Facebook. But then Grace isn't and wouldn't know how to find anyone. The kids could show her. But then, she could just ask her dad.

For now, she gets lost in a long list of Kate Bush tracks. When she – quietly – sings along to her favourite, a duet with Peter Gabriel called "Don't Give Up," she is singing the words to herself.

Finally, unbelievably, all the black has gone. Her work is done. She sits on the bath, happily exhausted. She'll sleep now. Without the need for codeine. It's a small victory. But a victory nonetheless.

nine

When Grace comes downstairs on Sunday morning, Des is at the kitchen table, nursing a mug of tea. The chair has gone from the back door. She wants to thank him for putting it there but, clearly, isn't supposed to know. With a smile, she joins him for a cup of tea.

"You cleaned the grouting," he says. "I was going to do that."

The guilt she feels is automatic. This is a matter of pride to him. Why didn't she think of that?

Well, because he has Parkinson's. He shouldn't be climbing into baths with toothbrushes.

Also, she has landed in on him with her kids; she should be pulling her weight.

She's about to explain all this when she stops herself. She has spent too many years excusing herself. It's time to stop.

"I enjoyed it," she says cheerfully.

"Are you mad?"

"You *know* I am."

They share a smile.

"Dad?"

"Yes, pet?"

"Whatever happened to Yvonne Barry?"

"Oh, she works below in the library. You should drop in to see her."

Her inner child wants to run there now. But it'll be closed. And what would Yvonne think anyway – that Grace is suiting herself now that she's back in town? She'll wait. Maybe they'll bump into each other in the village. And Grace can apologise for the bad friend she turned out to be.

"You could catch her at Mass," Des suggests.

Grace looks at him for a long time. "Gave up on God, long ago, Dad."

He squeezes her hand. Then pushes himself up into a stand. "I'll probably go myself."

So he's not completely avoiding the village. This *is* good news. But then Grace imagines him making his way along the narrow path, alone. She'd offer to go with him if he wouldn't be insulted and she could leave the children alone, which she's not going to risk.

"Take an umbrella!" He could use it as a stick.

"Why would I want an umbrella? Sure, isn't it a glorious day, out?"

Grace smiles. "Good point."

Outside, Des pauses. He hasn't been able to face Mass – or the village – since he retired. Today, though, he has the biggest incentive a man could have, the safety of his family. He wants a quiet word with Paddy O'Neill, the local police sergeant, and Mass is where he'll find him.

Des could take the car but that would seem mad – and weak – driving a few hundred meters. Anyway, he'd have to turn the car around on the narrow street, the car that he hasn't moved in two weeks.

The other option feels like a trek to the Himalayas.

Fine, if that's what it takes….

Out on the path, Des gives his body the usual instructions. He lifts his chin. A deep breath and he's off. He's doing the right thing. He and Paddy go back a long time; the family secret will be safe with him. The main thing is, he needs a heads-up in case they need to call on him.

Des hasn't gone far when Dolores Tracy, the lollipop woman at the local primary school, arrives alongside him in a furry leopard-print coat, purple boots and red ear muffs. Des wonders if the kids appreciate the colour she brings to their lives – a wild, new rigout every day.

"Dr. Sullivan!" she gushes. "'Tis great to see you out and about!"

"Sure, why wouldn't I be?" he asks, a little too defensively.

"No reason in the wide world," she utters, flustered. She looks like she wants to disappear. But they're both going to the same destination and to disappear would be to rush off on him.

"I'll let you go on ahead, Dolores. I'm a little slow," he says softly, sorry for snapping at her.

But politeness roots her to the spot.

"I'm grand, Dolores. Honestly. I like to say a few preparatory prayers on my way," Des lies.

"Oh, right so," she says in relief. "Of course." She shoots off like she's been relieved of a load.

Des watches her go with a benign fondness, then continues on, returning the waves, nods and smiles of other villagers heading to Mass. He pretends that nothing has changed. He's as fit as a fiddle. Halfway to the church, though, his legs feel so heavy that he has to stop. He peers into the window of Coughlan's, giving him an official excuse to rest. The fact that it's largely a hardware shop is never reflected in the window display. There could be sailing gear. Buckets and spades in the summertime. Fishing tackle. Today, amongst the eclectic mix, is the most beautiful blackthorn stick Des has ever clapped eyes on. It's standing there like it's calling to him, and only him. The blackthorn is the sturdiest of walking sticks, with a smooth round oak handle and a thick, knotted, black shaft. Des has always fancied one but has never treated himself. Now, he could really do with one. So his pride talks him out of it. Until, it occurs to him that the knots on the shaft would make it a fine weapon. That settles it! First thing tomorrow, he'll venture out to Coughlan's and arm himself. For now, he has a church to get to.

Des makes it to Mass on time and surprises himself with a long list of prayers. For Grace. The children. Fresh starts. Peaceful solutions. For love. And hope. And freedom. He even puts in a request to slow the advance of his Parkinson's.

Leaving the church, he feels calmer.

He still has a mission.

At the base of the steps, he is keeping an eye out for Paddy when, into his line of vision, comes a round-faced woman in her forties, dressed for the office, with a haircut Des has always considered unfortunate. Choir leader, Barbara Kelly, has a keen nose for gossip, something Des avoids like the plague. But there is no escape now; their eyes have met and Barbara is on her way over.

"I thought I'd see Young Dr. Sullivan at Mass!" she says. "I was looking out for her."

For a good auld gawk, Des thinks. "You did a great job today, Barbara. Great job."

"We put in a lot of hard work," she says proudly. "I think it paid off."

Des scans the crowd. He can't let Paddy get away. "Give my regards to Paudi," he says to Barbara, hoping she'll take the hint.

"I will indeed," she says and hurries off, already waving to – and making a beeline for – one of her cronies.

Tom Creedon, the amiable, ruddy-faced butcher, nods as he passes Des, a man of few words. Luckily, he has just two on this occasion: "Dr. Sullivan!"

"Tom!"

Des sees Tom's wife, Jacinta, deep in discussion with a group of women. Tom has clearly given up waiting and is heading home.

At last, Des sees Paddy. He is not the bear of a man he once was and his thick head of hair is fully grey but he looks a lot younger than Des feels. Sharp as a tack, the sergeant spots him. And comes over.

"Des, how're things?" he asks with his usual authenticity and warmth.

"Will we go for an auld scone in the Coffee Cove?" Des asks.

"Sure, that'd be grand, altogether. It's been too long."

Des feels he should mark his cards. "There's something I want to ask you about. In confidence."

Paddy frowns and nods. "Of course. Let's go."

Back at the house, Grace was going to make pancakes for the children. But she doesn't want to remind them of home. So she opts for a fry, something that was never allowed. The smell wafts upstairs like an upbeat alarm clock. She doesn't have to call them.

She watches them eat with so much love. And concern.

"How're ye doing?" she asks them, softly.

"Fine," they say together. It's their usual answer. They're always fine. Because she has never been.

"I'm so proud of you two."

Jack tenses as if sensing an agenda.

Grace wonders if she should leave it. Then reminds herself of the two faces of Jacinta Creedon.

"How do ye feel about starting school?"

"Fine," Jack says in an end-of-discussion tone.

"Hol?" Grace asks.

Holly shrugs, glancing at Jack.

"Well, *I'm* worried about starting off in the practice if that's any comfort," Grace says. "We all get nervous. Don't we, Jack?"

"Stop babying her!" he snaps. "She just needs to stand up for herself. To hell with everyone."

"Mum's only trying to help."

What Grace is *trying* to do is avoid them having to face what she already has. So, she persists. "I guess, if you want to blend in, you could tone down the Dublin accents a little."

Jack throws down his knife and fork. "I'm not toning anything down for anyone!"

"That's fine, Jack," Grace says calmly, her stomach twisting.

Holly looks at her mum. "How do I learn the Cork accent?"

That's when Grace realises that, in trying to protect them, she's just making Holly more nervous than ever.

"You know what? Jack's right. Don't worry about your accent. Don't worry about anything. You're perfectly fine just as you are. Better than fine. You're wonderful. They'll be lucky to have you."

Jack leaves the table and thunders upstairs.

Grace runs her hands through her hair and sighs. Hearing her father's key in the door, she makes for the kettle.

Des appears, looking invigorated. "How's everyone?"

"Grandad, can I borrow your radio?" Holly asks.

"You can of course, love."

Holly peers over at it on the counter as if it's from the ark. "Is it on a Cork station?"

He tips his head down and looks up at her. "You have to ask?"

She smiles. "How do I turn it on?"

"'Tis fierce complicated," he says. He takes it from the counter and places it on the table in front of her, then demonstrates with the flick of a switch.

"Brilliant, thanks!" She gets up and puts her plate in the dishwasher. Then disappears upstairs with the radio.

"You'll have a fry," Grace says to her dad.

"I don't suppose it'd kill me," he says, rubbing his hands in anticipation.

Jack has spent the day in his room, getting more and more worked up. It's after ten and he has lost count of the sit-ups as his thoughts continue to race. When is she going to stop trying to protect them? They're not babies. They're better – stronger – than she thinks. Suddenly, he needs to hear his father's voice, the father who always believed in him. He gets up, locks the door and puts his earphones in. Sitting on his bed, he takes a deep breath and inserts his old SIM. His stomach cramps at the stream of missed calls and voice messages that have been coming in, night and day. Way too many to be normal. This was a mistake; he shouldn't listen.

But how can he not?

"What the hell is going on, Jack? First you turn me into, into some kind of *monster*. Then you block me out." His father sounds desperate, hurt, lost. And Jack feels sorry for him.

"I'm your father, Jack. I've invested sixteen years of my life in you. You can't just stop all contact."

Jack closes his eyes and reminds himself to breathe. In. Out. In. Out.

With each message, his father grows increasingly irate. "She's making you do this? Isn't she?"

"You know what, Jack. I'm not paying maintenance for people who won't even call me back. And you can tell your mother that."

"If you don't return my calls, so help me, I'll come down there."

Jack flings the phone onto the bed like it's on fire. He interlinks his hands on the top of his head and presses down. Hard. How could he have forgotten his rage? How could he have forgotten the bullying way he tries to control everything? If Jack calls him, he becomes his tool. If he doesn't, he'll show up here in Killrowan. Jack can't let that happen.

Stomach knotted tighter than it's ever been, he picks up the phone. His thumb hovers over his father's number. Mouth dry, he stares at the screen. He takes a deep breath. Then pauses. If he makes this call, his father could still show up. Jack would become his tool. While also betraying his mother. She would be devasted if she knew that he kept the SIM, never mind talking to his father.

Phone in hand, he slumps onto the bed. He can't betray her. And he can't blame her for trying to protect them. She kept them innocent for so long. Jack had no idea – until he began to spend time at his friends' houses. That's when he noticed. Not all dads spoke to their wives like his did. They didn't criticise them. They didn't insult them. They joked and laughed and teased maybe, but fun teasing, that resulted in teasing back. When his father joked, it could turn at any moment. You could feel the tension in the air like ice particles, everything brittle, as if something was about to crack at any moment. And crack it would.

Jack wants to tell her he's sorry. But sorry is a word that his father used to get what he wanted. Sorry is a word that Jack doesn't trust.

He thinks back to the days before he knew. He'd burst through the school doors to find his mum waiting for him in the yard with a little box of juice and another little box of raisins. She'd pick him up and he'd throw his arms around her neck and lay his head against her chest. Then she'd whisk him and Holly off to the cinema or the beach or the amusements in Bray where he'd kill alien invaders with an enormous pink gun up against his shoulder. She was such a warm mum. She still is. He just stopped noticing, coloured by his father's view of her. She'd die for them; he feels that now, like a great force of truth. He wishes he could wipe out all the pain she went through. He wishes he'd stood up for her. He thinks he's so hard. But if he really is hard why didn't he step up? Why didn't he protect her like she protected him?

There's a knock on the door. He turns the phone on silent and shoves it under his pillow.

He opens up to see his mum. There's so much he wants to say. But he keeps it all in.

"Just wanted to say goodnight," she says, looking beautiful, if he's honest.

He forces a smile. "'Night."

She goes to him, cups his face in her hands like she used to when he was little – and he used to cup hers right back. He'd forgotten that. The memory touches him.

"I just want you to know that you can relax now," she says, looking deep into his eyes. "You can be a teenager, look out for yourself, have fun, be free. We're okay now. The hardest bit is over."

Suddenly, tears threaten. And he *never* cries. "Yeah, okay, gotta get some sleep." He won't sleep.

"Okay, sweetie, see you in the morning. Love you."

Maybe, someday, he'll be able to say it back.

Grace knocks gently on Holly's door. Opening up, her heart melts. Holly has carefully laid out her uniform on the back of a chair. Her school books are organised according to subject on the dressing table, ready to go into her bag. And she's tucked up in bed, listening intently to the sea area forecast and repeating the words exactly as they're said. Everything she has done today, she has done while listening to the radio. Grace smiles at her baby and sits on the edge of the bed. She opens her arms wide for a hug. Holly folds into her. Grace kisses the top of her head. That Holly was conceived in violence has never weakened Grace's love for her. If anything, it has made it more fierce, more determined.

"Love you to pieces."

"Love you too, Mum," she says in a strong Cork accent.

Grace pulls back. "That's so good!"

"Really?" Holly asks hopefully, continuing to sound like a native.

"Really!"

Holly turns down the radio and looks into her mother's eyes. "We'll be okay, won't we, Mum?"

Grace tucks a strand of hair behind Holly's ear and looks into her eyes. "We'll be better than okay. We'll be amazing." The minute she says amazing, it feels too strong, too unbelievable, too big a leap. Why didn't she just say "great"?

But Holly is looking at her like she really wants to believe it.

Grace pinches her nose. "New start. Clean slate. The world's our oyster."

"The sky's the limit," Holly says.

"If you can dream it, you can do it!" Grace exaggerates a shudder and they laugh. She puts her arms out again.

Holly clings to her.

And she clings right back.

"Do you think if I leave the radio on I'll listen in my sleep, subconsciously, like?"

Grace smiles. "It's worth a try."

Grace is lying awake at two in the morning, her mind swirling around on a worry loop. What is Simon up to? Does the fact that he didn't appear this weekend (when at his most outraged and off work) mean that he's not going to? Can she allow herself to hope that the law really will stop him? Maybe he spent the weekend with fat-cat lawyer pals preparing his backlash. What's the worst he can do legally? Get access? He can't force them back to live with him. That's what matters. She has to stop thinking about him. He's in the past. She has a future to worry about. Will the kids be okay at school and in Killrowan in general? How fast is her father's Parkinson's progressing? And is she up to taking over from him? That last question, alone, is a minefield. At the age of forty-seven, Grace is returning to work full-time – without the full educational credits she needs. The Irish College of General Practitioners has said that she can continue to gather them (with further courses and study) as she works. But what if she makes a mistake? Her experience is mostly with young mothers and children. The patients in her father's practice are, by and large, elderly. She could really do with a crash course in geriatrics. And that's just to be competent. Grace has to go beyond that. She has to be as beloved, as respected as the original Dr. Sullivan. For him.

But there are positives too; she has to remember that. She is returning to what she loves, full-time. Becoming independent again. She knows that Simon would never doubt himself if he was in her situation. He'd walk right into that surgery, head high, thinking everyone lucky to have him. It's disconcerting to realise: Grace should be more like him.

She looks at the hands on the clock. She really must sleep. She can't start work in a fog. Maybe one codeine. Just one. And just for tonight….

ten

Monday morning, Holly stands at her bedroom window, out of sight, looking down on the street at everyone heading to school. She whispers a thank you to the woman in the uniform shop – who was right about the skirts, shoes, coats, everything. Holly checks out – exactly – how the girls are wearing their hair. Straightened and in high pony tails. Luckily, she has just straightened hers.

She leaves the window.

The ancient (and kind of gross) dressing table is actually pretty handy. Holly can sit facing the mirror with somewhere to rest her hair things.

There's a knock on the door. Out of the corner of her eye she sees it open.

"I'm heading out now," her mum says. "Just wanted to wish you luck."

"Thanks," Holly says without taking her eyes from the mirror. Time's running out and she has to get this ponytail right.

"Give your mum an old hug."

"Haven't time!" Her eyes meet her mother's in the mirror.

"You look lovely," she says, smiling.

"I can't get my hair right," Holly says in growing frustration.

"Want me to do it?"

"No!" she snaps. Apologetically she adds: "I know the exact height."

Grace places her hands on Holly's shoulders and kisses her temple. "Have a great day, sweetie."

"Great? Not amazing?" Holly wishes she weren't so superstitious. Like, how can what her mum wishes her affect her actual day? It can't. So it doesn't make a difference if she wishes her a "great" day instead of an "amazing" one. That's not how life works. Hopefully.

"Amazing. Of course, I meant amazing."

Holly knows she's being dumb. Still, she smiles in relief. "You too. You have an *amazing* day too."

Her mum presses her nose. "I'll see you when I get home, chicken."

"See you then." First, though, she has a whole day to get through.

Jack is sitting on his bed, tying his shoes when his mum knocks and pops her head in.

"Good luck at school," she says.

The luck he needs is with his dad. "Thanks. You too."

"How about a hug?" she asks as if she's expecting a no.

And he is so tempted by that no. But he gets up and opens out his arms, out of loyalty to how close they once were.

She does a little pretend race to him, arms pumping. Laughing, he wraps his arms around her. Easier that way. She's tiny.

"This feels like a lucky hug," she says.

"It is," he lies. Jack doesn't believe in luck. And though he is surprisingly reassured by the closeness and the familiar scent of "Mum," he counts to five and pulls back.

She smiles up at him. "Better get that hair sorted. You look like a hedgehog."

Jack checks his watch meaningfully. "Thought you said you wanted to get there early."

"I do, I do. Okay, I'm gone!" She does another fake race to the door. Then she stops and turns. "I've left lunch downstairs."

"Go!"

She waves her arms in the air, mimicking panic.

"You're crazy," he calls after her, liking the person she is becoming. Or maybe returning to.

Holly has tried three different ponytail heights. At last, she deems herself satisfied. She checks her watch. Oh no! She grabs her bag and runs. Out on the landing she calls Jack. She's not walking up that road on her own.

He appears, looking like he has just dragged himself out of bed – having slept in his clothes. His shirt is hanging out and his tie is off to one side. The worst is his hair, though.

"Jack! Your hair!"

He ignores her, turning and making for the stairs.

She notices his feet and tries to save him. "The boys are all wearing runners!" Jack's in his old school shoes.

He turns around. "Do I look like I care?"

"Why are you always looking for trouble?" she demands.

He looks at her for the longest time. Then his expression softens. "Okay, look. If you try to fit in, you never will. Just be yourself, okay?"

"Easy for you to say. People love you."

"Because I don't care. Just don't care, Holly, and you'll be fine."

"You can't just click into not caring."

"I give up." He trots down the stairs.

"Ah, there he is! James Dean himself," Des says, like he's impressed.

"Who?" Holly asks.

"James Dean. 'Rebel Without a Cause.' Actor. Doesn't matter." He slides lunch boxes across the table. "I slipped in a little surprise for ye."

"Aw, thanks, Grandad," Holly says, shoving her arms into her coat.

"Okay, we're off," is Jack's goodbye as he heads for the door.

"Jack, make an old man happy and put on a coat. There's rain forecast."

"So, what else is new?" Jack grumbles, grabbing the coat his grandfather is holding out and walking off with it still in his fist.

"I don't know why we're walking so fast," Holly says to her brother. All around them kids are messing, pushing each other around, laughing, joking, teasing each other. "We look way too intense."

Jack slows down – for her.

"Aren't you nervous *at all*?" she asks, under her breath.

"Of a bunch of culchies?"

She glances around to make sure no one heard. "Shh!"

"You're as good as any of them, Hol."

When she looks doubtful, he walks ahead, jaw set, like he's ready to take on the world. Reaching her school, though, he stops and waits for her. "Break a leg, sis."

She brightens.

He stands, arms folded by her school gates.

"What?" she asks.

"Just waiting for you to go in."

"Aw. I'm touched," she jokes, hand on her heart.

"Go on, shoo!"

She takes a deep breath and heads in through the gates behind a swarm of girls. Reaching the entrance, she turns around. Jack raises an arm in some sort of crazy salute. She laughs and gives him one back, remembering. Family comes first. Family is everything.

Crossing the road to the boys' school, Jack imagines Ross and all the others at their lockers now, having the banter. Without him. He looks around him. He has nothing in common with these, these… farmers. How did they get their "guns" anyway, lifting tractors? He takes out his phone to text Ross. But there's no service. And the moment of weakness passes. What will he do with himself down here? A boy with red hair passes with a hurl on his back. Jack sure as hell won't take up hurling, the sport of culchies. He lifts his school bag higher, pushes his shoulders back and strides into the school. If anyone hassles him…

eleven

Grace runs her hand over her father's old desk. The surgery hasn't changed. Well, the computer is new. Outside of that, it's just as she remembers. She sits in the swivel chair, pushes back from the desk and turns in slow circles, absorbing everything, the way the light shafts in and dust motes rise, the warm chestnut wood of the desk and shelves, the way the room smells faintly of antiseptic. This is where her dreams of becoming a doctor first formed. By the age of ten, she knew how all the equipment worked. She could take a temperature, pulse, blood pressure. She knew what caused heart attacks and strokes. And she knew how to do the Heimlich manoeuvre.

She would visit so often that the surgery was like a second home. She and her mum would bring Des lunch and sit and chat with him for the short break he allowed himself. Her parents were so in love. Right to the end. It showed in the little things. How she'd never miss a day of bringing him lunch. How she'd cut his hair and how he trusted her to. And how he walked on the outside of the footpath so that if anyone mounted it, he'd take the hit. Grace never imagined that marriage would mean anything other than love.

She turns on the computer, puts her phone on silent and tosses it into her bag. Glancing back at the computer screen, her stomach lurches. She has no idea how to work this system. Why didn't she think to come in over the weekend? Such an obvious thing to do. She scoots the chair tight to the desk and tries to figure it out. She has to. She can't call any patients in until she works out how to bring up their files and add notes.

But the more she looks at it, the more she clicks, the more convinced she becomes that this system might as well be in Chinese.

She tries not to think of the waiting room filled with patients, already, at five past nine or the fact that there is no sign of her partner, Dr. O'Malley.

She needs help.

Unfortunately, Myra, the receptionist, has already proven herself immune to Grace's charms, her mouth a grim line as Grace introduced herself minutes earlier.

Well, it's Myra or sit there.

Grace hurries out to reception where Myra and her ample bosom are checking in yet another patient. Grace folds her arms to stop herself from fidgeting. More than anything Myra looks efficient. Her mostly grey hair is whipped up into a neat bun. A pen is tucked behind her ear like she means business. No make up. No nail varnish. And a sensible polo neck pullover.

"Take a seat inside," sounds like an order.

The patient thanks her and starts to move off.

Grace launches herself at the reception. "Myra, can I borrow you for a second just to get a quick intro to the computer system?"

Myra goes from efficient to irritated.

"I can't get started without accessing the patient files."

Myra sighs. Reluctantly, she leaves reception as if all hell will break loose without her.

As they pass the waiting room, Grace glances in. Her stomach tightens. It's heaving in there. And everyone's staring out at her.

"Has Dr. O'Malley arrived in yet?" she asks sotto voce.

Myra gives her a look. "We'll be lucky to see Dr. O'Malley before ten."

"But the first appointment's at nine!"

"Doors open at nine. And it's far from appointments we are, here. You're not in Dublin now."

"How do you avoid queues and lags without them?" she asks as she follows Myra into her surgery.

"Lags? Have you seen the waiting room? It'll be like that till tonight."

It's how Grace remembers it.

Myra sits at the desk and pauses. Her face fills with regret. "Ah, the place is so different without him." She takes a deep breath. "Right, let's have a look at this."

Myra moves at speed. Clicking this, clicking that. Grace struggles to keep up, wishing she'd thought to film it all on her phone. Too late now. If she takes her eyes from the screen for a second she'll miss something crucial. Plus, she knows what Myra would think of her resorting to her phone over her brain.

The receptionist stops suddenly and looks at her. "D'you think you have it now?"

Grace hopes so. She nods. "Thanks so much. You're a saviour." She glances towards the door. "You can send my first patient in now."

Myra looks straight at her. "You don't have any patients. They've all checked in for Dr. O'Malley."

Grace stares. "What about my father's patients?"

Myra shrugs. "They're asking for Dr. O'Malley."

"All of them?"

Myra nods.

Colour shoots up Grace's neck and face. Her heart starts to race. Is it the hair? The nails? The notions? The fact that she's been away for years? Don't they see her as one of them? Don't they trust her because they don't know her? Maybe they consider her too "young" at forty-seven?

And as she watches Myra take off, she decides that whatever their problem (or multiple problems) with her, she has to do something to change this. This partnership has to work.

Wearily, Myra returns to her desk. She loves this job. She loves the patients and – normally – the doctors. She had a special affection for Dr. Sullivan with his warmth and his calm approach to everything. Without him, it's like a light has gone out in the surgery, like the very air has changed. She watches Young Dr. Sullivan approach the waiting room like a lamb to the slaughter. Myra had hoped that she'd be like her father. Instead, she's like the young locums who come in to relieve the doctors every so often – filled with energy and bright ideas that never work. Every last one of them talks of appointments. Appointments how are you?! No one wants to see these young idealists coming to the rescue. Myra doesn't know what the point of them is, really. They don't ultimately relieve the doctors because no one will go to them. They just put pressure on her. They don't know the system, the subtleties, the locals. And no one trusts them. They're nothing but a thorn in her side. Until now, though, they have only been a temporary thorn. Manageable. She looks at Young Dr. Sullivan coming to a halt at the waiting room door with her silly hair and her city clothes. Her heart sinks. She'll open her mouth now and unleash that posh Dublin accent of hers. She may as well have a sign around her neck saying, "unclean."

At the waiting room, Grace feels like she's standing at the door to a party she hasn't been invited to. All eyes are on her. One woman nudges another with a surreptitious elbow that Grace – unfortunately – sees. Grace raises her chin and smiles professionally.

"Good morning, everyone. I'm Grace Sullivan."

There follows a round of: "Good morning, Young Dr. Sullivan."

"Anyone for me?" she asks aiming for Simon-confidence.

No one moves. A blink or two. Finally, a frail man of around eighty raises his hand like a schoolboy asking permission to speak.

"I'll wait for Dr. O'Malley, if you don't mind, love."

She forces another professional smile. Then glances around at the other patients. "Does anyone want to avoid a wait? I'm available now."

People look into their laps, at their fingernails, out the window – anywhere but at the new doctor. One woman suddenly rummages in her bag like the pressure's too much.

"Well, you know where I am if the wait gets too much."

Grace returns to reception. "Myra, if anyone's in a hurry, please send them in to me. Also, anyone who'd rather a female doctor." She stops short at "young." Desperation is not going to make her ageist. Anyway, she's already learned: "young" is relative.

twelve

Des is on the ground, where he has fallen. He can't believe how easily he came down. He was just turning around. He must be more aware of where he places his feet, must remember to keep them wider apart, especially when turning. He must be constantly aware of what he is doing.

The doorbell rings. Well, they can wait. If he rushes now, he'll come a cropper again. He rolls onto his side and, from there, onto his hands and knees. He grips the arm of the couch and pulls himself up.

The bell goes again.

"All right, keep your hair on," is not like him. And he scolds himself. He will not let this… condition… turn him into someone else.

Des opens the door to his grandson. And knows immediately that something's wrong. For starters, school's far from over. He's in his school shirt and tie – no coat. And he is shivering. His skin is chalk white, lips blue, fingers mottled. He didn't get this cold just walking from the school. Where has the boy been?

"Come on in out of the cold," Des says, standing back to let him in.

Jack heads for the stairs.

"Tea?" is a speedy attempt to stop him.

Jack turns and looks at his grandad for a long moment, sighs, then nods and goes to the kitchen table where he sinks into a chair like gravity is pulling harder on him than the rest of the world. He rests his head in his hands, his fingers splayed through his hair.

Des puts on the kettle. And the heat. "Back in a second."

Gripping the bannister, he makes his way upstairs, frustrated by his body's stiffness, slowness, heaviness. In his room, he takes his neatly folded navy round-neck pullover from the top drawer.

He roots around in the bottom one for a woollen cap he got from a patient one Christmas but has never worn. He snaps off the label. And makes his way back downstairs.

He hands Jack the pullover. "Put this on."

Jack doesn't argue.

"And this." He passes him the cap.

"I'm okay."

"Put it on anyway."

Jack tugs it over his cold red ears.

Des makes the tea and pops on two slices of toast. Things are always better on a full stomach.

He brings the snack to the table and sits at right angles to Jack. Face to face might seem confrontational.

Jack studies the grain in the pine table, following the swirl of a knot with his finger. Des wants to ruffle his hair and tell him that, whatever it is, it'll be okay. He thinks of Grace and wonders if the school has been onto her. If they had, she'd have been straight on to him. She's probably with a patient. Des hopes he can ease the boy's distress before she finds out. First things first. Distraction.

"Will you give your old grandad a hand putting in a new ballcock when we've finished our tea?"

"Ballcock?" Jack squints as if his grandad is having him on.

"For the cistern in the bathroom. I think it's the root of all that groaning when the toilet flushes."

"Oh, right. Okay," he says as if anything's better than going back to school.

Des looks into his milky tea. "So, do you want to tell me what happened?"

"Not really."

Des smiles. "Come on. I'm bored out of my tree. I need a little excitement in my life."

Jack sighs. "It was just some punk looking for trouble," he mumbles into his mug.

"In what way?"

"I don't know. Slagging me off. Being a smart ass."

"What did he say exactly?"

"Look, it doesn't matter."

"It might. Cork people are a law onto themselves. We say all sorts of nonsense that mean absolutely nothing."

Jack sighs. "He said, 'Ye boy ye.'"

"Sure, that's a compliment down here as in, 'Hup ye boy ye!' It means you did a good thing."

"It was the way he said it. Like he meant the opposite, like he was talking down to me."

"What else did he say?"

"Something about coming down from Dublin."

"That's it?"

"No. He started explaining to me that craic meant fun. As if I was from outer space. Of course, I know what craic means. I'm bloody Irish."

"Maybe he genuinely thought you didn't, though. Maybe he was having a go at himself to make you feel more at ease. Playing up the culchie."

Jack looks doubtful. "You can't take any rubbish, Grandad, especially on your first day."

Des tilts his head to the side. "True enough. But, once you decide not to take it, people will know that from your body language and leave you be. You can put a man in his place with just a look, a sentence, even silence."

"I know that." Jack stares into his tea, then looks up. "So, you really don't think he meant anything?"

"No. I don't," he says very definitely.

Jack flops back in his chair. "That's just great then," he says sarcastically.

"What?" Des asks.

"I hit him."

A pause. "So, apologise."

He scoffs. "Only wimps apologise."

"Only wimps *don't*. It takes guts to say sorry. And one 'sorry' can go a long way in defusing a situation."

"Not in my experience."

Silence falls. Des knows that the "experience" he means is the experience of growing up in an abusive situation. He wants more than anything to help this hurt and damaged boy who is nowhere as hard as he lets on. He fumbles for his wallet. With clumsy fingers, he takes out a photo of Jack as a baby that's been cut to passport size. He slides it across the table to his grandson.

"Your mum sent me that a long time ago."

Jack brings it to his face, smiling at the little person he used to be. Looking directly at the camera, too young to know to smile, he was a cute kid with his little heart-shaped face, hair blonde then, eyes green. Jack glances up at his grandad in gratitude, touched that he carries this photo with him. He passes it back.

"You were a right joker, back then," Des says with affection, tucking it back in his wallet.

"I *was*?"

Des chuckles. "You used to be always messing."

"*Really*?" he asks, encouraged.

"Oh yeah. Whenever we came up to visit, you'd be up to all sorts of tricks. You'd drop your bottle out of the cot just so your mam would have to pick it up. 'Twas a game ye played. Your gran thought you were a scream."

Smiling again, Jack asks, "What else did I do?"

"Oh, let me see." His face brightens at a memory and he chuckles. "You'd call your mam 'Dad' and you'd call your dad 'Mam.' You were barely talking. And, still, you were such a little blackguard."

"And what did I call you?"

"Poo – for a long time."

Jack laughs out loud.

"Come on, let's show this ballcock who's boss," Des says.

Jack looks at his grandad and laughs even louder.

thirteen

Grace familiarises herself with the computer system – just in case hell freezes over and she gets a patient. There's a knock on her door. She turns in hope.

But it's not a patient.

She gets up. "Dr. O'Malley!"

Entirely bald and dressed in a tweed jacket that has seen better days, he looks so much older than she remembers – as old as her father who, at seventy, is ten years older than his former partner. He has a little bit of egg yolk on his tie. Grace decides against pointing that out.

"Grace," he beams, smelling of hard-boiled clove sweets. He grips her upper arms and she tries not to flinch. "I can't get over you. You were probably, what, eighteen when I last saw you?"

She smiles professionally, then decides to face the elephant in the surgery.. "Sorry about the waiting room. You're a lot more popular than I am."

"Ah, probably just a case of the devil you know. Give it time. Show your face around the town. Oh and make an appearance at Mass. Always a good idea." He winks then he rubs his hands together. "Right, I better get to it. Time waits for no man. Welcome onboard, pet."

Grace tenses. Pet? Is that how it's going to be? Did he say it in all innocence because he has only known her as a child? Or is he putting her in her box? She wishes she could tell.

"Maybe we'll have a drink after work," he suggests.

She smiles politely but plans to get home as soon as she can to see how Jack and Holly got on at school. Poor Holly. It'll be hardest for her.

The door closes behind him. Grace checks her phone. And nearly drops it. Three missed calls from the boys' school. Plus, one voicemail. Before she can listen to it, her phone rings again. She answers immediately.

"Is this Dr. Sullivan?"

"Yes?"

"Jack Sullivan's mother?"

Grace freezes. "Jack Willoughby?" she clarifies, hoping there has been a mistake.

"No. Sullivan."

Grace closes her eyes and releases a long breath she didn't know she was holding. Wrong child!

"No wait. You're right. Sorry, it *is* Jack Willoughby. I see here from the records that he's enrolled as Willoughby. He was calling himself Sullivan."

Should she explain?

She doesn't get a chance. "This is Sinead Hannigan, the principal. We need you to come in. There's been an incident."

Her breath catches. "An incident?"

"Jack punched one of our best students, then marched out of the school and hasn't come back. That was half an hour ago. I should warn you, we're looking at expulsion.

Grace's hand goes to her forehead. "Where's Jack now?"

"We were hoping you could tell us."

"I'm at work. But let me call home. Then I'll be straight over."

"Bring Jack with you, obviously, if you can find him."

"Of course."

Grace kills the line. And immediately calls her father.

Des and Jack are replacing the ballcock, Des instructing, Jack implementing, sleeves rolled up, hands submerged in the cistern.

"Okay now, pop that in there," Des says. "And that should be it."

Jack does as instructed, then looks at his grandad.

"Good man! That's it! You did it!"

Jack, wearing a look of achievement, takes his hands from the water. Des passes him a towel.

"Did you know that your grandad was almost expelled from school once?"

Jack's eyes widen as he sits down at the side of the bath. "What did you *do*?"

"Chased a teacher around the classroom with his belt." Des smiles nostalgically like those were the good old days.

His grandson looks baffled. "What were you doing with his belt?"

"Oh, I snatched it out of his hand when he tried to whip me with it."

Jack's eyebrows shoot up. "He tried to *whip* you?"

Des nods. "They were always at it, back then. Corporal punishment they called it. To make it official, like. Well, that day I'd had enough. He needed a taste of his own medicine," Des says simply. "The coward ran. The class was in uproar. It was worth it just to see everyone's faces. Our one small victory. We'd all had enough of that weasel and his antics."

"Go you, Grandad. Wait. Why *didn't* they expel you?"

Des waves his hand. "Ah. I was up for a scholarship and they were due to get half. So, they didn't want to cut off the gravy train."

"Did you get the scholarship?"

"Oh, I did. Otherwise I'd never have been a doctor."

"Wow," Jack says looking at his grandad with new eyes.

Des replaces the lid on the cistern. "All I'm saying is, I was always in trouble and I turned out okay. Well, if you call a harmless auld fella fixing a ballcock okay."

"What else did you do?" Jack asks eagerly.

"I used to stand up to bullies when they were picking on the little lads. I was a little skinny lad myself but nifty with the old catapult."

Jack laughs, looking at his grandad in amazement.

"The school were always sending letters home."

"What did your parents say?"

"Oh, they never saw them; the big eejit of a principal trusted me to deliver them."

Jack pulls down his sleeves. "Wish there were more people like you," he says with regret.

Des wonders if he's thinking about his father. "All I'm saying is, don't worry about this. It's nothing in the grand scheme of things."

Jack grimaces. "Not sure that Mum will agree."

"Ah, we'll cross that bridge when we come to it. Now let's flush this baby and see if we've made any difference at all."

They're listening to the sound of groan-free flush – and sharing a victorious smile– when Des's phone rings.

They look at it, up on the windowsill, as if it spells doom.

"Well, that'll be your mother," Des says, reaching for it.

"Or the school."

Des answers, looking at Jack. "He's here."

"And you didn't think to call me?" Grace sounds furious.

Des draws a finger across his throat for Jack's benefit. "I thought you'd be with a patient."

"Put him onto me."

"He's holding something for me," Des lies.

Jack looks at him in gratitude.

"He assaulted one of the best pupils at school! Then left, just walked out. They're talking about expulsion!"

"'Twas a punch, love. And they won't expel him. Not on his first day. A man is allowed a mistake on his first day."

Jack's eyes are glued to his grandfather's.

"I'll have a chat with him now about what happened. Then we'll head over to the school to Sinead."

"First name terms?"

"Sure, I've been her doctor all her life."

"You can't dine out on that!"

"Grace, love, you asked me how we're on first name terms."

"I know but how can you be so calm?" she asks shrilly.

Des looks at Jack. "Sure, getting worked up never helped anyone."

"This is serious, Dad. Jack, of all people, knows you can't go around assaulting people." Her voice rises and wobbles as if tears are on the way.

"Look, 'tis all under control. You go on back to work. How's it going anyway?"

"I'm coming home."

Des and Jack exchange a defeated glance.

Driving too fast through the village, questions flood Grace's mind, all of them panicked. Is he turning into his father? Does he *want* to be expelled? Does he want to go back to Dublin? To his father? And why didn't she take the day off for their first day at school?

fourteen

"Neaten up, there, Jack," Des says as they wait for Grace to show up.

"I'm grand."

"Why antagonise the principal further by refusing to tuck in that shirt and straighten that tie?" Des shoves a tub of Brylcream in Jack's direction. "And here, tame that hair."

Jack would rather walk on nails. But, seeing as it's his grandad asking, takes the tub to the bathroom mirror and obliges.

When his mother's Jeep screeches to a halt outside the house, he is ready at the door. He goes out to her before she can come in.

But she's already jumping from the Jeep. "What in God's name were you thinking?"

Jack gives her a back-off look and climbs into the Jeep.

She jumps in beside him, then swings the car out as if she's starting a high-speed chase. "Why did you punch him?"

He turns and looks out his window.

"Jack!"

"I won't be bullied."

That changes everything. Her heart contracts. "Who was bullying you? Jack, look at me."

With a sigh, he turns to face her. "It doesn't matter. Grandad thinks I just took him up wrong."

"And you *punched* him?"

"Yeah, I punched him," he says defensively while still feeling sick about it.

"Ah, Jack."

"I don't have a Cork dictionary, do I?" he flares.

Grace hurries into the school. She stops, turns and whispers at Jack who is following at his own slow pace.

"Hurry *up*!"

She takes off again, the sound of her heels echoing through the corridor. How she hates schools. They always make her feel like she's done something wrong.

The school secretary looks at Grace's hair long enough for her to know that she is judging. Then she asks them to take a seat outside the principal's office.

They sit side by side looking straight ahead not a word passing between them.

The principal snaps her door open almost as soon as they've sat down. She's younger than Grace and her hair is purple. Maybe there's hope, Grace thinks.

She extends her hand. "Sinead Hannigan."

Grace shakes it. "Grace Sullivan. Sorry about this."

Jack tenses at the apology.

"Wish we were meeting under better circumstances. Come in."

The principal sits across the desk from mother and son. "Jack, what have you got to say for yourself?"

"He was bullied. In Dublin," Grace rushes before Jack can speak.

The principal turns to her in surprise.

"It's made him sensitive," Grace continues. "He misinterprets...."

Jack stares at her. "Mum!"

"I'm just saying that there are extenuating circumstances."

"Mum. Stop. Let me speak for myself."

The principal's face softens. "Go ahead, Jack."

He visibly swallows, his Adam's apple rising and falling. "It was a mistake," he mumbles. "My grandad – Des Sullivan – explained to me that what that boy said was okay. I thought he was slagging me. But he wasn't. It was just the way people here say things. I lashed out because you can't let yourself be bullied, especially on your first day." He bows his head. "But I'm sorry."

Grace knows how hard that "sorry" was. And wants to hug her son.

"I think now would be a good time to bring in Simon and his parents."

Grace panics. He didn't hit the boy because of his name, did he? She stares at Jack. Who glares back at her.

"Wait! Please," Jack says to the principal. He lowers his voice. "What my mum said... that's... private."

The principal nods. "I understand. Absolutely. What's said in this office stays in this office. You can trust me on that. Always." She gets up and goes to open the door. Looking to her right, where Grace and Jack sat, moments ago, she says, "Come on in. I'm sorry for keeping you."

Grace stands up. Reluctantly, Jack does the same.

The boy appears first. To Grace, there is something familiar about him. His eyebrows in particular remind her of someone. His mother comes into view and everything stops. When Grace had hoped to bump into Yvonne Barry, it wasn't under circumstances like this. Jack has punched her son. Now Yvonne is staring at her.

"*Grace?* Grace Sullivan? Is that you underneath that hair? I *heard* you were back in town!"

Despite everything, they laugh.

Grace checks out Yvonne's husband who has just appeared. "Pat Harte? Is that you?" Grace looks back at Yvonne. "You married Pat Harte!"

"She did," Pat Harte says proudly.

Yvonne shrugs. "Ah, sure, there was no one else left. They all went hightailing out of here." She links arms with Pat and tugs him closer as though she wouldn't have it any other way.

How much they've all changed. And yet, in so many ways, stayed the same. Incredible!

The boys look at each other, bemused by their parents.

The principal clears her throat.

They remember why they are there. Silence falls.

"Have a seat," the principal says. Sticking her head through the door, she says, "Irene, another seat. Thanks."

Two seconds later it arrives. Everyone sits.

"So, Simon," the principal says. "I think Jack has something to say."

Jack starts over, explaining the misunderstanding and how his grandfather put him right. This time, though, faced with the boy, he struggles with the apology. It doesn't materialise.

Grace wills him to say it.

But it's Simon who speaks. "C'mere, boy. We're cool alright? You're from Dublin; whatever like.' He shrugs to show no hard feelings.

Jack looks at him, at the honesty in his eyes. Then he takes a deep breath. "I'm sorry," makes its way out at last.

Outside the school, Grace and Yvonne quickly exchange numbers, everyone having to return to work.

"I'll call you!" they say together. And hug. It's like the years have fallen away. Suddenly, after a terrible start to the day, Grace is filled with childlike optimism.

"Mum!" Jack appears out of the school.

She pulls back and turns in surprise.

"I'll go on," Yvonne says.

"Great to see you," they say – in sync. Then, "I'll call you." Also, in sync.

Jack strides up to Grace. "The principal said I could talk to you for a second." He rubs his arms. "Can we sit in the car for a sec and put on the heat?"

"Yeah, sure," she says, wondering what this is about.

They climb into the Jeep.

Whatever Jack is about to say, Grace has to tell him, "I'm so proud of you. I know what you think of apologies."

But Jack is eyeballing her. "Why did you lie? I wasn't bullied."

She hesitates. "Well, we all were bullied – by your father."

"That's different."

"Is it? Because of him, we overinterpret everything, find hidden meanings–"

"Why do you have to find excuses for everything?" he raises his voice in frustration.

They both know why.

"What else was I to say?" she asks, feeling his distress.

"*Nothing!* You could have let me handle it. Trusted me to. Instead you turned me into a victim!"

She tilts her head back. He's right. In her panic, she completely undermined him. "I'm sorry, Jack."

"Stop, saying, sorry! And stop lying to get out of situations! There doesn't always have to be some sad excuse."

She knows he's right. She knows she'd do anything, say anything to avoid conflict.

"Why did you have to make a big deal of it? *Why?*"

"Because I didn't want you to get expelled! Where would you have gone? Back up to Dublin, up to your dad? Is that what you wanted?"

He stares at her like she's slapped him. "I can't believe you said that. If you knew how he's been wrecking my head all day, you wouldn't ask that!"

"What do you mean?" Grace asks with a frown.

"Nothing."

"What do you mean, Jack?"

Jack looks down. His voice quietens. "Nothing. I just think about him. Sometimes. That's all. I don't want to go back. I never want to go back." He jumps from the car and takes off. At least this time it's in the right direction, back towards the school.

Grace goes after him. "Jack! Come back! I'm sorry. I didn't mean–"

But he has already disappeared inside.

She fumbles in her bag for the Nurofen Plus. She takes two, without water, on an empty stomach. Not what she would advise her patients. She leans back against the Jeep. Across the road is the girl's school, silent and still and austere in the shade of great oak trees. She hopes that Holly is having a better start.

Des checks his old reliable leather-strapped watch. They're probably still at the school. He picks up the phone.

"Myra, how are things?" he asks with genuine affection.

"Oh, Dr. Sullivan!" she says like her spirits have lifted just hearing his voice. "Sure, 'tis crazy here but I'm grand altogether. How are you?" she asks in a more-importantly tone.

"Never better. Never better."

"Good, good."

"Are you looking after her for me, Myra?" Des has seen the welcome stand-in locums get at the practice and can well imagine the first day that Grace must be having. He didn't warn Grace. He doesn't want to mother her. If he comes to her rescue, she'll think he has no faith in her. And he has more faith in her than she has in herself.

There's a pause. "You mean Young Dr. Sullivan?" Myra asks.

"The very person."

"Well I… haven't had a second but I will."

"A woman after me own heart, Myra. After me own heart."

fifteen

Grace hurries back into the practice but then slows approaching reception, remembering that no one will be waiting for her. She looks at Myra, hopeful that maybe *one* patient might be in a hurry. Myra shakes her head with what seems to be genuine regret. Grace produces a smile. Turning, she notices a lime green, notice posted on the glass screen separating Myra from the masses. Having no memory of it, Grace scans the words.

> *Young Dr. Sullivan*
> *Specialising in women's and children's health*
> *Shorter wait time*

Grace turns to Myra in surprise.

"Thought it was worth a lash," the receptionist says, taking the pen down from her ear and tapping it against the counter.

Grace is genuinely touched. "Thank you. And that's exactly what I *do* specialise in. How did you know?"

"Wild guess." She waves her pen in the direction of the waiting room. "There's a sales rep in there. Will I send him in to you?"

Anything's better than sitting in silence, ruminating on what just happened at the school. "Do so. Though I won't have much of an effect on his sales."

Myra leans towards her conspiratorially. Quietly she says, "Give them time." Her voice dips to a whisper and Grace has to lean in to hear. "Might be no harm to show your face at Mass." She raises her eyebrows.

That's two voices now. Grace would be a fool to ignore them – despite the fact that she has given up on there being a god of any variety. She nods slowly. "Point taken. Thanks, Myra."

Conor Sweeney of Blackcastle Pharmaceuticals is a standard-issue rep, young, handsome, and well turned out. His handshake is firm but not crushing and he waits to be asked to sit.

"How's your dad?" he asks.

"How did you know Dr. Sullivan's my dad? Were they talking in there?" she asks suspiciously.

"Actually, your name gave it away, *Young* Dr. Sullivan." He smiles.

"Can't seem to shake it off. It was decided before I even got here. Dad's doing well, thanks." Out of loyalty, she doesn't bring up the Parkinson's. Des wouldn't want her to. Because it doesn't define him.

"He was one of my favourite calls."

Grace doesn't doubt it.

"We used to arm wrestle."

She laughs. "You did?"

"Oh yeah."

"Who won?" She's still smiling.

"I'm a medical rep. Who do you think?"

She laughs again. "I won't take you on so. There'd be no challenge in it."

"True enough."

From now on, Grace will have a red-carpet policy for reps.

He lifts his briefcase up onto his lap and starts to open it.

Grace braces herself for a detail aid of boring graphs, enough to send an insomniac into a coma. Already, she's reviewing the red-carpet policy. And yet, she has to keep up to speed with all new medications. So...

She struggles to focus on graph after startling graph. Then he mentions a new Parkinson's drug that Blackcastle has just received FDA approval for. Grace wakes right up, lobbing question after question at him.

He promises to send more data. "Some really encouraging papers."

Finally, he starts to pack everything back into his briefcase.

Suddenly, Grace doesn't want him to go – and leave her with her worries.

"So is Blackcastle a good company to work for?"

He literally ignites. "Amazing." He explains that they have given him shares in the company. "They're skyrocketing!"

Might explain his graph enthusiasm.

"I wonder why," she muses aloud. Maybe it's the Parkinson's drug. She hopes so.

"Well, great products."

"Obviously."

He laughs. "Would you like some product samples?"

Grace thinks about the visits she'll have to make to the clinic on Torc island. Three miles off the coast, the island has no pharmacy. Samples, antibiotics especially, would be really welcome. Especially as her first trip is tomorrow.

"Whatever you have would be great."

He unloads his case.

Grace gets a ton of samples, free pens, Band Aids with cartoon characters and a mug with the name of a drug on it.

The Band Aids bring her actual joy. "These are fab, thanks."

He gets up to go but then looks like he's having second thoughts and sits down again. "Dr. Sullivan, I hope you don't think I'm stepping out of line here but I just wanted to say…" He pauses. "This is a tough practice. Stick with it, though. They need someone like you."

"You think?" she asks doubtfully.

His nod is adamant. "I do."

She smiles. "Well, *you've* just earned my undying loyalty."

He laughs. "Buy the shares, though. Seriously. They're definitely worth a punt."

It'd help if she knew how to buy shares. "I'll look into it."

They shake hands. Who'd have guessed that a medical rep could help her state of mind.

As soon as he's gone, though, it's back to silence. Stillness. Worries. She'll make a coffee. Then again, does she really want to pass a room full of people who don't want to see her? She'll Google that Parkinson's drug, see if she can find out more. Then, she'll investigate how to buy shares.

sixteen

After a visit to the toilet that could no longer be avoided, Grace has to pass the waiting room. People are standing now, having run out of seats. She thinks of Dr. O'Malley in his surgery and the pressure he must be under trying to get through everyone. She has to do something.

She goes up to reception.

"This is ridiculous, Myra. Can you tell Dr. O'Malley that I'm going to write up the repeat prescriptions and text people their blood results?"

Myra nods, collects the relevant information and hands it to Grace. "I'll let Dr. O'Malley know."

Back in her surgery, Grace moves the mouse to wake up the computer. Before writing the scripts, she needs to check patient files to make sure each prescription is still relevant. It would be mad to prescribe blindly, knowing nothing about their condition.

She clicks into the first patient's file, telling herself how good it will be to at least *start* becoming familiar with the patients in the practice. Seeing other doctors' work will also help her revise her medical knowledge. This first script is for a teenager requiring Ritalin. After scanning his medical history, she checks to see if his liver function tests are up to date. They are and all is well. She writes the script and puts it aside.

Next is HRT for a patient who Grace confirms is doing well with no side effects. She adds another script to the first. Next, she clicks into the file of Fred Cronin, a man in his fifties who requires a variety of meds. She sees that he had an uncomplicated medical history until about five years ago. Since then he has been back to the surgery every few months with a growing list of complaints. Impotence. Joint pains. Fatigue. Dr. O'Malley has prescribed Viagra for the impotence. Nonsteroidal anti-inflammatory drugs for the joint pain. And iron for the tiredness.

Grace taps her pen against the desk. Dr. O'Malley has been treating all of the symptoms as if they are independent of each other. What if they're linked? She clicks to check the results of blood tests and is surprised to see that none have been taken. She checks for more symptoms. No more have been recorded. It's probably fine. Still, something is niggling at the back of her mind, a condition that was covered in great detail during a continuing medical education seminar. She gets up and goes out to Myra.

"Describe Fred Cronin to me," she asks quietly.

"Fred?" Myra asks, surprised, then sees in Grace's expression that there must be a medical reason for the question. "Fine big man." She tilts her head. "Though thinner lately it has to be said."

Grace mentally adds weight loss to the list of symptoms.

"Sallow skin," Myra continues like a thoughtful citizen trying to help a private investigator. "Probably from being out in the fields."

"Was he always sallow?"

Myra frowns. "Now that you mention it, he wasn't always. No."

Grace has a sinking feeling. "I need to talk to Dr. O'Malley."

Myra looks concerned. "Is everything okay?"

"Grand, grand," she says, reminded how fast news travels in Killrowan. She reassures herself that Myra is not the type to break patient confidentiality. If she was, she wouldn't have kept her job. "Can I go into him?"

"There's someone with him. As soon as she's out, I'll buzz you."

"Thanks, Myra."

Grace paces her surgery, telling herself to calm down. She could be wrong. There's no blood test. No proof. She's probably wrong. What if she isn't, though? What if this man could have been diagnosed five years ago and his condition halted? What if he's headed for cirrhosis? Liver cancer? Liver failure? What if cirrhosis has already started?

Five minutes of mad pacing and the phone rings.

"Pop in quickly," Myra says. "But I warn you. He's not in good form."

Grace runs.

In Dr. O'Malley's surgery, a faint whiff of BO hangs in the air, presumably from the last patient. The doctor glances up distractedly from fast typing with two fingers. He looks hassled. And he still has egg on his tie.

"What is it, Grace?"

"Dr. O'Malley. I was doing the repeat prescriptions, as you know, and noticed that Fred Cronin has never had bloods taken."

"So?" he asks impatiently, resuming his battle with the keyboard.

She has to be careful here. She doesn't want him to think she's checking up on him. Because she's not. "Well, I think we should run some tests to rule out haemochromatosis. He has a lot of the symptoms."

"So, call him in. Take the bloods." He glances up. "Is that it?"

Doesn't he *get* the significance of this? He has been giving the man iron. "Yup that's it. I'll call him so."

"And send in the next patient, would you?" he asks as if it's her fault no one wants to see her.

Grace stands at the door to the waiting room and calls, "Next!"

The usual lack of response kicks in.

"For Dr. O'Malley," she says as snippy as the doc himself.

An old woman gets up. "Thanks, love."

Grace goes straight to Myra. Hands on the counter, she leans in. "Myra, can you call Fred Cronin and ask him to come in for a blood test."

Myra pinches her lower lip. "Is he all right? Should he be worried?"

"No, no. I just want to check something." She produces what she hopes looks like an optimistic smile. "When he comes – if he can make it today – send him in to me."

As soon as Young Dr. Sullivan disappears into her surgery, Myra looks up Fred's number. She knows something is up. That much she can tell. She always liked Fred Cronin. They were at school together. They even did a line for a short time. He just lacked a bit of gumption in the end, she thought. But a good man. A good man. He'll probably still be milking now given the size of his herd. She'd better call the mobile.

Almost an hour later, there's a gentle knock on Grace's door.

"Come in," she calls.

A tall man with a trusting face and jaundiced (not sallow) skin comes in, taking off his tweed flat cap. "Young Dr. Sullivan?"

She gets up with a smile. "Mr. Cronin?" She offers her hand.

His shake is strong. "Fred. Please."

"Fred." She notices, with disappointment, that his dark and soulful eyes are jaundiced too. "Have a seat."

He sits heavily into the chair.

"How have you been feeling?" she asks.

"Tired. Fierce tired," he says, nodding as though to confirm his words. "I thought the iron might give me a boost, but nothing seems to."

Grace rubs her nose. "I want you to stop taking the iron for the moment."

Fred grimaces. "I actually gave up on it when it wasn't working."

Thank *God*, Grace thinks. "So, you were taking it for how long?"

"About a month. Are you going to give out to me, now, Doctor?"

"No, no." The absolute opposite. If she's right, iron is the very cause of his problem. Grace suspects that Fred Cronin has an inherited disease called haemochromatosis which leads to a lifelong build-up of iron in the blood that incrementally damages the liver. The recommended treatment is to regularly *lower* the iron by draining off blood through phlebotomy. Dr. O'Malley has prescribed doing the opposite.

"Why did you call me in, Doctor?" he asks, twisting the cap in his hands.

"I'd like to take some blood samples, Fred, if that's okay? And run a few checks."

"What I mean is, why now?"

She reminds herself that Dr. O'Malley was doing his best, under pressure.

"Well," she says as she struggles to find the right words, "I was writing your repeat prescription and I thought it was about time you had a check-up." This is true. She reaches for a blood form, needle and syringe and Vacutainers. "Technically, you should be fasting for these–" And he should. But, if she's right and he has haemochromatosis, his iron will be so high that fasting won't make a difference.

He brightens. "Well, you're in luck, Doctor. I was feeling a bit bloated this morning so I held off."

Bloating is not the good news Fred thinks it is. Later, Grace will have to add it to his notes as yet another symptom of the disease she doesn't want it to be. She snaps on her gloves, wishing she could turn back time.

Fred rolls up his sleeve. "How are you settling in, Young Dr. Sullivan?"

Grace looks him straight in the eye. "Fred, I may as well admit it. There's a room full of patients out there all waiting for the same doctor. And that's not me."

Fred nods slowly. Then he scratches his chin thoughtfully. "Have you tried going to Mass?"

She laughs. "I'll be there on Sunday. Front row."

"You'll want to be up at dawn to get the front row."

Grace smiles. What a lovely man. She has never wanted to be wrong more than now.

"Okay, you'll just feel a little prick." Despite everything, this statement has the same effect on her that it always does. She quells the urge to giggle. "You're doing grand," she says as she fills the last of the Vacutainers with blood, removes the needle and presses cotton wool on the injection site.

"What are the tests for, Doc?"

"Iron, liver function tests, full blood count…." She's not going to mention genetic testing unless she has to.

"I'll be in trouble with Dr. O'Malley if the iron is down."

Grace could shake Dr. O'Malley. "You were right to stop it if it wasn't having any effect." She tapes the cotton wool down. "Right, as soon as we have results, either myself or Dr. O'Malley will be onto you."

"Liver function tests," Fred says, thoughtfully. "So, you think it might be the liver?" Grace opens her mouth to speak. "My father died of cirrhosis," he adds before she can reply. "But then I'm not a drinker like he was."

Grace's stomach churns. She doesn't tell Fred that drinking may not have caused his father's cirrhosis. News like that should wait until she is one hundred percent sure.

"We'll know more once the bloods are back." She snaps off the gloves. "Thanks for coming in."

Fred gets up. "Thanks, Doc."

"My pleasure." Grace walks him to the door. "You take care," she says with so much meaning.

"You too. You too."

She closes the door and bites down on her fingers. She will die if she's right.

seventeen

Des puts on his tweed jacket and flat cap and reaches for his blackthorn stick. Jack's school finishes ten minutes before Holly's. They might have time for a short stroll – and a chat – before she gets out.

As he makes his way to the school, Des wonders how he ever managed without the stick. In a way, it's like a calling card. This man walks tall. This man has style. Best of all, this man is not to be messed with.

The boys are already on their way out. In groups of varying sizes, they respectfully greet him by name. He returns their greetings with fondness. He delivered most of them into the world.

At last he sees Jack emerge, chatting with a red-haired boy, his demeanour so much lighter than earlier. Des is thinking of making himself scarce when Jack spots him and his face lights up. Surprised and heartened, Des raises his stick in greeting. Jack says bye to the boy and strides over to his grandad.

"That was the guy," he says under his breath. "You were right. He's harmless."

Des smiles. "Harmless?"

"And actually okay."

"Glad to hear it." He glances up the road in the opposite direction to the bus stop where most of the boys are headed. "D'you want to go for a little stroll before Holly gets out?"

"Sure."

They take off.

Des breathes in the sea air, looking out towards the horizon. It's good to get out of the house alright.

"Thanks for today, Grandad. I'd have got expelled without you."

"Indeed and you would not." Des turns to his grandson. No time like the present. "I was wondering, though. D'you think that something might have been on your mind that caused you to lash out at the boy? 'Twas just a thought I had – now that I have all this time on my hands to be thinking." He says it lightly, like he's mocking himself.

Jack looks at him for a long time, then shoves his hands into his pockets and glances down at the ground.

"This isn't easy, all this change," Des nudges.

Jack looks up again, out over the graveyard to the blue of the sea. He sighs.

Des waits, hoping that the boy can get it out, whatever *it* is.

Jack turns to him. "You can't tell anyone."

"Of course, I won't."

"Especially not Mum."

Des stops walking. "Jack, you can tell me anything. I promise you it'll go no further."

Jack blows out a long breath. "It's my dad."

Des nods. Then listens intently as Jack shares with him that he has a SIM card he shouldn't have, giving him access to all that his father has been saying, threatening. Des's grip tightens on the stick as he listens. He pumps the ground once – hard – with it. "Now you listen to me. *That* is bullying."

"Yeah but what'll I do?"

The poor lad is in a state of panic. Des grips his wrist to snap him out of it. He looks deep into his eyes. "You've done the first thing, Jack. You've told your grandad. Now we're in this together."

Relief floods the boy's eyes.

Des taps the stick against the graveyard wall as he thinks, then he looks at Jack. "Right. The first and most important thing now is that we don't fall into his trap. We don't play his game."

"But he'll come down!"

"Let him."

"He'll kill her!"

Des grips his stick. "By God, he won't. I might kill him, though."

Jack smiles like he's found an ally. The tension in his face eases.

"You've done really well, Jack, holding off. If you'd given into him, he'd have hung this threat over you and manipulated you with it."

Jack nods.

"No. Let him come. Let him break the barring order. See what happens. This mightn't be Dublin with its fancy lawyers but we look out for each other in this village." A car passes and Des raises his hand in greeting.

Jack freezes. "But nobody knows, right? You haven't told anyone, have you?"

"Lord, no." Des reminds himself that telling Paddy is like telling the priest. "But if I need to call on someone, I can. So, don't reply, don't give in to him. Absolute thug, blackmailing a child like that."

"I'm not a child."

"No. But you're not eighteen either. Now, as soon as we get in home, I want you to give me that SIM card and I'll get rid of it." By "get rid of" Des means, he'll hold onto it and keep track of what that *creature* is up to. Then he'll keep that information well and truly to himself. He will, however, be prepared.

"Okay but you can't tell Mum I had it. You can't tell her anything."

"I've no intention of telling her." Worrying her.

Jack tenses again. "What if he doesn't pay the maintenance?"

The boy is far too young to be worrying about things like that. "Now, you listen to me. Your mother is an independent woman now, making her own way. She doesn't need or want to rely on him. It would be just one more thing to hang over her. And, sure, we're not living in a metropolis, here in Killrowan. What would ye want to be buying anyway?"

Jack smiles. "Where have you been all my life?"

Good point. Where *has* Des been? Beavering away in his surgery, not checking up on his only daughter. Well, he'll make it up to her now. If it's the last thing he does.

He checks his watch. "Right. Will we go meet Holly?" He turns around. "Ah, there they are, getting out now." A great swarm of girls spills from the school, a sea of blue.

Big steps, Des reminds himself.

Jack matches his slow pace.

Des nudges him with an elbow. "Not walking too fast for you, am I?"

"You are a bit," Jack jokes.

Des chuckles, loving that there is the tiniest Cork lilt in his grandson's voice. "By the way. You needn't worry that I'll be turning up at the school gates every day. I'll get some keys cut for ye all tomorrow."

"Turn up anytime you like, Grandad."

Jack spots his sister emerge from the school and something inside him lifts. The "loner" in Dublin, is talking animatedly with two girls, one on either side of her. They seem to be hanging on her every word. Jack reminds himself that it's just the first day. Still, it's like a huge neon sign saying: "This is going to work out." He feels like high-fiving her.

"Yeah, we probably shouldn't interrupt her," he says. "We can just take up the rear." He'd suggest leaving her to it completely – if she had a key.

"You're a wise man, Jack Willoughby."

"Sullivan," he corrects.

Des pats his grandson on the arm. "Now *that* is music to my ears."

eighteen

Grace has seen one patient today and still arrives home shattered. She drops her bag and kicks off her shoes, unable to get Fred Cronin out of her mind. But then she sees her daughter and her concerns become more feral. She opens her arms wide. Holly comes to her, fitting into her embrace like a matching jigsaw piece.

"How's my baby? How was your first day?"

"Grand. No bother," Holly says in a definite Cork accent.

Grace pulls back and looks into her daughter's eyes. The relief is huge.

"Holly, girl, you sound like you were born here," Des says, exaggerating his own accent.

Holly turns to him. "Fake it till you make it, Grandad," she sings, sounding more like a native with every word. A very happy native.

"You're a smart cookie, all the same," he says, ruffling the hair she has now taken down.

"I've got a second chance. And I'm going to make the most of it."

Grace snatches a fake microphone out of the air and starts to sing to Holly. "You bring meaning to my life. You're my inspiration."

Holly grabs another imaginary mic. "You bring feeling to my life. You're my inspiration."

"Want to have you near me. I want to have you hear me saying 'No one needs you more than I need you,'" they shout-sing together.

Jack rolls his eyes but happily.

Grace leans against the worktop. "I'm serious, though, Hol. You *are* my inspiration. You went in there and made the most of it." Grace remembers Jack's bumpy start. "I'm so proud of you both," she says with real emotion. "You were great today, Jack."

Holly lifts her head proudly. Jack bows his.

Grace rubs her hands together. "So! Who wants pizza?" In Dublin, takeaway would *not* have been acceptable to the plastic surgeon. Well, they're not in Dublin. There's no way she's cooking.

"You can *get* takeaways here?" Jack asks.

Des slaps him playfully on the arm. "Give it a rest, boyo."

Jack smiles. "Let's get two, extra-large. I'm starving."

Pepperoni pizza and vegan pizza. In Killrowan. Who'd have thought? They bring their plates to the blazing fire, this new family unit, tucking in and chatting. Jack and Holly discuss the nationalities in their class. Germans, English, Dutch. Killrowan is way more cosmopolitan than they'd expected.

Des turns to Grace. "How was everything at the practice?"

"Oh, fine. Just settling in." She doesn't want to let him down by telling him that no one wanted to see her. Or worry him about Dr. O'Malley's... oversight. Still, she'd love *some* insight. "How is Dr. O'Malley?"

He doesn't look surprised by the question. That's the first thing she notices.

"I thought you might ask." He shifts in the chair. "Tom's eye has been off the ball a little since his wife, Tricia, died last year. I was carrying him a little to be honest. You might have to put a bit of work in, there, till he gets over the worst of the grief. But he's a good man, Grace, and a great doctor. He'll get through this bad patch though he may be doubting that himself. That's where it's at with Tom."

"Right." That helps. Hugely.

"How was Myra?"

She smiles. "Thawed out as the day went on."

"Ah, good old, Myra. I'm fierce fond of her. D'you want to know the way to her heart?"

"She has one?" Grace swats the words away. "Ah no, I'm only joking. I actually like her. Even though she terrifies me."

He smiles. "Those giant chocolate chip cookies they have in The Coffee Cove. That's the secret."

"Giant chocolate chip cookies?" She raises her eyebrows. "I must get down there."

"I used to bring her one every morning. And she loved *me*."

Grace smiles. "I'll give it a try so."

Grace's phone pings. It's a text from Yvonne.

Don't suppose the blow-in is up for a drink?

Grace was planning an early night but finds her inner eighteen-year-old texting back:

I'd kill for a drink!
Ahern's at eight? Comes Yvonne's reply.
It's a date!

Grace sings in the shower about girls just wanting to have fun. It's like time has rewound and she's getting ready to go out with her best bud. She dries herself briskly, feeling a new energy rush through her body. But then she eyes her clothes, lying in a heap on the toilet lid, charcoal grey and conservative. It's like the music stops. The last thing she wants to do is put them back on.

The man who dressed her hated denim.

She opens the bathroom door and steam wafts out.

"Holly?" she calls.

Holly sticks her head out from her bedroom.

"Do you think any of your jeans would fit me?"

"I bet they would. You're tiny. Will I bring you a pair?"

"Why not?" Grace says like she's throwing caution to the wind. "Just not ripped ones."

"Okay!"

In the bathroom, Grace squeezes into a black pair of skinny jeans. And feels rebellious. She pops her head out again.

"Hol?"

A smiling Holly appears.

"How about a top?"

Holly laughs. "Sure." She disappears. Seconds later, she re-emerges holding up two options.

"I love you," Grace says, picking a black one. With sparkles. Then it hits her: how horrified she would have been as a teenager if her mother had started to borrow her clothes. "I'll buy my own stuff tomorrow, I promise…. Just tell me what websites."

"We could do it together! It'd be fun!"

"Oh wait, we can't tomorrow. I'll be on the island."

"How late do you get back?"

"About seven I'd say."

"We'll do it then!"

How did she get a daughter like this? Grace was nowhere as accommodating as a teenager. "It's a date!" she says, marvelling at this new life springing up organically, taking on a momentum of its own. She grimaces, knowing she's pushing it, now. "Could I try your makeup? Just for a change?"

"'Course."

"And some of that hair gel you use?" Holly is *bound* to kill her now.

But her daughter just laughs like she's delighted to see this new light-hearted side to her mum. "You're going crazy!"

"I am!" No one to stop her now.

Grace sets an armful of makeup into the bathroom sink. Clearing condensation from the mirror, she faces a pixie. And panics. It's not happening too fast, is it, all this change? Everything's not going to come crashing down, is it? Maybe she should stay in. Take things slower. Safer. But then, slow and safe kept her trapped for sixteen years.

nineteen

Ahern's hasn't changed since the day Grace left Killrowan. It's so old-world it's come back into fashion. The heavy, wooden bar stools could tell a few tales. The small, round tables dotted around don't demand much of people. "Come as you are," they seem to say. The fire is blazing and, no doubt, there'll be traditional music sessions on Saturday night. There is comfort in this familiarity, and for once, Grace feels at home with the locals, well, the local sitting opposite her, at least. She can't stop smiling.

"So, Pat Harte? Who'd have guessed?"

"It's always the quiet ones." Yvonne grins. She looks as beautiful as ever to Grace. Yes; everything has faded. Her hair is a gentler shade of red. Her cheeks have lost a little of their glow. She has laughter lines around her eyes. And she's a little heavier. But she's as sultry as ever, her thick and fabulous hair in a 1950's style. Her black fitted polo neck and skinny jeans hug her curves proudly. And, of course, that deep voice hasn't changed. Yvonne has always sounded – and looked like – a jazz singer. Grace thinks that she is lost in Killrowan. But then rethinks. She is the opposite of lost in Killrowan. She is like a beacon of glamour. "Ah, I can't complain," she says in husky Cork. "He gets better with age."

Grace wonders what it must be like for a relationship to stay good, maybe even get better, for your husband to keep loving you, respecting you, going to the school with you when there's an "incident."

"What about you?" Yvonne asks.

She shakes her head. "Didn't work out." She takes a sip of her beer. *Beer, Simon, beer.* She mentally flips him off.

"He was a consultant or something, I heard?"

She rubs condensations from her glass, then looks up. "Why didn't we keep in touch, Vonnie?"

Yvonne waves away the question. "Ah, sure. We were young."

"But best friends."

"Inseparable," they say together wistfully. It's what people used to say about them. All the time.

"'Twas my fault," Grace says. "I'm the one who left. I should have kept in touch, come home more often." Simon did soak up all her free time; he did isolate her *but* she had a say. And she chose him.

"Ah, sure look it."

If they'd had a traditional wedding, she would have invited all her old friends; they'd have got back in touch. But he had wanted to elope, selling her on how romantic it would be. She went along with it, like she went along with everything. Could she have been any more blind, any more naïve?

"Doesn't everyone go off and not look back? That's just the way of it. Our kids'll be the same."

Grace remembers the incident at the school. She's about to apologise for Jack when she stops herself. She won't do that to him. Ever again. "How's Simon?" she asks instead, wishing he was called something else. Anything else.

"He's grand out. Thinks Jack is the bee's knees."

"Really?" Grace is so relieved.

"Imagine if they became friends – our kids, friends!"

"That'd be so *weird*," Grace says sounding eighteen again.

"Great, though."

"Great but weird."

"Great weird."

They laugh.

Yvonne touches her arm. "It's great to have you back."

"It's great to be back." Even after the day she's had, it feels a hundred percent true. The power of friendship, she thinks.

"Have you bumped into Alan yet?" Yvonne asks.

Grace's face lights up. "Alan? No! Is he still here in Killrowan?"

"He is, though I don't see a lot of him. Life's busy."

Grace recalls his adorable, loveable face, his big blue, trusting, optimistic eyes. "We should ring him, tell him to come down!"

Yvonne checks her watch. "It's eleven."

"What? Already? So much for one drink!"

"It's the company."

Grace smiles. "So. What's he up to?"

"Odd jobs, really. He can turn his hand to anything."

"Is he with anyone?"

"Nope. Still single."

"We should arrange a night out, the three of us."

Yvonne smiles. "Let's do that."

They glance at the clock over the bar. But neither makes a move to leave. There are just too many unanswered – unasked – questions.

As the fire begins to dull and the bar begins to empty, Grace and Yvonne discover that they have girls the same age, not only that, but Holly and Molly share a birthday.

"We went into labour on the same day!"

"How weird is that?" they say together, and laugh.

"What about Holly and Molly? Like one letter different!" Yvonne says.

Grace bites her lip. "Your son has the same name as my... ex. But I won't hold that against him!" she jokes. Half jokes.

Yvonne wrinkles her face. "You must hate the name."

Grace matches her expression. "Not my favourite, to be honest."

"We all call him Ginge anyway."

"Ginge? He doesn't mind?"

"Wears it like a badge of honour. Loves his hair that boy. Vain like his mam."

Grace laughs. "You were never vain."

Last orders are called and they remember their responsibilities. Outside Ahern's, they hug like they're still eighteen and their futures will be different now. And, as they reluctantly go their separate ways, it hits Grace just how lonely she has been. For years and years and years. How did she survive?

twenty

Grace can't remember when she last had a hangover. Probably because she can't remember when she last had a drink. Simon frowned on alcohol – and on her if she drank it. Now, her body doesn't know what's hit it. The slightest movement and it feels like her brain is expanding in waves. Her tongue could be a carpet, thick and furry. And she has a thirst on her like a camel – assuming camel's get thirsty.

Doctor's bag in one hand and a bottle of water in the other, Grace approaches the pier with dread. How will she make it across to the island without throwing up? Sinking – slowly – into a squat, keeping her head very still, she sets her doctor's bag on the ground. And roots through it for an antiemetic, a challenge given the number of samples she has packed.

Samples out on the dusty ground, Grace is continuing to root, when a pair of male legs stops beside her.

"Young Dr. Sullivan! Is everything alright? Do you need a hand?"

"No, no, I'm grand thanks," she says, without daring to glance up. How unprofessional this must look, she thinks. Then reminds herself that throwing up on the boat would look more so.

"I'll leave you to it so."

"Thank you!" she says in relief.

Finding the Motilium – at last – at the bottom of the bag, she clicks one out of the blister pack and downs it with the bottled water. She tosses the samples back in the bag before anyone else comes along, then stands slowly, feeling like her head is going to explode. She squints in the light of a sun that seems way too strong for October. She should have brought her shades.

She makes her way to the spot where the ferry comes in. She is first, it seems. Wait. What about the owner of the legs? Where did he go? Did she imagine them? And why is there no one else here? Has she got the time wrong? She hasn't missed the ferry, has she? She checks her watch. No. There's still ten minutes. She closes her eyes, inhales the briny air and tells herself to stop panicking. She could do with sitting down.

Other passengers start to arrive in dribs and drabs, dropped off by a variety of cars. One tractor. Everyone is carrying something. A man in his fifties in dark overalls has an oily piece of machinery. A younger man with bad acne has a box containing a (live) chicken. An attractive, overdressed woman carries a gift-wrapped parcel. Island life, Grace thinks.

"Young Dr. Sullivan," says the man with the chicken – putting it down and his hand out. "Ted O'Driscoll."

They know her on the island too? "How are you, Ted?"

"Grand altogether. Aren't you the brave woman all the same?"

"I am?"

"Travelling out to the island with a storm forecast," he says looking towards the horizon like a Shakespearian soothsayer.

"There's a *storm* coming?"

"Eddie they're calling it. There's a yellow warning. Didn't you check the forecast before coming to the island?"

The answer is very clearly no. She was too busy catching up with Yvonne in the pub. "But *you're* going out to the island," she says, hopefully.

"Oh, I am yeah but I'm staying put when I get there. You were probably planning on going home after the clinic, though, were you?" He scratches his face like that might be a problem.

"You think I won't get back?" She has to – to the children, to her dad, and to the practice first thing tomorrow. But most worryingly – what if Simon comes down and she's not there! She scans the faces of the others waiting to board, all of them eagerly following the conversation. "What about you? Someone must be coming back."

"I am," says the man with the machine. "I'm dropping this out to my brother and hopping straight back on the ferry."

Everyone else nods in confirmation.

Grace looks out at the flat calm sea, then back at them. It suddenly occurs to her…. "You're pulling my leg!"

They look at her blankly.

"New doctor's first day on the island!"

"We wouldn't do that to you," Ted says.

All hope melts away. "When is it blowing in?"

"Afternoon, they say." Ted glances at her doctor's bag. "But, sure, when are they ever right?"

Should she cancel the clinic, ask Ted to pass the word? What if people need to see her urgently? It's two weeks since a doctor last visited. Maybe Ted's right. Maybe the storm won't hit till later. Forecasts are often wrong. Especially about storms. Grace has often found that they don't hit till hours after the warning began. They probably err on the side of caution. She takes a deep breath to calm herself – and the nausea. She'll talk to the boatman.

The ferry arrives with the rumble of an engine and a plume of oily smoke on the air. No one is in a rush. Except Grace. She hurries onboard and goes straight to the boatman, a ruddy, weather-beaten man in his sixties.

"Young Dr. Sullivan!" he says before she can introduce herself. He holds out a hand. "Ger Daly."

"Ger. Hi. I'm just wondering when you'll expect that last boat to leave the island," she rushes. "I need to get home to my family. I didn't know about the storm and don't want to let the islanders down."

"Don't you worry. We'll keep going till the wind blows up and the sea gets choppy. I'll be keeping a good eye out. I can have someone run up to the clinic and let you know when the last ferry will be leaving the island."

"Oh, that would be wonderful, thank you so much."

Grace takes a seat and a few more deep breaths. She opens her bag and starts to dust off samples with a tissue.

Despite all the vacant seats on the boat, someone sits beside her. Grace glances up. It's a tiny, elderly woman, wrapped up in an oversized coat, scarf and woollen hat. There will be conversation.

"Young Dr. Sullivan. Don't be worrying. Sure, you can stay over in Cooke's if all comes to all."

All can't come to all. "Is the clinic usually busy?" Maybe she can take a half day.

"Oh yeah, 'tis always mobbed. I'd say you'll be there till five or six anyway."

"I may have to leave early if the storm blows up."

The woman looks doubtful. "Well, you might be lucky and have a quiet day. God's good."

Grace turns around. Already, Killrowan is disappearing into the distance. From now on, she will take a keen interest in the weather.

twenty-one

Grace climbs the steep slope up from the tiny harbour, wishing she hadn't packed so much into her bag. Glancing up, she sees that there is already a line of patients outside the surgery. She tries to be positive. At least people want to see her here. She picks up her pace and feels for the key in her coat pocket.

She reaches the clinic, out of breath. "Sorry for keeping you," she rushes, inserting the key. "I won't be a moment."

Hurrying inside, Grace is greeted by a blast of cold air. She flicks on the light in the dimly-lit corridor and reaches for the radiator. She can't believe it's not on a timer.

"Come on in," she calls as she goes in search of controls.

There are just two rooms, one facing the other on opposite sides of the narrow corridor. The door to one is open and people start to file in. Waiting room, she deducts, then scans it, unsuccessfully for a control box.

An elderly man limps by. He could do with a warmer coat.

"I'm sorry about the cold," she says, rubbing her hands together.

"Oh, 'tis always like this," he replies cheerfully. "We're hardy, here on the island. Like mountain goats."

"Right." She's no mountain goat, though. "So, there's no way of turning on the heat?"

"I don't know if it's ever worked to be honest with you."

"There are radiators, though. There must be a way."

She turns the knob on the radiator in the hall clockwise, which she knows is wrong.

"You're wasting your time, Doctor," another arriving patient says.

He's probably right. The waiting room is filling up. She has to get started – if she wants to get off the island before the storm. She cups her hands in front of her mouth and blows into them. Could she wear her coat while seeing patients?

She knows the answer to that.

She opens the door to the surgery. And is relieved to discover how well-equipped it is. Even the computer seems modern enough. What Grace is most delighted to see, though, is a plug-in heater. With a, "Thank you, God," the atheist lunges for it and turns it on.

The computer gives her further reason to rejoice, linked as it is to the practice on the mainland. She can keep track of patients who go between the surgeries.

Checking her watch, she allows herself two minutes to investigate a box on the wall, which could be controls for the heating. She fiddles with the buttons. But nothing happens. No sounds of a generator kicking on. Nothing.

She needs to get started. She takes off her coat and jogs on the spot – fast. She rubs her hands up and down her arms. Then she takes a deep breath and opens the door.

No receptionist here. No waiting list. No idea who's first.

What would the most confident man she knows do?

She strides to the door of the waiting room and claps her hands. "Right! Who's first?"

"That would be me."

The American accent surprises her. All the tourists have usually gone by now. Thinking of the Oscar Wilde story about the swallow who stayed behind in winter and… died, she turns to the voice. This man couldn't look more out of place. At least twenty years younger than the average islander, he is expensively decked out in high-end outdoors gear, giving him the look of a hiker who washed up on the island. But then a battered leather satchel worn across his body confuses the image. Grimacing as he gets to his feet, he avoids rising to his full height so as not to hit his head against the ceiling of the cottage.

In the hall, Grace introduces herself. "Grace Sullivan."

"Wayne Hill." In his forties, she guesses, a few random strands of grey in his floppy dark hair, his eyes are striking in their blueness.

"Come on in."

In the surgery, she takes her seat and swivels to face him.

He sits slowly, carefully.

She produces her professional smile. "How can I help?"

He clears his throat. "I don't suppose there's a male doctor coming?"

"There's one in Killrowan if you want to get the ferry across." It would speed things up for her.

"No, no. It's fine. I'm being ridiculous." He smiles.

Grace thinks: STD.

"I have a wound," he says. "Between my legs."

What has he been up to? Grace wonders.

"It's become quite painful."

"Right. I'd better have a look." Grace gets up and starts to pull the faded yellow curtain around the bench. "So just remove your clothes from the waist down, hop up onto the bench and cover yourself with the blanket."

He flinches.

Maybe "hop" was a bit too optimistic?

Wayne Hill takes off his fleece, leaves his satchel by the chair and then disappears behind the curtains with the enthusiasm of a man going to the gallows.

To the sounds of undressing, Grace washes her hands, wipes down a metal trolley with alcohol swabs, sets up a sterile dressing kit and snaps on a pair of sterile gloves. It has all gone quiet behind the curtains.

"Ready?" she asks.

His, "Yup," borders on a yelp.

Opening the curtains with an elbow, she pushes in the trolley.

"You wouldn't mind folding back the blanket," she says to him. "My gloves are sterile."

He does as asked then averts his eyes to the wall beside him.

"Now if you could bend your legs and let your knees fall apart," Grace asks, feeling some tiny equality for all the women given this instruction every day by male gynaecologists.

Wayne Hill, eyes still averted and already pale, pales even further. He obliges with the grimace of a man in great pain.

Seeing the wound, Grace keeps her face impassive. No wonder the grimace. No wonder the yelp. Grace is looking at a roaring infection.

"You've put up with this a bit longer than you should have," Grace says.

His eyes dart to hers. "I was waiting for the stitches to dissolve!"

She keeps her gaze steady. "These aren't dissolvable stitches." Though they should be for this delicate area.

"*What?*" His already strong jaw looks suddenly stronger. "Dr. O'Malley said they were dissolvable!"

Once again, Grace hides her reaction. Could this really be her partner's second mistake in as many days? And if so, is it some fluke? More pressingly, what will she say to the patient?

"Don't worry. I can remove the stitches for you. But not now. You have an infection I'm afraid. That's the reason for your discomfort."

"*Discomfort?* I'd call it *pain*. And even *that* would be an understatement."

She understands his fury. But needs to move towards a solution. "So, I'm going to remove two stitches now, so that any pus that may have accumulated behind the wound can escape. Then I'm going to take a swab to send to the lab." She eyes the small fridge in the corner and hopes it's working. "I'll also start you on antibiotics and clean the wound. We may have to alter the antibiotics when the swab results come back."

He nods.

Grace gets to work. "Okay, I'm going to remove two stitches now. I'm sorry, this is going to hurt." Grace, as gently as she can, starts to remove a suture where the wound is at its reddest.

"Do you mind me asking how you acquired the wound?" she asks to distract him from the pain she's about to inflict. Also, she's curious. The edges are surprisingly jagged.

"I was climbing over a barbed wire fence," he says like it's the last time he'll ever be attempting that.

"Ah," she says instead of "ouch." "You've had a tetanus shot, then, I take it?"

"No. I have *not* had a tetanus shot," he says like he wants to jump on the first flight back to the US.

Grace doesn't understand it. Her partner is a hugely respected doctor. What was he thinking? Or not thinking? Is he just under too much pressure? When Grace gets back, she needs to start seeing patients fast, take that pressure off him.

She looks up at Wayne Hill. "In that case, you'll need to come to the surgery on the mainland for a shot, as soon as the storm passes."

"Don't you have one here, now?"

"No. It has to be kept in a temperature-controlled environment."

"What about the fridge?"

"Too cold for tetanus I'm afraid."

"This is ridiculous."

He's right. It is. But what can she say? "Right. That's two of them out!"

"Really? That wasn't too bad," he says in surprise.

"Now, I'm going to apply a little pressure. Sorry."

"Whoa!" His hands grip the sides of the bench.

A tiny bead of pus escapes and she catches it with the swab. She pops it into its container.

"I don't understand how it got infected!" he says desperately. "I did everything he said! Salt baths! Letting the air at it!" He looks suddenly mortified as though realising the visual implication of what he's just said.

Grace tries not to visualise him walking around in the nip and fails, becoming unprofessionally giddy in the process. "I'm sure you did everything you could. It's the area. It's incredibly prone to infection." She doesn't spell out that it's warm and moist. "I'm just going to clean the wound now. It's going to feel cold."

He flinches when the first saline-soaked swab lands.

"This should be cleaned twice a day with hydrogen peroxide and cotton buds. If you can't come to the surgery, you could do it yourself. As long as you can see it properly and–"

"I'll do it myself. Are cotton buds Q-tips?"

She nods, dropping the swab into a plastic bag she has attached to the trolley. "You can get everything you need in the pharmacy when you come over for the tetanus shot. You should get sterile gloves and dressing kits. And I'll ask them to order in silver dressings for you."

"Actual silver?"

"Apparently," she says, picking up another swab with the sterile forceps and dipping it into the saline.

"Well, I guess they deserve silver."

She smiles. "When you come for the shot tomorrow, I can show you how to dress the wound." Then Grace remembers his initial mortification. "You may want to go back to Dr. O'Malley, though, and that's fine."

"Not a chance."

Grace starts to cover the wound with a dressing. Not an easy task, given the area. "Cold packs might ease the pain – applied to the general area, obviously, not the wound itself." She snaps off her gloves and drops them onto the trolley. "You can get dressed now. No rush."

She pushes the trolley through the curtains, discards the dressing kit and swabs down the trolley again. She washes her hands thoroughly. Then retrieves antibiotics from her bag. Thank God she brought samples.

Wayne Hill emerges from behind the curtains, his jaw out of kilter again. She doesn't know if it was the pain of getting dressed or being alone with his thoughts but his fury is back and it's swallowing up the tiny room.

"Have a seat," Grace says.

"I'll stay standing if that's okay," he says grimly.

"Sure." Grace gets up, hands him the antibiotics and explains how to take them. She goes back to her bag and retrieves her Nurofen Plus. He'll need them. "Here are some painkillers. There's codeine in them so when the pack's gone move to plain Nurofen."

"Okay. Thanks."

"And you'll come across tomorrow for the tetanus shot – assuming the storm breaks?"

"I'll have to, won't I?"

She nods. "When the infection has cleared, I'll remove the rest of the stitches."

She checks to make sure she has the right telephone number for him on file in case she needs to change the antibiotic. That's when she sees that his occupation has been entered as a novelist. It makes sense. Only an artist would opt to visit Torc in winter.

"Okay, I'll see you tomorrow," she says.

Luckily, he pays in cash as there doesn't seem to be a credit card machine.

When he opens the door, she catches a voice from the waiting room call to him, "Lord above, we thought you were having open heart surgery in there."

Glancing at her watch, Grace realises the consultation took thirty minutes. She'll have to speed up.

twenty-two

It has taken Des half an hour to get that piddly little SIM card into his phone. Now he's staring at a barrage – a *blizzard* – of missed calls and messages, dating back to Friday, including school hours and the middle of the night. The man is either crazy or an out-and-out bully. There's no question that he's the latter. He's also, most likely, the first.

Bracing himself, Des goes back to the very first message. As he listens to each one, pain expands in his heart, the pain of knowing what they have had to live with for years on end. He's so glad they're not hearing this, so glad that Grace thought to pre-empt it. Anyone would crumble under this litany of threats, guilting, bribery, blackmail. Des wants to go up there and kill the man. Man is too kind a word.

One of his – many – threats is that he will come down to Killrowan. Given how unhinged he seems, Des has to take this threat seriously. He can't rely solely on Paddy – who could be anywhere at any given time. And he, himself, hasn't the strength he used to. In all honesty, he couldn't fight a flea. He needs to tighten security. Especially given the fact that he doesn't have any.

If Alan Wolfe had a nickname it would be "Not a problem." He arrives in his usual navy overalls, carrying his usual toolbox. A tall, affable man with a tendency towards weight, Alan can turn his hand to anything. Just as importantly, he is discreet; no one will know, unless they see for themselves, that he is installing a security system at Des Sullivan's place.

"So," Des says, "I want the best locks you can get on the doors and windows. And I want you to put in an alarm for me."

Alan licks a pencil and jots everything down in a small notebook. Then he looks up and smiles. "Not a problem. I'll just have a quick look around."

His "quick look" involves taking photos and measurements.

When he's done, Des offers a cup of tea.

And delivers it with scones.

Alan takes out his iPad, places it between them on the table, and goes through a selection of locks and alarms, explaining the pros and cons of each. Des makes his selections, then runs a hand back and forth over his mouth.

"You're not happy," Alan probes.

"No, I am, I am. I was just wondering… what would you think about chains on the doors as well?"

Alan looks automatically at the door. "I'm not too keen on the chains, myself, Des. They can be kicked in too easily. You'd be better off with one of them camera yokes to see who's at the door and then just not open it if you don't like the look of them."

Des nods slowly. "You're right. Let's get a camera." Again, his hand runs over his mouth. "You know what, put one on the back door too. Just to be on the safe side."

Alan looks at him as if to say: "Is it an Armageddon you're expecting?" Instead, it's a simple: "No problem." He takes the pencil down from behind his ear and adds 'two cameras' to his list. "Let's have a look at some options."

"I'll leave it to you, Alan."

Alan looks uncomfortable at that. "I'll do up a quote for everything and, when I drop by with it, I'll show you the cameras I've picked."

"Good man," Des says, not in the slightest bit worried. Alan knows what he's doing and never overcharges. In fact, sometimes Des wonders how the man makes a living at all.

They drain their cups. Alan gets up and dusts down his overalls as he always does when it's time to go. "Grand, so. If you're happy with the quote and everything, I can get moving on it straight away."

"I'll be happy, don't you worry." Des opens the front door.

Alan pauses. "I hear Grace is back," he says as though he has been meaning to all along.

"She is, yeah." The thought of that still cheers Des.

"Does she have a number at all?"

Of course, she has a number, Des thinks. The last thing she needs is men sniffing around. But then, she and Alan always were good pals. And she's a grown woman. If she doesn't want anything to do with men, she can tell Alan that herself. He gives him her number. "Don't be giving it out, obviously."

Alan looks horrified. "I wouldn't do that. It'd just be great to catch up. How's she getting on?"

"Oh. Settling in. She's out on the island at the clinic, today."

Alan frowns. "With the storm on the way? She'll never get back."

Des doesn't blink. "She'll probably have to stay over."

Alan nods. "That's what she'll do. Right, so. I'll give you a shout."

Des stands at the door, watching Alan climb up into his white van. They wave to each other and the van disappears off up the road. Des glances up at a sky that is darkening with angry, charcoal clouds, carried in on a blustery wind. He knew yesterday that the storm was on its way but didn't warn Grace. He wanted her to get to the island and see a rake of patients, one after the other – to get over her first day and kill the fear that comes with no one wanting to see you. He knew, too, that if she got to the island, she wouldn't get home; she'd be forced to have a night to herself. Away from everyone. The kids. Her old man. The lot. Grace won't find the person she was in one night. But one night is a start.

The sky is as dark as a fresh bruise. Down in the harbour, the sea is grey and choppy, white horses as far as the eye can see. A gale howls through a gap in the graveyard wall. In through it the three friends go, coats zipped up to their chins, Holly feeling like a musketeer – one who has just joined and hopes she can stay.

Round-faced, Aoife, turns to Holly and Jenn. "Have ye got yer sandwiches?" she asks with the confidence of a leader.

They nod quickly. Then all three girls root in their schoolbags.

Holly opens her lunchbox and produces half a sandwich she deliberately left uneaten. "I hope he likes peanut butter."

Jenn snaps open a Tupperware box. "I have ham if he doesn't."

Holly and Jenn hand their sandwiches over to Aoife like some sort of sacrifice. Then she turns to face the sea. "Come on!" she shouts over the gale. "Let's go." She darts into the graveyard.

Holly and Jenn race to keep up.

Aoife slows, glancing around.

"Where is he?" Holly asks, scanning between the tombstones.

"Over there!" Jenn calls, pointing.

Holly spies their holy grail: a black and white Border collie sitting like a Sphynx, gazing up at a tombstone. His owner, a woman called Sheila Crowley, died last week and he just won't leave her. People have tried to coax him away. Now they have started to look after him, here. There's a roster. But Aoife, Jenn and now Holly aren't on any roster.

Reverently, they approach.

Holly thinks of Benji. And knows how this dog feels.

The friends squat down at the edge of the grave, not wanting to invade his sorrow.

"He's so *gorgeous*," Holly says to her friends.

Aoife makes a face. "Gawd, you sound fierce posh all of a sudden."

Any other time, Holly might freak out that she's about to lose her new friends. Now, all she cares about is this dog. She feels his pain in her heart. It mirrors the ache she feels for Benji.

Aoife breaks the sandwiches and feeds him pieces. He takes them gently as if he's doing so to keep them happy not because he's hungry. Jenn tips out the water in his bowl which the wind has filled with leaves. She tops it up with her water bottle.

Holly is happy to just watch.

The wind howls through the tombstones. The sky is low and threatening.

Jenn glances around. "This is starting to get freaky."

"Yeah. Let's go," Aoife replies.

They grab their bags. "Bye, Benji," they say like their minds are already home.

"Wait! *What* did you call him?" Holly asks, not believing.

"Benji."

"*No way!*"

"What?" Aoife asks impatiently.

"That was my dog's name."

"Cool," Aoife says but not like she really cares. She turns and hurries away, Jenn at her heels.

But Holly can't leave. She moves onto her hands and knees and closer to Benji.

"Hey, come on!" Aoife calls impatiently.

Holly turns.

Her friends have stopped and are waiting for her. The sight lifts her.

She's still not leaving. "I'm going to stay for a while," she calls.

"Okay, cool. See ya tomorrow," Aoife says.

"Be careful," Jenn adds.

Holly waves then turns back to the dog. "Hey, Benji. How're you doing? How're you doing, boy?"

He looks up at her with sad eyes and whimpers.

"I know. I know you're lonely. It's so hard, isn't it? So unfair."

Benji lays down and Holly lays with him, her head against his side, rising and falling with every breath. "I don't have to go for a while," she says.

twenty-three

At five, Grace closes the door behind her last patient. She is exhausted. And starving. It has been full-on, all day. She worked through lunch to finish early. Never thought to bring a sandwich. Now, she snatches up her things. Grabs the pus swab from the fridge. Turns off the heater. And hurries out into the hall. She has been listening to the wind all day. And it hasn't been that bad at all. No one has come from the ferry. Another case of weather forecasters getting overexcited. She locks up and hurries down the hill.

Her phone starts to ring. Thinking it might be Des or the children she whips it out of her pocket. When an unknown number comes up on the screen, she freezes. It could be Simon. It'd be just like him to call on a different phone. But how did he get her number? The only people she gave it to are Des, the children, Myra and the schools. Her heart bucks as she watches it ring and ring. She keeps walking. If she doesn't answer, he can't get her. Twist her. Trample on her. She pockets the phone and picks up her pace. If it's someone else and urgent they'll leave a message.

At the bottom of the hill, she rounds a corner. A gust of wind slams into her, stalling her. She squints out to sea and her stomach churns. It's incredibly choppy. How could this be? But she knows how it could be. It's the direction of the wind. The clinic is sheltered from it because of how it's positioned. Still, it must be safe to sail. Otherwise someone would have come from the ferry.

The wind is howling in her ears, whipping at her hair, tugging at her coat like a wild and living thing.

She sees it then, the ferry, anchored in the harbour, being tossed by the waves, Ger Daly rowing away from it, with two people in lifejackets onboard. She can't believe it. She was relying on him. She could have left earlier…. Okay so maybe she couldn't. Still, this is a disaster.

She stands on the pier, arms folded, buffeted by wind and spray, waiting for them to reach shore.

At last, they do, faces red and lips blue. The passengers look shaken.

"What's happening?" she shouts over the gale.

"Ah, I'm sorry, love. It came up so fast in the end. We just got across. I couldn't even dock at the pier, it's so rough. Had to abandon her there. It's too dangerous to risk going anywhere now. We'll have to burrow in for the night."

Burrow in for the night? What about her kids, her dad, her job? "When's the first ferry back?"

He looks out to sea as if he can tell by looking at the horizon.

She wants to remind him that that didn't work this morning.

"Tomorrow afternoon at the earliest, I'd say. Why don't you go on up to Cooke's? Have yourself a nice meal and check in for the night."

She shakes her head in disbelief. Then resigned to her new destiny, she takes out her phone to call home. Before Des picks up, it occurs to her that they won't hear anything over this wind. With a sigh she hurries up to Cooke's which, admittedly, does look like a haven, yellow light flooding from the windows illuminating the rapidly darkening day, reminding Grace of novels she read as a child about pirates and hidden coves and mischief.

The wind barrels Grace through the door of Cooke's. On her left, is a simple pine table with a small plastic tent sign saying "Reception" that could have been picked up at any office suppliers. Beside it is a clashing, gold-coloured, old-fashioned metal bell with a slap-down button for attention. In between the two, is an open book for guest comments which Grace ignores. Beggars can't be choosers as her mother used to say. Past the table, on the left, is a light blue door through which float the muted sounds of conversation, tinkling glasses and occasional laughter. To the right is an oak staircase and, to Grace's immediate right, a corridor featuring another rudimentary sign pointing to "Toilets." She could be at a train station.

She whips out her phone. But there's no service. Muttering to herself, she moves around reception slowly, retracing her steps over and over till she finally picks up two bars at the end of the corridor just past the toilets.

Des answers on the third ring.

"Dad! I'm stuck on the island! Is everything okay there?"

"Everything's grand here, love," he says calmly. "The three of us were about to make dinner. How are you?"

"The ferryman thinks they won't get another boat out till tomorrow afternoon!"

"Well, Ger's pretty good with the weather."

Grace could beg to differ.

"Sure, check into Cooke's there for the night. Have yourself a nice meal and a glass of wine by the fire. We'll be grand here."

Grace bites her lip. "You didn't give my number to anyone, did you?"

There's a pause. "I did yeah. Alan Wolfe. I hope that's okay, love? He seemed keen for a chat."

Grace feels her whole body deflate in relief. "No, no. That's great, thanks Dad. It was just an unknown number and I thought…" She lets her voice trail off. "I'll call Alan back later." Her stomach knots again. "Dad?"

"Yes, love?"

"Don't answer the door, okay? Just in case. I know he won't come down from Dublin in the middle of the week but…."

"Don't you be worrying about that. I've everything under control here. Let your hair down for one night and we'll see you tomorrow."

She sighs. Nothing else she can do now. "Thanks Dad. I'll be home as soon as I can."

As soon as she hangs up, she calls Myra, explaining that she won't be getting in until the afternoon the following day. "Oh, and Myra could you make sure we have a vial of tetanus vaccine for a patient who is coming across."

"'Course I will. And don't you be worrying. Take your time tomorrow. There's no rush," Myra says like she runs the place.

Still, Grace is reassured. She remembers Wayne Hill's sample in her bag. Would Cooke's keep it in their fridge overnight? A sample of pus from an infected scrotum? Could she, in all fairness, ask them to?

Grace slaps the bell. No one appears. She waits. A good five minutes. Starving, and getting a bit shaky from what at this stage must be low blood sugar, she slaps it again. A sturdy woman in her fifties, in a navy apron, comes bursting through the blue door like a bear that has been woken from hibernation. Spying Grace, she delivers a look that implies a major inconvenience and, hands on hips, she comes marching over.

"Mrs. Cooke?" Grace asks with what she hopes is a disarming smile.

"Have you come for the restaurant or a room?"

"Both actually."

"Have you booked?" she snaps like she already knows the answer. The Cooke's are famous for their gruffness. In summer, tourists travel from afar to sample it. It's quaint, they think. Right now, it feels anything but quaint. Grace wants to remind her that she does plan on paying.

"No. I haven't. I'm Dr. Sullivan. I was here doing a clinic and got trapped by the storm."

Her face softens – ever so slightly. "I *may* have a single," she says. "And I'll have to check the kitchens to see what's left in terms of food. I know for a fact you'll have to share a table."

Grace nods. "That's fine. I just want to eat."

"Right. Let's get you sorted with food," Mrs. Cooke says, like she appreciates a good appetite. "I can show you to your room after."

An idea hits Grace that may solve her swab conundrum. "Do the rooms have fridges by any chance?"

The look she gets is murderous. "It's not the Hilton you're in now. Far from fridges in rooms…"

"It's fine. I just have to pop back to the surgery for a minute before dinner if that's okay?"

Mrs. Cooke tut-tuts. "You shouldn't have come till you were ready."

"Give me two minutes."

"It'll take five."

Wearily, Grace turns around and strides to the door.

Before Grace is halfway to the surgery, the skies release a monsoon of biblical proportions, a monsoon that the wind turns horizontal. Head down, she starts to run. Could the day get any worse?

She opens up the clinic, bangs on the lights and rushes the sample back into the fridge. Then she locks up again and it's back through the monsoon. Soon, rain starts to seep through her coat. Icy water trickles from her, now drenched, hair, down her neck and back. She could cry.

Bursting into Cooke's, Grace hurries to the bathroom. Where she is met with a surprise. Pretty flowers in a jar, L'Occitane liquid soap and hand cream, and a basket of fluffy face towels for hand drying. A beautiful, antique mirror reveals how wretched she looks. Like a drowned rat. She snatches a towel and pats her face dry, unintentionally removing the last of her makeup. Apart from her mascara which stubbornly clings to the area under her eyes transforming her to a rat/panda cross. She uses two cloths to dry her hair. Another on her briefcase. She slips out of her soaked coat and runs another cloth over the back of her neck and across the shoulders of her blouse. She glances down at her soaked high heel shoes and tights, wishing she had worn trousers.

This time, she doesn't ring the bell, just goes straight through the blue door. It's as if she has walked into a country kitchen that has welcomed in all the neighbours. It is cosy and down-to-earth and buzzing with relaxed conversation. But the best thing about the restaurant is the smell of lamb and roast potatoes. She closes her eyes and inhales while hanging her coat up on an old-fashioned wooden stand that could be as old as the building.

Mrs. Cooke comes bursting out of the kitchen carrying two plates of food. She slaps them down in front of an appreciative looking couple. Spying her, Mrs. Cooke marches over.

"Come with me," she says like a prison guard.

Grace follows obediently. She doesn't care where she sits as long as there's food. Warm, filling food. And wine. Plenty of wine.

As luck would have it, Mrs. Cooke guides her to a table right beside the fire. As misfortune would have it, it is occupied by an

American – the last American in the world Grace wants to see.

"Wayne Hill? Young Dr. Sullivan will be joining you," Mrs. Cooke states. And that's that.

Wayne Hill starts to choke. He reaches for his glass of red and gulps it back.

Grace will not apologise. She didn't ask to sit with the man. And she's not about to give up a seat by the fire for him. She yanks out the sturdy pine chair and sits down.

"Just pretend I'm not here," she says, matter-of-factly. She'd prefer if they didn't have to talk. She has too much to think about anyway.

He puts his hands up. "No, no. It's fine! Honestly. I just got a fright." He exaggerates a grimace. "I looked up from my lamb and felt physical pain."

She smiles. "I tend to have that effect on people. Seriously, though, we can totally eat separately. Just keep your eyes on your lamb and I'll do the same."

"Too late; I've lost my appetite."

Is he serious?

He grins.

She touches her heart. "Not funny. After the day I've had."

He pours her a glass of red.

She waves her hand. "It's okay. I'll get my own."

"Fine but get that into you, first."

She's not going to argue. "Thanks."

He raises his glass and they clink.

"To new starts," he says.

She closes her eyes as the wine hits. The air moves beside her and she hears the slam of a plate landing in front of her. She looks up. Mrs. Cooke is back.

"You're lucky there was anything left."

At Cooke's, there's no menu. You take what you get. But it's always good. So goes the legend. The lamb, roast potatoes and mixed vegetables do look like a feast to Grace right now. Then again, given her state, anything would.

"Thanks so much." She smiles up at Mrs. Cooke.

"Don't you have a change of clothes?" she asks with a look of derision.

Grace just smiles curtly and takes another sip of wine.

"Here, take my fleece," Wayne Hill says, when Mrs. Cooke leaves. "You're soaked through."

Panicking, Grace glances down at her breasts. The relief is gargantuan when she finds them dry. "It's fine. It's just my shoulders." And entire back but who's looking?

"You're shivering."

"I'm grand. Honestly." She nods to the fire.

He takes off his fleece anyway and hands it to her. "Go to the bathroom, take off your things and change into this. Then you can dry them by the fire."

She freezes at the order in his voice. "It's okay," she snaps. And hands it back.

He looks at her as though trying to understand the sudden frostiness.

She blushes and looks down. "I'm sorry. I'm fine, okay? Long day."

"Know the feeling," he says, putting his fleece on the back of his chair in case she changes her mind. "Thanks for the painkillers, by the way."

She smiles. "My treat."

twenty-four

Holly ignores the wind that is whipping around the tombstone and the darkness that is falling, listening only to the calm beating of Benji's heart. It seems to her to be matching her own. When she checks her pulse, it is.

Her phone rings, jolting her and Benji into alertness. They sit up together and Holly fumbles for her phone. Onscreen is "Grandad" – who she texted earlier to say that she was with a friend and would be home for dinner. It wasn't a lie. Benji *is* a friend.

"This storm is really blowing up, Holly. I want you home, now." He sounds worried.

"Okay, Grandad," she shouts over the wind.

"Wait. Where are you? Don't tell me you're out in it?" The worry in his voice grows.

"On my way."

"No but where *are* you? I'll come and meet you."

"Just out past the school. You don't need to come. I'm grand. I'll see you in a minute." She hangs up.

Benji is looking at her questioningly.

How can she leave him?

She kneels in front of him and places her hands on either side of his narrow head.

"You'll be okay, Benji. It's just wind. Nothing to worry about. I'll come and see you before school tomorrow, okay? I'll bring you something. I don't know what yet. But I'll know it when I see it." She kisses the top of his head. "I love you," she says with ease. Everything is easy with dogs. You don't even have to tell them you love them. They know. And they love you right back.

She picks up her school bag and smiles goodbye. She wishes there was somewhere for him to shelter from the storm. She thinks about calling him, seeing if he'll come home with her. But that would be taking him away from his family. And she can't do that to him.

"I'll see you tomorrow." She kisses him again.

Easier for both of them if she doesn't look back.

She squeezes through the gap in the wall, then, thinking of her grandad having to come out in the storm, she starts to run. She squints against the wind which is whipping dust and leaves into her face.

In the glow of a streetlamp up ahead she sees the outline of someone. But it's not her grandad. She slows.

"I thought Grandad was coming?" she shouts to Jack.

"Yeah, I said I'd come. Quicker. Who's your friend?"

"What?"

"The dog."

She swivels around and her heart melts. Benji is right behind her, gazing up at her with big, brown, questioning eyes. It's as if he's asking her why they've stopped and who this guy is. Smiling, she squats down and opens out her arms. He trots to her straight away. Tearing up with emotion, she flings her arms around him. He has chosen her.

"Come on!" Jack says. "Grandad's worried."

Holly gets up and turns to her brother. "You're not going to believe this story."

When she starts to tell him, Jack stops her. "Yeah, I heard about him already at school. Come *on*."

"Okay, well, you're not going to believe his name, then."

"Can't you go any faster? Holly seriously."

"Benji! It's Benji!"

Jack stops. "For real?"

Holly is nodding furiously. "D'you think Grandad will let him stay?"

Jack looks up at the gale whistling through the overhead wires, ripping through the trees, the charcoal clouds scuddering across the sky, the rain starting to fall. "Well, if he doesn't take him in today, he never will."

"I bet if he takes Benji in for one night, he won't want to let him go."

Out on the island, Grace thanks Mrs. Cooke, who has just added coal to the fire. Turning back to Wayne Hill, she meets questioning eyes.

"You haven't asked what an American is doing living on Torc Island but then you probably already know," he says with what sounds like a mix of suspicion and bitterness.

What's his problem? She didn't even know he was living there. More fool him. "All I know about you is that you like to climb over barbed wire."

He pulls a face. "Ouch. Just when I'd forgotten." He lifts his glass like he's hoping to forget again. Then he leans back in his chair and folds his arms, observing her. "You're different."

What's that supposed to mean? Is it a line? Or is he being condescending? She's so out of touch she can't tell but she wishes she'd kept her wedding ring on for times like this. She glances around the restaurant. Why didn't Mrs. Cooke put her sitting with a woman, for crying out loud?

"You're not curious like everyone else around here," he explains like curiosity is a crime.

"I don't have time for curiosity," she says, cracking pepper over her meal. She should be working out what to do if Fred Cronin tests positive. How to approach Dr. O'Malley. And whether or not to tell him about the mess he's made of Wayne Hill's scrotum.

"Good, because news spreads way too fast in this part of the world."

This part of the world is *her* part of the world. "Would you rather people were cold, aloof, disinterested?"

"Sometimes."

Okay, she actually knows what he means; she still hasn't got used to the need for people to know her business. But she's not telling *him* that.

"I came here to get away from people," he says.

People or person? Grace would like to know. Does *that* make her curious?

"But it seems that, instead, I've become a local celebrity."

She feels like telling him that not everyone cares about his struggle for privacy. People have their own stuff to deal with – if they could get a moment's peace. She stabs a broccoli floret. She'll eat faster. Finish up and go. "I've never heard of you, if that's any comfort."

"Give it time," he says with an air of defeat.

"Look, if you think that I'll be telling the world and its mother about your medical... condition, I can assure you that I'm a professional. I've taken an oath."

"What I'm actually saying is that it's a relief to be around someone who doesn't care about who I am."

Could the man be any more self-obsessed?

twenty-five

The storm rattles Des's window panes and the deluge pounds his roof. Even the draughts have draughts. A gust hits the house. He glances up from his grandson's biology book, open on the table in front of them, wondering how many tiles he has just lost. Beside him, Jack looks towards the window, then at him.

"Will Mum be alright, out on the island?"

"Oh, she will, yeah," Des assures him calmly. "Cooke's is sheltered from the wind. She'll be tucked in there now, lovely and cosy." Des goes back to the human heart. "Right, now, here's a handy way of remembering the blood flow. Always bear in mind that the wall between the two sides of the heart keeps the oxygenated blood separate from the de-oxygenated. That's the first place to start." Des points to the septum dividing the heart.

"So, the blood flows into the heart, here, from all over the body, gagging for oxygen." Des points to the right atrium, the chamber at the top right where the blood flows in. "Then, when the heart beats, it's forced down here into the right ventricle where it's lovely and muscly. Then, another beat and it's pumped to the lungs for oxygen." He follows the blood flow with his pen. "Then it's back to the heart, up here, in the left atrium. Then down to the muscly left ventricle then out all over the body again to deliver the oxygen. Pure magic!"

Des has always thought the body a miracle of nature, all its different systems working away together in silent harmony. Everyone just goes around, doing their thing, oblivious to all that's happening inside.

"Draw it. That'll help you remember." Des is loving this time with Jack, which began by trying to distract him from the storm. (Holly is so obsessed with the dog, she could be on the Ark and not know it.) Des loves seeing the wonder ignite in his grandson's face and hearing his many questions. The boy has smarts. Des remembers sitting with Grace like this at the very same table. He knew from her curiosity and fascination that, one day, she'd follow in his footsteps, though he never encouraged, never hinted, never asked. He let her find her own way. There's something very special about having passed the baton to her. There's something equally special about being here with his grandchildren. He hopes that he's making some small difference. He may have retired but he's not completely useless yet.

In front of the fire, Holly is brushing Benji.

"You're so gorgeous. And brave. And loyal. And patient," she says, as she drags her hairbrush slowly through his coat. She's not worried about the brush; she can buy another one tomorrow or just borrow her mum's. There are more important things than hair.

Benji's eyes are closing as the brush glides through his fur.

Holly takes it as a sign that he's relaxing. He must be so relieved to be out of the storm.

"We'll go back tomorrow to visit her," she says. "We'll go back every day."

Benji lifts his head and looks at her. It's as if he is saying, "Thank you."

All over Torc island, the lights go out. In Cooke's, conversation stops. By the light of the fire, Grace finds her phone and swipes up to turn on her torch. Other phones start to light up the tiny restaurant like fireflies. A few people flick cigarette lighters and hold them to the sky, reminding Grace of the Elton John concert she went to with Yvonne – before concerts ended for her.

Mrs. and Mr. Cooke appear from out of the kitchen with armfuls of candles.

"No panic, no panic," says a panicked Mr. Cooke, rushing from table to table in his chef's attire, setting down big, fat, white candles. There is something endearing about his concern for his customers. Mrs. Cooke may be equally concerned but she moves with the calm confidence of a woman used to people and things giving way to her.

"Light up them candles like a good man," she says to Wayne Hill.

To Grace's surprise, the contrarian gets to his feet and obliges without remark. He seems even taller than she remembers and, in the candlelight, his features look softer, boyish even. She has heard, somewhere, that the best time to sell a horse is at sunset. The same must be true of candlelight.

By the time Wayne Hill returns to the table, the restaurant looks so pretty that Grace hopes that the power will stay off.

"This is nice," she admits.

"Isn't it?" The guy actually smiles. Must be the wine. He tips more into their glasses. Then gazes at her. "So, did you always want to be a doctor?"

More comfortable when he was prickly, Grace shrugs with a silent tilt of the head, then reaches for her wine.

"Wow. Are you always so talkative?"

She looks into his eyes, daring him. "You were in the waiting room, this morning. You probably know all about me."

"Wait." He squints. "Are you *saying* you'd rather if people were cold, aloof, disinterested?"

She makes a "very-funny" face.

Wayne Hill tips back on his chair looking like he is indeed amused. "You *were* the news of the day it has to be said. Dr. Sullivan's daughter returns home to Killrowan."

Her life reduced to seven words. She lays her knife and fork down on her plate, done.

"As for the waiting room? I learned everything, in line, outside the clinic. Knew what you looked like before I ever saw you."

She raises an eyebrow. "And I thought you hated gossip."

"Blocking my ears would have been rude."

"So, you subjected yourself to torture." She swills the wine around in her glass then looks up at him. "You know, if you really wanted to avoid attention, you should have moved to New York City. Isn't that what they say? The best place to hide is right in the middle of a crowd."

"True." He lets his chair down and gazes into the fire. Then, as though talking to himself, he says, "Sometimes, though, a person needs to get away."

This she understands.

"Anyway, this part of the world is inspiring. I'm writing four thousand words a day. Sometimes six."

"Is that good?"

"Wait, is that an actual question?" he asks in mock horror.

She smiles and shrugs. "Just wanted to prove I'm like everyone else."

"You're not, though," he says, holding her gaze.

"So, what are you writing about here on Torc?" she asks to prove him wrong. And, admittedly, because she also is curious.

"It's a story about a man who travels to Ireland to find his birth mother."

Automatically, she wonders if this is his story. "Sounds good."

"There you go again, not asking."

"What?"

"If it's autobiographical."

She gives in with a smile. "Okay, the question had occurred."

He squints at her. "Is this some kind of reverse psychology you have for getting people to talk? *Don't* ask. *Make* them want to tell you."

She puts her hands up. "You're onto me."

He laughs. "Good trick. When people are nosey, I clam up. When they're not, I wanna talk. What does that make me?"

"Human?"

He shakes his head. "Definitely not."

"Obstinate?" she tries again.

"Getting warmer."

"Cantankerous?" A smile escapes.

"Warmer still."

"How about impossible?"

He points at her. "Yup! That's it! That's me!"

She laughs.

Heads turn.

She turns hers right back. She is so *tired* of taking things lying down.

"I can't believe I made you laugh."

"I *have* been known to laugh. Occasionally."

He rests his chin on his hand. "You know, when you were forced to sit down here and it was very clear that it was the last thing you wanted to do, I set out to make you laugh. It was ambitious. A lot of hard work. A struggle, in fact. I almost quit. The power cut renewed my energy. And finally, I did it. I think I deserve a medal. Or at the very least some chocolate."

"Wasn't the laugh reward enough?" she smiles.

"No. I need chocolate."

Grace glances around at the desserts that have started to be plonked down in front of other diners. "Oops! Looks like they're offloading their ice cream before it melts."

"Any chocolate flavour?" he asks, scanning the bowls himself now.

"I'm afraid, my friend, it is vanilla or strawberry."

He puts his hands to his face. "She called me friend."

She laughs and shakes her head and yet, weirdly, finds herself imagining that friendship with this grumpy, moody man might not be impossible.

twenty-six

Grace finds her way upstairs by candlelight, psyching herself up for a cold, dark room without heating. Though her clothes no longer feel damp, they probably still are. She'll have to sleep naked while they dry – if they do. She turns the quaint, old-fashioned key in the lock and opens the door to a complete surprise. She could hug Mrs. Cooke – and that's saying something. The room isn't just candlelit, it's candle-filled. Behind a screen is a blazing fire. It's probably breaking a million different health and safety regulations. Grace doesn't care. To her, this is better than any five-star hotel. And, for one night, it is all hers.

She drops her bag and coat inside the door, kicks off her shoes and hurries out of her tights. Then she goes straight to the fire and takes away the screen. She squats down, holds her hands up to the heat then breathes in and out deeply, taking air right into the ribs in her back. Then she remembers home – and Alan. She takes out her phone. But there's no service. Reluctant to leave the fire, she paces the room trying to find a signal – without success. She could go back downstairs and try the corridor again. But she's not leaving this room. She's just going to have to trust that they're okay till the morning. And that Alan can live without a call till then.

She pulls up a chair to the fire and considers the day that started so badly. It wasn't a total disaster after all. It was stimulating, challenging, and confidence-building to see so many patients, one after the other, without a break. And she was up to it. Nothing fazed her. Even the Wayne Hill situation resolved itself, in the end. She hopes. She thinks of him heading off into the storm to return to his cottage and how strange life is. The last thing she expected going out to the island was to meet another outsider, running from their past – another hater of gossip. Maybe she's even glad she had to stay over.

She's definitely glad when she checks out the bathroom. It is old-world beautiful, antique bath with little legs, farmhouse sink and big antique mahogany mirror. More flowers and L'Occitane products. Grace carries all the candles in, dotting them around the room. The mirror doubles them. Heaven.

Running a bath, Grace tips the entire bottle of the L'Occitane lavender oil provided (another hug for Mrs. Cooke) into the stream, closes her eyes and inhales. She could be in a spa. She slips out of her clothes and hangs them on the back of the chair in front of the fire.

It's so long since she's had a bath. It's always been a (quick) shower. She tests the water with a toe, then, in she goes, adding cold water and lifting her feet one at a time until the temperature is as hot as she can tolerate. Slowly, she submerges with a long breath out so that only her head is above the water. As the wind howls outside, Grace starts to play with the soap, humming a song from her childhood. "I Do Like To be Beside the Seaside."

Fingertips shrivelled and face flushed, Grace finally parts with bath magic. Maybe she'll have time for another in the morning. Then again, maybe not. She returns the candles to the bedroom padding around, wrapped in thick, white fluffy towels. Her mind starts to slip back to the threat of Simon, but she pulls it away. She will not let him invade this night. She scans Mrs. Cooke's mini library of books. It's so long since she read for pleasure. Everything has had a purpose: escape and the planning of it. Now, her fingers, running over the spines, stop at a familiar name. She eases out a novel by Wayne.

She wonders if it might be a little bleak: one man's fight to find a cure for his son. Opening it to scan the first page, she comes across his signature in a flourish of black ink. The book is autographed to Mrs. Cooke. Weird. Grace can't imagine the formidable woman asking for anyone's autograph. Maybe it was a gift.

Letting her towel fall to the ground, Grace climbs into bed naked. And gasps. The crisp white sheets are freezing. She pulls the quilt up to her neck and waits for her body to warm them. At last, she opens the book.

With every page, Grace is pulled deeper and deeper into this new world. The characters have become real. She feels for them.

Laughs with them. Cries for them. Mostly, though, she hopes for them. Every doctor should read this book. To see things from the patient's point of view. Not just the patient but the family of the patient. In college, they teach doctors empathy. This is the best lesson in empathy she has ever come across.

At four am, she wishes she had Internet. Could this, too, be autobiographical? She hopes not. Because this brave, fearless, warm and loving man has lost his fight to save his only child. His marriage is crumbling under the pressure. There are only five chapters left when Grace's eyes betray her and close, unable to stay open any longer.

Grace doesn't wake till eleven. She jumps out of bed and hurries to the window. The wind seems to have died but she knows now how deceptive it is on the island. She opens the window and listens. Nothing but the shrill cry of gulls. She wishes she could see the sea but then she's no sailor. She wouldn't know what she was looking at in terms of a ferry travelling.

She dresses quickly and shoots through the door, almost tripping over a breakfast tray that has been left on the floor outside her room. She carries in the mouth-watering selection of hams, cheeses, breads and coffee, places it on her little table, and then takes off again.

Striding down to the pier, the sea still looks choppy. Grace is reassured, however, to see Ger Daly preparing to row out to the ferry. She hurries up to him.

He turns. "Ah, 'tis yourself, Young Dr. Sullivan. Did you have a good night's sleep?"

That's when it hits her: it's the first time in years she has fallen asleep without worrying. She'll have to make bedtime reading a habit. "Great thanks. What time are you heading across?"

Ger Daly does what he does best; he looks out to sea. "I'm hoping we might be able to get away in an hour or so. I'll send someone up to Cooke's to let you know."

"Great, thanks." She'll come down and check for herself in forty-five minutes. Just to be on the safe side.

Over breakfast, Grace returns to Wayne Hill's novel, hoping to finish it before leaving.

At eleven forty-five, with one chapter left, she reluctantly, closes the book. She can't miss the ferry.

Downstairs, passing over her credit card, she risks the wrath of Mrs. Cooke and pulls the book from her bag.

"Mrs. Cooke, would you mind if I borrowed this until I'm back over in two weeks? I've just a chapter to go and I'm *gripped*."

The look of prison guard is back. "I don't normally lend my books. Especially my Wayne Hill books." She passes the credit card machine to Grace.

Entering her number, Grace remembers all the people who never returned her books. "I understand." She passes back the machine.

Mrs. Cooke tears off the receipts and hands one to Grace with her card. She folds her arms, observing her.

"*But*. It's a good chapter. In a great book. So, go on. Take it. But…" She wags a finger at Grace. "I'll be sending out a posse if I don't see it in two weeks." She raises her eyebrows. "I won't forget now, mind."

Grace crosses her heart. "I promise you'll have it back. I'll look after it like a diamond."

Mrs. Cooke looks down at the book in Grace's hand and smiles fondly. "His bark is worse than his bite, isn't it?"

"Wayne Hill's?" Grace asks in surprise.

"First time he came into the restaurant, I thought he was a grumpy old so and so." Not a million miles away from what Grace had thought of Mrs. Cooke. "But he's been in every day, since, for his dinner. And he'd do anything for you, anything at all. And he's a great tipper. I've grown fierce fond of him. Anyway, I won't hold you up. Thanks for staying at Cooke's. You're welcome back at any time."

"Thanks so much. I had such a good time. I'll be posting a review on TripAdvisor." It occurs to Grace that Mrs. Cooke has probably never heard of it.

But she clasps her hands together in front of her amble bosom. "Oh, that would be great altogether. Thank you, love."

"Better go. Can't miss this ferry."

Grace rushes up to the surgery to collect Wayne Hill's sample, then back down again. She's still first to board the ferry, which – though still in the shelter of the harbour – is markedly rocking. Making her way to a seat, Grace, at one moment feels like gravity is pulling too hard, then as if her feet are barely touching the floor. Dropping into a seat, she opens her bag and goes in search of Motilium.

Pill safely downed, she takes out the book and gets lost in words.

The engine starts with a rumble. Grace looks up. And finds herself alone. Would no one else risk the trip? Should she? She reminds herself that Ger Daly has been making this crossing for decades. He knows it like his own child. If, indeed, he is a father.

She returns to the book. If she's lucky, she'll finish it on the way across.

She is three paragraphs in when she feels someone come up to her. If she doesn't look up maybe they'll go away.

"Looks like a great book," an American voice says.

Her head shoots up and she smiles. "You owe me a night's sleep," she tells Wayne Hill. "I couldn't put it down. I've only a chapter left."

"Wait. You stole it from poor Mrs. Cooke?" he asks. Then the swaying boat plonks him down beside Grace.

"She let me borrow it but I don't think she wanted to let it out of her sight to be honest. Actually, if I finish it on the crossing, could you bring it back to her? Would you mind?"

"Sure. I'll leave you to it, then." From his battered leather satchel, he produces an orange moleskin notebook and pen.

"Great. Thanks." She glances back down at the novel, then up again. "You better not make me cry," she warns.

He puts his hands up. "Whatever I say to that will be a spoiler."

"Good point. Shut up and let me read it."

He laughs.

She zones in on the book. She wants to take her time, savour it but knows that she might not get it finished.

Then, reading, she forgets everything as she gets lost in his words.

Finally, she closes the book. She is very still. It's either surreptitiously wipe her nose on her sleeve or give the game away and go for a tissue. She wishes she still had her bob to hide behind. With a sniff and a defeated sigh, she opts for the tissue. She tries to blow delicately.

"That bad?" he asks.

She passes the book to him. "You've broken my heart," she says hoarsely.

"Bet you say that to all the boys."

She smiles. To herself. And sighs away the sadness that his words have brought to her heart. She's okay again. Or she will be in another minute or two.

"It is," he says.

She turns to him. "It's what?"

He shrugs. "Based on my life. You wanted to know, right?"

Compassion, respect and admiration swamp her. "I didn't want to ask."

"I know."

She wants to reach out. Touch him. Comfort him in some real way. She can't imagine life without Jack or Holly. She doesn't think she could live it. "I'm so sorry."

He smiles. "Me too."

She wants to tell him that he should go back to his wife, try again, maybe with counselling. It's so clear that they love each other but are just so broken. But what does she know? She hasn't walked in his shoes. She has read his story and thinks she knows him. Silence falls between them as Grace, once more, readjusts her view of this man she met just a day ago. Of course, he'd want to escape to a wild, grey, remote and unforgiving island. Of course, he'd shun the limelight. Of course, he'd be quick to anger – though in fairness any man would be angered by Dr. O'Malley's mistakes (plural). She wants to say sorry for all the judgements she had made. She wants to say sorry for his pain. Instead, she is silent. Whatever she might say, she knows that it would be too little.

twenty-seven

Grace offers Wayne Hill a lift to the surgery. She wants to tell him how much his book moved her. But she's already made *that* obvious. So, she gives him something else:

"I was thinking," she says, squirting water on the windshield to clear the Dried-in salt stains from the storm spray. "Maybe all those people who treat you like a celebrity just love your books." She glances at him. "It'd be hard not to."

"Hey, you've just read the one," he says with a self-depreciating smile.

"Well, it won't be my last." She looks at the road ahead. "I was wondering why you wrote it as fiction." She glances at him. "If you don't mind me asking."

He turns his mouth down and shakes his head. "To protect my wife." He looks out his window. "It still upset her. Sometimes I think I shouldn't have written it. But it was my tribute to Jason. And that still stands."

She wants to reach out, squeeze his hand. But who is she to do so? "It's a wonderful tribute and an important book. I want to tell the world about it."

He turns to her. "Thank you."

Arriving at the clinic, they become doctor and patient again. Grace hurries inside. Approaching reception, she remembers that there's probably no one waiting for her anyway.

"Myra, how are things?" she asks.

"Same as ever," she says with meaning.

Grace feels heat spreading across her face. "Do you have that tetanus vial?"

Myra nods and goes to get it.

Grace turns and smiles at Wayne Hill. "Don't bother with the waiting room. I'll see you now."

Myra hands her the vial.

"This is Wayne Hill," Grace explains to her. "He's Dr. O'Malley's patient but I saw him out on the island and he's due a tetanus jab," is the best way to put it. "Oh, and Myra," she says, rooting in her bag. "Could you get this swab to the lab asap. It's been in the fridge overnight."

Myra takes it from her.

"I'll take the repeat prescriptions too, thanks."

Myra passes them to her.

"One last thing. Fred Cronin's results. Have they come in?"

"No. I've been keeping an eye out." Myra tucks a strand of hair behind her ear as if hit by a sudden, un-Myra-like, uncertainty. Or is it embarrassment? "I knew you'd be looking for them," she adds unnecessarily.

Could Myra like *Fred*? Grace is not going to embarrass her by staring – though that's exactly what she wants to do, stand there staring until she figures it out. "Great thanks, Myra. I'll see Mr. Hill now."

Wayne Hill follows her into her surgery. "So, it's back to Mr. Hill?"

She turns and smiles.

"Wayne," he says.

"Wayne it is, so," she says awkwardly.

"Maybe I can drop the Young in front of Dr. Sullivan?" he teases.

"Grace. Please." She holds up the vial. "So! This goes in your shoulder muscle." She looks at the layers of clothes he's wearing. "I'm not sure I can get your sleeves up that high though."

He pulls two pullovers over his head at the same time. His T-shirt rides up, accidentally revealing an actual washboard stomach. Heroically, Grace tears her eyes away.

Yanking the T-shirt down, he asks, "Is there any part of me you haven't seen now?"

"I don't think I've seen your feet."

"Don't tempt fate. I'll probably drop something on them on my way out."

Smiling, Grace washes her hands and draws up the injection, flicking air bubbles to the top of the syringe and squeezing them out with the plunger until a droplet of tetanus sprouts out.

"You're not squeamish about needles?"

He shakes his head.

"Great!" She locates the injection site and swabs it.

She looks into his ridiculously blue eyes. (Is he wearing coloured contacts or something?). "On the count of three, I want you to take a deep breath." She gives him the shot on two.

"Hey! Sneaky!"

"It was over before you knew it, though."

"I don't know if I can ever trust you again," he jokes.

She smiles. "I presume you've had all your childhood vaccines?" she asks to rule out the need for more boosters.

He nods.

"Great! That's it! I just need to show you how to do the dressing."

"I kind of know what to do," he says like a child trying to avoid homework.

She smiles. "I just want to make sure that you do it in as sterile a way as possible."

Grace pulls around the curtain. While he disappears behind it, she gets the dressing kit ready.

She shows him how to clean the wound then watches him in action.

"Perfect. I'll let you get dressed."

When he comes out from behind the curtain, Grace is writing out a list of what he'll need at the pharmacy."

He smiles, glancing at it. "I feel like a little boy about to go to the store."

She doesn't tell him that he looked like a little boy last night by candlelight. "Make sure to get yourself a lollipop."

"Will I get you one?" he asks in all seriousness.

She laughs. "You'd have to bring it all the way back."

"You're worth it," he jokes.

She hands him the list. "You can have my one. By the way, the peroxide might sting a little."

"I can take it." He gets up.

"Don't pay Myra on the way out. I'll let her know you covered it yesterday."

"Okay! I guess I'll see you when the stitches come out."

She raises her eyebrows. "No more climbing over fences."

"My love affair with fences is over."

Grace walks him to the door. "So, call me if the wound doesn't start to improve. And I'll be in touch if you need to change the antibiotics."

His, "Thank you," sounds like an apology for their first consultation.

"My pleasure."

"I hope not."

"Ha!" she barks. She's about to call herself a sadist when she stops short. What is *wrong* with her?

Des might be making progress on the *Southern Star* crossword, open in front of him on the kitchen table, if he weren't revelling in the sounds of life in the house. Being Wednesday, the children have a half-day from school and Holly has arrived home with two friends – Barbara Kelly's youngest, Aoife, whose appendix almost killed her when she was eight and Jenn Ahern whose grandad, Bill, owns the pub. They're on the floor, fussing over the dog like new parents.

"Where's Jack?" one of them shyly asks. Without looking up, Des suspects it's Jenn, the more quietly spoken of the two.

"Oh my God!" exclaims the other – definitely Aoife. "Jack is so *mint*."

Des has never heard of "mint" but it sounds like a positive.

"Does he have a girlfriend?" Jenn asks, sounding a strange mix of shy and forward.

There's a pause.

The urge to look up is killing Des but he can't let them know he's listening.

"I don't *know*. It's not like he'd tell me." Holly sounds snippy.

"Nah. If Jack had a girlfriend we'd have heard," says Barbara Kelly's daughter.

It's a lifetime ago since Des was a teenager but he remembers it like yesterday. The tension, the excitement, the hoping. Then, first love. Was there anything like it ever again?

He wonders how the subject of the conversation is getting on at the hurling. Jack arrived home shortly after one, bolted down a sandwich, hurried into sports gear and took off, saying he was going to borrow a hurl and a helmet from someone called Ginge.

Hope is a feeling that had started to die for Des. Six days ago, it came back into his life. Hope is what keeps a man alive.

There's a knock at the door. Des takes his time. He looks through the camera Alan installed this morning and sees the man himself returning from his lunch break. Des opens up.

"Still working okay?" Alan asks of the camera.

"'Tis, indeed. I keep going over to check it," he says like a kid with a new toy. "Don't know how I lived without it."

Alan smiles. Then he rubs his hands together. "I'll finish installing the alarm so. Then I'll start on the window locks. I thought the deadbolts might have arrived home by now but no sign, there. It might have to be tomorrow before I get to them, Des."

"That's fine, Alan. Sure, I'll have my alarm. I won't know myself."

"Grand so."

Every time Alan comes to do a job, Des is reminded why he chooses him. He just gets to work in a quiet, unruffled way, tapping away at whatever he's at without the need for blaring music or chatter. And nothing is ever a problem.

twenty-eight

The afternoon has dragged. After Wayne Hill left, Grace went through the repeat prescriptions. She texted patients their blood results, then revised the notes of everyone she saw on the island, making sure she missed nothing. She rang home (all well), called Alan (it went to voicemail), checked her bank balance online hoping for a miracle (no miracle, no maintenance payment). In a moment of craziness, she set up a stockbroking account and bought a tiny amount of shares in Blackcastle Pharmaceuticals. Conor Sweeney was just so enthusiastic.

Now, she's drumming her fingers and looking around the surgery.

When her phone pings, she snatches it up.

"*Want to meet for coffee?*" Jack's text says.

This is an absolute first. And highly suspicious. Grace wonders what it could be about. She checks the time. Just after four. She's so hungry, she's starting to get shaky. That's when it hits her. She never had lunch.

"*Meet you in five at The Coffee Cove,*" she texts back.

It's unlikely she'll need her doctor's bag but it would be handy to have in case a house call comes in – she can go from there. Which means she should also bring the car.

Out at reception, she tells Myra she's popping out for a late lunch but that she has her phone.

In the car park, she takes a moment to breathe in the sea view, the fresh air, the peace. Today, the gulls seem to be crying, "Why?

Why? Why?" She rolls her shoulders back. Living amongst all this beauty must be good for the health. It's certainly good for the soul.

The Coffee Cove is Manhattan chic with pale wood, white walls, low-hanging, metal light fittings and paintings of the area. Though it's October and the village is quiet, "the Cove" has attracted a crowd like a cosy fire. School kids nursing mugs of hot chocolate. Older people brightening their day. There's "lovely" Jacinta Creedon with a boy of about five; if it's her son, she had him late. No sign of Jack.

To get to the counter, Grace will have to pass Jacinta. She is about to get a table and wait for Jack, instead, when she notices how unwell the boy is looking. He is worryingly pale and his breathing seems to be off. Grace should say something. If Jacinta were anyone else, she would. She tells herself that she shouldn't punish the boy because his mother is a cow. Just as she is forcing herself to go over, Jacinta turns and sees her.

"Young Dr. Sullivan, I'm glad you came over," she says in a hushed but relieved voice. "That was so awkward in the supermarket–"

"Hi Jacinta," Grace cuts her off. "Who's this?" she asks smiling at the boy.

"This is my son, Matthew," she says with all the softness in the world.

Grace squats down to the child. "Hey, Matthew. How's it going?"

He holds his throat.

"We're on our way to the surgery," Jacinta rushes.

Grace keeps her eyes on the boy. "Good idea. I'd say you have a temperature, little man." His eyes look watery.

"He just wanted an ice cream to cool his throat down, first."

He hasn't eaten any of it, Grace notices. "I won't hold you up," she says because, by the looks of Matthew, they shouldn't delay. "Tell Myra I said you could skip the queue when you get there. I'll text her now." The receptionist will probably kill Grace on her return. Time she started living dangerously.

There's a tap on her shoulder. She swivels round automatically, arms rising into a defensive position. Seeing Jack, she continues her arms in a smooth upward arc to her hair and smiles to cover her reaction.

"Hot chocolate?" she asks. Her heart always lifts to see one of her kids.

"Hey, I asked *you* for coffee. I'm buying."

Wow, her little boy is growing up. "I'll have a latte so. Thanks, sweetie."

"If they have them here," he says looking towards the counter.

"Of course, they do. West Cork has the finest food in Ireland." He'll learn.

"You sit down," he instructs.

"See you later," she says to Jacinta and winks at Matthew. "Hope you're feeling better soon."

Grace finds a table and positions herself with her back to the wall. No one can steal up on her that way. She wonders if she'll ever feel relaxed enough to just sit anywhere, do anything, with anyone. One day at a time, she reminds herself.

She glances around the café, loving the little touches. Old-fashioned, glass milk bottles hold tap water with mint leaves. Smaller bottles act as vases for pink peonies, red roses and sprigs of tiny wild flowers. Sugar bowls and milk jugs are turquoise, glazed pottery – Dunbeacon, Grace discovers, on inspection.

She glances over at Matthew. His breathing is becoming visibly laboured. She wishes Jacinta would forget about the bloody ice cream and get a move on. Grace is distracted by the approach of her handsome young son. How did he grow up so fast?

"They had those homemade chocolate chip cookies that you like so I got you one."

"Wow! It's huge." She can totally see how one of these a day would win a person's loyalty. "Thanks, love."

Jack unloads the tray and sits down. He worries his hot chocolate with a straw then glances up at Grace. There is a tiny bit of mud over his eyebrow. Grace reaches across and scratches it away with her thumb.

"A tiny bit of mud," she says. "How was the hurling? Grandad told me you were giving it a try."

"Ferocious!"

"Is that good or bad?" she asks cautiously. Hockey was his life.

His face lights up. "Mad! Totally vicious. And fast. They're all crazy! You can whack that ball as high as you like. You could take someone's head off. It's brilliant!"

She laughs.

He sucks on his straw, like he has lost years. And darkness.

"This is such a lovely idea. I'm so glad you suggested it. I never get to talk to you alone."

He drops his gaze and goes back to stirring the straw.

She has ruined the moment. As she always seems to do with Jack, somehow. Anxious, she breaks the biscuit into pieces. And takes a sip of coffee.

Finally, he looks up. "So." A pause. Followed by a deep breath. "I just wanted to say sorry for blowing up at you on Monday. I was just so stressed."

"Hey, it's okay, sweetie." She is so incredibly touched by this, especially given how hard sorry is for him. "I completely understand."

His eyes burrows into hers. "You're not just saying that?"

"No! Our lives are changing so fast. No wonder we're stressed. But you handled the situation at school amazingly well." She pauses. "I learned a lot from you." She holds the sorry.

"Let's make a deal," he says without softening his gaze. "I'll chill with people. And you trust me."

She reaches across and squeezes his hand. "I do trust you."

He pulls it away. "You know what I mean. Have *faith* in me," he says earnestly as if this is the real reason for the coffee.

"I *do*. So much. Look at you, bringing me for coffee and apologising. I have total faith in you."

Still, he doesn't soften. If anything, he grows more intense. "No lying, okay? You've got to face the truth, whatever it is, Mum."

She raises her eyebrows. "This is one tough coffee," she jokes to lift the mood. But her smile is fleeting. She knows how important this is to him. "No lying," she says firmly. She will really, really try.

"Deal," he says, sitting back in his chair, the tension visibly leaving his body.

Grace holds out the plate of cookie pieces to her son. "Peace pipe," she says.

"What?"

"Peace offering. Olive branch."

"Oh. Right. Cool." He takes a piece. "Wow, yum."

Grace closes her eyes as the cookie melts on her tongue. Heaven.

"So, you and Ginge's mum were besties?"

She smiles automatically. "Ah, we were great pals."

"There you go again, talking like a Cork person."

She smiles. "I keep telling you. I *am* a Cork person." What she *doesn't* tell him is that he is very slowly starting to sound like one too. "So, what's he like?"

"I was wrong about him; he's actually okay."

Grace is encouraged. "Okay" is about as enthusiastic as Jack gets about anyone.

"He let me borrow his hurling stuff. He's such a good player. Total lunatic." Jack remembers his hot chocolate, sucks on the straw then looks up. "I might have been wrong about hurling, too."

"And culchies?"

Jack just smiles.

It's like a shaft of light entering Grace's world. Out of the corner of her eye, she notices Jacinta hurrying Matthew into his coat. Turning, she frowns.

"What?" Jack asks as she gets to her feet.

"Back in a sec," she says, already rushing over.

Jacinta looks at her in panic. "He can't swallow the ice cream. He keeps spitting it out. And his breathing is off. See?"

Grace nods. She feels his forehead. He's burning up.

"What's that?" Jacinta asks of the high-pitched wheezing sound Matthew has started to make.

"It's a stridor. Something is obstructing his airflow. Sit forward, pet," Grace says to Matthew, squatting down to him.

He leans forward and his breathing eases a little.

Grace looks at Jacinta. "This all came on suddenly, right?"

Jacinta nods, her face a worried question.

"And he didn't swallow anything other than the ice cream? Popcorn? A hard-boiled sweet?"

"No. Nothing."

"Okay, take off his coat, Jacinta, and sit him on your lap, please."

Jacinta removes his coat and scoops him up.

"I'm just going to have a quick look at your throat, pet. Open wide." She activates the torch on her phone and shines it into the back of the child's mouth to rule out a foreign body. She hasn't the tools to see right down the back of the throat to the epiglottis; she has to trust her gut, here. She smiles at Matthew, then looks over his head into Jacinta's eyes to calm her. She keeps her voice steady as she says, "Okay, it looks like Matthew may have epiglottitis and his throat is becoming blocked by swelling. It's a medical emergency. I'm going to call an ambulance but we must be ready to act if we have to, okay?"

Jacinta nods frantically.

Grace grabs the car keys in her pocket. "Jack!" She throws them to him. "Run and get my bag from the boot of the Jeep!"

He bolts.

Grace calls for an ambulance, knowing it will take at least twenty minutes if it's coming from Bantry, forty from Clonakilty and Lord knows how long from Cork City – an hour and a half? She introduces herself and tells them her exact location. "I have a little boy, here, aged about five, with suspected epiglottitis. I need an immediate ambulance. If you don't get here on time, I may have to perform a tracheostomy." Technically a cricothyrotomy but she's not sure who she's talking to and most people are familiar with tracheostomy.

Jack has arrived back with her medical bag.

Silence has descended on the café, all eyes glued to the unfolding incident. Because it's very clear that this child is fading fast. His breathing, alone, has people gasping for breath.

From her medical bag, Grace retrieves sterile wipes, a scalpel, swabs and sterile gloves. Jacinta keeps telling her little boy he's going to be okay. He's going to be okay. But the child goes quiet, breath sounds stopping completely and he collapses into her arms, unconscious, skin translucent, lips blue.

"Lie him on the table," Grace instructs in a voice empty of emotion. "Tilt his head back and support it. If you're queasy, close your eyes. I have to operate now." She calls up to the counter. "I need straws! Don't take off the wrapping."

The pretty waitress of about sixteen grabs a fistful of individually wrapped straws and runs with them to Grace who has already donned the sterile gloves. Grace opens the scalpel and the sterile wipes. Then swabs the boy's throat.

"Open a straw but don't touch it," she instructs the stunned waitress. "Grip it by the paper and hold it out to me when I ask."

Eyes closed, trusting her fingers, Grace feels for the hard edge of the thyroid cartilage. She makes an incision just below it.

"Straw!" she says. It appears right by her. She whips it out of its wrapping and inserts it into the hole she has made in the child's neck. There is a noisy inhalation and his chest expands.

Though he is still unconscious, Matthew's colour improves with every breath.

Grace, still holding the straw, looks up at Jacinta reassuringly. "He's out of immediate danger but we need to get him to the hospital. The ambulance is on its way."

Jacinta bursts into relieved tears.

"Are you okay to stay supporting his neck? Or do you want Jack to take over?"

"Stay." She closes her eyes and inhales deeply to regain control.

Grace knows that she'd be the same if it were Jack lying on that table. She looks down at the child. "Poor little fellow."

"I know!" Jacinta says, fresh tears threatening.

Grace understands the easy guilt of a mother when something happens to her child. "You were great, Jacinta," she reassures, keeping her eyes fixed on the straw that she continues to hold; she can't afford to move it a centimetre. "This condition blows up so fast, it always catches people out."

"It was just a sore throat this morning," Jacinta insists. "What did you say it's called again?"

"Epiglottitis. Inflammation of the epiglottis, that little flap of tissue at the back of the tongue that covers the entrance to the lungs when we swallow. It's a great little flap of tissue. But when it gets inflamed, well…."

"What caused it to get inflamed?" Jacinta asks, looking down at her little boy.

"Most likely infection. When Matthew gets to the hospital, they'll start him on antibiotics."

"I don't know what I'd have done if you weren't here!" Jacinta's voice wobbles.

"But I was," Grace says, not wanting Jacinta to go there in her mind.

"Can I go now?" the waitress asks.

"Oh, sorry. I forgot you were there," Grace says, without looking, not daring to change position. "Of course. Absolutely. Thank you. You were great."

The pretty brunette flashes Jack a shy smile before hurrying back to the comforting normality of coffee and cakes. The other customers aren't sure quite what to do. An air of shock pervades. There are one or two timid offers of help which are politely declined. A woman excuses herself apologetically to pick up her child from piano lessons. Everyone else stays, as if loathe to abandon the boy and his mother. Grace understands. This is the community she grew up in. It might be claustrophobic, at times, but people stick together, look out for each other. She's glad of the reminder. Maybe this is the best place she could have brought her family. Time will tell. For now, she wishes that ambulance would hurry up and get here.

twenty-nine

Before Grace can step down from the ambulance, Jacinta throws her arms around her, clinging to her with a touching ferocity, her entire body trembling.

"Thank you," she whispers. "Thank you for saving my baby."

Grace pulls back, conscious that the ambulance needs to get going. "I'll call the hospital later to see how you're getting on."

Jacinta looks into her eyes. "I'm sorry. For everything."

Grace nods. "I know."

"No. I was a disgrace," she says, eyes welling.

Grace pats her arm. "You're in safe hands now."

She climbs back onto the street where Jack is waiting.

"Will he be okay?" he asks, eyes filled with concern.

Grace puts an arm around him. "Barring complications, he should make a full recovery."

Jack smiles down at her. "Never knew you were a ninja."

Arriving home, Grace kicks off her shoes and drops her bag. Closing her eyes, she tilts her head back, stretching out the tension in her neck. Thank God, she thinks; thank God we got him back. Until now, she hadn't let herself consider any other option but it had loomed over her like a dark shadow as she struggled to save the child. Taking slow and measured breaths, she understands Jacinta's relieved tears, emotional herself now. What if....

She feels something cold in her palm and glances down in surprise to see the most gorgeous creature by her side, offering her comfort without even knowing her. The dog's eyes seem luminous, as if he is exposing his soul. Grace looks up to the sound of Holly's laughter.

"Isn't he gorgeous?" she asks before excitedly revealing a story of life and death and the fine line between the two, a story that fills Grace with emotion.

"It feels like fate," she whispers, her hand on her heart.

"There's something else!" Holly enthuses. "His name is *Benji*."

Grace squints at her. "It's *really* Benji or you're just calling him that?"

"Yeah, no. It's Benji," Holly says like she can't believe it either. "It was always Benji."

"Wow," Grace whispers, her throat burning. "Wow." She squats down to this beautiful creature and feels her heart expand.

"Ah, so you've met the new member of the family?" Des asks cheerfully, walking into the kitchen.

Standing up, Grace eyeballs him. "Are you sure? You haven't been pressured into this?" She looks at Holly here.

"Sure, who'd pressure me? Amn't I my own man?"

"Have we the room?" In other words: "You won't trip over him?"

"The more the merrier."

"It's only till we find our own place," Grace reassures him.

"Maybe we don't need to find our own place," Jack says.

Grace looks at him in surprise, Jack who loves his comforts, the finer things in life.

He shrugs. "I like it here with Grandad."

Des places a hand on his shoulder. "Well, I like having ye here."

Jack looks at Grace with so much hope. She needs to explain to him that they can't land in on Des permanently. But now is not the time with Des listening in. He'll only be polite. And, so, she jokes, "I go away for *one night* and you adopt a dog."

Holly looks her in the eye. "Benji adopted us, Mum."

Grace touches her heart. She smiles down at the dog. "Welcome to the family." This is just what they needed.

"Wait till ye hear what happened at the Coffee Cove!" Jack says.

As he recounts every detail in one hurried breath, Grace squats down and pours her gratitude into the dog for showing up for them.

"You should have seen her," Jack finishes.

Grace glances up to find him looking at her – in an entirely new way. Her son is looking at her with pride.

This day!

"Do you know how long Jacinta and Tom were trying for that child?" Des asks.

Grace starts working back from Jacinta's age.

"Fifteen years," he says before she can work it out. "Matthew is their miracle boy."

Grace is so glad she didn't know that.

Grace promises herself that next week there will be no takeaways as she orders another, this time fish and chips. She simply hasn't the energy to turn around and cook. Simon would have had a fit. But Simon's not here. And Simon didn't save a life today.

"Apparently, you're a mint, Jack," Des says.

"A *mint*?" Jack looks confused.

Holly is rolling her eyes. "He's not *a* mint. He's *so* mint. And that's a matter of opinion."

"Holly, translation please," a baffled Grace says.

"It means he's cute," Holly explains like she's seriously bored.

Jack looks the opposite of bored. "Who thinks I'm mint?"

"Everyone. As usual," Holly snaps.

The intercom buzzes.

"They couldn't be that fast!" Jack says.

"Did you change the bell?" Grace asks Des at the same time.

"I did, yeah. We've got an intercom now. Come have a look," he says proudly like a child showing off a toy. They look at the screen.

"It's Alan!" they say together.

Des opens the door.

"Would you believe the deadbolts were there when I got home?" Alan says to Des, failing to notice Grace. "Thought I may as well get them in now if I'm not disturbing you."

"Alan Wolfe!" Grace says.

Alan looks past Des and his face ignites. "Gracie Sullivan! Would you look at you! Sure, you're only gorgeous!"

Grinning, Grace goes in for a hug. She rests her head against the chest of the best hugger in West Cork. In Ireland, possibly.

Des closes the door, while Holly and Jack stare, first, at each other, then at their mother.

Alan pulls back, holding Grace at arm's-length and taking a good look at her. "'Tis better looking you're getting Grace Sullivan."

"I tried calling you back, earlier," Grace says. "What are you doing here?"

Alan defers to Des with a look.

"Putting in an alarm system for me," Des says. "Paddy O'Neill was telling me there's been a spate of burglaries in the area so I thought I'd better be on the safe side."

"Here in Killrowan?" Holly asks, coming over.

Jack comes too but not because of the burglaries. He glares at Alan protectively.

"Well, out by Goleen and thereabouts," Des hedges. "I wouldn't be worrying, pet. Probably just a few messers bored out of their trees. Anyway, I thought I may as well get my house in order."

Grace, watching her father closely, guesses what he is up to. And she is so grateful. She didn't know how to ask. She turns back to her childhood friend. "How're you *doing*? Yvonne was saying that we'll have to catch up for a drink."

"Will we see if she's free tonight – after I put in the deadbolts?"

Grace looks at her family, from whom she has just spent a night away. "Maybe not tonight."

"Why don't ye go for one?" Des suggests to Grace. "After the day you've had."

Grace and Alan look at each other. Alan waits for her to decide.

"Maybe a quick one," Grace says. "I'd love to catch up."

"One it is, so," Alan says. "Soon as I finish up here."

The intercom buzzes again.

Almost as if he can smell the fish and chips, Jack shoots to the door.

"Jack, look who it is before opening up," Des says with a note of warning in his voice.

Jack just about nods as he takes in the food.

"Have you eaten, Alan?" Grace asks.

Jack's head swivels but Grace misses it, waiting for Alan's reply.

"I have, yeah," he says. "Thanks anyway. You take your time. I'll just get these locks in."

Grace can't get over the difference in him – from boy to man, really. But with the same gentleness in his soulful, brown eyes. Alan has always reminded her of a seal. He still does. A trusted, adored seal. "D'you know, I was thinking the other day," she says, seamlessly resuming the easy banter they've always shared. "I've been away from Killrowan longer than I've been here. Isn't that mad?"

"Gas altogether. Right, let me get to work. The sooner I'm done, the sooner we can have that drink. I'll start at the back and leave ye in peace." Alan heads for the back door.

Jack opens his mouth to say something then changes his mind.

Des puts a hand on his shoulder. "Old pals," he explains.

thirty

Grace waits while Alan flings his overalls into the van, then they stroll down the village together. The old-world street lamps cast warm pools of light, illuminating the pinks and blues and yellows of the shopfronts. A gentle sea breeze stirs the air. Grace closes her eyes and inhales it deeply, grateful for the easiness of her breath after what happened earlier. She stops abruptly.

"Oh, no. I forgot to ring the hospital."

Alan looks concerned.

"It's okay. It's just Jacinta Creedon's little boy, Matthew. He had a bit of a turn today. Just want to check up on him."

"Fire away. I'm in no hurry."

Grace wants to hug him. With Alan, nothing's a drama. Being in his company is like being carried along in a gentle stream. Grace makes the call and the news is good. She hangs up smiling. "He's doing great."

"Ah, that's great." No questions with Alan. No nosiness.

Grace tips her head back in relief. "Wow, look at those stars! I've never seen so many." It seems like a mistake, the most beautiful, magical mistake of nature. "You never see this many in Dublin with all the light pollution."

"If you really want to see them, we could walk out to the graveyard where the street lights stop."

She links his arm. "Let's do that so."

They lean into each other.

"'Tis like you never left," he says. "Already."

"It is." Not for the first time, Grace wonders what life would have been like if she'd never met Simon, if, instead, she'd met someone like Alan, someone kind. She catches herself sighing.

Alan doesn't miss it. Neither does he ask.

"I left my marriage." She gives him that.

He stops walking. "Are you alright?" he asks, like that's all that matters.

She stares as she realises, he's right. It *is* all that matters – as long as "you" is taken as a plural. She smiles. "It's great to be back, Al. It's great that I get to start over. And it's great to be here with you, like this, just hanging out, like the good old days."

He unlinks his arm, puts it around her and squeezes her to him. And suddenly there's no need for words.

They stroll out to the graveyard. And she tells him the story of Benji.

"'Tis a miracle," he says. "A real miracle. You've no idea how hard I tried to coax him away from that grave, poor little fella. But you know what? He was waiting for the right person."

She swallows. He always did understand.

They sit on the graveyard wall, gazing up at nature's display.

Grace elbows him. "So, what have you been up to?" She means on the romance front.

"Staying out of trouble."

She looks at him. "What does that even mean?"

He chuckles. "Ah, I'm happy with a small life, Gracie. Some of us aren't ambitious. Some of us just want to keep things simple."

"That makes total sense to me." It's what she wants now. A smaller life. That's exactly it.

The breeze picks up. Grace feels it on the back of her neck like the grip of a cold hand.

"Right, Ahern's let's be having you," she says and jumps down from the wall. Alan's right; it's as if the years have melted away.

They wander back towards the village, linking arms again.

A car passes, headlights dipping. They wave automatically, as you do in West Cork, even when you've no idea who it is.

"The tongues will be wagging now," Alan says.

"What d'you mean? Don't they *know*?"

He shakes his head. "You're the only one I've ever told apart from my parents."

"But *why not*?"

He sighs. "Mam and Dad didn't take it well. They begged me not to tell a soul. So, I never did."

"Alan! You've lived your life in secret!" But, then, who is she to talk?

"It's grand. I make little trips to Cork, Dublin, even London sometimes for secret get-togethers. My social life is at weekends."

Most people's social lives are, when Grace thinks about it. "So, there's never been a special person?" What is she talking about? Look at how her special person turned out.

"There was one but I would have had to move away."

She pulls him closer. "Why didn't you?"

"Mam hasn't been in the best of health. And I couldn't do it to her. She's on her own now. I couldn't leave her."

Grace nods. She is not one to judge. She stayed stuck for almost seventeen years. "Let's get that drink," she says to the most giving man she has ever met.

"Are you sure?" Alan asks. "What about the tongues?"

Once again, he's thinking of her.

"Let them wag," she says with a vengeance.

Jack could put his fist through the wall. First, his mum gets all cosy with this handyman. Then, his father doesn't deposit his pocket money into his bank account. He's used to a hundred euro a week. What's he supposed to do now?

In her room, Holly is looking at her bank balance. Where's her fifty euro? She tosses her phone onto the bed. Then reminds herself of her whole new life. She never imagined it would be this easy. She's still waiting for it to turn, flip over, fall apart. But it mightn't! The girl in the mirror has changed. Her head is high, her eyes alive, hopeful, confident. Fifty quid a week is a small price to pay for this new person. She turns in the direction she imagines Dublin to be and flips off her dad. Keep your precious money. There are more important things. Like dogs. And friends. And happiness.

Alan leads the way into Ahern's. Heads turn and the conversation dips. They find a table in the darkest corner of the pub. Grace grabs the seat with the back to the wall. Alan, still standing, glances at the bar.

"Tell me you're not still drinking snowballs," is his way of asking what she'll have.

She laughs, remembering. "How did I ever?" she asks. "I'll have a beer. Peroni if they have it. If not, I don't know, Heineken?"

Alan turns and bumps into Bill Ahern, who has owned the pub for as long as Grace can remember.

"What are ye having?" Bill asks, his paunch straining the buttons on his Hawaiian shirt.

"The usual, Bill, thanks," Alan says. "And a Peroni for Grace."

"Grand so," he says and heads back to the bar.

Alan lifts his eyebrows at Grace as he sits down. "I'll have to hang out with you more often. I've never, in all my days, seen Bill Ahern come out from behind that bar for anyone."

She puts her hands up. "Don't look at me. I don't know why he served us. And would people ever stop staring at us?" she whispers.

He looks around, then leans towards Grace, voice low. "Confirmed bachelor, Alan Wolfe, out with a woman is big news."

She squints. "D'you want to go?"

"I do not. We're having our drink and ignoring the lot of them. He lifts a beer mat and starts to tap the table with it.

She smiles. "Wow, you still do that?"

He looks up from the mat and his thoughts. "It seems I do!"

"It is so, so good to see you, Al." She doesn't know why she's getting emotional. Been a long day, she guesses.

"Tell me you've had a good life, Gracie," he says with so much hope.

She wishes she could say she had – for him. She looks down at a knot on the table, a fascinating, intriguing knot. She wants to tell him. He trusted her with his secret all those years ago. And she trusts him now. She'd trust him with anything. But she can't take that giant step. She can't convert all that's happened into words and release the truth of them. She just can't.

Bill Ahern sets the drinks down. Both Alan and Grace go for their wallets. That's how it's always been with them, a race, a fight almost, to pay.

"On the house," Bill says, looking at Grace. "For what you did for young Matthew in The Cove earlier."

"Aw, thanks, Bill. That's very kind but there's really no need. I was just doing my job."

"That's my godson's life you saved," he says with a wobble in his voice. "I'll be forever grateful." His eyes water, then he turns and hightails it away.

"You never said you saved a life!" Alan says. "Sure, that's what they're all looking at. I've been sitting with a hero and I didn't even know it."

The responsibility of a child's life shakes her once more. "I was lucky, Al. So many things could have gone wrong." She mightn't have been able to find the right spot to go in. She might have gone in wrong. "I was very, very lucky." She takes a big gulp of beer.

"No luck about it. Unless you mean that Matthew was lucky you were there. Or that we're lucky to have you here in Killrowan." He raises his glass. "To Grace Sullivan! Welcome home, me old segotia."

Her spirits lift. "Cheers, Big Ears," she says, like old times.

He laughs and clinks her glass.

She puts down her drink and, though she knows no one can hear, she whispers. "Al, not one patient has come to see me. I'm sitting in there twiddling my thumbs all day. I don't know how much longer it can go on Dr. O'Malley can't manage the practice alone. There are just too many patients."

"They'll wisen up. They always do."

She tells him what she overheard Jacinta Creedon say in the supermarket about her notions and her accent.

Alan puts down his drink. "Look. You're going to get that. Some women will see you as a threat. Gorgeous creature like you rocking into town stealing husbands."

She laughs. "Stop."

"It's true. I don't say much but I see everything. And I know what I'm talking about. Anyway, you'll have made a friend of Jacinta today. That's for sure."

Another round of drinks lands down on the table. "From Mick Farrell, up at the bar," Bill says.

Grace and Alan turn automatically. It's an older man with an Aran sweater, grey beard and a Guinness moustache, drinking alone. He raises his pint like an ad for Ireland.

Grace lifts hers and mouths a "Thank you" to him.

"I'll have to carry you out of here," Alan says. "This is only the start. Wait till it livens up in here."

"I thought we said one drink."

"You can't stop a village now, can you?"

Grace can feel the second hangover of the week already. She thinks of how horrified Simon would be. And smiles.

thirty-one

Grace is suffering. Alan was right. Last night, the free drinks kept coming. Until it became a political quagmire. She couldn't refuse one when she had accepted another from someone else. So, she paced herself, letting the glasses mount up on the table in the hope that people would get the message. They never did.

Now she sneaks downstairs before the alarms have gone off and starts to put on a fry. That is what she needs. That is what everyone needs. It's Thursday, which means they've made it through their first week. Time to celebrate.

She hears a familiar thudding and smiles. She knows it's Jack before he appears. And she knows that his stomach is driving him. She turns as he appears.

"Are you cooking a fry?"

"Yup! We're celebrating. A week here today."

"Wait! Tomorrow's Friday."

"Yeah, I know. Count up, though. Friday, Saturday, Sunday…." She counts on her fingers till she gets to Thursday. "Seven days. One week."

"Cool!" He sits at the table.

"Will you set the table, love?" It's so important to Grace that Jack won't be like his dad and think himself above helping out.

He groans but does get up. He is setting a fork on the table when he looks at her sideways. "So, who's this Alan dude?"

She turns and smiles. "One of my oldest and dearest friends." She'd like Jack to spend more time around him so he can see that there are good men, gentle men, giving men.

"As long as he stays just friends." There is a warning tone to his voice.

Grace stares at him. "Jack, Alan is like the brother I never had. I could *never* see him any other way. We used to climb trees together.

Sail boats together. Have snowball fights together. There were three of us. The three musketeers. Me. Yvonne Barry. And Alan."

"Is he married?"

"No."

"Tell me he's gay."

She could. But that would be breaking Alan's confidence. And burdening Jack with another secret. So, she looks her son in the eye.

"You asked me to trust you, Jack. And I do. One hundred per cent. Now I'm asking you to trust me when I say that there is no room in my life for a man in the way that you mean. There is room only for friends. Alan Wolfe is the nicest of men, the kindest, most thoughtful. And I want you guys to be surrounded by men like that." The rest of what she wants to say, she silently wills to her son: "So you know they exist, so you know how to be one, someday."

"Okay," he says. He gets to his feet and goes to inspect the fry. "Is it nearly ready?"

She smiles. "Nearly."

Grace passes a brown paper bag from the Coffee Cove in through the cubby hole to Myra.

"All good traditions should be kept up."

"Ah, you shouldn't have."

Grace squints. Myra's voice seems incredibly loud today. Everything does. It's like the whole day is too loud, too bright, too irritating. She wonders if she could have a little nap in her surgery. She can't imagine anyone would notice.

"I'll take the repeat prescriptions, Myra thanks. And let me know if Fred Cronin's results come in." Surely today, she thinks.

"So, you don't want me to send in your first patient?" Myra asks.

Hands on the counter, Grace (slowly) leans in. "I have *a patient*?"

Myra tucks a strand of escaping hair behind her ear. "You have half a waiting room of them." She beams as she reveals the surprise that she has been holding in. "Here's your list so far. I printed it out just in case you didn't believe me but it'll be up on the computer inside." She passes it through the cubby hole.

Stunned, Grace takes it.

"You're the talk of Killrowan, by the way," Myra says, like a proud mother.

Grace risks raising her eyebrows. "Maybe I won't have to go to Mass, after all," she whispers.

"Oh, that's non-negotiable," Myra says without expression.

Grace can't figure out if this is black humour or basic fact. Well, she has three days to work it out.

She taps the list. "Just give me a few minutes to warm up the computer." And drink a pint of water.

Grace eases past the waiting room without looking in. She's not about to tempt fate.

In her surgery, she turns on the computer, looks at the list and smiles.

Leaving the house for school, Jack spies Nicky, the girl from the coffee shop, disappearing into the newsagents. She is seriously cute, like a young Mila Kunis. He got a definite vibe, yesterday. But he was distracted then. Now, there's nothing in the way – apart from a possible late – which he can handle.

"You go ahead," he tells Holly. "I'll catch up."

She raises an eyebrow, hooches her schoolbag higher and takes off without him.

He saunters across the road and down into the newsagents, where he queues behind Nicky at the checkout and grabs a packet of (banned at school) gum. He watches her take money from her pencil case to pay for her bap.

"Micky Mouse?" he says. "Seriously?"

She turns and instantly blushes. Still, she eyeballs him. "What are you, the Disney police?"

He laughs, loving her spunk. "In my spare time."

She's next in line. He has to move fast before she turns and goes. "So, yesterday!" he says, two words that automatically connect them.

Her eyes widen. "I *know*!"

And, just like that, he's in.

Grace, grateful for a morning of back-to-back patients, sees a large number of children (who all get a Disney Band-Aid to take home) and an equally large number of sore throats. There's even a phantom sore throat. Grace is not sure if Dolores Tracy really believes her (non-inflamed) throat to be sore, if she just came for a good gawk at Young Dr. Sullivan or if, perhaps, there is something more sinister worrying her that she is struggling to bring up.

"How are you feeling in general, Dolores?" Grace asks, in case it's the latter.

The lollipop woman starts to fiddle with the clasp of her pink, furry handbag – encouraging Grace to probe further.

"You know what we should do," she says gently. "Give you a general check-up, seeing as you're here. We all look after our cars, giving them the old NCT every year. But we forget ourselves. What do you think?"

Dolores seems to perk up.

Grace starts with the basics, checking her blood pressure, pulse, temperature.

All fine.

"Do you ever check your breasts, Dolores?"

"Indeed I do not," she says like it's a crime.

"Well, why don't I show you how and then you can check yourself once a month."

"I'm getting hot flushes!" Dolores blurts out, anything to save herself the indignity of a breast check. "And I'm sweating something fierce at night. I have to change all my clothes. More than once. And keep moving around in the bed to escape the wet sheets. It's awful."

Grace nods. "Go on."

"Sometimes, I get so moody I could kill small animals. Or big people. Or any people at all actually. Well, except the kids at school. They're safe."

"Dolores, that's all totally normal."

"Oh!" Dolores says, surprised. And encouraged.

"Let's talk through some options." Grace discusses changes that occur during menopause, including the impact that dropping oestrogen can have on the bones and heart. "Have you ever had a bone scan, Dolores?"

"No."

"Right. We'll set one up for you. Any family history of osteoporosis?"

"I don't think so, no."

Dolores's mother died of a heart attack though, so Grace takes blood for cholesterol and general screening. Finally, she prescribes a low-dose HRT patch for Dolores.

"So, you need to apply a new patch every day, anywhere below your waist. Usually anywhere on the bum is fine."

"I'm normally a very nice person," she insists, still dwelling on the mood swings.

"Trust me. The menopause can create monsters, Dolores. Hopefully, you'll see a big improvement with the patch."

"You won't tell a soul!" she blurts out.

"Not a soul. Now, I'm going to give you a month's supply of samples. See how you get on. Come back to me if you've any problems. All going well, I'll see you at the end of the month for a review." Normally, Grace would make an appointment. But she knows what Myra would say to that. "Actually, why don't you put it in your diary now, for just under four weeks. If we're happy with how it's going, you can get your next month's supply in Skibb or Bantry. But let's see how you get on, first."

"Thank you, Doctor. You're lovely. Despite what anyone says."

Grace tries not to think what that might actually be. She smiles professionally, gets to her feet and starts to pull around the curtain. "Now why don't you hop up here on the bench and we'll do that breast exam."

Dolores looks appalled. "What? I thought we wouldn't need to do that now."

Grace tilts her head. "It's a good idea to keep an eye on things, Dolores. Generally speaking. And as I have you here...."

Dolores flaps her hand. "I've taken up enough of your time. Why don't we do it at the next visit?"

"Dolores, I'm sorry but I really should do a breast exam before prescribing HRT."

Her eyes plead to be let off.

"It'll take five minutes. Won't hurt at all. And it's nothing I haven't seen before. At least I'm a woman, right? You haven't had that option till now."

"I wouldn't be here otherwise, Young Dr. Sullivan."

"Good. Come on then, let's do it. You'll be glad afterwards. I promise."

With a sigh and a nod, Dolores gives in.

Dolores gets the all-clear. And looks thrilled. She seems to be about to say something, then stops. Grace spots her hesitation. This might be important.

"Is there anything else you want to tell me, Dolores?"

"I love your hair," Dolores blurts out. "I think it's gorgeous."

Automatically, Grace touches it. "Really? Oh, my goodness. That doubles the number of people who do!"

"No, no. That Jane is a pure artist."

"That's true."

"And look at your nails! They're so *daring*."

Grace splays her hands. "They're a bit mad, aren't they?"

"They're only gorgeous."

"Well, I love your style too, Dolores. The whole shebang. Top to toe." Pink furry top, today, to match the bag. "You take care, now, and call me if you're having any problems whatsoever. There's always a settling in period."

"I will, Young Dr. Sullivan, thank you so much," she says as if a huge weight has been lifted.

As Grace walks her to the door it hits her: *This* is why she chose medicine. *This* is the difference she wants to make in people's lives.

thirty-two

Fred Cronin's blood test results are in. And Grace could cry. His iron levels are through the roof. His liver function tests are elevated. She can't tell how badly damaged his liver is until he has further tests, a biopsy, ultrasound... He needs to see a consultant as a matter of urgency. More than one. A haematologist. And a hepatologist. First, though, Fred needs to see Dr. O'Malley. Grace picks up the phone and tells Myra she needs to speak with her partner urgently. Then she paces the surgery, tapping the chestpiece of her stethoscope into her palm over and over. How can she tell him? How can she look him in the eye and deliver the news that will deem him negligent? He has failed in his duty of care. He should have asked more questions, taken a family history, linked the symptoms, taken bloods (especially after prescribing iron for a man for over a year). He should have started phlebotomy five years ago. But that's easy for her to say. She hasn't been under the pressure he has.

The phone rings and she jumps.

"Go on in," Myra says.

Grace hangs up slowly, then wipes her palms on her trousers. This is her first week and already she's telling her partner where he went wrong.

She knocks on his door, hyperaware of her reputation as having notions.

Dr. O'Malley turns from the computer and smiles. Even behind his glasses, he looks tired and bleary eyed. "Here she is! The village hero!"

She doesn't know if he's genuine or mocking. So, she gets to the point.

"Dr. O'Malley–"

"Tom. Please."

"Tom." She takes a deep breath. "The bloods on Fred Cronin are back. His LFTs and ferritin levels are raised. Markedly so. His profile is pointing to haemochromatosis."

His smile fades. He removes his glasses and looks at Grace for a long time. Then he turns back to the computer, replacing the glasses on his nose. He pulls up Fred's file and checks the blood results, which Grace has inputted.

"Jesus," he whispers, interlocking his fingers at the top of his head. "This is a malpractice case waiting to happen."

"I don't think that Fred... if you explain..."

"You're here a blind day," he snaps, whipping down his hands. "You don't know how people get when there's a sniff of compensation."

She really doesn't see Fred Cronin in that light. "Regardless, we need to get Fred in. Set up consultants' appointments. Line up phlebotomy as soon as possible."

Ignoring her, he picks up the phone. "Myra, get me Des on the line."

Grace goes cold. Is her father complicit? Did he see Fred, too? They divide their patients. But what if Des saw Fred when Dr. O'Malley – Tom – was away? Grace never thought to check.

"Okay, keep trying him," he says into the phone and hangs up. He looks back at Grace.

"Right," he says. "You call Fred in and see him."

She remembers her promise to Jack. "No. I can't lie to the man. If he asks me if this could have been prevented, I'll have to say yes. And that's no good for you; if this comes from me. It has to come from you. With an apology. Otherwise I wouldn't blame him for suing you." Dr. O'Malley's face flashes red. He looks apoplectic. She's going to be booted out of the practice. "Look," she says, as calmly as she can. "Fred's going to work this out for himself as soon as he learns that he has too much iron in his blood. He knows what he was prescribed. He knows that he came to you with symptoms five years ago. Fred's a good man. He deserves honesty. And he deserves the very best of treatment now."

He puts his hands up. "All right, all right." He sighs deeply and picks up the phone. "Myra ask Fred Cronin to come in for his test results."

Grace thinks about Wayne Hill. Now is not the time to bring up about his stitches. Or the forgotten tetanus shot. She hopes that these are flukes, one-off mistakes that will never happen again. And that learning about Fred Cronin will make her partner pick up his game.

The first thing Grace does when she gets back to her surgery is scan Fred Cronin's file to make sure Des hasn't seen him. She scrolls back through five years of records, conscious of the growing number of patients waiting for her outside.

She has to know.

Finally, she gets to the initial consultation, five years ago. And almost collapses in relief. Thank God her father never saw Fred. Had he, though, he would have picked it up. She's sure of it. But then he's human. And so is she. There will be mistakes in the years ahead. By the law of averages. But, *hopefully*, knowing that will keep Grace alert, keep her always looking for that crucial symptom, that unasked question, and always continuing her medical education. Determined, she gets up and calls in her next patient.

Outside the Coffee Cove, Ginge stops.

"I don't know about this."

Jack scoffs. "Are you a man or a mouse?"

"A hundred percent mouse."

Jack laughs. "It looks like I came to Killrowan just in time." He opens the door to the coffee shop, then stops and turns around. "Let me do the talking."

Jack strides up to the counter. Ginge, in his wake, stuffs his hands in his pockets and keeps his head down.

On seeing Jack, Nicky blushes. "Hey, it's the Disney police," she says with her usual sass.

He grins. "So, you're going to give us a freebie, right, Nick?"

"*Nick?*" she asks cynically.

"Short for Nicky," he says as if she's misunderstood.

She fights a smile.

"So, the freebies?"

She shakes her head. "No way. I could get fired."

"*If* they find out."

"It's okay, I'll pay," Ginge says, looking up at last.

Jack widens his eyes at him.

"It's alright, Ginge," Nicky says. Then *she* widens *her* eyes at Jack. "This is a once-off, Sullivan."

He gives her a killer smile. "Thanks, *Nick*."

She eyeballs him. "You're welcome…. *Sully*."

Grace is typing up patient notes when there's a gentle knock on the door. It's so timid, she calls, "Come in."

It's Fred. And he looks crestfallen.

Automatically, she stands. "Oh, Fred. You've been in to Dr. O'Malley?"

He nods, his cap twisted in his great big, practical hands.

She goes to him, touching his arm. "Come in. Sit down."

He nods again and takes a seat.

Grace sits opposite. "Would you like a coffee? I was literally just going to have one."

He shakes his head. "I just wanted to thank you."

Grace touches her heart. This man. "I did nothing." She wishes she were here five years ago.

"No, no. Because of you, I'm on the right path now."

"You have your consultant appointments?"

"I do. I'm going up to Cork tomorrow to meet the haematologist. The hepatologist is next week. And every second week, I'll be giving away some of my blood to the Blood Transfusion Service. Other people can benefit from it. Isn't medicine great in its own way?"

Not for the first time, she wants to hug Fred Cronin.

"Well, I won't keep you," he says, putting his hands on his thighs and pushing himself into a stand.

Ever thoughtful. "I'll walk you out."

As they pass the reception, Fred pauses. "Thanks, Myra." He taps the counter with his hand as if he's going to say something else. Instead he nods to himself and turns to go.

"You know where I am if you need anything, Fred," she says very quickly, as though she has forced herself to say the words.

Fred turns in surprise. "I might call you sometime just for a chat if that's alright?"

"I'd like that," Myra says.

So would Grace. What a rock Myra could be for him. And he for her. Grace crosses her fingers and makes a wish.

At the door of the practice, Grace watches Fred get into his muddy Volkswagen Passat Estate. She raises an arm as he drives off, beyond him sky and sea. Crows and rooks fly up out of the church ruins. And the sun peeks out from behind a great white cloud. While, overhead, the gulls cry, "Yeah, yeah, yeah." What she wouldn't give for a book of seagull translations. She inhales deeply and goes back inside.

Passing reception, a mad urge grips her and she leans in across the counter to Myra.

"When are you going to make an honest man out of Fred Cronin?" she whispers.

Myra chokes on a sneaky bite of chocolate chip cookie.

"He's the most gorgeous man in Killrowan," Grace adds.

Recovering, Myra points out, "You don't know any of the men in Killrowan."

Grace raises a finger. "Maybe not but I know a good one when I see one."

Myra leans forward, her voice and eyes searching. "You don't think he lacks a bit of… gumption?"

"That man has more gumption than, than… I don't know. Anyone."

Frowning, and more searchingly than ever, Myra asks. "Will he be alright, Young Dr. Sullivan?"

Though she knows Myra's concern is genuine, Grace must respect Fred's privacy. "He'll need a few more tests, Myra but the news could have been better," is as much as she can say.

Myra looks towards the door that Fred has just left through as if she wants to go after him, as if she has more to say.

thirty-three

Thursday evening and Grace is so relieved to be home with the family she feels she has barely seen all week. Des, by the fire, is doing the *Southern Star* crossword, calling out clues that unite everyone in brain struggle. Jack is lying at his feet curled up with the dog like he's never heard of a thing called television, or heaven forbid, Netflix. Holly and Grace are side by side on the couch, Holly opening her laptop with great enthusiasm.

"So, I've put loads of stuff in the baskets of lots of good sites."

"Really? Aww."

"So, see what you think of these," she says, clicking into the Abercrombie and Fitch website.

"Oriental warrior. Five letters," Des calls out.

The united mental effort is almost tangible. Then:

"Ninja!" Jack and Holly say together.

Des smiles and writes it in. "Maybe we'll win the twenty-euro voucher yet. We'll go mad."

"What do you think?" Holly asks Grace of the items she has selected for her.

The clothes seem a little young to Grace but she nods. "Good, yeah."

"We can go back to general women's section if you like."

"Okay, let's give it a try."

Holly starts scrolling down through the jeans.

"Ooh, I like those," Grace says, pointing to a pair of faded skinny jeans.

Holly immediately clicks the picture.

"Would anyone like a cup of tea?" Des asks, pushing himself up with the arms of the chair.

"I'll make it," Jack says, getting up.

"You're grand. Stay where you are. I need the exercise."

"I'm actually fine thanks, Dad," Grace says, peering at black skinny jeans.

"Just me, so," Des says. "I'll bring back a few bikkies."

In the kitchen, Des puts on the kettle. He glances out the window at the dark and silent street. A carbon stick for drawing. Eight letters. So, not pencil. Not crayon. Charcoal? The phone rings. Who, Des wonders, could be calling at ten at night? Taking deliberate strides, he makes his way to the big, black ring-dial telephone that's so old it's gone out of fashion and come back in.

He lifts the receiver. "Hello?"

"Des, how are you?" comes the smooth voice of a man he used to trust. A man he used to love really. The son he never had.

Des's stomach contracts and his body tenses with rage. "Don't you Des me," he spits, voice low, glancing at the door to the sitting room. "And don't ever call here again." He slams the receiver down, his heart pounding. How dare he bring his brutality here? How dare he intrude on their peace?

Des is two steps from the phone when it rings again. Turning and reaching for it, he stumbles. He grips the table just in time and reminds himself to breathe. Then he lifts the receiver, kills the line and leaves the phone off the hook. Hands flat on the table he takes a deep breath to try and regain control. His blood really does feel like it is boiling. He'll change his number first thing Monday. In the meantime, the phone will stay off the hook.

"Everything okay in here, Dad?" Grace asks, wandering into the kitchen.

"A carbon stick for drawing. Eight letters," he says to distract her. "Oh, and will you get the biscuits, love, while I make the tea? Kettle's just boiled."

"Sure. Pencil?"

"Eight letters," he says. "You sure you don't want a cup?"

"Actually, yeah, go on."

He smiles.

"So not crayon," she thinks aloud. "Charcoal?"

"That must be it," he says, marvelling at how her thought process matched his.

He places two mugs of tea on a tray and Grace adds a plate of chocolate Digestives.

"Here, let me carry them in," she says.

"Thanks, love."

After the shock he's had, Des reaches for his stick before following his daughter back into the sitting room. Seeing his family, gathered together, with their cheeks rosy from the fire, his heart is broken for what was done to them.

Friday morning, as soon as Grace has left for work and the children for school, Des puts on his jacket and reaches for his walking stick. Benji looks up at him expectantly, tail wagging.

"Alright, so. Come on." He hopes the dog has been trained to heel because he doesn't have a lead and the paths in Killrowan are as thin as paths get.

He sets the alarm and opens the door.

Benji trots out onto the street with his chin in the air, sniffing all the smells of a new day.

"Heel," Des says, in what he hopes is a commanding voice.

Benji moves in right by his heel.

"Good boy!" Des says. "Good *man*!"

Benji looks up to acknowledge the praise.

Down through the village they go. People, seeing man and dog together, smile even wider than usual.

"I heard from Barbara Kelly ye managed to get him away from the graveyard," says Seamus McCarthy, Killrowan's token Kerry man, known for saying, after a few drinks, "I'm a fine catch with a boring name."

"Benji decided himself. Followed my granddaughter home."

"So I heard. So I heard. That's great altogether."

"I better keep going, here, Seamus. Want to give him a decent walk." Truth is, Des has arranged to meet Paddy O'Neill at half past nine and doesn't want to keep him waiting.

There are three more obligatory chat stops along the way but Des manages to reach the station on time. As arranged, Paddy is sitting in the squad car outside, where they can talk in private. Des forgot about that plan when he decided to bring the dog.

"Ah, sure let him come in too," Paddy says, setting his hat on the dashboard. "I'll pull back the front seat and he can sit by your feet."

Luckily the seat goes way back. Benji hops in, then looks expectantly from man to man as if to say, "So, what now?"

Des gets straight to the point. "What's the best form of self-defence out there, Paddy, do you know?"

The policeman looks at him searchingly. "D'you think he'll be trouble?"

"I honestly don't know. He's been leaving a lot of irate messages on Jack's phone. Last night, he rang the house. I just want to be prepared. You know yourself."

"Of course, you do," Paddy says like he's seen it all before. "Was he very hard on her?" is a question between friends.

Des sighs and looks out the window as he thinks about his little girl, his child, bearing the brunt of that man's brutality. "She couldn't tell me in any great detail. And I couldn't push it," he says looking at a car go by on the road outside. The dog rests his chin on Des's lap and looks up at him with soulful eyes. Des rests a hand on his head.

"It doesn't bear thinking about," Paddy says. "From a self-defence point of view, you'll be wanting Krav Maga. A few of the boys have done it, here. Military units all over the world use it as well."

"Self-*defence?*"

"Close combat. Counter assault. In Krav Maga, the attacked becomes the attacker."

"I might have a go of it myself!"

Paddy takes out his phone and his glasses. He starts Googling. After a while, he looks up. "There's a course next weekend in Dublin. Two full days, Saturday and Sunday."

"Dublin." Des is unsure.

"If you want to learn the techniques quickly that's your best bet," Paddy says, scrolling the site. "There are three places left."

Des scratches his head. Then remembers the voice of the charmer invading his home. "Sign me up, there, for the three." Des gets out his credit card. He can always get a refund if Grace and the children are against it.

In minutes, they have three courses booked.

"She'll probably kill me," Des says.

"She will not! I'm sure she'll really appreciate it. She's lucky to have you." The policeman takes his hat from the dashboard and twists it in circles through his hands. "How are you, these days, Des?"

"I'm well, Paddy," he says thoughtfully. "It's great to have the company. Before they came down, I was at a bit of a loss to be honest. Now, the house is alive. And I have a mission. I'm going to make up for not being there when they needed me."

"Ah, now. Don't be so hard on yourself. Weren't you way down here with a busy practice? And weren't they way up there? And… *you didn't know.*"

"No. But if I'd gone up at weekends…."

"He wouldn't have made you welcome. Or he'd have organised for the family to be elsewhere. I know how these men work. You were the port in their storm. They're here now with you, making a home." Paddy glances at the dog. "How are they getting on?"

Des cheers. "I can't get over them, Paddy. After all they've been through, they're great people. Just great. I get prouder of them every day." His voice fills with emotion. "Jack is angry, of course, and worried his father will show up, but he's managing it. Holly is the most determined little thing. She's inspiring. I think they'll be okay, Paddy. As long as that thug stays away."

"And Grace?"

"Is my hero."

Paddy smiles. "How about an auld pint, one of these days?"

"A pint would be grand – maybe when they're up in Dublin at the self-defence." If they go…

"I'll tell you what. Let's pop in to the Coffee Cove for lunch before then."

Des smiles. "It's a date."

thirty-four

Grace is dashing out to the Coffee Cove for a toastie when, passing reception, she realises that she has never seen Myra take a break. She's a permanent fixture at reception like the clock above her head.

"Myra, aren't you taking lunch?"

The receptionist glances at Dr. O'Malley's door and lowers her voice. "I have to stay in case the doctor needs me." She holds up a brown paper bag. "I have a sandwich."

"You're entitled to a lunch break, though. I'll talk to Dr. O'Malley if you like." He's going to love that – Grace rocking the boat again.

But Myra's eyes widen and she holds up her hands. "Oh, no, no. He doesn't ask me to stay. I just… should."

Wrong. "It'd be good to clear your head, though, wouldn't it?" However much she wanted to, Grace herself, couldn't keep going.

Myra looks like she's in pain. "Yeah but if he needed to go out, there'd be no one holding the fort."

"Couldn't he ring you if he's desperate? Anywhere in the village and you'd be back in five minutes."

Myra starts pinging the hairband around her wrist. "What about the patients who'd arrive in? Who'd sign them in?"

It's a novel concept but: "Themselves?"

"Oh, I wouldn't be comfortable," she says, looking… uncomfortable.

Grace is starting to feel like this is one she's not going to win. She's just stressing Myra out. "Okay. Well, you know what to do if you change your mind. Just pop the list up on the counter with a note."

Myra breaths out in relief looking as if the very *thought* of a break would be torture.

Wayne Hill's swab has grown staph aureus, the bacteria most commonly associated with wound infections. This is good news. It means that the antibiotic Grace prescribed on Tuesday has been working away and he won't need to take the ferry across to Killrowan for a new script. Grace could just text him the news. Given his experience of the practice, though, she needs to go one better. A call with the scientific name of the bug might reassure him he's not dealing with amateurs. Anyway, she wants to check how he is managing with the wound care.

He answers after three rings.

"Hello?" he shouts over the sound of the wind.

She should just have texted. "Hi, hi. It's Dr. Sullivan."

"Not Grace?"

She smiles. "Grace. Can you get out of the wind at all? I can hardly hear you." She realises she's shouting herself.

"Sure. Hang on." There's a (wind-filled) pause. Then blissful silence. "Any better?"

"Much." She gives him the staph aureus news.

"Best news I've had all day. *Only* news I've had all day."

She finds herself smiling again. "How are you getting on with the dressings?"

"Good. I'm calling myself Nurse Hill. I don't know what I'll do with myself when it heals. It'll be like not having to make up babies' bottles anymore."

A silence falls as they both remember what happened to that baby, that little boy.

"So. Yeah. Steady as she goes," he rushes to fill the gap. "The swelling has gone down. So has the redness. And it's not as sore."

"That sounds very good alright. Why don't you come back to me this day week and, all going well, I'll remove the sutures."

"Can't wait," he deadpans.

"I'll give you a Disney Band-Aid."

"Can I have two?"

"If you're good!"

He laughs. And she is so, so glad.

"I better go, here."

"Okay, I'll get back to the wind and the bleakness and the solitude."

"Just stay away from barbed wires."

"Mention barbed wires one more time…."

"And?"

"I'll think of something."

Smiling, she hangs up.

thirty-five

Saturday morning, Grace wakes with the rising sun. A sky of pinks and blues calls to her. She hurries into her clothes and down the stairs. Benji jumps to his feet, wagging his tail as if to say, "Wherever you're going, I'm coming too." Grace takes out her phone and googles: "Do border collies like water?" She follows that up with, "Do border collies retrieve?"

"Wow." Not only do they love to do both but they can be trained to rescue people from drowning, even jumping from rescue helicopters to do so. "We are going to Barleycove, my friend!" she tells Benji.

She places an old towel in the back of the Jeep. She looks at Benji wondering if he'll jump or if he needs to be lifted. With a bark of excitement, he leaps right in.

"Good *boy*!"

The drive to the beach, alone, is a treat. So much sky. Inlets of Caribbean blue. Headlands of green with grey, limestone edgings. Tiny fields dotted with black and white cows. Occasional sheep. Windy roads. Soaring birds. All bathed in a pinky glow.

In the deserted carpark, Grace jumps from the Jeep with the energy of a child. Facing the sea, she closes her eyes and inhales the uplifting air of this place. There is something very special about Barleycove. It's food for the soul.

Grace opens the door for Benji, who leaps out, sniffs the air and barks. She half-expects him to bolt for the sea. Instead, he trots obediently by her side as she takes off along the wooden beach path. Feeling a new energy, she breaks into a run. Reaching the pontoon footbridge that crosses the small estuary, Grace slows. She has always loved this bridge, which rises and falls according to the height of the water. Halfway across, she jumps up and down so that it bounces. Benji barks, making her laugh. She feels years fall away.

Over the dunes, pockmarked with rabbit holes, they go. And then it is there in all its glory, her favourite beach in the world. White sand stretching left and right. And the sea coming in between two headlands.

She runs down the dunes to the beach. Benji decides it's a race and takes off, barking. She glances around for a stick for him and has to walk a bit before finding one. She'll have to buy him a ball.

She takes off her shoes and socks and rolls up her jeans.

The water is like ice on her feet. Which just makes her feel alive. Would it be crazy to go for a swim? She didn't bring her togs. The towel is for Benji. And the water is Arctic.

She starts to undress. Swimming was a passion curtailed by the strategic placement of bruises. Her thighs were his favourite. He didn't want her to venture anywhere in a state of semi-undress, especially without him. She could have met and gone off with anyone. (If he actually knew her at all, he wouldn't have worried; the last thing she'd have wanted was to risk life with another man.)

One by one, she drops her clothes onto the sand like a mini-rebellion. The old her would have folded them.

Looking at her thighs, she promises them: "From now on, you'll be two colours only – white or tan. If you go blue, it'll be from the cold."

Down to her underwear, she scans the beach, then the road in the middle distance. For now, they're empty. She thinks of how appalled Simon would be if she stripped naked, then does exactly that and runs into the sea, screaming at the cold. Benji races alongside her, barking and leaping through the water until he is out of his depth when he swims beside her, glancing at her every so often, like a canine bodyguard. Then she is swimming too with great strong strokes, plunging her face into the water and out again. She can't remember when she last felt so alive.

Finally, she has to come out or die.

Opting for dog hair over hypothermia, she swipes up Benji's towel with an apology, shakes off sand and wraps herself in it. Semi-dry, she hurries into her clothes. Raising her fists to the sky, she calls to the horizon, "Go me. Go me. Go me." She laughs.

Benji is looking up at her and barking, then looking at the sea. He wants *more*?

Fully dressed, partially numb, Grace fires the stick out as far as she can. He bounds in after it, jumping waves until he's swimming. He snatches the stick out of the water, turns and comes paddling back to her.

"Where did we get you?" He really does feel like a miracle. She worries that he'll get too cold, though. "Ten times, max," she promises.

Finally, she dries him off with the damp towel. And they sit together staring out to sea. Her teeth are chattering. Her fingers are blue. But Grace is not moving from this spot. Right now, staring at the horizon, she feels so free. Her headaches have gone. Her breath is easy. Her body no longer feels like it's going to snap with tension. Her jaw is relaxed again and she has stopped grinding her teeth at night. Grace is shocked to realise the full effect that Simon has had on her body alone.

Little things about him start to flood her mind. The vigorous way he brushed and flossed his teeth. The way he farted when he woke. The way he peered into *his* illuminated magnifying mirror as he plucked his eyebrows. He chomped. Why is she only realising now how much she hated all those things?

The answer comes easily. When she was with him, it was all about what *she* was doing wrong, how *she* was irritating him. He made her feel lucky to be with him. There were actually times when she believed that she didn't deserve him. Now, she wonders if all his putdowns were a smokescreen to distract her from his own faults. Did he knock her to elevate himself? She'd believe that of him – easily – if he wasn't so in love with himself.

Why is she still thinking about him?

Because she has to figure it all out. Why he did it. Why she stayed. She was a confident person when they met. How did she let him erode that away? It started with looks, looks that began with pregnancy, looks that implied she was no longer attractive, no longer desirable. In public, he cut across her, talked over her, answered for her. At first, she called him on it as soon as they were alone, but his anger was such that it became easier to say nothing, to let things go. She didn't want to distress the baby she was carrying, the baby she was responsible for.

She thought that things would improve once Jack was born. In fact, they got worse. And she was so tired. So shattered, really, that she turned into herself, focusing on her little chubby-cheeked, round-eyed boy – who loved her unconditionally. After that, it became about the children and keeping her husband from exploding. Slowly but surely, the person that Grace was began to slip away.

What she doesn't understand is that he *wanted* kids. And he loved them. Why did her becoming a mother turn him against her? Was he jealous that he had to share her? Just as he had always been jealous of other men. Maybe it wasn't just the pregnancy. Maybe that's just when he ramped things up – when she was at her most vulnerable. Before that? Yes, he had been controlling. But he had never physically hurt her. She'll have to read up on this. Buy books online – not at the local bookshop or library. The main thing is, she needs to know, needs to understand, and maybe someday forgive herself.

Benji nuzzles into her like he senses her pain. He smells like wet dog. Which makes two of them. She kisses the top of his head, treasuring his comforting presence and unconditional love. Her throat burns, remembering her other beloved Benji. Dogs are simply the best.

Finally, aware that Des and the children will be getting up soon, she drags herself away.

Coming out from the carpark, heat blasting, Grace waits for a car to pass. It's a muddy Volkswagen Passat Estate. She raises her hand in greeting. But Fred Cronin doesn't see her, laughing as he is with the person beside him. Wait! Was that *Myra*? Grace slaps the steering wheel with a, "Ha!"

thirty-six

Arriving back in the village, Grace lowers a window for Benji, then nips into the Coffee Cove for scones for Des. The estate agent next door is opening up when she hurries out, armed with confectionary. She glances at the properties in the window, then at the Jeep. She really needs to start looking at what's available. Benji will be okay for a few more minutes.

The door pings as she scoots inside.

An attractive woman in her thirties comes up to the counter and smiles. "How can I help?"

Grace leans on the counter, accidentally sprinkling it with grains of sand. "I'm looking for somewhere to let... three bedrooms," Grace says, working out her priorities as she goes. Here's a big one: "Nowhere too isolated. Ideally, something in the village." Surrounded by people.

"Hmm," the estate agent says, tapping her pen against the counter like this is a big ask. "How soon would you need the property?"

"Well, I have a few weeks yet." Unless the unexpected happens and a maintenance payment comes in.

"Let me take your details in case something comes up. In the meantime, I'll give you a few brochures for the closest properties I have to what you're looking for."

Grace leaves with five brochures, all for homes at least five miles outside the village – and all isolated. She tries to be positive. At least, she has started to look. She breaks off a piece of scone and lobs it back to Benji who snatches it out of the air like a pro.

She arrives home with scones, brochures and a damp and sandy dog. Everyone's at the table having breakfast, the children still in their pyjamas.

"Were you at the beach?" Holly asks. "You should have woken me up!"

"I will next time – now that I have your official permission," Grace smiles.

"Did you actually *swim*?" Jack asks, glancing at her damp hair.

"Yup," she says proudly. "Who's for scones and croissants?"

"Ah, a woman after me own heart," Des says.

She flings the brochures down on the worktop, pours water for Benji, washes her hands and puts the scones out on a plate.

Jack's hand moves at supersonic speed.

Des looks at him fondly.

Grace makes a coffee and joins them at the table.

"Will you make sure I'm up early for Mass tomorrow," Holly says to her, sounding borderline anxious. "I've joined the choir."

Jack laughs.

"Good woman!" Grace says, hiding her surprise. Holly has only ever sung in the shower. And not very often. There wasn't much singing in their house of tension. "Jack are you coming to Mass to hear your sister?"

"I've hurling training," he rushes.

"I thought that was today," Grace says.

"It is – with the school. Club hurling is tomorrow. My coach said to show up."

"You'll probably need a stick."

"It's a hurl, Mum," he corrects her.

Holly laughs. "I thought hurling – and *hurls* – were for culchies."

For once, her brother doesn't have a comeback. Getting up to relieve the fridge of what's left of the Gubeen cheese, Jack spies the brochures. Cheese instantly forgotten he brings them back to the table. While he scours through one, Holly reaches for another. They flick through all five with growing concern. Jack looks up from the last one like his mother has lost her mind.

"We're not staying there!"

"No. We're not," she says calmly. "The estate agent handed me the brochures and I didn't want to be rude."

Jack gives her a look.

She feels like telling him she'll get more assertive. Eventually. "Who's coming to the library with me? Holly?"

Holly pulls a reluctant face. "I think I might try camogie. Aoife and Jenn said it's great craic."

"Now who's the culchie?" springs the comeback king.

"Isn't it great that ye'll be playing the sports of your ancestors?" Des muses, taking a bite of his scone.

Simon would have a fit. Though he married a "culchie," his view of all things rural is derisory at best. It would never occur to him that people in Dublin play Gaelic sports too.

Light filters in through the sashed library windows in shafts, dust motes rising. Old-world bookshelves and herringbone wooden floors remind Grace of happy days she spent here with Yvonne and their beloved stories, words, imaginings. If blindfolded, Grace would know where she was by smell alone.

"Hello stranger," comes a familiar voice.

She turns and smiles at Yvonne. "I should have known one of us would end up working here."

An austere-looking woman sitting at a reading table shushes them with a frown.

"There's one everywhere," Yvonne whispers to Grace.

"I'll have a look around," Grace whispers back. "You free for coffee at any stage?"

"I'll make myself free."

"Brill," the eighteen-year-old Grace says.

She wanders around, pulling out books, browsing, sliding them back, looking for something she can nod off to. She finds herself in the H section. Wayne Hill has three other books!

She takes them all from the shelf and brings them to a table. The last thing she needs is someone to come along and help themselves to one before she can choose.

They all look good. Maybe she'll take all three. She might overdose on Wayne Hill though. It has happened to her with other authors. And she doesn't want to go off him. Hmm. Which one?

Yvonne sits down beside her.

"Ooh! You're reading our local celebrity?" she whispers.

Grace prickles at "celebrity." Annoyed for him. Which is ridiculous. "I read his other one, *For Charlie*. It was amazing, Yvonne." She can hear the emotion in her voice.

"It was good alright."

Good? *Good?* "It was based on *his life*."

"Yeah, I know."

"Didn't it *move* you?" Is she a robot?

"It did, yeah. Clearly it moved you too," she says with meaning.

Grace rolls her eyes, annoyed again.

"Why are you so defensive?" Yvonne asks like she's enjoying herself. "You'd swear you'd written it."

What? "He's a good guy. He's been through hell. That book is better than good, Yvonne."

"Sooooo, when you say he's a good guy, are you telling me you've actually *met* him?" Her eyebrows pop up.

"You mean you hadn't heard?" Grace asks with an edge to her voice.

"News hadn't reached me yet, no." She winks and stands up. "I better go do some work. Come and find me when you're ready and we'll go for that coffee."

The Coffee Cove is packed. Yvonne dives for the only free table.

"Survival of the fittest," she says triumphantly.

"What are you having?" Grace asks.

"A latte and a Rocky Road."

Grace will be remaining loyal to the chocolate chip cookies.

At the counter, she smiles at the pretty dark-haired girl who produced the emergency straws for Matthew. She smiles back like they've connected now. And when Grace pays, she tips her well.

Back at the table, Yvonne looks annoyed. "I heard you and Alan went for drinks without me."

"*What?*"

Yvonne grins. "Just teasing. How is he?"

"Great." And for the record: "He was working on the house for Dad. We went for one then got swamped by people buying me drinks because of what happened with Matthew. I presume *that* news got to you?" She looks at her sideways.

"Oh, it did. And all the gory details." She puts a hand up. "Please don't expand. Just tell me how you met The Celebrity."

"You do realise that he would hate you calling him that."

"*Really?*" she asks, like she's fascinated. "You know him so well."

Grace shakes her head like she's dealing with a hopeless case. Which she is. "He's a patient."

Yvonne stirs her latte, scoops some white from the top and slips it into her mouth. "I don't suppose you'll tell me what's wrong with him?"

Grace laughs. "I took an oath, Yvonne."

Yvonne cuts her Rocky Road into bite-sized pieces. "So touchy." She pops a cube of confectionary into her mouth. "I suppose you'll be going to his book launch, so?"

Grace puts down her coffee. "He's having a book launch?"

"Next week."

He said nothing about a book launch – and they were talking about books. Doesn't he want her to go? Why *should* he invite her, though? She's just his doctor. She doesn't know why she's so… irritated? Hurt, even? She's being ridiculous. Worry and self-doubt creep up her spine, where they love to hang out. Has she been isolated for so long she's forgotten how to deal with people? Is she blowing everything up, taking things too seriously? Is she in fact a little unhinged?

"Did *you* get an invite?" she can't help herself.

"Oh everyone's invited. There are posters going up. I've a stack of them back at the library. Got lumped with the job of putting them up. Wanna help?"

"No." If he didn't invite her, she's not sticking up his bloody posters.

She's not annoyed. She is so not annoyed.

"What's wrong?" Yvonne asks.

"Nothing!"

"You look miffed or something."

"Why would I be miffed?" And who uses the word "miffed" anymore?

"You tell me."

"Yvonne Barry, you haven't changed one bit."

Yvonne sucks her teaspoon and points it at her friend. "Sure, isn't that just as well? I wouldn't want to lose my fabulousness, now, would I?" She grins, renegade chocolate on the corners of her mouth.

Grace gives in to a smile. "Or your self-confidence."

"That'd be a tragedy altogether."

Grace, knowing just how true that statement is, puts a fingertip to the corner of her own mouth and raises her eyebrows.

Her old pal knows what to do. "Thanks, bud."

"You're welcome, bud. Gotta stay classy."

thirty-seven

The children are still out when Grace gets back. Des is standing over Benji, who is lying on the floor looking up at him with total focus.

"Roll over," Des commands.

Benji flips over then looks at Des as if to say, "What else have you got?"

Des tosses him a treat and turns to Grace in amazement. "He knows them all: sit, paw, lie down, heel. Where did she get him, the circus?"

"We'll have to keep him stimulated so he doesn't get bored." She takes off her coat and puts her bag on the table. Then she frowns. "Why is the phone off the hook?"

"What? No reason," Des says – too innocently.

Staring at it, every muscle in Grace's body tenses. "He called, didn't he? Of course, he did!" She should have thought of that, prepared for it. Her mind starts to rewind. "That was him last night, wasn't it? When the phone rang once. Then again." Her arms cross her chest. It's as if he has entered the room and the temperature has dropped.

"Okay, he called. But I hung up. That was it."

"What did he say? What did he want?"

"He didn't get to say anything. I cut him off. I'll change the number first thing Monday."

"So, he said nothing? Nothing at all? Tell me, Dad, I need to know exactly what he said."

Des sighs and wearily takes a seat at the table. "He said, 'Hello Des. How are you?'"

"That's it?"

Des nods.

She joins him at the table, her eyes searching his. "How did he sound?" She hears the craziness in her own voice.

Des's jaw tenses. "Like the snake he is."

She runs her hands through her hair. "D'you think he'll come down? What if he comes down?"

"That chapter of your life is closed, Grace," he says firmly.

She's back pacing. "What if it's not? What if he shows up here?"

"I had an idea. You'll probably think I'm mad." Des tells Grace about the self-defence course. "I just thought it would be good for you all to do – in general – you know, for life. And that."

She bursts into tears.

"I'm sorry; I'll cancel it. I shouldn't have–"

"No, no! I want to do it. And I want the kids to. I just, I just… It's just… I'm not used to people…. I'm not used to… this kind of support." Any kind of support. "That's all." She can't stop crying.

Des goes to her. He places his arms around her shoulders and rests his head on the top of hers. "I'm sorry I wasn't around more."

"No! I should have come down more. I should have stood up to him. Stopped this sooner." She's growing hysterical. Benji comes over to lick her hand. She hardly notices. "I was trying to appease him, prevent the boat from rocking." She bows her head. "I was trying to do the impossible."

"But now you've left. You've made a stand. It's over and I'm so proud of you. Now, let's get you feeling stronger, being stronger, and being able for anything. Invincible."

She nods and takes the pressed and folded handkerchief her father is offering her like he used to do, a very long time ago.

She wipes her face and blows her nose.

"Will you be alright going back up to Dublin?"

Grace looks at him for the longest moment, then the cogs in her mind start to spin, the same cogs that got her out of there, that planned everything, got them free. "What part of Dublin is it?"

"Dublin 8."

"He wouldn't be seen dead there. We'll stay in some cheap hotel nearby, park underground and leave the car there all weekend." She nods, deciding. "It'll be fine."

"That's my girl."

"Thanks Dad. For everything. I know why you put in the alarm by the way and I appreciate it so much," she says, her voice rising as tears threaten again. "I don't know what I'd have done without you."

"You'd have found a way. You were determined. And when you get determined, nothing stops you, Grace Sullivan."

She smiles sadly. That is how she used to be. Maybe, someday, she'll be that way again. For now, this is a start. They are Dublin-bound.

By the time the children get home, Grace has had a shower and removed all evidence of tears. All four of them travel to Drimaleen to buy hurling and camogie gear. On the way home, Grace is restless, Simon on her mind. If he shows up, they can't be at home.

"Who's coming for a walk with me out to Sheep's Head?" she asks cheerfully.

"I'm bate after the hurling," Jack says.

Grace's eyes dart to the rear-view mirror. "You're *what*?"

Jack drops his gaze to his phone.

"He's tired," explains his sister, like the local language expert. "That's what everyone says down here."

Grace knows what bate means; she just never thought she'd hear it from her son.

Holly looks at Jack in glee. "The culchies I mean."

"Holly, what about you?" Grace persists.

She rests her head back. "Bate too. And anyway, Aoife asked me over."

"Is Jenn going too?" Grace asks, not wanting her to be forgotten.

"Of course!" she says with disdain. "You don't think we'd leave her out, do you?"

"Good girl." She shouldn't have doubted Holly – who knows more than most what being left out is like.

Grace cancels the idea of a walk. She needs to be home with Des and Jack in case they have a visitor. She glances at her hands on the steering wheel, at the indent left by her wedding ring. She *has to* stop letting Simon dominate her every thought, her every action. If she lets him, it'll be like she never got away. That's why she got rid of the SIM cards. She should go for a walk herself if she wants to. But when she actually considers it, she admits to herself that she's a bit "bate" too after the early start, the tearing around all day, and the week that she's had. He won't risk breaking the barring order. He won't risk prison. She'll stay home because she wants to stay home. It would be nice to sit in front of the fire with a good book. And she has three Wayne Hills in her possession. She must remember that she has time, now, time to do things for pleasure.

thirty-eight

Half-ten, Sunday, and Grace looks at Holly in surprise. She wants to leave for the church thirty minutes early. Hair straightened, she's wearing her favourite outfit and is heading for the door.

"Mass isn't till eleven," Des points out.

"I need to be there now!" she stresses. "It's okay. I'll go myself."

"No, no. Let's all go," Grace says. This enthusiasm is new and precious. In Dublin, Holly was reluctant to do anything, go anywhere. Not rebelliously so. It was more that she had just accepted that life wasn't going to get any better.

Now, she makes for the door.

"Holly, your coat!"

"Don't need one."

Grace lets it go. They'll be driving right up to the church anyway.

Des, looking smart in his tweed jacket, grabs his blackthorn stick.

Jack was up and out before anyone.

They arrive at the church twenty-five minutes early. The choir is assembling, everyone in their Sunday finest.

Holly shoots off with a quick, "See ye later."

Standing at the back of the church, Grace takes in the scene. It's just as she remembers it, though everything seems smaller: the simple no-frills altar, the stained-glass windows, the mahogany confessional boxes and matching mahogany pews and the army of candles flickering under statues of St Anthony and The Little Flower. She remembers the superficial things she prayed for when she was little and smiles inside at the innocence of them.

She had forgotten just how peaceful churches are, how still and silent and restful. Well, unless there's a choir setting up.

"Let's sit down," Des says.

"The front row's free!" Grace says almost as a joke to herself.

"Surely, you don't want to sit right up there?"

Actually.... "Why not?"

He looks bemused. "All right, so."

No sooner have they seated than the choirmaster shoots over to them, beaming.

"Des, how are you?" she asks.

"Grand, Barbara, thanks."

But she has already switched her attention to Grace. "Great to see you at Mass, Young Dr. Sullivan! I'm Barbara Kelly, the choirmaster." She extends a hand.

Grace shakes it. "Grace."

"Your Holly has a magnificent voice."

"Really? Wow. That's great to hear." Automatically, Grace glances over at the choir. Holly is chatting to a round-faced girl with freckles to her right and a timid-looking girl on her left who could be from Scandinavia with her colouring. It's the first time that Grace has seen Holly with her friends and her heart lifts.

"She and my daughter, Aoife, are great pals." Barbara gives the girls a little wave.

"Oh, you're Aoife's mum?" Glancing over again, Grace sees a resemblance to the girl on Holly's right. Proof though is when she is the only one of the three to roll her eyes instead of waving back.

Des absently taps his walking stick repeatedly against the kneeler.

"Right! I better get back to it," Barbara says as if she is urgently needed.

"Lovely to meet you," Grace says.

"Likewise." Barbara hurries away.

"She seemed nice," Grace whispers.

"Stay well away. And by that, I mean avoid her like the plague. Biggest gossip in Killrowan," Des whispers back.

Grace thought she had met the biggest gossip in Killrowan. She wonders what he thinks of Jacinta Creedon. But, then, asking would make Grace just like her.

The church begins to fill with the sounds of shuffling, mumbling, coughs and whispers as people steadily filter inside. As eleven approaches, there's a hush. Everyone stands when the priest arrives at the altar in all his robes. The sight of Fr Desmond, so old now, jolts Grace back to a time when she would sit at the back of the church with her parents, revelling in the bird's eye view this gave her of everyone, including whatever boy she fancied at the time. How simple life was then. How hopeful.

Behind her, she hears the congregation move. She doesn't know whether they've sat or kneeled and has to glance at Des to see what he's doing. She can't believe she never thought of that when choosing the front. Not only can she not see what everyone else is doing, *they* are seeing her hesitation. It's eighteen years since Grace was at Mass. She married a man who was above religion. Dismissing it elevated him. Grace's lack of belief stems from something entirely different. What God would allow such terrible things to happen? She still has no answer for that. She bows her head. But lifts it again, in case people think she's praying. It's one thing going to Mass to be part of a community. It's another pretending to be religious.

Grace follows her father's lead for the entire service, standing, sitting, kneeling whenever he does. She's surprised by how much of the actual prayer she remembers, though. She doesn't join in because she doesn't believe in it. Until they get to the Our Father – which she has always instinctively loved. She says the words aloud but stops when they reach the section about forgiving our trespasses. She just can't say those words.

She doesn't go up to the altar to receive Holy Communion. But watches those that do. It would be hard not to; they're passing right in front of her. This is the last time she'll sit at the front. If she comes again. Which she probably will. For Holly. And because it's expected of her. In fairness, the singing is lovely.

And here is Holly now, hands joined in prayer, approaching the priest. Grace's heart expands with love and pride. Why, though, is it still so hard to believe that this is real? That they are here. That they got away.

When the service ends, Grace and Des wait outside for Holly. There's a lovely, friendly atmosphere as people mingle, reminding Grace that Mass in Killrowan is so much more than a religious service. It's a gathering of people, a way of keeping in touch for so many, a lifeline for some. From miles around they come, older, single farming men who probably haven't seen a soul all week, island people, families who live out of town. There is a special energy, like a village fair. Humans are sociable; we're meant to mix, Grace thinks. Isolating a person is going against human nature. It really is.

Her gaze is drawn to a couple leaving the church grounds before anyone else. In their thirties, they're dressed as though going to a funeral or business meeting. She is beautiful, blonde and delicate, like Princess Grace of Monaco. He, on the other hand, has a head like a potato with small eyes and a mean mouth.

Yvonne, arriving beside Grace, follows her gaze.

"Jack O'Driscoll, the bank manager, and his wife Mia," she says with distaste. "Always leave immediately. A cut above the rest of us it seems."

But Grace is watching the careful way Mia O'Driscoll holds herself, the brittleness of the air around her, the grip her husband has on her elbow as she smiles encouragingly down at their little girl of around six. Grace sees a different story here. But then she can't let her past colour everything.

"Come on woman," Pat says to Yvonne. "You want to see Ginge play, don't you?"

"I do. I do." Yvonne gives Grace a hug. "I'll call you."

Watching them go, Grace reminds herself that Jack has always hated spectators. Suddenly, she beams. Because Myra and Fred Cronin are coming her way – arms linked! Myra looks so cheery and vibrant. Fred, all dressed up in wax coat, chinos and loafers, looks like he's walking an inch from the ground.

"I see you got the front row, after all!" Fred grins. "Would I doubt you?"

Grace laughs. "I had to fight a few people off but I got there in the end!"

"I'd say it was brutal."

"Oh yeah. Blood everywhere. We managed to clean it up, though, before Mass, luckily enough."

There's a pause of uncertainty.

Then Myra and Fred break into laughter together.

Grace feels like she's coming out of a fog as she is reintroduced to a quirkiness she used to have – before it was reigned in, eroded away and then forgotten. Could it be making a comeback? And is this actually a good thing?!

"I suppose we better get going," Fred says.

Myra looks up into his eyes and smiles like he's the only man in the world. If Grace had come to Mass solely to witness this, she would have been more than happy.

Looks and nudges spread like ripples through the crowd as Myra and Fred make their way out of the church grounds. This must have been Myra's plan – get the news out of the way quickly rather than have people wondering and guessing.

"Still no sign of Holly?" Grace asks Des, conscious that he's been standing around for long enough. "Will I go inside and see where she is?"

Before he can answer, a giant of a man approaches. He takes off his cap and holds it in giant hands. He bows his head.

"Young Dr. Sullivan, Tom Creedon. You saved my son's life this week. We'll be forever grateful. Jacinta is over at the hospital with Matthew. He'll be coming home this week, thanks to you."

"Oh, I'm so glad. Please tell them I said hello."

"I will, surely," he says then replaces his cap, bows again and hurries away.

"Those are the most words I've ever heard out of Tom Creedon's mouth," Des says. "Be prepared for a lot of free meat."

Grace remembers that he's the butcher. And smiles. It may not be perfect but there is something very special about Killrowan.

Then Holly is out!

Before Grace can even tell her how great she was, her daughter is asking, "Can I go to Aoife's? We'll study."

Grace doesn't care that this is an exam year for Holly. Study is not a priority over friendship. Happiness comes before everything.

Sunday afternoon, Grace manages to get the children to agree to a walk – not the long, wild and beautiful trek that is Sheep's Head but the shorter beach stroll that is Barleycove. Benji, and his amazing retrieving skills, get them over the line.

On the beach, there's no actual walking, just standing at the water's edge, throwing. Competitive throwing. With Jack and Holly each trying to outdo the other in getting Benji to swim out furthest.

Grace perches on the rug she's brought, arms around her knees, watching them, her heart expanding with love and hope.

Eventually Benji tires. Then all four of them sit, looking out to sea, Jack dusting sand from his feet in vain. Grace laughs. He has always hated the feeling of sand on his skin.

This is not a moment Grace wants to ruin. But she'll have to ruin *some* moment and the sooner she brings up the self-defence course, the better. It's only five days away.

"These will be really good skills to have – in general," she concludes.

Holly and Jack look at her like they know – exactly – what she means by "in general" i.e. the opposite.

"You think he'll come here, don't you?" Holly asks.

Grace takes a deep breath. "I don't think he'd break the barring order, hon. But we should be prepared for anything, right? We've taken the biggest step. From now on, it's just little steps."

Holly nods. "I'll go."

Jack looks wary. "Is it for girls?"

"No," Grace says adamantly. "Look at the website. Military units all over the world use Krav Maga. And the police."

Jack takes out his phone and starts Googling. "Looks good," is the conclusion he finally reaches.

"So, you'll do it?" asks Grace hopefully.

He frowns. "As long as I don't get selected for the club team and miss a match."

"You are *officially* becoming a culchie," Holly says, like she's welcoming him to an exclusive club.

Grace puts an arm around each of them and pulls them to her.

thirty-nine

Des leafs through the estate agent brochures. None of the properties is anything like the home they have left. Most, however, are better than his place. How did he ever let it get so dated, *so jaded*? The house in Dublin would lift your soul. The ceilings were high, windows enormous, everything modern, open plan. Well, there's nothing Des can do about his ceilings. The same goes for the windows. No room can be made bigger. But he'll work on what he can. Grace's walls were white, her floors wooden. She had cream blinds instead of curtains. There were paintings, everywhere. Des knows nothing about art. The bathrooms were pure luxury with those fancy power shower things. Well, he can get a new bathroom, white, of course. The wallpaper can be painted over, he's sure. Wooden floors can be put down, blinds put up.

Des looks around his modest little home, glad of the money he put into pensions (plural) when the government introduced tax incentives to encourage people to save for retirement. He takes out his phone and calls Alan.

Fifteen minutes later, the very man is having a look around.

"No problem," he says. As expected. "I'll get some of the lads in and we'll turn the place around. We'll give it a complete makeover. You won't know the place. All that'll be missing is the TV cameras."

Des laughs at the thought.

Alan glances around the kitchen like something's bothering him.

"If you don't mind a suggestion, Des?"

"Fire ahead."

"Would you think of giving the kitchen cupboards a lick of paint and changing the handles? It'd make all the difference. I'm thinking of a lovely warm cream colour that would tie in with the white walls and wooden floors."

Anything has got to be better than the way the kitchen is now. "Sounds good."

Alan smiles like Michelangelo getting the go-ahead for the Sistine chapel. "Ah, great. Honestly, you won't know the place."

"There's one thing I don't want touched," Des says. He walks Alan to the kitchen doorframe where tiny pen marks of various colours and lengths record Grace's journey from child to adult.

"Ah, Lord," Alan says. "Of course."

"You know yourself," Des says then realises that Alan doesn't know himself. "I mean–" he says, flustered.

Alan smiles calmly. "So, when were you thinking of getting started?"

Des grimaces. "That's the catch. I need it all done over a weekend. Next weekend."

"The *whole lot*?" For once, Alan looks like he may have a problem.

"Or as much as you can. Definitely the bathroom. And the floors. And the walls...."

Alan tilts his head. "I don't know, Des. It'd be very tight. But you know I'll do my very best. I'll get as many of the boys in as I can. They'll be delighted with the work. What time would we be able to kick off?"

"Well, this is a surprise for Grace and the children. They're leaving for Dublin on Friday when Grace finishes at the clinic. And they'll be back no earlier than midnight Sunday."

Alan starts to think aloud. "Well, if we order everything right away, get them delivered to my place by Friday and have the boys ready to go, maybe...."

Alan takes off his cap and scratches his head. "Give me a call the minute they leave on Friday and we'll come straight over and get cracking on the bathroom. We'll work flat out. Through the night if we have to. First thing Saturday, we'll start on the floors. Then we'll paint like mad, walls upstairs and down, kitchen cupboards. Then we'll get the blinds up. We could do it. If we're lucky."

"Sorry for the short notice."

"Not at all. Sure, this is right up my street. I love a good makeover. Honestly, Des. You won't know yourself. It'll feel a lot bigger and brighter with all the walls white and the floorboards down," he says like he can see it all. "Right so, have you got time now to pick everything out – floors, blinds, bathroom, fittings, paint colour?"

"Well, the paint is white. So that's that."

Alan laughs like he's hilarious. "D'you know how many shades of white there are?"

"Then I'll leave the paint to you. Knock yourself out."

"Ah, sure I know the one I want already. It's a beautiful shade. The bathroom and the floors are the big things. Let's start with them." He pulls out his iPad.

Des wonders if he has bitten off more than he can chew. "Let me put on the kettle."

As soon as Alan has gone, Des tackles his next challenge – to find a B&B owner who'll take a dog. He does know one dog lover but he hasn't seen MaryAnn Randall for a very long time. And, given their history, he can't just pick up the phone.

He hasn't driven for two weeks. And is hesitant now. He knows that, at some point, the Parkinson's will stop him driving altogether. Well, that point hasn't come yet. He can't let his confidence slip.

He reaches for his stick, then changes his mind and leaves it behind. He sets the house alarm and locks up.

The minute he sits into the car, he wonders what he was worried about. He indicates, checks his rear-view mirror and pulls out. So glad to be back in the driving seat. Out along the coast road he goes, past the graveyard and almost to the next pier along. Seeing the B&B sign, he slows. He doesn't want to be presumptuous and park in MaryAnn's drive but there is only one other car there and plenty of room – as opposed to the narrow road outside. Slowly, he turns in.

For a moment, he sits in the car, admiring the pretty and manicured garden. In the porch, windchimes and stained-glass art sway gently in the sea breeze, chiming every so often.

Getting out of the car, Des reminds himself to straighten up and *stride*.

Maybe this is too much, he thinks, calling to her door out of the blue. Maybe he should have phoned, after all. But, then, what if she has seen him pull in? He can't back out now like some kind of fool.

He's raising his hand to ring the bell when the door opens. Des smiles automatically. She always did go mad with the hair. This time, she has a streak of bright blue at the front. He feels a fondness for her and her unique way of looking at the world.

"How are you, MaryAnn?"

"I'm well, Des, thanks," she says, like she's wondering what he's doing on her doorstep.

"I was just wondering if you might have a room available, next weekend? I'm doing some renovations on the house."

"Come on in out of the cold." She stands back and opens the door wide.

The smell of baking wafts out on warm air like a welcome.

Des holds the doorframe as he steps up. All he needs now is to fall.

MaryAnn closes the door, then leads the way down the hall, moving like the girl he knew and loved at seventeen. Des remembers how it felt to hold her hand – like he was floating. The strength of the memory hijacks him. He reminds himself that was a lifetime ago.

The house is warm and cosy. In so many ways. Des wonders if he's making a mistake, getting rid of the carpets. Maybe he should just get new beige ones like these. And her wallpaper is lovely. He never thought of that – wallpaper with modern designs. But then that would probably take ages to put up. He imagines Alan ordering everything right now. He'll leave well enough alone. It'll be tight enough, as it is, to get it all done.

MaryAnn shows him into her sitting room. The view! How peaceful it would be to sit and look out at the sea every day. MaryAnn always did seek out calm. Well, good for her.

They sit opposite each other and she smiles.

The years have been kind to her, Des thinks. But then they are always kind to fun-loving people, he has noticed. MaryAnn was always quick to laugh. And even quicker to laugh things off. She was his first love. Is that why she is etched, clear as a fingerprint, on his mind?

"You'll have a cup of tea?" she asks. "I've just taken scones out of the oven."

"I'd never turn down a scone, MaryAnn."

She smiles. "Back in a sec."

There she goes again, flying around like a teenager, Des thinks. He's glad he didn't bring the stick.

Des glances at the photos of MaryAnn's family on the mantlepiece, like a record of time passing. He wonders vaguely about the alternative life he might have had if they'd stayed together. Not that he has any regrets. He's just mildly curious. Her hair was pink when he went off to college – when no one in Ireland was dyeing their hair – any colour. They kept in touch by letter. And there were some gorgeous letters that first year. But Des found it harder and harder to write back. College was like a different world. A different universe. It seemed like he had left village life far behind. There was no toing and froing to home all those years ago. He was up in Cork on scholarship and he had to knuckle down or he'd be out. And there were the girls, the smart, funny, witty girls that he let himself get distracted by. By the time he got home to set up in practice, he was already engaged. MaryAnn was married.

She returns, now, with a tray of tea and scones.

"Where did life go?" Des thinks aloud. "How are we here, already?"

MaryAnn just smiles and sets down the tray and starts to unload it.

Why did he say that? He sounded so *old*. So washed up. He'll stick to business. "So, d'you think you can fit me in next weekend?" he asks, awkwardly.

She bites her lip and tilts her head. "I'll have to check, Des. I have a group of stamp collectors coming down from Kinnegad."

"Stamp collectors!" He's also fascinated. "What would be bringing stamp collectors to Killrowan?"

Her laugh is as loud and carefree as ever. "Nothing at all. I was just pulling your leg. I won't have a sinner here, next weekend.

After September, apart from the odd fluke, things get very quiet. I'd be delighted to have you, Des. You know that."

"I don't suppose you still love dogs?" He grimaces. "I was hoping to bring a companion."

"What breed?"

"Border collie," Des says, unable to read her expression.

"Ah, lovely."

"Benji's his name. Couldn't be better behaved."

"Not Sheila Crowley's Benji who never left her side?"

Des nods. "Followed my granddaughter, Holly, home one day."

MaryAnn looks confused. Des remembers how she was never one for gossip – and has never attended his practice.

"My daughter, Grace, has moved to Killrowan with her kids," he explains. "They're staying with me at the moment."

"Oh, so will they need rooms too, this weekend?"

"No, thanks, MaryAnn. They'll be away."

MaryAnn nods. "Well, I'll be delighted to have you and Benji. We're old pals, Benji and I. I was very fond of Sheila. You didn't bring him along to see me?"

"He's over in Barleycove with Grace and the kids."

"They'll never get him out of the water!" MaryAnn smiles. "Well, he's welcome, here, anytime."

"Ah, that's great, MaryAnn, thank you." When she'd mentioned the stamp collectors, Des had wondered where else would take a dog. "You're a star."

"I'm glad you haven't forgotten," she jokes.

Being here with her, he realises that there's a lot he hasn't forgotten.

forty

On Monday morning, Myra looks different. There's a colour in her cheeks that Grace is heartened to see.

"Young Dr. Sullivan–"

"Myra," Grace interrupts. "When are you going to start calling me Grace?"

The receptionist looks like she's developed a sudden toothache. "I'm just a bit set in my ways, Young Dr. Sullivan. I wouldn't be comfortable."

"How about leaving it at Dr. Sullivan then? Do we really need the 'Young'?"

"Well to distinguish…"

Grace gives up. "Sorry, did you want to ask me something, Myra?"

"Young Dr. Sullivan," she says like she's starting into a prepared speech. "Do you think I might have every second Friday off, only I have to go up to Cork for… something."

Grace wants to hug her. She's going up with Fred for his treatments.

"I haven't been taking holidays, you see," Myra continues, wrapping her pearl necklace around her finger.

"Myra, you're entitled to holidays."

"I know but Dr. O'Malley is used to me being around. He relies on me, like. So do the patients."

"Every second Friday is no problem whatsoever," Grace says. She has no idea who she'll get to fill in but there must be *someone* looking for work in rural Ireland.

"And you'll tell Dr. O'Malley?" Myra confirms, glancing at his door, as though she hates to disappoint him.

"I will, of course. I'm sure he won't have any problem with it."

"But he might."

"Then I'll just remind him of all the backpay you must be due for not taking holidays," she says simply.

Myra leans back, releasing her grip on the pearls. "I used to think you were a pussycat, Young Dr. Sullivan. But you're no pussycat."

"You're right. I'm a tiger!" Grace growls and scratches the air with imaginary claws.

After a disconcerted pause, Myra breaks into laughter. "I got you all wrong, Young Dr. Sullivan."

The thing is, Grace *is* a pussycat or at least she knows a man who thinks she is. Well, that man is gone. She can go tiger – sometimes.

"So, would you like this Friday off, Myra?"

"I would, please, if that's alright."

"Of course." Who'll Grace find by Friday though? She doesn't know anyone in the village. Except Yvonne who has a job. And Alan…. Hmm. Would her old pal do her a favour until she finds someone more permanent?

As soon as she gets to her desk, Grace calls Alan.

"Hello, cupcake!" he says.

"Hello, lambchops."

"Lambchops? Is that actually a compliment?"

Grace laughs. "It is if you like lamb." Then her smile fades. She twirls the wire on the phone. "So. How busy are you these days?"

"Why?"

So Cork – answering a question with a question. "I might have a tiny job for you if you're up for it."

"Shoot."

She shoots, fully expecting him to say no. "It'd be just every second Friday."

There's a pause. She shouldn't have asked. He's insulted.

"I'd love that. Welcoming everyone in, putting their minds at ease."

There's a lot more to it than that. Grace should warn him. "It's busy enough."

"Busy is good. Things have been quiet." There's a pause. "But then, something always comes along when I'm on the verge of starvation," he says cheerfully.

She's still cautious for him. "Would you like to chat to Myra, see what's involved, then decide?"

"Okay but I can't see myself changing my mind."

"Great! I'll put you through to her now. Call me back and let me know."

"Will do. Thanks, sweet pea."

"Don't mention it, sugar puff."

Smiling, Grace puts him through.

While Myra and Alan talk, Grace figures out how to break the news to Dr. O'Malley. Tom.

Minutes later, she's knocking on his door.

"Enter!" he calls.

Grace assumes he's joking. And "enters."

"Ah, Grace," he says peering at her over his glasses.

"Tom. Myra's going to be taking every second Friday off until her holidays are used up. Alan Wolfe will stand in for her." Best, she felt, to deliver the news as a fait accompli. "Myra has a huge backlog of holidays due."

"Right so," he says simply. "She'd better show him the ropes."

"That's all arranged."

He looks thoughtful. "It'll be nice to have a man around the place."

Clearly Grace won't be passing that comment along to Myra.

forty-one

When Grace gets to the surgery on Friday morning, Alan is already installed. Dressed in a crisp, blue shirt, open at the neck, he looks like a newsreader. She imagines him in boxer shorts from the waist down.

"Dr. Sullivan!" he greets her cheerfully.

"If you're going to go all formal on me you better make it *Young* Dr. Sullivan."

An eyebrow lifts. "I'm not calling someone older than me by three months *young*."

"I can tell you're going to be trouble, Wolfe. Thank God for that." It's so lovely to have him here, Grace thinks, handing him his chocolate chip cookie.

"What's this?" he asks excitedly.

"A surprise. Are there many inside?"

"A good few," he says clicking into business mode and sliding the list through the cubby hole. "I've put Dr. S. beside the ones for you. I know it's all up on the computer but Myra said you like a physical list when you get in." He sneaks a look into the brown paper bag and touches his heart. "Awww."

Grace looks up from all the Dr. S's. "I'd have preferred silver stars."

"Don't tempt me. You know the special affection I have for stars."

"How could I forget?" Grace feels like he has always been there.

"Actually, I was thinking," he says, seriously now. "I'd love to give everyone a little present, you know, something small, to cheer them up because they're not well."

She eyes him incredulously.

He puts his hands up. "Out of my own money."

"Are you mad? Have you seen how many people we get a day? You'd be broke."

He looks confident. "I'll think of something."

"How about air?"

He smiles.

She points the rolled-up list at him. "You're too nice, Wolfe. That's your problem."

"The world needs nice."

That she will not argue with. She winks at him, "See ya later, alligator."

She can't think of a better stand-in for Myra.

The first patient on the list is Mia O'Driscoll, the bank manager's wife. When Grace calls her, the delicate-looking young woman lowers her eyes as she stands, then moves like she's afraid of disturbing the air. Grace notices that she's wearing a polo neck, covered by a scarf. A knot starts in her stomach. She tells herself that people are allowed to wear polo necks without it meaning anything.

In the surgery, Mia waits to be asked to sit. When she does, it's almost apologetic. She removes her coat but not the scarf.

Grace smiles encouragingly. "How can I help, Mia?"

"I've done something to my ear," she says, looking into her lap.

Grace remembers all the times she sat in her GP's surgery, blaming herself for something her husband did using those exact words: "I've done something to…" Fill in the blank as required. These words should be sent to every doctor in the country with a red flag warning.

"My right ear," Mia clarifies, this time meeting Grace's gaze.

"So, when you say you've 'done something'….?" Grace's voice rises in a question.

Her eyes lower immediately. "Oh. I tripped and fell against the corner of the table."

An excuse Grace herself has used. "You'll need to take off the scarf, Mia."

Slowly, carefully, as though every little movement hurts, Mia unwinds it.

Grace tries to stay impassive in the face of too many pieces fitting together. "When did this happen?"

"Last night."

That would be right. Kids in bed. No one around to disturb him. The knot in Grace's stomach tightens. "What are your symptoms, Mia?" she asks lightly.

Mia makes eye contact. "Pain. There was watery fluid on my pillow this morning with tiny bits of blood. And when I blow my nose, it's as if air is coming out my ear."

Grace nods. She takes her otoscope from its unit on the wall and applies a fresh cover.

"I'll just have a little look," she says, though she knows what this is.

Lifting Mia's hair, she pauses at the sight of a large black bruise behind her ear. Grace's heart breaks for this sweet and timid woman. She wants to take a picture, record the evidence but that would just send Mia running for the hills. She has to tread carefully.

She rests her hand gently on Mia's shoulder as she inserts the otoscope. Mia immediately flinches. Grace lifts her hand like the shoulder is on fire – which it probably is.

"I'm sorry. Did I hurt you?"

"No, no! It's okay!" Her whole body is rigid.

Rage rushes through Grace, rage at a man with a potato head. She tries to control her shaking hands. And focus on how she can help. She asks herself what her own doctor might have done differently all those times she visited. What could he have done that might have encouraged her to speak up? Grace would have needed two things: an absolute reassurance of confidentiality and a guarantee that nothing would happen without her say so.

"Did you hurt your shoulder too?" she asks.

"I must have," Mia mumbles. "But I'm not worried about that. Just the ear."

Grace nods, somehow managing to keep in all that she wants to say. She inserts the otoscope.

No surprises. That respectable pillar of society (she can think of other names) has punctured his wife's eardrum.

"Let's check that shoulder."

"It's fine! Honestly!" Mia recoils, eyes wide, like a startled animal.

Grace immediately backs down, returning the control to Mia.

Returning to her seat, Grace faces her patient. "So. You have a perforated eardrum," she says rather than: "You have perforated your eardrum." Because she's not going along with the lie.

Mia looks alarmed.

"It sounds worse than it is," Grace says gently. "The eardrum usually heals itself, though it can take up to three months. I'm going to prescribe antibiotics to prevent infection entering the middle ear. You'll need to avoid further trauma." Grace pauses, looking right into Mia's eyes willing her to speak up, end this.

Once again, Mia drops her gaze.

So, Grace continues. "You'll have to keep the ear dry. No swimming. A fully waterproof shower cap in the shower. Don't put anything into your ear whatsoever. You can take Panadol or Nurofen for the pain. Stay away from Nurofen Plus. It has codeine." It occurs to Grace that she hasn't needed to buy another pack since giving her last one to Wayne Hill. One small victory. Which won't help Mia.

"So, I'll be okay?" she asks now breaking Grace's heart.

"Your ear should heal up fine. But if you have any problems do come back to me."

"Thanks, Doctor," she says, putting the strap of her handbag over her left shoulder.

"Mia?"

"Yes?" she looks at Grace for an unguarded second.

"I just want to reassure you that this is a safe space. Anything discussed here is completely confidential."

The same look of alarm flashes across Mia's face.

"Is everything okay at home?"

"I don't know what you mean!" She shoots to her feet.

Grace stays seated.

Mia is too polite to leave.

"Sit for a moment," Grace says kindly.

Mia sits at the edge of the chair, like she's about to bolt.

"How is your little girl?" Grace asks with meaning.

Mia looks at her for the longest time, her face so sad, so guilty. She seems to be faltering.

For your little girl, for your little girl, Grace wills her.

But then Mia's eyes lower and Grace knows she's lost her.

"She's fine," Mia mumbles.

"Mia look at me," Grace says gently.

Slowly, she raises pleading eyes. Grace can't tell if they're pleading her to back off or push harder to get her to speak up.

Grace leans in. "I want you to know that I'm here for you. You mightn't want to talk now. And I understand that. Trust me. I do. But you can call me at any time. Anytime." She hesitates before picking up a pen and writing down her mobile number on a post-it pad. "This is my private number." She tears off the sheet and hands it to Mia. "Please don't share it. I don't normally give it out."

Mia nods. Holding the note in two trembling hands, she looks at the number, then up at Grace again as if she still might do it, detonate that grenade in her life. Then she shakes her head as if to herself, snaps her bag open and shoves the little yellow square of paper inside. And the moment is gone. With a "Thanks, Doctor," she shoots from the room with her head down.

Grace can't sit still. She paces the surgery, gripping her head. She has failed Mia. That thug will carry on hurting her, controlling her, weakening her, punishing her, ruling her... *owning* her. What if he goes too far? Grace inhales deeply, then exhales slowly, reminding herself that no one would have made her leave, either. The decision – a huge one – had to come from her. It will be the same for Mia. Grace has told her where to come. At least, in her mind, there is a starting place, a refuge – if she chooses it. Now, Grace must do all she can to get ready for a day she hopes will come, the day Mia O'Driscoll decides, "Enough!"

Grace's medical records were crucial in fighting her case. In fact, they could have been so much more helpful. The most valuable thing Grace can do for Mia is document this consultation meticulously.

At her desk, Grace records the time of the appointment and the time of the injury. She documents not just the diagnosis, but the bruising behind Mia's ear and the tenderness of her shoulder. She wishes she had been able to take a photograph. But she had weighted up the risk and made a choice. She doesn't regret it.

She notes the demeanour of the patient – fearful, protective, defensive. Then she scans Mia's file for other signs of domestic violence. And finds them. More so-called falls. Persistent headaches. A broken wrist. She has no doubt that she will be recording further injuries if Mia doesn't do something to stop this.

Afraid of what she'll find, Grace goes through Mia's daughter's file, a six-year-old girl called Faith. With each consultation, she grows a little more hopeful. Until she finally collapses back in her chair in relief. There is no evidence of anything other than normal childhood ailments.

Grace runs her hands up and down her face. Should she have a word with Paddy O'Neill? Not without breaking Mia's confidence. And what could he do anyway as long as Mia denies it – just put her in more danger? Maybe Grace should talk to her father. Mia was his patient. Did he suspect anything? Do anything? But then what could he do? And what can Grace do beyond what she has already done? How can she save someone who doesn't want to be saved? And what right does she have to interfere?

forty-two

Feeling shaken and too close to her past, Grace has only one option, to keep going, keep her mind on work. She hopes that the next patient has something simple. A sore throat. Skin condition. Pregnancy. She checks the list and closes her eyes in relief. Wayne Hill. Removal of sutures.

When she calls him in, his smile is wide. No grimace, now, when he stands.

"How are you?" Grace asks as she leads him across the hall.

"Cautiously optimistic."

She smiles.

Entering the surgery, Wayne Hill glances at the bench like he's facing his nemesis.

"Think of the Band-Aids," she says and starts to pull the curtain across.

"You should have been a motivational speaker." He ducks behind the curtain.

Grace sets up a dressing tray and sterile gloves.

The sound of rustling stops. "Ready!" he calls.

"Gosh. You're very chipper." Chipper is just what Grace needs. She pushes the trolley through the gap in the curtain.

"It's the Band-Aids – plural – in case you forget."

She tries not to smile. "You *do* know that those Band-Aids are conditional on good behaviour."

"Oh, they'll be mine."

"Folding back the blanket will help your case," she says, gloved hands in the air.

He does as asked. And, despite the jocular mood, looks just as mortified as the first time.

"I have to ask you to open your legs."

"Of course. Sorry."

"Great, thanks," she says in her professional doctor voice, equally mortified – and mortified that she's mortified – so more mortified. Luckily, he's now looking up at the ceiling.

She removes the dressing, noticing that his fists are clenched.

"Oh. That's healing up very nicely. Good job, Nurse Hill."

He looks at her and smiles. "All in a day's work."

"Right, I'm going in. As they say."

"Who? The CIA? A SWAT team?" he jokes but braces himself, his hands gripping the edges of the bench.

But the hydrogen peroxide has done a great job of cleaning up the wound and sloughing away any debris that might have made suture removal tricky. The stitches slide out easily.

"That's it," Grace says, whipping off the gloves.

"Seriously? They're out?"

"You're a free man."

"Excellent." He replaces the blanket.

"I'll let you get dressed."

Grace clears away the dressing and gloves, wipes down the trolley and washes her hands.

From behind the curtain, he says, "I think I deserve some sort of honorary nurse's badge or something."

"I'll write out a certificate."

His laughter sounds like colour. Then the curtain is being whisked back. "I'll take my Band-Aids now."

She squints at him. "I'm *considering* giving you an extra one. For good behaviour."

"Can I pick the characters?"

She laughs. "You can pick the characters."

"You better have Bambi."

Until now, she thought he was joking. "I have no idea who's in there. Have a look." She gestures to the packet on her desk.

He goes straight for it. He empties the packet, roots through the Band-Aids, frowning in concentration. Finally, with a triumphant look, he holds up three. They are different images of Dory from *Finding Nemo*. "The inventor of 'Keep on swimming.'"

That's *her* motto. Her credo. "Dory is my hero!"

"Me too!"

"Those words have got me through the darkest times," she thinks aloud, her mood darkening as she remembers.

His eyes search hers as if he'd like to hear about those times.

"You never invited me to your book launch!"

He looks thrown. Which was the plan. But now he probably thinks she likes him or something. Why did she open her big mouth?

"Have you ever *been* to a book launch?" he asks.

"No. But I was just joking."

"Okay, good. Because watching paint dry would be more entertaining."

Still. Doesn't he want her to go?

"It'll just be people – mostly me – talking about the book. I'll probably have to read from it," he says like he'd rather have a lobotomy.

"Then why do it?"

"The bookshop owner, Jenny Mallin, is keen to sell a few books. Things get quiet for her in wintertime. This will get people back into the shop. Let me give you a copy of the book. Save you the pain."

He *sounds* genuine. "No, no. I'll buy the book." Feels only right after getting three from the library.

"I'd like to gift you one. For saving my life."

She smiles. "Hardly your life."

"My crown jewels are my life."

Grace bursts out laughing. "Crown jewels? What age are you?"

"Eighteen. Inside." He looks at the door. "Okay, I better get out of your hair."

"Are there many waiting?" she asks, though she could just check the list.

"Full house. And all saying good things about Young Dr. Sullivan – in case you care."

"Don't tell me that. I'll just feel pressure."

He lifts the strap of his satchel over his head. "So, this is it, Doc. Our relationship is officially over."

"As long as you stay healthy."

He grins. "I'll have to get sick so."

If Wayne Hill was anyone else this might feel like flirting. Grace knows from the book that, just like her, the last thing he wants is another relationship. Like her, all he wants is peace.

"As your doctor, I can't condone that," she says.

He grimaces. "Are you telling me I'll have to invite you to a boring book launch, then?"

"No, no. Don't invite me. Let me gatecrash it. We need *some* excitement in Killrowan."

He smiles. "Deal. But don't say I didn't warn you."

forty-three

Grace has no problem persuading Alan to take a lunchbreak. They leave a sheet of paper on the counter with a short note asking patients to sign themselves in. Then they wander down to the Coffee Cove, Grace inhaling the briny air deep into her lungs like an elixir. She circles her shoulders and gazes at the sea until it disappears behind the village.

The staff in the Coffee Cove always look a little scared to see Grace. She feels the same, as if at any minute someone's going to choke, just for her.

She knows it's not healthy to order coffee and a chocolate chip cookie for lunch and that it's not exactly the example she should be setting. She's feeling increasingly rebellious with every day she is away from Dublin.

They've just sat down when Alan bringing his huge bap up to his mouth mutters under his breath. "Brace yourself. Here comes Seamus McCarthy."

"Who?" Grace whispers, eyeing a tall, lanky man with a face like a horse, coming their way.

"Hot Kerry man with a boring name. His description. Not mine."

The hot Kerry man arrives at the table. "Alan Wolfe!" he exclaims. "Great to see you out with a woman."

Grace prickles.

But Alan's unruffled. "Wait, what's a woman again?" He scratches his hair for effect.

Seamus chuckles. "'Tis quicker you're getting, Wolfy. So, do I get an intro?" he says, looking at Grace.

"Seamus McCarthy, *Young* Dr. Sullivan, my boss. Young Dr. Sullivan, Seamus McCarthy."

Grace gives the hot Kerry man an icy nod.

"Ah, I can see ye're busy," Seamus says and slopes away, all six foot four of him.

"You put the run on him," Alan exclaims.

"He's unbelievable," Grace whispers crossly.

"Ah, 'tis just a little bit of harmless slagging. We're always at it, the two of us."

"You're very forgiving."

"I give as good as I get. Want to know my name for him?"

Grace nods.

"Fifty Shades of Seamus!"

She laughs out loud. "So, he's a player?"

"He likes people to think he is. But actually, he's harmless. He has a lovely daughter who keeps him on the straight and narrow. So!" Alan says, rubbing his hands together. "I've thought of a present I could give everyone that won't cost me a penny."

Grace can't help but smile. He looks like an enthusiastic puppy.

"Pebbles from the beach!" he says in a ta-da tone.

That's *it*? "Couldn't people just get them themselves if they wanted to?"

"They wouldn't think of it. That's the brilliance of the idea."

Grace thinks of him down on the beaches everyday gathering pebbles. "Better watch out for the environmentalists. That's all I can say." She shrugs.

Alan holds his chin and looks up, as if for a solution. "I'll just find them on the road, then," he says, simply.

"Road stones? There'd be a big run on them alright, I'd say," she says as if it's the worst idea she's ever heard. It's definitely up there.

He scratches an eyebrow. Then his face brightens again. "I'll paint them!"

She smiles in disbelief. "You're actually serious about this?"

"I am, yeah." He bites his lip. "What'll I paint on them?"

"Rainbows. Stars. Flowers. Little whirlwinds…" Grace starts to get into it.

"Can't be going for the rainbows."

"Oh. Right. I hadn't thought of that." She finishes her coffee and dusts crumbs from the corner of her mouth. "So, what are you up to for the weekend?"

"I've a date with a house."

"Meaning?"

"Big D.I.Y. job. Should be good." Alan has a glint in his eye. He has always loved his interiors.

"You'll have to let me know how it goes," she says with genuine interest.

"Don't worry. You'll be the first to know."

Returning to the surgery, Grace and Alan find that the system has worked seamlessly. While Alan inputs the names into the computer, Grace goes to call her first patient. She is sorry to see that Dolores Tracy is back already. She was hoping that the HRT would be a success. But then, Dolores has a medical card and won't have to pay. Maybe she's just coming for reassurance.

Crossing to the waiting room, the first thing Grace notices is a surprising lack of flamboyance. Dolores is wearing navy. No bright colours whatsoever. And nothing fluffy or feathered.

"Everything okay, Dolores?" she asks sympathetically as soon as the lollipop woman has seated in the surgery.

She shakes her head wildly. "'Tis worse off I am. I'm bloating something fierce. My tummy, even my... you know..." She gestures to her breasts, which do, indeed, look bloated. "They're... tender... as well. In all honesty, they feel like they're going to explode."

"We can't have that."

"And look at the state of my *ankles*. The courage it took to even get here."

Grace nods sympathetically. "Anything else?"

"I feel sick in my tummy." She rests a hand on it. And burps.

"It's definitely not agreeing with you."

"You can say that again. And all the hopes I had for it." She shakes her head tragically.

Grace stands up. "Right. Let's take off the patch."

Dolores looks at her. "Which one?"

"What do you mean?"

"Well, there must be at least ten of them on there, by now. That's the other thing," she says irritably. "I'm going to run out of space."

Grace wants to hug Dolores. "I think we may have found the problem. Let's have a look at the patches."

Poor Dolores's rear end reminds Grace of the patchwork quilts her mother used to sew.

"I'm just going to take these off."

"'Tis a pity," Dolores says sadly on an outward breath.

Grace removes patch after patch. "That's it!" she says as the last one comes off. Grace bins the patches and washes her hands. "That should solve the problem, Dolores."

"What should?"

"Removing the patches. You're only meant to wear one at a time. You were getting too many hormones. When you're applying a new patch, Dolores, you have to remove the one that was there."

"Ooooooh. I seeee. Oooooh. Grand, so." She gives Grace a confused look. "You should have told me that, Young Dr. Sullivan."

Grace thought she had. But then she remembers all the trouble her own mother took explaining to her about getting her period. Grace wondered what all the fuss was; she could cope with a period. Later, to her horror, she discovered that, actually, your period was a regular visitor.

"So, just to be clear. When you're applying a new patch, you take off the one you've on. And place the new one in a different spot."

"Maybe that's what confused me. The different spot."

"Maybe."

"So, I can keep going on the patches so?" she asks hopefully.

"I think it's worth sticking with them and seeing how you get on. But let's give you a week without patches to allow your levels to return to normal. Then, start again. So, mark your calendar for next Friday. And pop on the first patch. Come back to me if you have any problems whatsoever."

"I'm so glad now I came, Young Dr. Sullivan. I was just going to put up with it."

"Never put up with anything." Grace words hang on the air. If only she'd taken her own advice, years ago.

Dolores's smile is like the sun coming out. "You're right."

Grace understands now what Alan was saying about presents for the patients. She'd like to give Dolores something. Not a stone, though. Painted or otherwise. She needs to give this some thought. Maybe on the drive up to Dublin....

Grace looks at the list. The patients are slowing to a trickle. Her day is nearly over. She goes out to call in the next patient. Seeing Alan's smiling face, she stops at reception.

"You know, Al, I'm beginning to come around to your idea."

"What idea?" he asks, vacantly.

"The gift idea."

"The gift idea?"

"Yeah. The gift idea." What's wrong with him?

"Dr. Sullivan," he teases. "Do you *actually* think I'm a bit simple?"

"What?"

He dips his head so his eyes are looking up at her. "You really think I was going to go around giving everyone presents?"

"I'll kill you!"

He laughs.

She reaches in through the cubby hole to strangle him.

He shoots his swivel chair back, hysterical now, holding his belly and bending over.

A throat clears behind Grace.

She turns.

It's the woman that Jacinta Creedon was gossiping with in the supermarket, pinched face, tight mouth and judgemental eyes all present and correct.

Grace gives her a cold look, turns back and points at Alan. "Behave yourself, Wolfe. Your position is very wobbly as it is."

He's still laughing.

Grace locks the door to her surgery, hating the thought of the drive to Dublin. She goes over to Alan and leans on the counter.

"You okay?" he asks.

"Am I mad, going back up?" she asks, reminding herself that he doesn't know.

"Come in here to me."

She opens the door and goes into the little reception office, wishing for a moment that Alan was a permanent fixture. She hooches herself up on the counter, legs dangling, feeling at home in his presence like she always does. She wishes she could shrink him and carry him around in her pocket.

"So, what are you up to this evening?"

"Heavy date."

"Wow! I'm almost jealous," she says, looking at the indent left in her finger by her wedding ring. She wonders how long it will take to return to normal.

"You better get going," he says, starting to tidy up.

She looks at him. "Trying to get rid of me?"

"Long journey," he adds.

She sighs. "You're right. I better get going.

"Not without a hug, though."

She jumps down. Then clings to him like a life-sized teddy bear. She knows that once she hits the road, she'll be okay.

"Not at work, folks. Not at work."

They turn to see a visibly unimpressed Dr. O'Malley looking in at them. Alan drops his arms. Grace knows it's for her sake. She doesn't try to explain. Couldn't anyway. Not without hurting Alan. A friendly hug is a friendly hug. If her partner wants to read more into it that's his own creative mind.

forty-four

In a large room with a bank of mirrors covering one wall and a floor of soft spongy material that's clearly designed for impact, Grace and the children wait for the course to start. About fifteen others have gathered, over half of them men. Jack looks relieved about that. Seeing people of colour reminds Grace how cosmopolitan Dublin is compared to Killrowan. She misses that. She also misses the energy of the city, the buzz tangible from the moment they arrived last night.

Standing with his back to the mirrored wall, the trainer introduces himself as Patrick Cumiskey and asks everyone to form a circle. A short, cuddly man with mischievous eyes, he takes them through his training as both a psychotherapist and Krav Maga instructor. Though her stomach is knotted with nerves, something about him reassures Grace that they are in good hands.

He starts the instruction by describing the psychology of attackers, zoning in on how they pick their prey, always going for the easiest targets, those who will give them least trouble. What, Grace wonders, earmarked her as an easy victim? Her size? The fact that she was so easy going, always fitting in with what he wanted? He *did* love her once, though. She really does believe that. It wasn't all about finding someone to control. Was it? She reminds herself that, Patrick Cumiskey is talking about a different kind of attacker. The opportunistic stranger.

"They prey on kindness. Many ask for help with something – like directions – to lure you into a vulnerable position and get close. If someone invades your body space be ready."

Getting close, invading body space, is a language Grace understands. She feels her body tense as every word brings Simon more and more into the room. She glances around her. Everyone's listening intently as if this is all very interesting but all very distant to them. Except for Holly and Jack. Who are watching her intently as if checking that she's okay. She smiles encouragingly, wanting to put her arms around them and hold them close. She feels her throat burn at the thought of all that they have witnessed. Maybe this was a mistake. Maybe this is the last thing they needed to hear.

Jack slips from his position in the circle and walks on the outside of it until he gets to her.

"We're doing the right thing," he whispers, putting an arm around her.

Her heart swells.

From across the circle, Holly offers a brave smile, her eyes welling.

Meanwhile, Patrick is explaining that Krav Maga is not self-defence; it's counter-assault. "Self-defence implies that you're a victim. With Krav Maga, you are a counter-attacker. Big difference."

Jack gives her a supportive squeeze. It hits her then that the three of them are together now. A unit. As long as she stayed stuck, they were apart because she spent all her time trying to hide it from them. Now they have a shared truth. A shared bond. A shared goal. Survival. Life.

She raises her chin. That is a goal worth fighting for.

She zones in on Patrick who is demonstrating how to take up a defensive position for counter-attack. His hands are up in front of his chest, elbows bent, knees also slightly bent with one leg in front of the other. He moves from here – so easily – into a block position, then a strike to an (imaginary) face. Then strike after strike after strike as if he is in his element. He stops and looks slowly around the circle, person to person. "Sometimes, you have to strike first," he says, with barely contained glee.

This is an entirely new and wholly uncomfortable prospect for Grace but she can't dwell; they have to adopt the position. Lining up, facing the mirror, they also have to mimic his facial expression – one of outrage, fury, and a desire to fight. Bring, it, on.

In her reflection, Grace sees someone new. Someone powerful. Someone taking control. This Grace owns herself, body and soul.

They divide into pairs to practice moves that Patrick is going to show them.

Jack gets a small woman of about thirty.

Holly gets a boy not much older than her.

Grace faces a giant of a man, no stranger to the gym. Why he needs self-defence she has no idea.

"Everyone wants to fight the big guy," he explains quietly, like he can read her mind.

"Oh. Right. Wow." Must be a gentle giant, she thinks – hopefully.

Des is finishing up a gorgeous fry. He had planned to walk Benji but the rain is really coming down outside. MaryAnn clears away his plate. He tries to remember the name of that orange stone she's wearing, that stone she has always loved, that stone that is so her. It escapes him.

She lifts his plate.

It doesn't feel right that she's waiting on him. "Why don't you join me for a cup of tea?"

"I will, so. I've just made a mug of ginger and lemon." She takes his plate. "Need anything else?"

He pats his belly. "Not a thing, MaryAnn, thank you. That was fabulous."

MaryAnn returns with a purple mug that she couldn't possibly have bought in a shop. Catching him eyeing it, she chuckles. "My one and only attempt at pottery."

"It's… unique."

"Well, it has one thing going for it…. imperfection – which is why I love it."

"There's some hope for me so," he jokes.

"Will you stop it," she says crossly, surprising him. "You're forever putting yourself down."

"I am?"

"You are."

He didn't know. "It smells nice," he says of her tea.

She blows on it and takes a sip, then looks towards the window. "You were lucky to catch me here. I travel a lot in winter."

"Is that right? Where would you be heading off to?"

"Oh, anywhere. I've been known to take a cruise or two. They visit all the best places, Alaska, Cuba, Bermuda, the Caribbean–"

"You've been to all those places?" he asks in amazement. It strikes him that he has never lifted his head up from his work.

"Well, Alaska, Bermuda and Cuba."

"Wow."

"And what do you do… onboard?" He always thought cruises sounded, at best, boring, at worst, claustrophobic.

"I usually go for cruises with a meditation guru onboard. You meet great people."

Doesn't sound like his cup of tea at all. But then, he didn't think he'd like that alternative health column in the *Southern Star* till he started reading it. Now he wouldn't be without it. Maybe someday he'll surprise himself.

"Are they expensive?"

"Not when you factor in all that you're getting. I read about a woman whose life is back-to-back cruises. It's cheaper than a retirement home. With great company. And you get to see the world."

"I like the sound of her."

"There are doctors onboard and everything. But living on a ship wouldn't be for me. I like to get away, but I love coming home. I have to be able to go where I want, when I want. You do start to feel a bit trapped on the cruises after a while. Next trip will be a safari. That's why I'm home now. Saving up," she says, sipping from the endearingly imperfect mug. "Safaris – the good ones – are pricey. But then you don't want to get eaten by a lion, do you?" She grins.

It strikes him then. MaryAnn isn't just alive, she's *living*. Lining up the adventures still to be had. He, on the other hand, has let illness and retirement make him feel like it's all over. But he's only seventy. He still has some kick in him. He had planned on walking Benji a few hundred yards up the road and letting him sniff around in a field. But if MaryAnn can go on safari, surely he can make it to Barleycove. He'll have to collect his stick. And wait till the rain stops. The orange stone attracts his gaze again. Amber! That's it. He has no idea why it cheers him so much to remember.

forty-five

Des has walked Benji on Barleycove beach. His feet are still tingling from paddling in the ice-cold Atlantic. He has checked up on Alan. He and the men are *flying*. He has met Paddy for lunch in the Coffee Cove. Now he is back at MaryAnn's to take his medication and have a little nap.

She offers him tea and – crucially – a scone.

He wanders around the sitting room, looking at the art. They are all watercolours. Landscapes. He doesn't know anything about art but he likes these. He puts on his glasses to read the signature.

"You did all these!" he says as MaryAnn comes in, carrying a tray.

"Ah, they're no Picassos."

He looks at her in admiration. "You always loved the old art."

"Ah, 'tis nothing. Keeps me out of trouble."

"I'll buy the lot."

The tray clatters as she lands it down. "All of them?"

He nods, trying to visualise the best place to hang each of them in his home. A difficult task given that he's not quite sure how it will look when it's all done.

"Good Lord. I'll have to give you a reduction."

It's turning out to be an expensive weekend. But if Des can't spend his money on his family, what can he spend it on? The word cruise comes flying into his head.

On their way to the restaurant, Grace rolls back her shoulders trying to ease the tension in her body. All day, she, Jack and Holly learned how to escape from different situations – headlocks, chokes, being pinned to the floor. Every time Grace was held, it was by Simon, not her partner. She could hear his breathing, smell his breath, feel his iron grip. He was with her, whispering in her ear.

She kept telling herself it was her partner; she was being ridiculous. But her body refused to believe it, as if it could not let her take the risk. Every muscle tensed as though expecting the worst. Her eyes kept darting to the kids, checking they were okay. Jack had his arm around his partner's neck as though it was the last thing he wanted to do. Holly was a tiger, lashing out with heel thrusts, whacking the protective pad while roaring, "No, no, no!"

Roaring, they learned, energises, reminds you to breathe and makes the attacker fear that they will be discovered and, hopefully, leave you be.

They finished at five o'clock. Wrecked physically and emotionally, they hugged each other. Grace knew Jack was okay when he suggested food.

They have stayed local. Grace saw a place earlier that looked nice. Arriving, now, and going inside, it reminds her of the Coffee Cove, just more bohemian, with a younger crowd. Everyone is in their twenties and thirties, chatting and laughing, like they're blissfully aware that their lives are just beginning. A waitress with a nose ring directs Grace, Jack and Holly to a seat far from the window. With a direct view of the door, it couldn't be more perfect.

Jack has the menu in his hand before they even sit.

"That was so good," Holly says, with fire in her eyes. "I think I'll join the army!"

Jack laughs. "Yeah, right."

"I'm serious."

Jack looks up from the menu at his mum. "You okay?"

She can feel both sets of eyes on her.

Smiling, she nods. She reaches out and squeezes their hands. "I'm so proud of you guys. So, so proud." She gets a little teary. "You were amazing in there."

"So were you," they say together.

"I know that starting over was such a big ask but you've never once complained. You've just gotten on with it. You're amazing."

"It wasn't a big ask," Holly says. "It was a big answer. I prefer West Cork. I really do."

Jack glances around the restaurant. "It's good to be back in Dublin, though."

No one has given up more than Jack. He was the popular one. The one with the soulmate friend. Grace doesn't want to go backwards but she owes it to her son.

"I could drop you out to Ross if you like," she says, dreading the risk that would involve, going anywhere near their old home.

Jack brightens. "I wouldn't mind seeing him."

"Great!" Grace tells herself it'll be okay. What are the chances of bumping into Simon? "Give Ross a call. See if he's around. And I'll drop you out."

"I'll just go call him," Jack says, getting up.

Grace smiles at Holly, sorry that there is no one for her to see.

Holly's return smile is wide and innocent. It's as if she has forgotten her life in Dublin.

"Want to watch a movie when we get back to the hotel?" Grace asks.

Holly nods enthusiastically.

Grace has no one to see in Dublin, either, even if she wanted to. Yes, there were people she was friendly with. None were friends. Simon made sure of that, always checking up on where she was and who she was with, constantly interrupting with texts and calls, embarrassing her. If she didn't respond, he'd make her regret it later. If he got wind that she was meeting someone, he'd force her to cancel because of some sudden "urgent" job he had for her. Alternatively, he'd lash out the night before so she wouldn't be able to face anyone for fear she might break down. It became easier not to arrange things, not to have friends. Once, long ago, she did open up to a fledgling friend. The woman was so distressed that Grace wouldn't leave the situation, she cut all contact. It was too hard, knowing and not being able to help. Grace understood. And never opened up to anyone again. It was just too much to land on a person.

Jack goes outside to make the call but stalls, his thumb hovering over Ross's name. What if Ross has plans for tonight, plans he won't want to include Jack in? What if he has moved on, forgotten Jack? Worse, what if he's narked with him for not returning his texts or calls? Jack glances into the restaurant of laughing, chatting friends. He can't just give up. He has to take the risk. If he doesn't, he and Ross might never see each other again. What has he got to lose? Nothing that he hasn't already lost.

He takes a deep breath, depresses his thumb on Ross's name, puts the phone to his ear.

All the time it rings, he holds that breath like hope.

Ross doesn't pick up.

Before he can talk himself out of it, Jack calls again.

It rings out again.

Jack pockets the phone with a sigh and an ache in his heart.

What did he expect? He's blanked Ross too many times. Now, he expects him to jump to attention just cause he's back in town. He deserves this.

Opening the door of the restaurant, he tells himself it doesn't matter. He needs to stick to his plan. New life. Don't look back. It was working fine till he got to Dublin and realised just how much he misses his old pal, his old life.

His mum's eyes meet his questioningly. He shakes his head and shrugs.

"Probably good to get an early night anyway," she says. "Tomorrow will be a long day."

forty-six

It's six-thirty and the sun is setting. The new bathroom has been put in. Now the wooden floors are going down. Everything has been moved upstairs and the men are working efficiently and to deadline. The front door is wide open. Alan is heading out to bring in the new skirting boards when in saunters an expensively dressed and stunning-looking man with floppy, greying hair and piercing blue eyes.

"Can I help you?" Alan asks. Des put in security for a reason. Alan is not about to let any stranger waltz in, no matter how good he looks.

"Is Des around?" he asks, checking out the work in progress.

"I'm afraid not, no."

"Where is he?" he asks, like he's used to getting his own way.

Alan, folding his arms, wonders if this could be Grace's ex. He's the right age and certainly has the arrogance of a consultant. "I have no idea."

"How about his daughter, Grace and her children? Have you seen them?" he asks, like he's talking to a serf.

So, Alan plays the serf. "I'm just the workman. Sorry but I can't help you."

"How can I get in touch with Des?" he asks, anger replacing the smooth.

Alan may not be a smart man but he knows people. And this is not a good one. "Why don't *you* give me *your* number and I'll get it to Des?"

For the first time, he looks hesitant, caught out. Then he raises his chin. "I don't give my number to just anyone."

"Then I can't help you. And now, I have to ask you to leave. This is a work site."

Squinting, the man takes a step towards Alan. "Wait a minute. I know you. You're Alan, right? Grace's *gay friend* from back in the day."

Alan flinches, hoping the others didn't hear over the hammering, and hurt that Grace would have shared his secret so casually. But then this is clearly her husband and couples share everything. Alan is sure she didn't use the same dismissive tone when she spoke about him to this... twit.

"D'you have a number for her, pal?" he asks, condescendingly.

"Look, you've got the wrong person. And I don't have Des's daughter's number. I'm working for Des."

"I never forget a face. Goes with the job. *You* were all over Grace's old photo albums. So, you're telling me she didn't catch up with her best buddy now that she's back in town?" His smile is cruel.

Alan has never used his physical strength against anyone. Now he straightens up to his full height and takes a step towards this arrogant so and so. He's at least four inches taller and a hell of a lot stronger. "I asked you to leave. Now you're trespassing. If you don't go, I'll have to call the police. Pal."

Pouring himself a beer at the Coffee Cove while he waits for Paddy O'Neill to join him for dinner, Des can't remember when he last felt so hopeful. The men are transforming the house; he can't wait to see Grace and the children's reaction. He's out and about, catching up with old friends. Driving again. And it's been especially wonderful spending time with MaryAnn. He wonders if he should call her now and invite her along to dinner with them. He's taking out his phone when it starts to ring. Seeing Alan's name, he wonders if there's a problem back at the house. Maybe he just has a question.

"Alan?"

"Sorry for disturbing you, Des. Nothing wrong here at all. Just thought you'd like to know that a man called to the house. Looking for you. And Grace."

Des looks, automatically, out the window of the café. "What did he look like?"

"Handsome. On the smug side to be honest. Walked right in like he owned the place."

Des's breath catches. "What did you tell him?"

"That I didn't know where anyone was. That I'm just the workman."

"Good man." Des's breath returns. "Where did he go?"

"Got back in his car – a Jag, if that helps – and did a U-turn down into the village. He wasn't happy."

Des gets to his feet, eyes on the window. "Don't say a word about this to Grace."

There's a pause. "'Tis family business. Not mine."

"Thanks, Alan."

So, he's here, and prepared to break the barring order. Thank God, Grace and the kids are in Dublin. Des reaches for his stick. He has to put a stop to this now. But how? First thing's first. He has to find him. Then he'll warn him that he'll face the full force of the law if he tries to see them again. He tries to be positive. By the time Grace gets home tomorrow night, Simon will have to have left to be back in Dublin in time for work.

He hurries outside. Scanning the street, he sees no sign of the Jaguar. He takes off in the direction of the surgery. It'll be closed, of course, but it's all he can think of. Halfway there, the police station comes into view. He remembers Paddy.

He whips out his phone and calls his old pal. Who pulls up beside him in less than two minutes.

They cruise around in the squad car in search of the Jag, going a few miles outside the village in all directions, then turning around and coming back.

"Where would he go?" Des asks.

"Well, if he's looking for you and you're not staying at the house…"

"He's probably checking the B&B's!"

One by one, they visit them all, including MaryAnn's but there is no sign of his Dublin-registered car. They return to the main street.

"Go and have your meal, Paddy. I might go sit in my car and just watch the street for a while."

"Sure, why don't we sit here together in the squad car? I'll pop in, grab us some grub and bring it out."

"You're a good friend," Des says.

"I'm only being selfish. There's nothing I love more than a good old-fashioned stakeout."

Des smiles, grateful for the lie.

The two friends watch the street for over an hour. Paddy lowers the window to clear the smell of food. The cool October air invades the car and he turns on the engine for warmth, leaving the headlights off.

"He must be gone," Des says at last, not wanting to waste any more of Paddy's time. "We can't have missed him."

"Unlikely, alright."

"Go on home. Sorry for wasting your time."

"Sure, I was going to be out with you anyway. You've only added a bit of excitement to the evening. Let me drop you to your car."

"Right so, thanks, Paddy."

Paddy does as promised. "Make sure and call me if he turns up."

"Will do. Thanks, Paddy. Safe home."

Des sits motionless in his car for another thirty minutes. Sure, at last, that the brute is gone, he drives slowly back to MaryAnn's.

Out front, like a bad smell, is the Jag. So, he was checking the B&B's after all. He must have turned up here when Des and Paddy were on the main street or checking the other B&B's.

He kills the headlights and parks out on the road.

Approaching the house in the dark, he gets a clear view into the sitting room, illuminated with lamp light. There he is, the thug, in full charm mode, being waited on by poor MaryAnn. He's even getting the scone treatment. Gripping the knob of the stick like he's crushing a skull – and not just any skull – Des thinks about calling Paddy. But he doesn't want a scene at MaryAnn's. Doesn't want to inflict that on her. No. He'll go in, stay calm, keep his cool, and warn Simon about the barring order and the police.

MaryAnn must hear his key in the door because she comes rushing out into the hall.

"Oh Des, great! Simon's here!" she says as if she's known him all her life. "He wants to get back together with Grace. Isn't that wonderful?" Des has to remind himself that his son-in-law had him fooled for years. He can't blame MaryAnn for believing whatever line he's spun her. "When he saw workmen at the house," she continues, "he decided to try the B&B's. I said you'd be back and you could tell him where Grace is."

Let me at him, Des thinks. "Thanks, MaryAnn. I'll handle this."

"Is everything okay?" she asks, reading his face with concern.

"Fine, fine. I just want a word with Simon, alone, if that's okay?"

"Of course. I'll, I'll just be in the kitchen if you need me," she says like she knows she's made a mistake.

"Great, thanks. I'll go on in so." Des makes for the sitting room.

He opens the door. Benji gets to his feet and wags his tail. But then stops, his tail disappearing between his legs.

Simon stands. "Des, thank God."

Des thinks of all the times he has been played, like he's being played now. "Thank God, what?" he asks coldly.

"How are they?" he asks, his voice filled with concern.

"Hunky dory," Des says flatly.

He clasps one hand with the other, and moves them up and down pleadingly. "I need you to talk to them for me, apologise, I've made so many mistakes…" The bastard manages to look contrite.

Des taps his stick repeatedly on the ground, trying to reign in his fury. "Right. I'll pass on the message. You can go now."

"I was hoping that you might get Grace to rethink the access."

"I won't be doing that, Simon."

He grips his head. "They lied! I never hurt the children! I wouldn't. I love them–" he rushes, like he's the wronged party.

Des tightens his grip on the stick. "There's more than one way to hurt a child. And, mark my words, you've done your bit. If you have an ounce of love left for Holly and Jack, you'll leave them be. They deserve their peace now. They've had enough."

"I'm their *father*! They need to see me. The courts recognise the importance of fathers and almost always grant access. It was their lies–"

"If Holly and Jack wanted to see you, they'd be seeing you. Let me give you a hint as to why they mightn't be so keen on having you in their lives. There's the manipulation, the lies, the undermining of their mother, the bullying. Oh, and might I add there's growing up in a house of violence!" Des's voice has grown louder with every word.

"That's why I'm here, to apologise, to admit to my mistakes. Look, I'm trying to give Grace a chance here. If she doesn't rethink the access, I'll have to appeal this ruling – and bring up the fact that she perjured herself. The punishment for perjury is imprisonment."

Des squints at this *creature*. "Let me get this straight," he says slowly. "You are trying to blackmail my daughter – using me as messenger."

Simon raises his palms. "No, no, no. You've got me all wrong. I'm trying to go easy on her."

"Do I look stupid to you? You've certainly treated me as if I am, for all these years. Well, let me tell you, I won't be your messenger. And let me also remind you that there is a barring order against you. If you go near Grace or the children, you'll risk your precious appeal. How dare you show up here! How dare you try and use me to get to them! But mostly how *dare* you lay a finger on my daughter." Des's blood boils at the thought and he advances, not sure what he's going to do but prepared to do whatever he has to.

Simon, eyeing the stick, stands up with a sneer, towering over Des. "You haven't a hope, old man." His eyes have turned mean, cold and hard.

Des can see it now, all of it. Guilt swamps him, guilt that he let this happen.

But he can't let that – or anything – stop him. He straightens to his full height. Which is still way too short. "You're in Killrowan now," he says, injecting calm and foreboding into his voice. "The police, here, watch out for their own. They've been warned about you and are on the lookout."

"Which is why they're here now, lights flashing," he sneers sarcastically. "Keystone cops in the backwaters of West Cork." He holds out a hand and, fingers splayed, produces an exaggerated tremor. "Look, I'm shaking."

"Mock them all you like but if you ever show your face in this village when Grace is here, they'll be down on you like a ton of bricks."

"So, Grace *isn't* here? Is that what you're saying?" he asks, like the smartass he is. Then, like a smooth gear change, his voice switches to threatening. "Where is she, Des?" He takes a step towards Des.

Benji goes on full alert, his eyes locking onto Simon.

"Is she in Dublin?"

Des's face gives nothing away. "Yeah, she's in Dublin. Called up to see you," he says like Dublin is the last place she'd be. "Pity you're down here."

Simon steps right up to Des now.

Des is not a violent man but is considering a sharp upward jab of the stick when Benji starts to growl.

Simon turns. Seeing the dog, his Adam's Apple rises and falls. He addresses Des while keeping his eyes on the immediate threat. "Right, well, you tell her that this isn't over. Perjury is perjury. And I've the children's medical records to prove it. Your precious daughter will be seeing me in court. Very soon."

"The last thing I'll be doing is passing on your threats. Get out of here before I set the dog on you." He looks at Benji, hoping for something, anything.

To his relief, Benji starts to advance, teeth bared.

Simon points at Des. "This isn't over." He backs towards the door, eyes fixed on the dog.

Benji follows him until he hurries through the door and shuts it firmly behind him.

Des hears the front door slam and then, seconds later, an engine start up. Headlights flash into the room. Des stands, facing them, chin high.

The lights recede as the car reverses, then point towards the village and the car speeds away.

Des collapses into a chair. For once, his tremor has nothing to do with Parkinson's. Benji returns to him like a dog to a farmer after herding sheep. Des puts a hand on his head.

"My hero," he says.

Benji sits at his feet.

There's a gentle knock at the door and MaryAnn appears. It's clear from her shocked and guilty face that she's heard it all.

"I'm so sorry I let him in! I thought…! He said…! I believed…! I'm so sorry for your daughter. I'm so sorry for Grace. And I'm so sorry for overhearing. The walls…. Oh, Des. What a horrible man. I'm shaking."

He smiles. "So am I. Come and sit down. He's gone now. Good riddance to him."

"He had me completely fooled," she says, sitting in the chair beside him.

"He had us all fooled, MaryAnn," he says with regret. "He's a very persuasive, very cunning man." He looks down at Benji and rests a hand on his head. "Good dog. Dog among dogs." Des looks up at MaryAnn.

"I'll get him a bit of scone," she says, rising to her feet. "And something stronger for us."

"MaryAnn?"

She stops and turns.

"Please, not a word to anyone."

Her hand goes to her heart. "You know me, Des. I'm no gossip."

"I know. I'm just nervous for Grace and the kids." He thinks of Simon, driving back to Dublin. It's not very Christian but how easy it would all be if his car just went off the road?

In Dublin, it's eleven, and Jack is in bed when Ross calls him back. He sits up and bangs the light on.

"Hey, man. How's it going?" Ross asks, slurring a little. He sounds so… *American* to Jack. Is that how Jack sounds to the kids in Killrowan? How has no one floored him at school?

"Only saw your call now," Ross says.

Yeah, no one leaves it that long without checking their phone, Jack thinks. Still, he'd be the same if Ross went silent on him. He wants to tell him he's in Dublin but it's too late tonight and he's doing the course all day tomorrow, then leaving straight after.

"No worries," he says. "What's the craic?" He wants to know everything he's been missing. He feels it suddenly, like a great big gap in his life. Maybe it was a bad idea to get back in touch.

"I'd given up on you, man," Ross says.

"Sorry," comes easier now. "I don't know. I just thought: what's the point? Six hours each way, like."

"Whoa, dude! You sound like a culchie!"

Jack laughs but is stunned at how condescending and dismissive the word sounds. Is that how *he* sounded only two weeks ago? Like a complete dick. But he knows Ross and knows he's not a dick.

"Yeah, culchies aren't so bad, it turns out." He won't bring up the hurling, though. Ross isn't ready for that. "Maybe you could come down for a weekend sometime." There's still the issue of where he'd stay – and what they'd do with themselves. Ginge might have some ideas.

"Cool," Ross says. Just one word but Jack can hear all this: West Cork'd be such a trek when there's so much going on in Dublin.

"So, no craic?" Jack asks to fill the silence.

"You've been gone so long I don't know what you know and what you don't know."

So long? Two weeks? "Try me."

Ross goes through a list of who's going out with who. And who isn't any more. It does seem distant after all. And Ross really does sound drunk now.

"Yeah, I better go, here," Jack says at last.

"Okay. Cool. Talk soon, dude."

"Take it easy," Jack says and hangs up.

He looks at the phone and wonders how so much could have changed in two weeks. How *he* could have changed.

forty-seven

"You haven't been to *Drombeg*?" MaryAnn asks Des, setting down coffee and lifting his breakfast plate. "In all your seventy years?"

Des shrugs, his mind still on Simon. Can he appeal? Could Grace be accused of perjury? Is the punishment really imprisonment? Or was it all a bluff? Des needs to talk to a lawyer. Fast.

"Des Sullivan!"

"What?"

"There's a stone circle, three thousand years old on your doorstep and you haven't seen it"

"I'll get around to it, MaryAnn! Don't you worry. Just tell me where it is." He takes a sip of his coffee to keep her happy.

"You'll get around to it today. Because that's where I'm bringing you."

"Sure, there's no need to do that."

She points a fork at him. "Oh, but there is. If you go on your own, you'll look at the rocks and you just won't get it. No, Des Sullivan. We're going. Soon as you've finished your coffee."

"Haven't you got plans?" MaryAnn was always planning something.

"I can't think of anything more important than showing you this, this incredible legacy built by our ancestors, three thousand years ago and still standing – well most of it."

Des supposes that, for a few hours, he can put thoughts of Simon on hold. What can he do, anyway, on a Sunday? "Well, if you feel that strongly."

She actually claps her hands. "I do!"

Rocks of different sizes and shapes, the tallest close to six foot, stand silent and still in a Megalithic circle. Des and MaryAnn stand, equally silent, equally still, gazing at them. She was right, of course. This is something very special. And "special" doesn't do it justice. Des feels the history. He feels the people, their spirit lingering. And he feels that this spot, on raised ground with a view of the sea, was chosen for a reason. A sacred reason.

"Tell me about it," he says, his words a reverent whisper.

MaryAnn starts to point out various rocks. "So, these are the male rocks. And these are the female. On certain days, like the Winter Solstice, the shadow from each of the male rocks falls on a female, entering her."

"*MaryAnn!*" Des is mortified.

She laughs. "What? Our ancestors worshipped fertility. And weren't they right to? Isn't it an absolute miracle how babies come to be?"

Des has always thought so. It was one of the reasons he chose medicine. He almost studied obstetrics but wanted to be in the community. And here he is, now, embarrassed by shadows falling on rocks.

"Don't you think it's amazing, that people were here, three thousand years ago, living their lives, just as we are living ours now, doing their best like we're trying to do." MaryAnn has gone all dreamy and ageless.

Suddenly, Des wants to sweep her up in his arms and … he doesn't know what… or where the urge has come from… but he'd like to do something mad. The truth prevents him. Because the truth is this: he left her behind. In seeking a better life, he discarded her. And that's the truth. He loved his wife; he loved Miriam so very dearly. There's no question about that. But he loved the right person, the person whose parents funded him to set up in general practice. It was a love with benefits. He suited himself. He let MaryAnn down.

"I'm sorry," he says, feeling it deeply.

"For what?" she asks, turning. Seeing his face, realisation dawns in hers. She swats her hand through the air. "Don't be ridiculous. I've had a very good life, Des. I wouldn't change it for a second. And that's the honest truth."

"I'm glad. I'm still sorry."

"You did what you had to do," she says, without emotion, like she knew him better, back then, than he knew himself.

He gazes at the stones, remembering the star-gazing, nature-loving, barefoot-walking teenager he used to be. But then, he'd have gazed at anything, loved anything and walked, barefoot, anywhere with MaryAnn by his side.

Grace can't imagine gouging anyone's eyes out. And she says so to Patrick who has been highly recommending it as a means of escape.

"Look," he says to her. "Your attacker wants to hurt you. All you are to him is a desire to be satisfied. If you can't fight for yourself, then fight for the people you love, the people who need you to stay who you are. Fight for them. Escape for them. Be okay for them."

She nods with a new determination. It makes sense that he's a psychotherapist. He knew exactly how to make her fight.

He demonstrates new moves.

Everyone practices, in their pairs.

All morning, they spar, yelling, "No! No! No!" as they block and attack.

Finally, just as Grace was beginning to doubt that they'd ever break for lunch, they do. She is heading over to Jack and Holly when an arm encircles her neck from behind, forcing her into a headlock. She reacts on impulse, twisting and whacking her attacker three times in the groin as they've been practising.

"Whoa! Whoa! Stop!" The "stop" comes out as a high-pitched yelp. And Grace is immediately released.

Leaping away, she can't believe what she has done. Neither can she believe that she had it in her. Hands to her face, she watches her partner crouch over, groaning like a dying animal.

"I'm *so* sorry."

Jack whoops and Holly breaks into hysterical laughter while everyone else looks on in stunned silence. Grace wonders if she and her children need therapy. Have they been exposed to too much for too long?

Patrick is on his way over.

"I don't know what came over me," she says. "I got such a fright I just lashed out. I wasn't thinking. Something flipped. I'm so sorry."

"No need to be. You did well." He bends down to her partner. "That was out of line, mate. You deserve what you got, in fairness."

"I was just trying to help," he squeaks. "Introduce the element of surprise."

"How did that work out for you?" Patrick helps him up. "Leave the surprises to me, okay? We do everything very deliberately, very carefully here. For a reason."

Grace goes to Holly and Jack and puts her arms around them. "Sorry about that. I–"

"Are you kidding?" Jack says, staring at her. "Mum, you were a ninja. I've never seen you stand up for yourself before."

That floors her. Because it's true. All she has taught her children is to roll over and take it; the same lesson, year after year after year. Getting away, she realises, is only the first step on the road to their recovery.

forty-eight

Des doesn't know why he's annoyed. MaryAnn is as entitled to date as the next person. The fellow who came to pick her up, though.... Des reminds himself that there's no law against dating younger men. Or hippies. Or vegetarians with Rastafarian hair. Where were they off to at eight o'clock on a Sunday night, all the same? Probably star-gazing, he thinks, feeling sorry for himself.

"You big eejit, Sullivan. Why should you care? There are bigger things to worry about. Much bigger things," he scolds himself.

Benji snuggles up to him, like a silent agony aunt.

'Twas good of MaryAnn to let him stay on until Alan and the lads finish up at the house. That's what he should be focusing on instead of having a go at the Romeo who showed up on a BSA motorbike with an extra helmet. Des had a wonderful time with MaryAnn today. He should be grateful for that. Instead of wanting more. If he wants more. He doesn't want more.

And anyway, he needs this time to track down a family law solicitor. He goes through his patients in his mind. There has to be one. He remembers Theresa Dempsey, a former patient who grew up in Killrowan then moved to Cork to practice family law – if Des remembers correctly. He looks her up. And finds her! Based in the Mall in Cork, she *is* practising family law! He takes down the number of this lovely, lovely girl. Woman, now.

He goes back over everything Simon said. From the beginning. Then writes down a list of questions for Theresa, covering every eventuality.

Then he pauses. He can't call on behalf of his daughter, not when this is about perjury. He'll say he's calling about a patient who came to him suffering from stress. He hopes that news of his retirement has stayed local.

It's quarter past midnight and Des is dozing off when the call finally comes from Alan.

"Well, we did all we could," he says in a disappointed tone.

"I'm on my way," Des says, anxious to leave. His small bag has been packed for hours, out in the car with the wrapped-up paintings. "Let's go, Benji."

He quietly lets himself out.

Des is speechless. Alan was right about everything. The place looks bigger, brighter, cleaner, more modern. The kitchen cupboards look like something out of a catalogue. It's as if Des has walked into an entirely different house.

"I can't get over the place," he says to a beaming Alan.

"It's great, isn't it?"

Des frowns. "I thought you said you'd done all you could?"

Alan grins. "Which was everything. My favourite is the bathroom. Fit for a king, it is. Come on and I'll show you."

The thought of climbing the stairs is daunting but Alan looks like an excited puppy and Des can't let him down. He's dying to see the bathroom anyway. Smiling back at Alan, he drags himself up by the bannister.

It was worth the effort. A gleaming white bathroom with all the mod cons stands proudly waiting for inspection.

Des pats Alan on the back. "You've surpassed yourself, Alan. You really have."

"I'm delighted with it," Alan says, as if he has transformed his own home.

"There'll be a bonus in it for you and the lads."

"Ah, they'll be delighted. I just sent them home. They were shagged altogether."

Back downstairs, Des glances at the couch, which looks grim and saggy against all the newness. "It's too late to do anything with the couch, I suppose?"

Alan smiles. "'Tis a little. But we can get to that tomorrow, if you like."

"Lovely."

Des has to sit down. Normally in bed by now, his Parkinson's medication has worn off and he feels like he's run out of batteries. He takes an extra Sinemet, washing it down with a glass of water. He should really go to bed but can't miss the surprise.

"This calls for a beer," he says, getting up and going to the fridge.

Alan rubs his hands together. "It does, yeah."

Des loves that there is no false modesty here. There's no place for it.

They clink bottles.

"Cheers!"

They sit in amiable silence, Alan holding his neck every so often and tilting back his head.

"You must be shattered," Des says.

"Ah, I'll sleep in, tomorrow. Nothing like a job well done to give a man a lift."

Des's eyes fall on the empty walls. He remembers the paintings. But his limbs are just too heavy to lift. "Alan, would you do me one last favour? Would you hang a few paintings for me?"

"'Course I would. Where are they?"

Alan carries in and unwraps the art. One by one, he stands the paintings against the wall, appraising them.

"These are gorgeous, Des."

Des thinks of MaryAnn and her free spirit. He wonders if they're home yet, herself and Romeo. Then puts them from his mind. "Hang them wherever you think is best, Alan. I haven't a clue."

"Sure, we'll do it together."

They try out various places for each painting, then decide. Alan gets his hammer.

Des thinks of Una and Pat next door and hopes their hearing aids are turned off. He'll get them some wine tomorrow.

Finally, Alan stops hammering and they deem themselves happy with the result.

Des can't believe the place. He'd never in a million years have done this for himself.

The kids are asleep when Grace pulls up outside the house, close to sleep herself. Any longer and she'd have had to stop. It's almost one in the morning and all the lights in the house are on. Her automatic reaction is to panic. Is her dad okay? Did something happen? Maybe he just waited up. But why *all* the lights?

"Guys, we're here," she says and hurries from the car.

She lets herself in.

Two men are having a beer in a house she doesn't recognise.

Taking it all in, her hand goes to her mouth.

A grinning Alan catches it on camera.

The children, appearing through the door, lose their grogginess.

"Wow," Jack says, doing a full three-sixty.

Grace is going from painting to painting. "These are gorgeous." She looks at Des, entirely stunned.

"Nothing like you had in Dublin but it's a start, nonetheless."

She looks at him. "Dad, *Simon* chose the art. I never liked it." In fact, she hated it. Her understatement is for the children. Simon's taste was stark, modern, vulgar. Nothing had any warmth. He bought whatever was on-trend and expensive. "These are *really, really,* lovely, Dad. These are *home*."

"We're not moving now," Jack says, looking at her.

Everyone does. All hopefully.

"Guys, there are three of us – and a dog."

Holly, Jack and Benji all looks at Des.

"Sure, I love having ye here. But only if ye want to. Ye might want yer own space. And, sure look, I'm delighted with the makeover even just for myself. I love the place now. Why don't ye have a chat amongst yerselves, tomorrow. There's no rush."

"Ye haven't seen the bathroom," Alan bursts like he can't help himself.

The kids thunder upstairs, Benji in hot – and barking – pursuit.

Grace turns to Des. "Dad, seriously, please tell me if it'd be too much. Teenage energy–"

"There nothing I love more than teenage energy." He looks wistful. "Gracie, when ye came, it was just me and the fire. I wasn't even warming the place up." He glances around. "Look at me now.

I would really, really, hand-on-heart, love ye to stay. But only if you think it's the right thing for you and the kids."

Grace hugs him and gets a little teary. If she hadn't left Simon, they'd never be having this moment – or so many moments. If she had carried on, continued to suck it up, she'd have missed this closeness to her dad – and the children's closeness to him. Imagine if he had died without.... With a shudder, she kills the thought and pulls back. Only then does she notice that Alan, Holly, Jack and Benji are all standing looking at her, awaiting her decision.

She smiles then glances from one to the other. "I think we all want the same thing." Jack and Holly run to her and create a whole new family hug.

"This would have been perfect for 'Room to Improve,'" Alan says, taking another photo.

forty-nine

Reaching up for the Cornflakes is a challenge for Grace. The muscles in her arms are so sore that she can barely lift them. Her pecs are even worse. All that pounding into protective pads has taken its toll.

"Are your muscles killing you?" she asks Holly and Jack. "I literally can't lift my arms." She realises that she's also hoarse from all the shouting.

Jack glances at his mum's skinny arms. "You need to work on your upper body strength, Mum. Seeing as you have *none*."

"*I'm* kinda sore," Holly says in sympathy.

Grace winks at her. Then looks at Jack. "How would a person work on their upper body strength?" Not that she's committing to anything.

"Do weights. Find a gym."

Grace bites her lip. She still hasn't organised one for Jack. "There must be one around here somewhere. We need one for you, anyway."

"Yeah, I'm losing all my bulk."

Holly rolls her eyes.

But Grace knows how important the gym is to Jack, how it – and sport – have always been his escape. "Why don't you ask the guys at school where they go?"

A look of sudden horror crosses his face. "Wait! If *I* go to a gym *you* can't go there!"

Grace smiles. "Let's just sort a gym out for you. And I can build my…" She puts her fingers in quote marks "…upper-body strength, at home."

"I'll show you some moves. Press ups. Sit ups. Plank."

"Can't wait," she says with irony. But she knows she needs to do it, just as she needs to build her fitness. How is she meant to strike and run when she can't actually run?

"Hol, do you think I could borrow a pair of leggings? I might go for a run at lunchtime."

They look at her like she's told them she's a secret spy.

"Sure," Holly says. "Do you want runners?"

"Nah, I think the ones I have will do, thanks."

Des said little over breakfast, his mind focused on the conversation he's about to have with Theresa Dempsey. As soon as Grace and the children have left, he takes out her number and his list of questions. He gets as far as a secretary who explains that Theresa is in court. A good time to call back would be after four. Des can't call when the kids will be home.

"Does she ever take calls at lunchtime?" he asks hopefully.

The secretary sounds doubtful when she says, "You *might* be lucky."

Des never relies on luck. "It's her old GP, Des Sullivan, calling on behalf of a patient. It's a bit urgent, to be honest."

"Let me give you her mobile."

"Ah, that's great, thanks a million."

"Not at all. It's nice to come across a GP that cares so much about his patients."

Des feels bad, then reminds himself he *would* have done this for a patient. He's done lots of things like this for his patients. And a very big part of him misses not being able to, anymore.

Myra is humming. *And* she looks different.

"Myra, you look amazing," Grace says, staring at her, trying to figure out what's changed.

"Do I?" she asks, touching her hair, self-consciously. It's been cut short and turned a lovely shade of plum. "I'm not sure about the colour. Is it too much?"

"No! It's stunning. You look… Dutch or something."

Myra laughs.

But it's more than the hair. "Your eyebrows!"

"Are they terrible? I got the shock of my life when I saw them first. They looked like two slugs but I've gotten used to them by now. Do they stand out a mile? They're permanent, you know," she says, touching them, worriedly.

"So, you'll be permanently gorgeous. They're really, really lovely. They frame your face. Together with the hair, you look ten years younger. At least!"

"Ah, go on outta that." But she's grinning.

"Did Jane do all this?" Grace waves her hand around Myra's general aura.

Myra shakes her head, then leans towards Grace conspiratorially, lowering her voice and glancing around to make sure they're alone. "Actually, we went a bit mad when we got up to Cork. Stayed over and everything," she says like she has to tell *someone*.

"Oh, did ye now?" Grace raises her eyebrows teasingly. "Shameless, absolutely shameless." But joking aside, "I'm delighted for you, Myra. You know what I think of Fred."

"Who said it was Fred?"

Grace laughs out loud. "Hidden depths, Myra. Hidden depths."

"You don't know the half of it," she jokes. Then she grows serious. "D'you think if I popped out for lunch Dr. O'Malley would think I'd lost the run of myself?"

Grace feels like high-fiving her. "Myra, you know the answer to that."

"What about Dr. O'Malley, though?"

"I'll tell Dr. O'Malley. Not that I need to. Alan did it last Friday and 'twas fine. People just signed in themselves."

Myra looks relieved. "That's great altogether."

"Hot date?" Grace teases.

"Ah, just Fred."

"Don't you 'just Fred' me. Most gorgeous man in Killrowan. I'm so happy for you, Myra."

"Yera, stop. 'Tis only early days."

"Hey, the early days are the best." Grace is living proof. Though Fred is no Simon.

Grace calls her first patient since she got back from Dublin, a Brigid McCarthy. A girl of about fifteen stands up. Automatically, Grace wonders if she's in Holly's class. Beside her, Alan's friend, Seamus sends Grace a worried-parent look but he doesn't stand up. His eyes seem to say, "Look after her, won't you?"

Grace smiles reassurance, then turns to Brigid. Like Seamus, she's incredibly tall, incredibly lean with a long thin face and bright blue eyes. Unlike Seamus, she's not a smiler.

"This way," Graces says, unable to stop smiling, herself, for Myra and Fred.

"I know."

Right, Grace thinks.

In the surgery, she offers the teenager a seat.

She sits on the edge with her schoolbag on her lap, as if she's not planning to stay.

"So, Brigid, how can I help?"

"It's Bridge. And you can't. My dad thinks this is a medical condition. And it's just not."

Grace nods like she understands but has no idea what "Bridge" is talking about. "What is a medical condition?"

"My period."

"Ah." Phenomenal relief. For one crazy, terrified second Grace worried that she might be dealing with a teen pregnancy.

"We don't actually have to talk about it," Bridge says. "I'm a big reader. I get it, like. Even if I wasn't a reader, he got me a DVD – which was terrible."

Grace smiles.

"He's just, like, terrified so I said I'd come. So, he can relax, like."

"I see." Glancing at Bridge's file, Grace sees that she's only fourteen and that Seamus is a single parent. This has to be challenging for them both.

"Do you have any questions at all, Bridge? Just to get some value out of the consultation."

"Nope."

"Right. Let me think of some that might crop up."

Bridge starts to drum her fingers on her schoolbag.

"If you feel moody coming up to your period, that's perfectly normal."

"I'm moody pretty much most of the time anyway."

Grace smiles. "Aren't we all? If you get cramps, also normal. Some people get them more than others. Some escape with no pain whatsoever. If cramps *are* bothering you, just take Panadol or Nurofen and follow the instructions on the pack. Never take more than they say in any twenty-four-hour period. And never go for Nurofen Plus or Solpadeine. They have codeine in them. And that's not good." Grace hasn't had a Nurofen Plus in almost two weeks. It's amazing how that makes her feel. She wonders how Wayne Hill is doing, then flicks her mind back to Bridge, who has actually started to nod.

"For some, periods are irregular and that's perfectly fine." Grace tries to remember the kinds of questions she had way back then. "And you know there's more than one, right?"

"One what?"

"Period."

Bridge stares her. "Yeah, like. Of course."

"It's just that some people…." She points a thumb at herself. "Thought that there was going to be just the one."

Bridge bursts out laughing. "That's hilarious."

"It wasn't at the time."

They both laugh now.

Grace's awe of the body comes into play. "And you know why we get periods, right? Physiologically? It's just the womb getting ready for pregnancy and then discarding all that preparation when we don't actually get pregnant."

"I still can't believe you thought there was just one."

Grace grins and shrugs. "There's a fool born every day." Speaking of birth, she has to ask. "And you know all about the birds and the bees, right?"

"Ooooh yeah."

Grace smiles. "Okay. What else can I say? It's a good idea to keep a few pads in your bag. Just in case. And you know you don't have to stop anything you normally do. You can use tampons, if you want to go swimming and whatever."

"Yup."

"Okay, well, I think you are going to take this in your stride, Bridge."

"Sure hope so." She raises her eyebrows. "Because there *is* more than one!"

Grace laughs. "You're not going to let me forget this, are you?"

"Nope."

Grace thinks of her heading towards womanhood without a mum. "Okay, listen. I'm going to give you my number just in case anything crops up. Give me a call anytime. If I'm with a patient, I'll call you back as soon as I can. Okay?"

Bridge's eyebrows knot together. "You do this for *all* your patients?"

"Just the cheeky ones."

It turns out Bridge is a smiler after all.

They walk out of the surgery together.

At the door to the waiting room, Bridge eyes her dad. He gets to his feet immediately.

"Can I have the car keys?" she asks.

He hands them over, looking at her questioningly.

"It was *fine*," she says impatiently.

"Good, good. I'll just pay so."

Grace feels a sudden rush of fondness for the man she had dismissed as obnoxious. Here he is doing an amazing job at trying to be mum and dad for his little girl. His concern touches her and she lingers, in case he wants to talk.

He turns to her, his eyes filled with worry. "Is she alright?" he whispers.

"You've done a great job, Seamus. Bridge's a super kid."

He looks so suddenly hopeful. "I just wanted her to chat to a woman. Just to make sure I've covered all the bases."

"She could give a lecture on periods."

He blushes at the word.

"I've given her my number in case anything crops up."

"You're a saint." His "Thank you," is laced with relief.

"My pleasure."

He goes up to Myra to pay. "Janey Mack, Myra, you're getting fierce glam altogether."

She touches her hair. "Ah, just making a bit of an effort for a change."

"Oh, it's not just the effort, Myra. You've got a glint in your eyes, girl." Something about the way he says it reminds Grace of Alan.

Myra lowers her eyes.

"Could there be love in the air?" Seamus asks.

"Go on outta that, Seamus, you old codger."

The more she stays in Killrowan, the more fond of everyone Grace is becoming.

To his relief, Des catches Theresa Dempsey at lunchtime. Her secretary messaged ahead to say he'd be calling. Sweetheart that she is. After a brief catch up, Des outlines the crisis that his "patient" is experiencing. Theresa listens in silence.

"My first question is, can the father appeal?" Des asks.

"Yes, he can. It would be de novo, an entirely new case, going through all the evidence again. He'd be entitled to introduce new evidence."

Des closes his eyes. "What about the perjury situation?"

"Well, firstly, the fact that the medical records don't show physical evidence of abuse is not itself evidence of perjury. The child would have to make an admission under oath that he or she had lied for it to be perjury. Otherwise, it is not foreseeable that a court would deem it perjury. The court *may* seek to punish a parent if it is established that she put the child up to lying."

"It seems to have been the other way around."

"In that case, the court would not seek to punish the child."

"So, your advice would be not to give in to his blackmail?"

"One *could* assume from his approach that *he* doesn't have confidence in an appeal."

"That's very encouraging. Thanks so much, Theresa," Des says in relief. He was right not to worry Grace with this. If Simon does appeal, the worst-case scenario is he gets access. Why give it to him on a plate now? "You've been a great help. How much do I owe you?"

"A drink, if you're ever up in Cork," she says with a smile in her voice.

"Ah, you're a star. Thank you." He'll send her some flowers.

"As are you. I hope it works out."

"Me too. Thanks again." Des replaces the receiver and stares at the phone, deep in thought. Simon will probably appeal. But there is nothing Grace can do now to help her case. And her solicitor has proven herself more than capable. The best thing for Des to do is say nothing. The less the man is in her head the better.

His mobile rings.

"You're not going to believe it!" Grace says.

"What?" he asks cautiously, though she sounds over the moon.

"He's paid the maintenance! I can't believe it. What's got into him?"

Des knows exactly what's got into him – an appeal.

"Oh, that's great, love."

"I can pay you back some of the money!"

God love her, he thinks. That is the least of her worries.

Grace throws a hoodie on over Holly's leggings and finds "The Eye of the Tiger" on Spotify. Maybe a Rocky vibe will get her through the ordeal that lies ahead.

"Don't laugh," she tells Myra on her way past reception.

Myra pumps the air but her words are drowned out by Survivor.

Grace better start running before the song is over and she loses momentum.

The jog down to the pier is doable – "down" being the operative word.

Birdsong fills the air. And the sky is everywhere.

Out past the pier, Grace runs, jumping over cow pats and slowing as she goes, her breath already a pant. She shoves up her sleeves and starts to blow out each breath, though she knows that's not right. When the path stops so does she. She *could* cut up through the graveyard and get out onto the road....

Tackling what she thought was a gentle incline, she starts to really feel the pull on her leg muscles. It's like she's lifting lead. She opens her coat and welcomes the cool air on her chest. She knows she should be breathing through her nose but she just can't get enough air.

Head down, teeth gritted, she pushes, pushes, pushes, herself until finally, she slows to a stop, bending over, hands on her thighs. She takes off her hoodie and ties the sleeves around her waist, her breath a burning pant, her mouth parched.

Recovered somewhat, she begins to walk, telling herself that at least she's doing *something*.

At the top of the incline, she stops and turns, hands on hips, taking a moment to look out over the sea, sparkling in the sun like flash photography. She could be in the South of France. She understands why West Cork attracts so many artists. She wishes she could paint. Instead she fishes her phone out of the sneaky pocket inside the waistband of Holly's leggings and does her best to capture the beauty of this place with a click.

Feeling the pull of the surgery, Grace turns around and starts to retrace her steps. Downhill now, she remembers to kick out her legs with every stride like she learned, years ago, in junior athletics. The bigger the stride, the less work to be done. She tilts her head back and enjoys the feeling of her shoulders loosening as her arms pump. And, just for a little while, running feels like freedom.

fifty

After a particularly long day at the surgery, which included diagnosing a young mum with cancer, Grace is not feeling up to Wayne Hills' book launch. She just wants to get home and collapse. Locking the door to her office, she remembers his many arguments for not going. She rolls her shoulders. Did he even want her there in the first place? No. It was she who brought it up. She'll ring Yvonne and bow out. Her friend will still have Alan for company. The three of them had planned to go together.

"Ready?"

Grace turns and sees Yvonne, looking stunning in a black swing dress, her hair up and glitter on her cheekbones.

"What are *you* doing here?" Grace asks. "The launch isn't till seven."

"I texted you. Thought we could nip to Ahern's for a quick one, get us in the mood."

Yvonne's energy is exhausting.

"It's been a really long day, Vonnie."

Yvonne immediately links her arm. "You are *not* backing out of this. Come *on!* There's *nothing* to do in this town."

"There's recovering from a long day."

"Don't go boring on me." As an afterthought, Yvonne adds, "There'll be free wine!"

"You don't even like wine."

"And it'll probably be plonk but I have to show up. I'm the village librarian," she says, sounding suddenly responsible. "And *you're* the GP. We'd be conspicuous in our absence."

Grace sighs. She did *say* she'd… gatecrash. Maybe he'll be expecting her. He *is* her patient. But the real reason Grace gives in is the glitter on her friend's cheeks. She just can't let her down. Not with that glitter.

"Alright but I need to get food first."

"Ahern's do a gorgeous toastie."

"I might nip home, though. And change."

"You are *not* denying me a beer with my grub. You look grand."

"I look manky. He's my patient–"

"Lucky you."

Grace rolls her eyes. "I'm just saying I should make an effort if I'm going to go. And look at you. You're gorgeous."

"You're gorgeous anyway."

Suddenly, Grace couldn't be bothered arguing. Or actually changing. She looks at her glittery friend. "Okay, okay. You win. As always."

Yvonne grins. "I do. Don't I?"

"Don't tempt me."

It's six when Jack is leaving the school with his hurling coach. After training, Mr. Lyons took him aside to give him an extended one-on-one session to familiarise him with the rules of the game and to show him some tricks. Coming through the school gates, the thin, balding, track-suited man turns to Jack.

"So, what position would you see yourself playing, Jack?" he asks in a thick Cork accent.

Jack stops walking. "Wait. You think I'm good enough for *the team*?"

"You're a natural athlete. And you've taken to it like a duck to water. You'd have to start as a sub though, prove yourself to the lads."

Jack is speechless. He didn't think he could do it, pick up a whole new sport at sixteen and make a team – potentially. He loved it, yeah. Never expected to be good enough.

"I've been watching your form. Personally, I think you'd make a good forward," Mr. Lyons says. "You have the hunger."

It's true that Jack's natural instinct is to shoot for goal. With hurling, he'd have two options, goal or over the bar. Whack the living daylights out of the ball wherever's handiest.

"I'd love centre forward." But Ginge plays centre. And it was Ginge who encouraged him to play. "Maybe right corner-forward? Or left."

The coach smiles and pats his shoulder. "Forward it is. We'll figure out the details as we go along. Right, d'you need a lift?"

"I'm only up the road. Thanks."

"See you tomorrow, so."

Jack grins. "See you tomorrow." He feels like actually skipping.

"And Jack?"

"Yeah?"

"Well, done, son."

Jack is grinning again.

Mr. Lyons flings his sports bag into his VW Golf and himself in after it. Jack waits till he pulls away, raising his hand like a local. What's he talking about? He *is* a local. Now.

"Wow," he says aloud. He turns for home. And stops dead, his stomach contracting to a point. "What are you doing here?" he asks his father, the words coming out slowly in disbelief. Emotions swamp him, guilt at the lies he told, fear of what his father will do and an overriding desire to protect his mum.

"Waiting for you to come out. Luckily, I'm a patient man. What were you *doing* in there?" His father smiles. "And who's your man?" he jokes dismissively.

Jack's mind is racing. Should he text his mum, warn her? Or should he see what his dad wants? Maybe Jack can handle this himself. Get him to leave – without trouble. "Training."

His father makes a point at looking at the hurl in Jack's hand. "Never thought I'd see the day."

Jack just shrugs.

"I've missed you," he says, looking into his son's eyes.

Jack bows his head. He's missed his father too – just doesn't want him to know it.

"Why did you lie?"

Jack looks up in sudden panic. Could he be wearing a wire? He tells himself not to be ridiculous. This is Ireland. Stuff like that doesn't happen here. Taping someone probably isn't admissible in court anyway. Entrapment or something. Still he's not going to admit to a lie. So, he just sighs.

"I'm sorry," his father says. "About everything. I made a lot of mistakes. Can we go for coffee? Just one coffee?"

There'll be people at The Coffee Cove; he won't be able to do anything. Maybe if Jack goes with him, gives him his time, he can persuade him to go, do the right thing. He can't think of a better plan. So, he nods.

"Okay."

"I saw a place called the Coffee Cove. Is that *it* in this town?"

Jack nods. He doesn't remind his father that it's actually a village.

"Incredible."

Jack knows what his father is doing. Trying to make him miss Dublin.

"Let's go," Jack says, taking control. He hopes that no one from his family comes along, not Holly, not Des and especially not his mum. He can do this. He knows he can.

Alan is driving home from a job, half a donut in his hand and sugar on his lips. He has plenty of time before the book launch. Not that he's in a rush. What he's looking forward to, this evening, is catching up with Grace and Yvonne when all the hoo-ha is over. It'll be like old times.

Almost at the school, he squints at two people coming towards him on the path. They have the same walk, heads tipped down, posture identical. It's Grace's kid, Jack, with…. Wait. Alarm bells go off in Alan's head. Des clearly didn't want his son-in-law around. Could *he* have been the reason for the security? But why security for Grace's ex? Alan's hands grip the wheel as an option strikes, an option that doesn't bear thinking about. If he touched her, if he harmed her, if he's back for more…. Heart racing, Alan slows and, a hundred yards beyond father and son, pulls in. He takes out his phone to call Des but remembers that his battery died half-an-hour ago. He hurries out of his overalls, watching them in the rear-view mirror. He jumps from the van. And follows at a distance.

"The house is so empty without you," Simon says to Jack as they round the corner onto the main street.

Jack thinks of his old room. Then every room in the house.

He grew up there. It was home.

"You guys made a lot of noise!" his father smiles with a sadness that seems, not just real, but apologetic. "Now, it's like a cemetery. Almost spooky." He sighs deeply. "It's like someone has stolen my family."

If this goes on much longer, Jack will have to walk away.

"So! How are you?" he asks, more cheerfully.

Jack's not telling him anything. Because that would be giving him ammo. "Grand."

"Happy?"

Jack nods.

"Good, good." He looks around the village, as if he has no idea how anyone could be happy here. Reaching the Coffee Cove, he holds the door open for his son. "The usual?" he asks once they're inside.

Spotting Nicky at the counter, Jack avoids eye contact. Maybe this was a bad idea. "I'll have a Coke. And a chocolate chip cookie," he says like a vote for his mum.

Simon nods and heads to the counter.

Jack takes a seat far from the window. He checks his watch. Half past six. His father will have to hit the road soon or he'll never get home. Jack wonders, again, if he should text a warning to his mum. Once more, he decides against it. She'd just try and come to his rescue. When she's the one who needs rescuing. Maybe that's what his father wants, for Jack to lure her to him. His stomach cramps. He has to stay calm.

At the next table, Jack overhears Matthew's mum, (Jacinta?) and his dad (who dropped a load of meat off at the house) talking about the book launch Jack's mum is going to. He leans over.

"What time's the book launch?" he asks realising that he has to get his dad out of town before then.

"Oh! Seven," Jacinta says, excitedly. "Are you going?"

He shakes his head. "Not my scene. Just wondered."

"Probably just as well. It'll be mobbed. Wait, you're Young Dr. Sullivan's son! Jack isn't it?"

He nods.

"How is she?"

Oh, oh. "Fine, thanks."

"We'll be forever grateful."

Jack produces a smile. "How's Matthew?"

"Oh wonderful. Truly wonderful. At home eating ice cream with his auntie. We thought we'd get out for the night after the week that was in it." Jacinta glances at her husband. "We should probably go on over soon, Tom, to get a spot near the front."

He checks his watch. "Plenty of time."

Jack panics. What if Jacinta meets his mum at the launch and tells her he's at The Coffee Cove with his dad?

"Is that your dad?" she asks now, watching him carrying a tray their way. "Fine looking man."

"My uncle," he lies and takes out his phone to kill all further conversation.

Jack's dad reaches the table. Jacinta and her husband return his smile, Jacinta curiously. Jack knows what they see: Respectable. Intelligent. Handsome. Well-dressed. Charming. His dad ticks all the boxes for a good guy. Jack wishes he could magically suck out that one bad thing. How easy everything would have been then. Would still be.

He unloads the tray and goes up to return it. Watching Nicky smile at him turns Jack's stomach. He wants his father out, away, gone. He reminds himself that the best way to do that is to play this game, do this dance, match every step his father takes with a counter-step that's a little more cunning.

Heads turn as his father walks back. Heads have always turned. The man is a walking ad for quality plastic surgery. And he knows it.

Behind him, the guy who did up Jack's grandad's house is going to the counter. Nicky looks surprised to see him.

"I'll have another latte, Nicky, thanks," he says, loudly. "All that sugar has done me in." He pats his stomach gently.

"For here or take away?"

"Here, this time. Shake things up!"

Smiling, she goes to make the coffee.

He glances over at Jack then immediately away again when their eyes meet.

Weird.

"Jack?"

"What?"

His dad has sat down and is zoning in on him like he's the only person in the room. It's a trick he has. Like a politician. Jack's not fooled.

"It's so good to see you," he's saying now.

Jack breaks up the cookie to avoid looking at him.

"I love you."

The words floor Jack. Because he believes him. And loves his father back. He looks up.

"I'd never do anything to hurt you," his dad says so earnestly. "You know that. Don't you?"

Jack can't speak, for fear of crying.

Next to them, Jacinta has stopped talking. Is she *listening*?

Tom stands up, lifting his eyebrows at his wife. "Coming?"

"We're grand for a while." She widens her eyes at him.

"Thought you wanted to get a good spot." Tom lifts his coat from the back of the chair and starts to put it on. He winks at Jack. "Good luck, son," he says and turns to go.

Rolling her eyes, Jacinta grabs her faux fur and hurries after him.

Jack feels a sudden fondness for Tom and a massive relief that they're gone. He looks back at his dad.

"But you did hurt me. Hurting Mum hurt me. Hurt us all."

He shakes his head at himself like that is the great regret of his life. "I don't know what made me do that. And I'm sorry, so, so sorry. But I've changed, Jack. I'm having therapy."

Hope rises in Jack. But he flattens it down again. His father's lies are fluid and slippery things.

"I'm going to appeal, Jack. I have to."

Jack hides his panic.

"It's not good for you to be without your dad and it's not good for me to be without you and Holly. It's just not natural. All I want is access, just to see you. It won't involve your mother. I won't ever need to see her again. And I won't bring her up ever again."

Jack doubts that.

"But can you please, *please*, when you're being interviewed by the psychologist or whoever for the Section 20 Report, can you please tell them that you lied? Otherwise we'll never see each other again. Even now, I shouldn't be talking to you but I had to risk it. Is this what you want? Really, Jack? For us to be apart forever? We love each other. I'm your *dad*. Let's start over. Courts never punish children. They just want to do the right thing by them. Let me do the right thing by my children. Please Jack, just tell them you lied. We all lie."

It's a lovely speech. But he's asking Jack to undo everything, stab his mother in the heart. If he admits that he lied, then that will make her a liar too. Because she backed up their lies. And maybe courts don't punish kids – and he's not sure he even believes that – but they definitely punish adults. Lying in court is a big deal. It's perjury. Even Jack knows that. He's not about to land everyone in trouble. Especially as his father's last three words are the truest of all. Jack can't trust him. And, so, he looks him in the eye. "I can't do that."

Outrage flares suddenly in his eyes as if someone has flipped a switch. "I didn't deserve those lies!"

And it is so clear to Jack that, whatever he says, he hasn't changed. Maybe people like him can't. He wishes so much that they could.

Already, he has switched back to calm. "There's another option, bud. You could come home. Live with your old man. No hassle. Just the two lads. All you'd have to do is tell them what you want."

He has called Jack "bud" for as long as he can remember. The word has always come filled with love. Jack swallows. It would be kinda cool, just the two of them, no hassle, at home in his room, his old life back....

"You want to come home, don't you, bud, away from this... backwater?" He glances around.

All he'd have to do is… ditch Holly and his mother. He raises his chin. "I like this backwater."

"Don't you miss your mates? Your hockey? Your school? Your life?"

Jack misses it all. Of course, he does.

"I'll up your pocket money. Two hundred a week. All you'd have to do is say you want to live with me. That's it."

He should have kept the money out of it. "Dad. You say you've changed. But you're still trying to manipulate me." Inside, Jack is crying. Because he wants his father in his life – but as a part of a happy family. And that can never happen.

"So, you're not going to do it," he says accusingly.

Jack presses his lips together. So much pressure. So much guilt.

"Maybe *Holly* will do the right thing. Maybe Holly will admit that she lied," his father says coldly, like a threat. "She was always a good kid."

"You stay away from her!" Jack flares.

With a sneer, his father stands up. "Thanks for your time, Jack."

Jack jumps to his feet and races from the coffee shop, leaving everything behind, his bag, his coat, hurl, sports gear.

Jack flies past the bookshop, all lit up and buzzing with life. He doesn't dare glance in; he might direct his father to his mother. He hopes that she's deep into the shop, surrounded by people. Invisible. He has to keep going. It's Holly his dad is after. Only she and Jack can change things. So, he keeps on running.

fifty-one

Village Books is heaving. It seems like the whole village is crammed into the quaint little bookshop. Especially the female contingent. Standing room only. If that. Grace spies Jacinta Creedon and her husband, Tom. Mia O'Driscoll is there with her potato-head husband. Even Paddy O'Neill is putting in an appearance. The only person she can't seem to see is the author. She smiles, watching Yvonne push her way through the mob to get to the wine table. Heroic.

Remembering that there will be speeches and possibly a reading, Grace puts her phone on silent.

A voice in her ear whispers something she can't hear. She swirls around, bringing her hands up to her chest and bending a little at the knee. Smiling in relief, she runs her hands through her hair as if that's where they were headed all along.

Wayne Hill, wine glass in hand, is looking officious. "I'm sorry, madam but this is a private party."

"I can see that," she says, glancing at the crowd. "How did you get such a big turnout?"

"I'm thinking boredom played a part. Must have."

She tilts her head. "Maybe you're just popular."

"Well, there *is* my magnetic charm."

Grace remembers that first consultation on the island. And laughs.

"What?" he asks, like he's offended.

"I'm just remembering that first time you came to see me."

"You know, a sore... groin... can really affect a man's mood."

"I bet."

He smiles. "Here. I brought you wine." He hands her a glass. "See? I'm much nicer now."

"You *are*!" She raises the glass and the corners of her mouth. "Congratulations on the book." She takes the copy she has just bought from her bag and hands it to him. "You'll have to sign it."

He flicks to the title page where he writes in a flourish of black: "To the woman who saved my crown jewels. Happy reading." He signs it, Wayne. Just Wayne. Then hands it back to her.

Her laugh is a surprised bark. She tucks the book away. She'll have to hide it when she gets home. People might get the wrong idea.

Someone is tapping a microphone. They look up.

"I better go," he says.

"Good luck!"

He grimaces. "I'll keep it short."

"Don't! We're out for the night." She looks for Yvonne. Is she growing the grapes? And where is Alan?

"You and?"

"My friend, Yvonne. She'll be raging she missed you."

"Well, maybe I'll see you guys after?"

"That'd be nice," she says, hoping the others won't mind. She wonders what Alan will make of him. When Alan finally shows up. She watches the author disappear through the crowd. And finally sees Yvonne coming in the opposite direction. She gives her a "where-have-you-been?" look.

Yvonne is giving her an entirely different one back.

"He *likes* you," is the first thing out of her mouth.

"*What*?"

"Wayne Hill, likes, you," she says, handing her a glass of wine.

Grace starts to panic. "No, he does not." She tries to put down the wine glass the author gave her but can't see anywhere to put it. So she stands holding two, like she has issues.

"Me thinks she doth protest too much," Yvonne cheerfully says. "You're probably on the death list of every single woman in the shop now. And some married ones too."

"Stop, Yvonne, *okay*?" she snaps, shoving the glass into the hand of a passing shop assistant.

Yvonne squints at her friend. "What?" she asks gently. "What is it?"

"Nothing. Forget it." She's shaking. And close to tears.

"No, seriously, what?" Yvonne asks apologetically.

Grace leans towards her and, in an urgent whisper, says. "I've just left a marriage, okay? I'm trying to get my life back. Not give it away again to some *man*."

Yvonne nods like crazy. "I understand. I'm sorry. I wasn't thinking."

"Forget it. Let's just enjoy our night, okay?"

"Okay but can I just say sorry for being such an eejit?"

"Alright. But you're my eejit and I love you."

"Love you too." They hug. "I'm so glad you're home."

Jack bursts into the house, slamming and locking the door behind him. Des and the dog turn.

"Where's Holly?" Jack demands, running to snap down the blinds.

"Upstairs, studying. Why?" Des asks in concern.

Jack thunders upstairs.

Des follows at his own restricted pace.

Holly looks up as Jack bursts in.

"Okay," Jack says, aiming for calm. "Don't panic but he's here. Dad's here in Killrowan. He's appealing the case and wants us to say we lied."

Holly stands up looking very Joan of Arc, calm, composed, strong. "Well, we just won't. And he can't make us."

Jack nods like he needed to hear those words. "He can't do anything as long as we don't open the door."

Holly's eyes widen. "What about Mum? Where is she?"

"Probably at the book launch. I'll call her." Jack takes out his phone.

At the door to Holly's room, Des is taking out his own phone and calling Paddy O'Neill.

"D'you think I've time to go to the loo?" Grace asks Yvonne.

"See if you can hold."

Grace makes a face. "Don't think I can."

"Okay, well, hurry up. It's about to start." Yvonne looks around. "Where is *Alan*?"

Grace squeezes her way through an entire village. Opening the door to the bathroom, she sees two women, ahead of her, waiting for the one and only cubicle. Deep in conversation, neither sees her. She reverses out, holding the door half open so no one cuts in front of her.

"She's cute out," a voice slips through the door. "Getting Alan into the clinic where they can make eyes at each other!"

What? Grace's heart stops.

"You wouldn't mind if she kept it at that. Did you see her flirting with Wayne Hill, just now? As if our own Alan isn't good enough for her. As if she'd be off in a shot if she got the chance."

Grace stands frozen, gripping the door she knows she should close. She doesn't need to hear this. And yet she does.

"Then again," one says, "Who'd blame her when it comes to Wayne Hill? They *say* he has a six-pack."

"Six-pack or not, one man's good enough for most of us."

The toilet flushes.

Then Grace hears the unmistakable – and currently enraged – voice of Jacinta Creedon. "I thought it was the pair of ye!"

"Well, we knew it was you by the shoes."

"So ye thought I'd be fine, hearing ye deride a good woman. Ye ought to be ashamed of yerselves."

Suddenly, Grace is being yanked into the bathroom, as Jacinta opens the door with Herculean energy. Face-to-face with her detractors, Grace doesn't know who has turned palest, them or her.

"Get in here, Young Dr. Sullivan, and use the loo," Jacinta bosses. "These two deserve to hold."

With a sigh, Grace makes for the cubicle. Just before she opens the door, though, she stops. Then she turns and eyeballs the pair like she has reached the end of her patience. "Wayne Hill does have a six-pack. For the record."

The intercom starts to buzz. And buzz. Holly looks at Jack whose phone is to his ear.

"She's not answering!" he exclaims.

Des is having the same problem with Paddy O'Neill.

Downstairs, the intercom keeps buzzing.

Holly goes to the top of the stairs. "Well, if he's here, he can't be with her, right?" she says so calmly that Jack and Des exchange a glance.

She starts down the stairs.

"Don't open it!" Jack warns.

"D'you think I've lost it?" she asks, turning. "I just want to see him." She goes to the intercom, pushes the button on the video screen and takes a sharp intake of breath at the sight of her father, looking up into the camera.

His voice invades. "Holly! It's Dad. Open up. I just want to talk, love."

She lets the button go and swivels around. "Can he see me?" she asks her grandad.

"No."

"Then how did he know I'd pushed the button?"

"He didn't," Des says. "But it's you he wants to talk to so he's just talking."

Holly pushes the button again.

"How are you, sweetie?" he continues.

Holly turns back to Des, releasing the button again. "It's like he can see me."

Des goes over to her. "He can't, though, pet. He's just chancing his arm like he always does."

Halfway up the stairs where there's still service, Jack hits redial on his phone.

"Holly, love. I'm sorry," her father is saying. "For everything."

Des puts an arm around her. And Benji joins them.

"Open up, pet. Let's talk."

Silence.

Simon bangs on the door.

Holly jumps. Des holds her tighter. And Benji starts to bark.

"Grace! Are *you* in there? Open up! I want to talk. I made a mistake. I'm sorry. Okay?"

Holly wraps her arms around herself. Her grandad kisses the top of her head.

"Grace, come on. Let me in. I love you. Let's talk. I've driven all this way. Twice."

"Twice?" Holly looks up her grandad.

Who shrugs.

"I need to see you. I need to see the children!"

The only response is a protective bark from a dog who can read people.

"Jack! I know you're in there. Open up, bud. Come on! This is ridiculous! Grace? Come on, now." His voice is growing more and more impatient. Holly hopes that he'll give up and go away. "You've made your stand, Grace. And I've taken it on the chin like a man. Now come home, all of you!" His voice eases again. "It's not the same without you. I'm sorry. I was a fool. I've changed. Okay?"

Holly looks at Jack and whispers, "Do you think he means it?"

Jack shakes his head. And tries his mother again.

On the screen, Alan walks up to Simon. "Stop harassing this family."

Startled, Simon turns to face him, then relaxes. "Oh! It's the workman!" he sneers. "Hello, workman!"

"Workman, concerned citizen, I don't think the police will mind either way." He holds up his phone.

The two men stare each other down.

"Alright, don't get your knickers in a twist," Simon says. Then he turns and walks away back towards the village.

Jack and Holly look at each other.

"Mum!" they say together.

fifty-two

Grace emerges to a room hushed by the voice of Wayne Hill at the microphone. She'll have to stay put till he's finished. Which is fine. She's in no rush anywhere.

"So, I escaped to West Cork," seems to be the punchline of a joke because everyone laughs.

Grace notices how short his hair is at the back. That he's had a haircut for the occasion endears him to her. Was he nervous about it, after all?

"I was getting away," he says, growing serious. "*Running* away, to be honest." He pauses.

Grace wants to reach out, tell him he's not alone. Which would be pretty stupid, given that he wants to be alone. He gathers himself and resumes with an endearing openness and honesty. When he thanks people for welcoming him into their heavenly piece of the world, Grace feels them taking him into their hearts. From her vantage point, he seems happy. She hopes he is. Even if just for tonight. Because you don't leave the past behind, ever, really. You can't. No matter how hard you try.

This is what she's thinking when a hand slips into hers and grips it like a vice. She freezes, knowing instinctively that her own past has shown up, like she always knew it would. He would never be satisfied with presenting the world with a shattered image – no more perfect marriage, no more perfect wife, no more perfect family.

To anyone watching, this is love, this beautiful man slipping his sculpted hand into hers.

"Come with me," he whispers into her ear like a lover. "I've got the children." He looks into her eyes and smiles, the man with the upper hand.

She could escape his grip in two swift, Krav Maga seconds but he has trapped her with words, words that kill all resistance. He has, like every good predator, gone straight for the jugular, her greatest weakness, the children. Across the room, she sees Paddy O'Neill. For a second, she thinks he sees but then his gaze floats back to Wayne Hill at the microphone and he laughs at something the author has said.

Simon's other arm grips her elbow and she is being shunted forward. People look surprised that anyone could be leaving. But, behind Grace, Simon must be reassuring them with winning smiles because, one by one, they look at him and smile before moving out of the way. A path clears before them like the parting of the seas. All Grace can think of is the children. What does he mean he's got them? Has he taken them, tied them up? Or have they gone willingly? Are they okay? That's all that matters. Are they okay?

Passing Wayne Hill, the author looks at her questioningly for the briefest of seconds before Simon turns her and faces her towards the door.

Outside the cold air is like a slap in the face.

"You don't need to hold me," Grace says. "You've got the children."

But he doesn't loosen his grip, just leads her forward and away from the bookshop. She knows it's a mistake to go with him like this; knows that this is when abusive men are at their most dangerous, when their victims have made a break. But Grace can't do anything until she knows where the children are, until she is sure that they are safe. She'll die for them if she has to.

Alan comes to, lying on his back on the path outside the supermarket. Holding his head, he sits up. It takes a second but he does remember what happened. That sly so and so turned suddenly and thumped him so hard in the face that he went down. Like a typical cheat, his fist was rock hard, like he had something in it. Alan scrambles to his feet, his head throbbing. On the street up ahead, he sees Paddy O'Neill leave the book shop. That's one man who needs to know.

Headed towards the edge of the village, having crossed the road, Simon pulls Grace even closer.

"I've missed you, Grace," he says in that sickly placating voice he used whenever he wanted to make up to her. Which was after every time. She's not sure which she hated most. The violence or the voice. Because it was the voice that kept her there. The reasoning. The apologies. The promises to change. Empty, empty, empty. His aftershave invades her nostrils and a wave of nausea hits. How did she think she could get away? How did she think this would ever be over? He has controlled her for, well, actually, nineteen years if she's honest. He knows no other life.

"We love each other, Gracie. What were you thinking, taking the kids from me?" His voice is silk. Like it always was. Even when he hit her, he did it calmly, skilfully, beautifully he probably thought.

But he has just reminded her of the one thing she has on her side, the one thing that got her away. The law. Will it be enough now?

"Twelve months in prison, that's what you'll get for breaking a barring order," she tries. "Give the children to me and leave and I won't report you."

He laughs. "I won't be leaving without you or the children. You're mine. That's what you've forgotten. You've had your little rebellion, Grace. Now it's over."

What does he mean? What's he going to do? Is she facing her biggest fear, the one that kept her stuck?

"Look at you with your pathetic hair, thinking you're something. Well, you're *nothing* without me. And you know it. You fail at everything you do. What kind of mother takes her children from their father, their school, their friends?"

They've reached the car park. Though its poorly lit, Grace spies the car tucked into a corner. Her stomach turns at the stark reminder of the past. So many things were done to her in that car.

She squints trying to see into it, trying to see the children. All she sees is black. Closer now, Simon, bleeps the car open. The inside lights up. Grace sees that the car is empty. Panic grips her.

"Where are they? What did you do with them?"

Ignoring her, he tries to force her inside but everything she learned at the self-defence class is screaming at her not to go with him, not to co-operate, not to get in. Pulling against him, she fumbles for her phone. She'll call Jack! See if they're okay. Simon could be bluffing; of course, he could. Why didn't she think of that sooner? But as soon as she produces the phone, Simon slaps it from her hand and it skitters across the ground.

"Sometimes you have to strike first." The words come to her clearly. Calmly. She moves like lightening, freeing herself in two swift movements, then swivelling round and striking upward, sharp and fast, the heel of her hand to his perfect chin. Then the other heel to his nose. Then back to his chin.

"No!" she screams with every jab, no to the past, no to the present, and no to whatever future he had planned. Each one comes from a place of strength, a place that means: no more.

"Okay, Grace, that'll do." It's the voice of Paddy O'Neill.

Grace turns in shock to see not just the sergeant but Alan. And Wayne Hill. And behind him, Jacinta Creedon. And Yvonne. And behind them a whole village of people, standing together in silence on this cold October night. Mia O'Driscoll holds Grace's eyes. Something passes between the two women, something silent and strong. Something like sisterhood.

"The children!" Grace says.

"Are okay," Alan reassures, coming towards her. "They're safe at home with Des."

"Thank God!" she says, bursting into tears of relief. "I thought…" She falls into his arms.

"You're under arrest," Paddy O'Neill says.

"*Finally*!" Simon declares triumphantly.

"It's you, Simon Willoughby, who's under arrest," Paddy says, striding towards him. "For breaking your barring order."

"*She* assaulted *me*!"

"I saw a clear case of self-defence."

"Me, too," Wayne Hill says.

"And me." Mia O'Driscoll, fire in her eyes, steps away from her husband. Grace fears that she'll suffer for this later and her heart floods with appreciation at the risk she has taken. She prays that she can pay her back.

"If you think some small-town cop–" Simon starts to bluster.

"We have cuffs here, too," Paddy says cheerfully. Cuffing him. "Now, if you don't mind, I'll read you your rights."

Jack comes racing into the car park. "Mum!"

Alan releases her immediately.

"Oh, sweetheart. Thank God you're okay. Where's Holly?"

"Coming. With Grandad." Seeing his dad in cuffs, Jack's face fills with regret.

Simon holds up his bound wrists. "You can blame your mother for this."

Jack turns from him and hugs his mum, his head resting on the top of hers.

She has never been more grateful for a hug. How did her little boy get to be so big? How did he grow so strong? Over his shoulder, she sees Holly, hurrying around the corner, linking her grandad's arm. Grace's eyes fill with tears of relief as her gaze falls over Wayne Hill, Jacinta Creedon, Yvonne, Mia and the entire bookshop of people who came to her rescue. She is swayed with gratitude. She is home.

fifty-three

Back at the house, everyone's talking over everyone else.

"He's going to appeal!" Jack tells Grace. "He wanted us to admit we lied but we wouldn't do it."

Grace looks from him to Holly. "Did he hurt ye?" is all she wants to know.

They shake their heads.

"He was just trying to persuade us," Jack reassures.

Des hurries his navy jumper and cap into Grace's hands. Shaking with cold and a million other things, she gratefully pulls them on, yanking the sleeves down over hands she can no longer feel. Smelling her dad in the wool is like being a child again, wrapped up in his arms. It calms her. She wishes something could calm the children who are a mix of hyper energy and shock, Holly chewing the cuff of her jumper, something she hasn't done since they were in Dublin. It's a habit she reverts to when nervous or distressed or both. The cuff of her last school jumper was in tatters.

"Everyone, sit down at the table," Des says. "I'm making hot chocolate."

Grace complies first, hoping the children will follow.

To her relief, they do.

"Is he going to prison?" Holly asks, suspiciously quietly.

"I don't know pet," Grace says. "How would you feel if he did?"

She bows her head. "Not good."

Grace would love him behind bars, away, safe. But then he'd use it to manipulate the children. She reminds herself to breathe. At least Paddy is holding him for the night. What was he going to do to her? Where was he going to take her? She can't think about that. "I'll call our lawyer first thing in the morning."

Des sets down a mug of hot chocolate in front of everyone, then joins them at the table in silence.

Everyone takes a sip in weird synchronicity. At least Holly has stopped chewing her sleeve.

"D'you think he'll still appeal after what happened?" Jack asks.

Grace shakes her head. "I really don't know, sweetheart. It can't be good that he broke the barring order," she says hopefully. "And knocked out poor Alan."

The doorbell rings. Everyone looks at each other, each thinking the same thing: What now?

Jack goes to the intercom. "It's Alan," he says and opens the door.

Alan comes in with his palms up. "I don't want to disturb ye. I just want to ask your mam a quick question."

Grace jumps to her feet. "Alan, your eye!" It has closed over with swelling and the skin around it is bright red. Grace examines it. "Let's get this X-rayed."

"I'm grand, I'm grand. I just–"

"Sit down." She gets a packet of frozen peas from the fridge, wraps it in a tea-towel and puts it to his eye.

He holds it in place. "Grace, I was just wondering if you want me to press charges. I'm happy enough not to. In fact, it wouldn't be my style to. I just want to know what's best for ye. It could end up in the paper, you see."

Holly and Jack exchange a worried glance.

"Not about us!" Grace rushes to reassure. "They can't report on a broken barring order. Just what happened with Alan."

Jack nods.

Grace looks at her childhood friend, so grateful that he thought of this. "I'm not sure, Alan; it might help. Just in case we need to prove he was violent…" She looks at the children.

Holly is back chewing.

Alan frowns but only one eyebrow moves due to the swelling. "I was thinking that. Even just to make him think twice about coming back down."

Everyone – even Holly – is agreed on that.

Grace takes a photograph of Alan's face and pings it to his phone. "In case you need it for evidence."

He smiles. "You think of everything."

Grace wishes she could think of a solution to the threat of Simon. What if he gets off with a fine?

Alan gets up and hands the pack of peas to Grace. "Well, I won't keep ye."

She pushes it back to him. "Keep it. And drop into the surgery in the morning when the swelling's gone down and I'll see if you need an X-ray."

Alan nods.

"Thanks, Alan, for everything," Grace says.

"Yeah. Thanks," Jack says a little grudgingly.

Alan winks at him with his good eye. "Sure, I did nothing but dent the footpath."

"You did more than that," Holly says. "You're a bit of hero, actually."

He waves the bag of peas dismissively. "I'm nothing of the sort," he mumbles.

"Take the compliment, Alan," Des says. "How often are you called a hero?"

Alan smiles at Holly. "It's a first."

fifty-four

Grace finishes speaking with Freda Patterson at eight-thirty in the morning, her body a knot of tension, her mind in a time-warp. She knows that, downstairs, Holly, Jack and her dad are waiting to hear. She takes a deep breath and tries to get everything clear in her head. Then she makes for the door.

Halfway down the stairs, she's met with three pairs of hungry eyes.

"What did she say?" Jack eagerly asks.

Grace can't give them any certainty and doesn't know how to tell them. "Let's sit down."

"I'll make tea," Des says.

Grace, Holly and Jack sit where they were last night. And it's like déjà vu.

"Can he appeal?" Jack asks.

Grace nods. "But breaking the barring order won't help his case. He's in breach of a court order."

"What does that mean – won't help his case?" he asks impatiently.

Grace scratches an eyebrow. "There's no real certainty till you're in court."

"Great," he says sarcastically.

"You know there's no certainty with the law. You're used to it."

"Don't have to like it," he says moodily.

Holly looks up from nibbling the sleeve of her new school jumper. "What about prison?"

Grace tries to condense Freda's legalese. She really needs that tea.

Right on time, Des sets it down in front of her.

"Thanks, Dad," she says, wrapping her hands around the mug.

"Mum!" Holly reminds her.

"Sorry." She's back at her eyebrow. "Okay. Freda said that prison is usually unlikely in cases like this but as he seriously assaulted Alan… that would be factored in."

"We have to tell Alan to drop the charges!" she panics.

"Hmm," Grace says. "I actually asked Freda about that. She said that Paddy O'Neill will have sent a file to the Director of Public Prosecutions – and only she can decide to prosecute or not. Not Alan. He could *withdraw* his statement but…"

"Well, let's ask him to do that!"

"Wait, Holly. Slow down," her brother calmly warns. He looks at his mum. "What happens if he *doesn't* go to prison?"

"He'll probably get a small fine. The fact that he's an eminent plastic surgeon who does pro bono work will probably go in his favour but even that's not certain. Nothing is, to be honest."

Jack looks at Holly. "He could still come back."

"Not if he's appealing!" Holly says. "He won't risk it again!"

"Yeah but what if he loses the appeal and *then* comes back, madder than ever?" Jack asks. "Think, Holly."

"I don't want him to go to prison!" she says on the verge of tears.

"Guys," Grace reluctantly interrupts. "There *is* another way." She looks from Jack to Holly. "You could agree to access. Holly? Maybe you want that? Maybe now that we're away and you've had space–"

Holly shakes her head wildly. "No. I just don't want him to go to prison. That's all. Prison's awful."

"We don't want access, we don't want him wrecking our heads trying to get at Mum, we want a new start, we want *peace*." Jack says it all in one galloping earnest breath.

Grace nods. "Okay." She had to ask. For them.

"So, what do we *do*?" Holly asks, eyes welling.

Grace feels her own eyes sting with frustration.

Jack drums his fingers on the table, fast, like some incredible pianist.

Hypnotised, everyone watches.

At last, he looks up. "Okay, I've an idea." He looks from Grace to Holly. "But you'd have to be okay with it."

Grace approaches the police station wishing she'd avoided breakfast. Any minute now, the contents of her stomach are going to make an appearance.

She pushes in the door. And in the main office is surprised to see Paddy O'Neill. He looks shattered, his hair all over the place and an impressive combination of shadow and bags under his eyes. But those eyes are sparkling with merriment.

"Paddy, haven't you had any sleep?"

"Oh, I have. Slept like a log here at my desk to a lovely soundtrack of abuse." He chuckles.

"Can I see him? Would that be okay?"

He frowns. "Are you sure you want to after his performance last night?"

She nods. Though she's anything but sure. "I can stay outside the cell, right?"

"Oh Lord, yeah."

"Thanks, Paddy."

He unlocks the door to a stark area containing two cells, side-by-side, in front of them a corridor. Outside Simon's cell, the sergeant places down a stool for Grace.

"I'll be right outside, pet," he reassures as if she's still eighteen. "Visitor," he says to Simon.

He sits up from the cot he was lying on. And Grace thought Paddy looked rough! Simon seems to have aged overnight, as if all his plastic surgery has abandoned him and his grey hairs have had (many) babies. His early morning stubble is patchy and weak – with little bits of red he has always hated.

"Well, look who it is," he says mockingly.

Grace keeps her face impassive as she sits on the stool.

"I spent a night in a cell because of you!" Simon spits.

"No. Because of you," she corrects, calmly. Because, facing him now, she remembers every "no" from last night. And the fact that they meant "no more."

"You have no idea of the shitstorm I'm about to bring down on you!" he threatens. "You *assaulted* me."

She doesn't mention Alan or the years of abuse. "I have a village of witnesses who say it was self-defence. But I'm not here to talk about that. I'm here to ask you to leave us in peace. Just walk away, Simon."

He gets up and walks towards her, threateningly. "They're my kids too."

She doesn't blink, flinch, move. "And if you let them get on with their lives, they'll see you when they're eighteen. Jack wanted me to tell you that. He's happy to see you when he can look into your eyes man-to-man. That's in just one-and-a-half years."

It's as if she hasn't spoken. "You lied under oath and I'll prove it," he says. Then he smiles triumphantly. "There's no medical evidence to say that the children were hurt. That's what you've forgotten."

She's tried to be fair. Now, she has to end this. She stands up and faces him across bars. "If you appeal or if you ever come down here again, I'll go public."

His eyes widen. For a second, he's speechless. When he recovers, it's with his usual arrogance. "You wouldn't do that to the children!" he says like he's dealt a winning card.

"Actually, it was Jack's idea."

"So what?" he explodes. "You're his mother! You can't expose him to that! The family courts are held in private to protect children!"

"Which also protects the abuser," she calmly cuts across his rant.

"Don't call me an abuser!" he shouts, a droplet of spittle flying through the air in slow motion. It lands on the lapel of her jacket.

She flicks it away with the same disgust that she'd flick him away.

"You're bluffing," he says as if he's having a Eureka moment. His faces relaxes.

"The news is already public here in Killrowan because of you. The children have had to face into school this morning knowing that there will be questions, knowing that their secret is no longer theirs. You've blown their privacy away. We have nothing to lose by going public because everyone we care about already knows now. You, however, will have to look your precious patients in the eye, your esteemed colleagues, hospital management. The man on the street. But if that doesn't convince you maybe this will."

She opens her bag and, from it, produces an envelope, on it, one word: Dad.

Simon stares at the envelope being passed through the bars to him. Something tells him not to take it but he can't resist the word "Dad."

He slips his thumb under the fold and rips it open.

> *Dear Dad,*
>
> *I love you. But Holly and I need peace now. We can't go back to the muffled sounds of violence and tears. We can't have you climbing into our heads and trying to turn us against Mum. We love you and we love Mum. That's the saddest thing. All we want is a happy family. And we can never have that. You say that access is best for us. It's not. Because you can't help yourself. You always end up trying to influence us, manipulate us, wreck our heads. Maybe you don't even know you're doing it but it kills us, you know?*
>
> *I've lived with so much guilt, guilt for not standing up for Mum, guilt for all the mean things I said to her, guilt for almost becoming you. I'm just not going to do that anymore. I'm just not. If you try for access, I'll fight you every step of the way and you'll lose me. Forever.*
>
> *Think about it. All you're fighting for is one-and-a-half years of my life – and probably just every few weekends. But if you walk away now. If you leave us alone, then when I'm eighteen, I'll make contact because then we can start over not as father and son but man to man. There's so much we could do together.*
>
> *I'm messed up, Dad. This is my chance to start trying to unpick that by living a normal life. I'll fight with everything I've got for that normal life. I deserve it. We all do.*
>
> *That's it. That's the deal.*
>
> *Jack*

Simon seethes. She has turned them against him. That's what's happened, here. He should have known. She always was manipulative, always did put herself first, the worst kind of parent. He wants to ball the letter up and throw it at her. But he knows his son, he knows that Jack, above all, means what he says, a great kid despite his mother. Simon doesn't want to lose him. Won't lose him. A few snatched weekends versus a lifetime.

He looks up. "I won't appeal."

The relief on her face makes him want to lash out.

"Thank you," she whispers. And as she turns to go, it hits him: He is watching his wife, life, family walk away.

fifty-five

Grace crosses the road and struggles up the slope to the clinic, feeling like she's already put in a day's work. Rounding the curve in the driveway, she sees Wayne Hill sitting on the clinic wall, a bunch of flowers in his hand. Her stomach tightens. It's such bad timing. Especially after what Yvonne said last night. Grace doesn't need this. Whatever "this" is.

He jumps down from the wall like his inner eighteen-year-old is alive and kicking. Then he starts to amble towards her.

She doesn't know what to say to him. She can't be rude.

"I've no idea what these are," he says, handing her the colourful bouquet. "I asked for their cheeriest flowers."

They are, actually, gorgeous. She inhales their uplifting scent. "I've no idea what they are either but they're lovely. Thank you." She'll give him that.

He shoves his hands in his pockets and looks down at his feet – maybe he really is eighteen inside.

"It was either that or a signed copy of a book you already have." His eyes come up from his shoes to meet hers. He grows serious. "Are you okay? I didn't know whether to come or not. I decided to be bold."

She smiles and nods.

"You ruined my book launch," he says with a lopsided smile.

She did not expect to be laughing right now but it feels good. Very bloody good. "I did warn you about gate-crashers."

"This is true."

Still, she hates the thought of ruining his big night. "I hope the party carried on afterwards?"

"I've no idea. I checked into my B&B and worried about you. Kept wanting to ring but I'm sure everyone else did too. And you had your family. How are they, by the way, your children?"

She nods slowly. "They're good." And when she gets to share the news with them, they'll be even better. "I can't believe how resilient they are. They surprise me every day. They're going to be okay," she says and absolutely believes it, suddenly. Something inside her lifts. They're all going to be okay.

"Will he get time?"

"I don't know. But he won't be bothering us again. That much I know."

He breathes out a long breath, as though he'd been genuinely worried for her. He's a good guy, she thinks. But then she knew that from his books.

"There are good guys in the world," he says co-incidentally. "I'm not saying I'm one of them. Just that they exist. Don't give up on us."

She thinks of Alan and Des. "Oh I know. I won't." She really is sorry she ruined his night. "You didn't stay in Killrowan last night just to see if I was okay?"

"No, no. I was planning on a few drinks on Ahern's. As it happened, I ended up having a lovely chat with – your dad's first love."

"Whaaat?"

He smiles and winks. "I'll tell you sometime. Till then…" he nods towards the surgery. "You better get in there and fix, I don't know, random crown jewels."

She laughs. "Not one of my commoner complaints, thankfully. Sorry. I didn't mean…" She holds up the flowers. "Thanks so much for these."

"Hey, thanks for coming to the launch. You didn't have to."

"I really do apologise for–"

"Don't." He reaches out and gently taps her arm like he wants to say more. "You take care."

"I will," is a promise to herself.

Grace approaches the surgery with growing apprehension. How will people react after last night? Will they pity her? Think less of her – as a person and as a doctor? Maybe no one'll want to see her.

She takes a deep breath and goes inside.

The minute she sees Myra her hand shoots to her forehead. "I forgot your chocolate chip cookie!"

Myra stands up and does a very unusual thing – she leaves the reception. She comes up to Grace and, without a word, opens her arms and folds her up in them.

Breathing out, Grace lets her body relax. And for the loveliest moment, it feels like she has a mother again.

"Does anyone want to see me?" she asks, her voice small.

Myra pulls back and looks into her eyes. "Only everyone." She grins. "Go on in and take a minute. I'll bring you in a coffee – with the chocolate chip cookie I bought you." She winks. "Oh, I nearly forgot. Alan left something in for you."

"Wait! Is he gone? I was going to see if he needed an X-ray!"

"He said he was grand. Looked atrocious though." An eyebrow lifts. "But very manly."

Grace laughs. "I won't tell Fred you said that."

Myra wafts the air. "Go away outta that. Let me get the box."

Box? Grace wonders.

Myra hurries back behind the counter then passes through a box of about six inches by six.

Grace picks it up. "Ooh. It's heavy."

"That's what *I* thought," Myra says, peering at it curiously. "And whatever's in there, moves around."

Grace smiles at her detective work. "I'll keep you posted." She takes it inside. And opens it straight up. "Awww," she says, aloud. A box of smooth round stones painted with cartoon clouds, stars and daisies. And a note saying. "Checked for environmentalists and risked the beach. Hope you're okay. Chat later. Love you, Alan."

She takes out her phone and sends him a thank you with a stream of emojis. Then she reaches for her favourite stone – a simple heart – and puts it in her pocket.

On her way to call the next patient, she holds it up to Myra. "Stones!"

Myra squints in confusion. "*Stones?*"

"Stones." Grace tries to peer at the upside-down list. Unsuccessfully. "Who's first?" she asks. "I forgot to look."

Mia bursts out laughing. "He does look like a potato." But then her face changes. "Can I ask you something?"

"Of course." Grace is expecting a did-he-do-this-to-you? question. And that's fine. She'll answer anything if it helps. She can talk about this. She can tell Mia all that happened to her – if that's what she needs. Her secret is out now and there's freedom in that. She's going to tell Yvonne everything – because Yvonne *will* ask. And Grace wants friendship, real friendship, no secrets. She'll tell Alan too, if he can take it. He may not want to know. Lovely, lovely Alan.

"Why us?" Mia asks, her eyes suddenly huge and lost. "I keep asking myself 'Why me?' Did he see me coming? Am I just too soft? Did I give in too easily from the beginning, fitting in with his plans, doing what he wanted?"

The truth hits Grace like a punch to the gut. "Everyone becomes vulnerable when they fall in love. That's what love is. Opening up and trusting that we'll be okay. Some of us get lucky. Some of us don't. I think we just got unlucky."

Mia's face fills with hope. "You think? I just feel so stupid, so blind, so weak–"

"Because that's what he's done to you. Let's not blame ourselves anymore. We've done our time," she says, like domestic violence is a prison sentence. It is. "Now let's get you out of this situation. Let's get you free."

"Would it be okay to hug you?" Mia asks uncertainly.

Grace grins. "I'd love a hug."

They cling to each other. One survivor. One future survivor.

Suddenly, Grace sees a beautiful irony in all that has happened. Because of Simon, another woman has decided: "Enough!" This is where everything starts to change. This is where a new life begins.

"So, the first thing we do is…"

THE END

"Mesmerised as you were by the stones," Myra says ironically.

"Exactly."

Myra checks the list. "Mia O'Driscoll."

Grace's blood runs cold. What has he done to her?

Grace calls Mia's name. Across the waiting room, two women exchange a long and silent glance. There's so much in it. A common bond. An understanding. A sympathy. A compassion. When Mia rises it's without guarding herself and without any obvious pain. Grace starts to hope; maybe the visit is for an ordinary medical complaint.

Grace smiles warmly when Mia reaches her. "Come on in."

In the surgery, Mia takes a seat without being asked to and looks at Grace with concern as she, herself, sits. "I came to see if you're okay."

Her kindness touches Grace deeply. "I'm really well, thank you. It's over," she says as the reality of her visit to the station hits her. "He won't be coming back." She wants to shout the words.

"I'm so happy for you."

It's Grace's turn for concern. "How are you, Mia?"

Mia's chest rises. "I'm going to leave him."

It's not her words so much as the look of determination in her eyes that convinces Grace.

"Oh, Mia! That's the best news!" It's a day of best news.

"Can you help me?" Mia asks. "Tell me how to do it. Get away without him killing me first."

Grace moves her chair right up to Mia, takes her hands and squeezes them in encouragement. Looking into her eyes, she says, "You've done the hardest part. You've decided. Now, I'm going to be right beside you. Every step of the way. You're not alone in this anymore. We can do this. We *will* do this."

Tears of relief and gratitude fill Mia's eyes. "Thank you," she whispers.

"Potato head won't know what hit him."

"Potato head?"

Grace scratches her head and grimaces. "That's what I call him. The bank manager."

About The Author

Aimee Alexander is the pen name of award-winning, internationally bestselling, Irish author, Denise Deegan. Originally from Cork, she lives in Dublin with her family where she regularly dreams of sunshine, never having to cook and her novels being made into movies. West Cork holds a very special place in her heart.

Also by Aimee Alexander
The Accidental Life of Greg Millar
Pause to Rewind
All We Have Lost

Checkout Girl: free short story available on Aimee's website: www.aimeealexander.com

Writing as Denise Deegan
Through The Barricades
And By The Way
And For Your Information
And Actually

Acknowledgements

This book would not exist without my author friend, Jean Grainger, who encouraged me to "just" sit down and write two thousand words a day, every day – or I'd hear from her. She was true to her word. Thanks, Jeannie.

Huge thanks to Siobhan Cronin and the fabulous *Southern Star* crew for answering all my crazy questions about West Cork life – and in such an entertaining way. Packing my bags and moving!

Heartfelt appreciation to Carrie McDermott whose patient replies to my many legal questions forced me to be even more creative with the plot because the law was not going my characters' way. Thanks, also, to my old school pal, Carol Leland for directing me to Carrie.

Grateful thanks to Rebecca and Dr Niall Maguire for your invaluable guidance on the life of a rural family doctor.

Forever grateful to Lisa Marmion, from Safe Ireland, for your insight into domestic abuse and for checking that I accurately represented the harsh reality that many women sadly face.

The trio of Clodagh Murphy, Keris Stainton, Sarah Painter deserve thanks and hugs for motivating me to get this story out to the world. You would not believe the amount of things I allowed to stall me, from book covers to confidence.

Speaking of book covers, many thanks to Anne Marie Cronin, photographer extraordinaire, who patiently offered me so many beautiful photos of West Cork.

So appreciative of my fabulous crew of advance readers who not only advised on story but on an endless stream of covers and titles. Sandra Baxter, Karla Bynum, Diana Coursey Davis, Marca Davies, Melanie Evans, Nancy Frank, Terry Hague, Valerie Judge, Patricia Kieran, Heather Lewis, Colleen Malito, Alison Mink, Bev Morris, Miriam Newton, Carole Olson, MaryAnn Randall, Claire

Rudd, Melanie Evans, Nikki Weijdom and Ciara Winkelmann. Angels on my shoulders. Both shoulders.

To all the wonderful book bloggers and online book club members who tirelessly spread book love to the wider reading community, I don't just thank you, I love you!

Joe, Aimee and Alex, thank you for reading things you really don't want to read and remaining honest at the risk of our relationship falling apart! Not always easy to be the family of a writer.

Thanks, of course, to my lovely readers – so many of you have become friends. Special gratitude to those who take the time to review my books, highlight them on social media and recommend them to friends.

Thank you, West Cork, for existing and for offering me solace so many times.

Printed in Poland
by Amazon Fulfillment
Poland Sp. z o.o., Wrocław